LOVE YOU MADLY

CORTNI MARIE

CORTNI MARIE

Salvisa, Kentucky

LA FLEUR DE LIS TRILOGY

BOOK ONE
✦
LOVE YOU FOREVER
October 2024

BOOK TWO
✦
LOVE YOU MADLY
December 2025

BOOK THREE
✦
LOVE YOU TO DEATH
TO BE DETERMINED

To my Nonna, who instilled a sense of imagination and adventure in me, without judgment or fear for the wild places my mind took me.

You would've loved these books.

"Ciao bambina"

AUTHOR'S NOTE

At the time of editing this book, an act of cruel and unjust malice has been brought down on the community of New Orleans. Because of the recency of these events, the subject matter within this book might be hard to read for those affected by this tragedy. My heart always goes out to those victims of senseless crime and injustice. What happened in New Orleans on New Year's Day **should not have happened.** My voice on institutions in cities like New Orleans and St. Louis has been loud from the beginning of this series. I am critical of the social services meant to protect and serve its citizens and yet fails to do just that. A biased government is no democracy. Importance to people's lives and safety should not be weighed by their net worth nor their zip code.

Further note — at its surface level, this is just a made up story about two people existing in a world where vampires are trying to take over. Dig a little deeper and you'll see the bigger picture: the corruption, the greed, the lengths at which people have had to go to *survive*, and the lengths others have gone to thrive in the adversity of others.

As such, I do like to spell out certain subject matter that might be cause for pause before you read. This is an adult urban fantasy that while lighthearted and funny at times, is also quite dark.

This list may contain spoilers:

- Imprisonment and torture
- Blood/vomit/gore
- Body horror in graphic detail (brief)
- Open door/in the bed sexual content
- Mentions of violence against women
- Drug and alcohol use/abuse
- Mental health struggles/depression/suicidal thoughts

PROLOGUE

She's *alive.*

✤

CHAPTER ONE
IZZY

Sinking her teeth into the soft, inked flesh of Charlie's neck had become a new pleasure that nauseated Izzy Ciampi.

His broad hands grasped her waist, keeping her upright as she leaned into him sitting on the stool at her kitchen counter. She drew in the warm, crimson blood she required. *Craved.* A moan dared to slip from her throat. His grip tightened and she hissed.

The entire fucking situation was miserable. Heady and addictive and fucking miserable. As if nothing had changed between the two of them.

"Enough, Izzy." His voice vibrated gruff through her lips. She bit down harder. A swear tore from his vocal chords as he shoved her backward, detaching them roughly. The ragged wound left behind had already begun to heal, the skin stitching together while the flow weakened to just a small drop down his neck. A neat trick of the virus that had turned her into this abomination. Nothing wasted, nothing ruined. Charlie's ocean eyes scowled at her as his hand pressed to his neck. There would be a bruise though.

His fault for speaking, she thought as she licked her lips, the metallic, citrus flavor of *him* roiling through her. Swiping the back of her hand against her mouth, she turned and walked into her bathroom.

They had simple yet strict rules for this arrangement: hands off and shut the fuck up. He failed at least one of those every week they met up but she had no other options. It felt worse than an affair.

As she washed her hands and mouth out, she didn't hear the telltale sound of the door opening and closing to signal Charlie had left. She watched the red tinged water drain down the basin, letting out a heavy sigh.

"You can leave now," she called out. She didn't dare look at her reflection. No sense in torturing herself further, seeing the way the blood livened her. Plumped her lips, colored her cheeks, set her green eyes to an alluring, almost electric glow. Why try to see the good in something so appalling? Why look for the appeal that led the world into this mess in the first place?

Footsteps sounded but stopped in front of the bathroom door. Fuck, he could never follow directions, could he?

"I'm serious, Charlie. You can go, we're done here," she said, tired. Sated. Exhausted. Revived. This game had become torturous and she needed to be alone.

"Izzy—" The door opened with a slow whine that echoed off the white walls of the small space. He looked how she felt. She gave him a grim smile.

"What do you want?" He flinched at the stiff sting in her words.

"Are you...are you okay?" He rubbed the black and yellow bouquet of daisies on his forearm, their stems held in the tight grip of a jet black king snake. "I mean, all things considered, are you doing okay?"

All things considered. She scoffed and looked back at the sink, a small faint pink puddle around the edges of the drain. "Get out, Charlie."

He never hung around like this, feigning concern for her. She glanced to the mirror, her brain snagging on the changes to it over the past six months. Six months since they blew up the old St. Louis library.

Six months since Noah disappeared without a trace.

Six months since she woke up as a monster.

Six months since Charlie murdered the only family she had left.

She shook her head and slipped past Charlie, out of the bathroom. She glanced to the floor to see his combat boots still next to the door. Slumping into the couch, she threw her head back and an arm over her eyes to block out the last remnants of sunlight trying to peek through her heavy linen curtains. She hated the darkness.

"Is there seriously no end to your torment on me? Don't you think I've had enough?" she seethed, keeping her eyes covered. He didn't move from his spot.

"I only agreed to do this because I care about you and I didn't want to see you succumbed to using one of those blood banks. Or worse," he responded, turning around to face her. She tsked in disgust and removed her arm to glare at him. Like he had the right to care about her anymore. Like he ever really did.

"Oh, please. Save your bullshit for the next girl. You are here because it's the closest thing to having control over me you can manage now." She stood up, taking an intimidating step toward him. Still he didn't falter. She stared up into his azure eyes. They fucking infuriated her. "I *chose* you because you're at the bottom of my list of most trusted individuals. I respect you so little that I'm willing to sit here and drain you, put your life on the line, because I just don't fucking care about it. I want you to leave. Your one use to me has been accomplished. We're done. Am I making myself clear yet?"

The muscles in his neck tensed. "As clear as the fucking Mississippi," he said through his clenched jaw.

She turned on her heel and slumped back into the couch, cradling her face in her hands. Every ounce of energy she gained from the past fifteen minutes of feeding felt like it seeped out of her pores. The space next to her sagged and she peeked an eye out as a heavy sigh left Charlie's chest.

"I'm not trying to argue with you, Iz. You have every right to hate me. You have every right to kill me. I've made my mistakes, God, I've made them good. But, as much as it pains you to hear it, I know you. I know you don't want to need me or anyone for that matter. But if you're going to have to do this, I know you would rather hate the person you're doing it to and I'm happy to be that for you. I deserve that. But you don't have to kill yourself for it. What's the point of living despite this if you're just a shell of the person you once were?" He rested his elbows on his knees, rubbing a hand over his mouth, eyes lost in thought as he stared at the empty screen of her television.

She didn't know if she should be livid or endeared by how well he had read the situation. Guess that's part of what made him such a good gangster. Walk into the room, see every scenario before it unfolds, take control from the start. Take control. Fuck.

She nodded her head once. "Fine. But can you please leave now? You being here isn't necessarily improving my shell state."

His gaze flicked to her and he studied her for a moment, a shared breath held between them as she felt the waves of emotions course through him. Then he stood and silently made his way to the door. The only lock he needed to unlatch was the main bolt.

"Just—" he started to say, hand on the handle. "If you start to feel so lost you can't get out, please call me. I know I'm the last person you want to talk to about anything but I'm here for you, regardless."

The silence grew between them like air in a balloon. Her hand absentmindedly went to her neck, to the spot where her golden cross usually sat. To guard her. To ground her. She had scoured the apartment looking for it over the past six months, to no avail. Her empty fist clenched in the hollow space left there.

Charlie nodded his head and walked out the door, softly closing it behind him. And damn her if a tear didn't fall from her eyes when he did.

❧

Adorned in her new wardrobe of a black hoodie over black jeans and black boots, she stalked along the shadows toward campus, sunlight filtered through her dark sunglasses. McMillan Hall rose before her, the garden above the basement labs buzzing with the spring blooms and promise of longer days. Fucking lovely. She longed to lay out, feel the soft blades of grass beneath her hands as she let the sun caress her winter tired skin.

But those were daydreams from a past life. With a sigh, she slinked down the stairs into the dark hallway of the basement corridor. Walking into the lab space she shared with Barry, she was hit with the pumping drumbeats of a Mexican Top Hits playlist.

Squinting into the dimly lit space, she called out, "Barry? What is going on in here?"

He popped out from the closet to her left, a sombrero over his perfect hair and a rainbow knit poncho to match. *"Ilega el cinco de mayo*[1]*! Izzy, vamos!* You are a storm cloud on the celebration of my ancestors!" He shook a maraca in her face as he twirled past her, shaking his hips side to side in time to the music before sitting down at his desk. Barry's family moved to the United States from Puebla, Mexico when he was a toddler, a couple years before shit hit the fan and the world devolved into immortal chaos. A simpler time. A happier time.

"I'm not feeling very *bonita* this year, Bear," she said, pulling back her hood and removing her sunglasses. When she broke the news to him about her predicament, he embraced her with such ferocity she had wept into his emerald velvet shirt for a solid five minutes before he broke the hold to ask, "So, whose neck are you sucking on these days?"

He had not-so-secretly hoped for a modern day retelling of Interview with a Vampire starring Noah as a role reversed Louis de Pointe. When she told him about Noah's sudden disappearance, they had wept together.

He threw a ball of gauzy paper on her desk and it unraveled into a mass of red, white, and green strips. "No worries, once you take a bite of the *tres leches* I will pour my entire soul into at Uncle Landy's penthouse this weekend for our rooftop celebration, you will be renewed."

Her spine stiffened at the mention of Lando and she started unpacking her bag. "You're still planning to stay the night with me?" she asked, dusting as much cheer as she could muster into her tone. It felt like ash on her tongue.

Barry's face looked a little crestfallen. Normally, her couch would be occupied by Vahagn and they would've made a sleepover out of it, complete with his famous margaritas. Her own heart ached, deeply, for the life she had lost. "I'll be there. I'll even consider sharing the covers with you."

She smiled. "As long as you're not a kicker, I'll give you all the covers you want."

"Oh honey, what I'm known for in bed is certainly not kicking." He winked at her and turned back to his laptop. Some might deem the salacious photos on his computer not safe for work, but that *was* his work as he scrolled through images of what looked like small statues in various sex positions she wasn't sure her body could bend in.

She sat at her desk and stared at the black screen of her own laptop. Her research had taken a turn over the last few months. Anything that had to do with women's roles in World War I went to the wayside as she poured her attention and time into studying the middle ages. Specifically, the reign of one Charlemagne. Shrouded in mystery, her efforts had been fairly fruitless. After finding Noah's notes tucked into The Ramblings, she had hoped to uncover some more information about the supposed army of immortals. Even just a mention of them or what had happened to them. Instead, it was the same old repetitive toting of triumph for the man. It felt worse than researching tales of the bible.

Powering on her laptop, she typed in "old St. Louis Public Library" hoping to uncover more about that secret cave entrance Noah had taken her to. Maybe there was something there, missing right underneath her nose. It couldn't be a coincidence that the walls were essentially covered in evidence to support Noah's claim. Her leg started to bounce at the thought. Had he known all along? Had any of it been real?

The search results popped up with black and white photos of the magnificent building when it was completed in 1912.

Candlelight shined in its cathedral arches, images of the high ceiling entrance and chandeliers that appeared to be floating in the air. God, it had hurt to destroy it. To see the pain it caused Noah when he realized her plan to do so. She never got to ask him what the place meant to him but she could tell it held some importance to his story. His journey to this damned city. Into her damned life.

She almost slammed the laptop shut on the images when one she had never seen before caught her eye in the bottom corner. A man, walking through a small wooden door held open. He wasn't facing the camera, maybe unaware it was even there underneath his dark top hat. She zoomed in on the door, to the carvings within it. To an image of a man kneeling to the moon.

Zooming back out, she studied its surroundings. That wasn't the same entrance Noah had led her through. This was in a different part of the library entirely, a part she never got to explore. A part she wouldn't have known existed and therefore wouldn't have told Lando about in their distraction plans…

She pushed back from her desk, standing and simultaneously pulling her phone out as she started packing her stuff up.

Barry broke out of his focused trance and said, "Where are you going now?"

Her finger hovered over the Call button of Lando's contact information. She was frozen. Her heart raced in her chest. There had been no phone calls between them since The Society ambushed her that fall. The cold snippets of talk they shared could barely be classified as conversation. She pocketed the phone, throwing away the notion that things could ever return to normal and tucked a loose curl behind her ear as she slung her bag over her shoulder.

"Um, out," she replied to Barry.

To her surprise, he stood, sombrero still perched on his head but a determined scowl on his face. "No," he said, voice defiant.

She had been pulling her hood on when he spoke and stopped, nose crinkled as she stared at him in bewilderment. "What do you mean 'no'?" she snarled, wincing at her tone.

He took his sombrero off, placing in gently on his desk, then readjusted his poncho before gathering his things into his bag. "I mean, no."

She sighed. "Barry, come on. I still don't have the telepathic capabilities you're determined to force upon me."

He spoke calmly as he finished packing his things, "I have spent the better half of the last six months watching you wallow in self pity. It's unbecoming and quite frankly, I'm sick of it. You are not alone. You are only down a few numbers. But that's no reason to lone wolf it. It's like you learned nothing from Game of Thrones. You're such a Jon Snow." He turned to face her, a smug smirk on his face and eye brow raised, challenging her to argue.

Her mouth opened then closed. This repeated a couple times as her mind whirled around his words. She stopped trying to form a response and glared at him. He rolled his eyes, waved a hand at her and trudged toward the door.

"Oh, whatever. Your bark is worse than your bite from what I understand," he said, pushing through the door and into the hallway.

Flustered, she hurried after him, hissing at the sunlight beckoning the exit from the hallway.

"How would you even know that?" she demanded as she fumbled her sunglasses onto her face.

"Charlie and I talk." He winked over his shoulder and

kept on moving toward that wretched golden light. She tightened her hood over her head.

"You don't talk to Charlie," she scoffed.

He sighed. "Yes, I do. Unfortunately, it's all mostly about you." He slowed so they walked side by side and then he eyed her warily as he said, "You know he regrets everything that happened between you two and with Vahagn."

"Good," she said, staring ahead. Barry stopped. She kept walking. He put his hand out in front of her.

"Izzy, wait." She turned to face him and hated the look she saw when she did. Hated the words she knew he was about to say. "You should talk to him. Just listen to what he has to say. He does care about you."

She snorted. "He has the worst way of showing it."

Barry sighed. "I know. I don't deny that. He was an asshole. Still probably is, deep down. But maybe just hear him out."

She studied the sincerity on his face, in his words. A moment passed. Then another. "Fuck, fine," she growled and continued up the stairs.

Not looking to press the issue more, he asked, "So, where are we heading?"

"The old library," she tried to say nonchalantly.

"Oh, Izzy," Barry said, theatrically. "And you were going to go by yourself? Oy vey, you're lucky I was in before you." He looped his arm into hers as they hit the street, hugging the shadows despite the chill they offered. How she missed the warmth of the sun.

❧

CHAPTER TWO
NOAH

Six months ago,

"I'm sorry, The Anti-what?" Noah tilted his head, eyes squinted as he tried to comprehend the vision of his dead brother standing in front of him. He pulled against the restraints again, the fresh bite of the rope letting him know this was all pretty fucking real.

"The Antisociété. When you meet Adette, you'll understand the name better." Benji beamed at Noah. "It's really a rather funny name once you think about it." He ran a hand through his curly blond hair, hazel eyes dancing in the distance as his thoughts catapulted through him. His mouth had never been able to keep up with his brain and the image convinced Noah this *really was* his brother. Alive. In front of him. On a fucking boat. Benji snapped and Noah focused again, his mind teetering with an unsteady grip on his reality. "Oh, and you'll meet Henry too. He's an absolute genius. Sheesh, and Malik will want to meet you." Benji grinned at him. "All in due time, brother, all in due time."

Noah let out a nervous laugh and sighed, looking to the rusted iron grate above him. He leveled a stare back on his brother and said, "So, I'm sorry, but how the fuck are you alive, Benji? I thought you died. I fled the city believing you were gone. That was over a year ago." The words choked on their way out and moisture threatened to spill over his eyelids. Fucking hell, he blinked and looked around to found something tangible to steady his mind. He settled on the dark, dusty brown shelves around the room, holding up cans of grease and chemicals to keep rust at bay. Humorous.

Benji stepped forward and Noah caught the concern in his brother's eyes, pulling at his heart. Jesus, his brother was *alive*. Noah was no longer alone.

You hadn't been alone with Izzy. His thoughts invaded him and his eyes widened, afraid Benji might've overheard them.

"Noh, my brother, I'm so sorry for worrying you. I should've told you at the time but," he rubbed the back of his neck, giving Noah a sheepish grin. "We couldn't risk anyone finding out. Adette found me a couple weeks before the riots. We planned the whole thing, to fake my death when we took down The Society so there wouldn't be any heat on you. But, fuck Noh, you weren't supposed to run? I figured you would stay and then we could use you as an in with The Society. You know, help us finally take them down."

The way Benji's words whirled with Noah's thoughts nauseated him. He didn't even know how to respond to his brother, his idiotic brother that he was so absolutely elated to see alive. Noah pulled against the ropes again and let out an exasperated exhale.

"And now what? I'm a prisoner because, unbeknownst to me, I was the keystone in a hostile takeover situation between two vampire gangs?" Noah said, his words clipped.

Benji's gaze shifted to murderous edges and betrayed shadows, weaponizing Noah's childhood nickname as he practically growled, "Don't call them that, Noh. They aren't vampires. They are fighting the immortality curse that's turned this world to shit."

Noah stared in disbelief at his brother, studying the stoic way he stood his ground. "Oh yeah? And how's that, Benji? Because as far as I can tell, you're still in knee deep with a psychotic French savant with a penance for world domination."

"You don't know what you're talking about, Noah. You never did. All you did was sit in your corner, running your calculations, making your little judgmental observations, and scoffing at every idea." Benji ran a frustrated hand through his hair, eyes shooting to the ceiling.

Five minutes. Five minutes was all that lasted of their warm reunion, come and gone and replaced with the old animosity Noah had held onto all that time. What scared him most was the way he blamed Benji for leaving him. For being a martyr in a stupid fucking scheme, without even telling Noah. Without trusting him enough to let him in on it all. It had been a ruse, with Noah as the butt of the joke.

Noah shifted against his restraints and Benji looked at him with downturned lips pressed firmly together. "Right, well then. Do I at least get to know where I'm going to be kept hostage?" Noah asked, his temper simmering enough to keep his thoughts to himself but not sound happy about it.

"Home, of course. Good ol' NOLA!" Benji said, the muscles in his jaw relaxing as he gave Noah a smirk.

"You've got to be kidding me," Noah murmured, shaking his head.

"But you're not being held hostage. I'm actually here to show you to your quarters," Benji said, walking behind Noah and working the knots around his wrist free.

Rolling his wrists and rubbing the raw spots, Noah

glanced up at Benji. His brother looked no worse for the wear. If anything, he seemed to have thrived in this new organization. There was a slight glow to his russet skin, his complexion always a touch darker than Noah's despite his sunshine colored hair. He had remained fit and his peppered golden eyes still created that scowl that made Noah feel approximately six years old every time he saw it.

As if the thought of being a child somehow sparked a thought, he reached down to check his pockets for his phone. Empty.

Benji marked the movement and said, "Ah, yes. That. We had to confiscate it. For security, of course. You'll get it back."

"When?" The words fell out on a frantic note. He needed to get ahold of Izzy. Needed to let her know he was alive. They were in the building when it exploded.

Would she even care?

"Eventually," Benji replied as he removed the last rope around Noah's ankle. Noah stood, wobbling a moment and putting his arm out to steady himself. Benji grasped it. It sent a shockwave through him. Shit, his brother was *alive*.

Noah turned his head to look Benji in his golden eyes, a near identical shade to his own. Benji gave him a reassuring smile.

"It's good to see you, Noh," Benji said.

Noah returned with a tight smile that grew into a genuine one. "Yeah, Benji, you too."

"Come on, let me walk you to your quarters."

Noah followed behind Benji as he walked out the little room, glancing once more to the grate nestled above the chair. How many secrets were being kept on this boat?

⚜

"So, they converted all the blood houses into food

pantries that also hold educational meetings to discuss the health effects of 'donating' blood too frequently and to hand out resources for those looking for alternative sources of income or seeking assistance with getting out," Benji explained as they traveled the tight corridor through the belly of the boat. Which actually turned out to be a retrofitted barge, commandeered to keep their operation mobile in case situations like this arose. When Noah asked what type of situation had sent them to St. Louis though, Benji deflected the question to show him the hot engine room.

The most disorienting aspect of being on the barge was the people. They were everywhere, constantly squeezing past one another to get somewhere in a hurry. At one point, Noah stared directly into the bright green eyes of a woman with mousy brown hair as they squeezed past each other, her features morphing into another that caused him to trip and bump into Benji in front of him. His brother righted him, gripping his shoulders and the woman disappeared down the hallway with a blush on her pale cheeks. Noah felt out of his depth by the sheer crowd around them.

"And what about the immortals? They just let you take the blood houses? They didn't fight back against this change?" Noah asked, returning his focus back to his brother.

Benji's face lit up. "Noh, that's the amazing thing! Henry and Adette developed this, like, cure to the immortality. They call it the *recours*. I don't know the details but I guess it makes it so they don't need blood as often. Most switch over to intravenous donations like once a month but some stop all together. It's incredible." His smile grew as his eyes twinkled in the lights lining the hull.

This stopped Noah in his tracks, causing a small pile up.

"How?"

The crowd pushed Benji along, ignorant to the fact Noah was no longer behind him as he said, "Oh, it's better if you hear it from her."

The flaky grey metal walls shifted, tilting around Noah. A cure. To vampires. To the monstrosity that plagued their world and ruined their lives. His heart clenched as Adette's voice filtered back into his mind.

He is the sickness and the cure.

Benji finally noticed Noah's absence behind him. He hadn't moved. Shit, he hadn't breathed. Benji turned to eye his brother like he had grown a second head.

"But do you know how they make it?" Noah croaked out, his words falling just above a whisper. By some chance, the hallway had suddenly become empty, as if everyone wanted to avoid the spectacle waiting to be unleash by his sheer presence.

Benji walked toward him, slapping a hand on his shoulder. This jolted Noah from his trance.

"Like I said, brother, you have to hear it from her. It's a crazy story, lots of science that goes way over my head, but you'll love it. Now come on, let me show you where you'll be staying."

⚜

Tucked down a hallway no different from any of the dozen others they had passed along the way, Benji twisted the handled wheel of a metal door and pushed into a musty room, barely larger than a walk-in closet. A small mattress sat atop a built-in platform with storage underneath along one wall, the corner of it stopping the door from opening fully. There was a small washroom built into the other corner with a sink and a metal rod hung into a small alcove above it that could hold no more than five hangers. A solitary chair took up the rest of the floor space that was swallowed by both Broussard brothers hulking forms. Thankfully, the chair looked to be foldable.

"The communal washrooms with showers and such are down the hall," Benji said.

Which one? Noah thought as he slumped onto the mattress. A spring stabbed him in the ass. He sighed. At least he was no longer tied to a chair. This new prison had a bit of comfort in mind.

Benji spun in a circle, taking in the space in one fell swoop. "I have you working in the kitchen but you'll have the rest of this evening to yourself. I'll bring you food later and take you to the showers. Then I'll be back in the morning to take you down for your first shift."

Noah raised a brow but said nothing. The leash had only been let out so far and he could still feel the tension around his neck.

Benji continued, ignorant to Noah's internal monologue. "You'll like the kitchen staff. Everyone on the boat has to work, its part of what makes the crew so solid. Everyone holds their own around here. Everyone is equal."

Noah coughed to cover the scoff that nearly escaped his lips. Gripping the scratchy canvas blanket beneath him, he took a moment to appraise his brother. Even when they were in The Society, Benji would talk about how change was coming. That it would get better, they just needed to get through the shitstorm with the immortals. Something good, something better, was always on the horizon for Benji Broussard.

"Will I be working with you then?" Noah asked, finally finding his voice in the cramped space.

Benji met his gaze, manic joy twinkling in those golden orbs, though his tone shifted to a serious nature. "Nah, I work directly with Adette." His lips curved into a slight proud grin but remained shut. No further explanation needed.

Great. His brother literally escaped death only to crawl right back into the same scenario that got him there, except with a different Dumas. Did Benji even know Adette had been married to Emilien?

Running a hand through his hair, fingers sticking in the knots coated with a concrete layer of dust, sweat, and potentially blood, he tried to pry more information from his brother. "How long has she been working in the states?"

Benji stepped toward the door, dismissing his question. "Save it all for when you meet her, Noh." He turned around, the glow of the single exposed bulb in the room reflected in his pupils. "You'll be amazed."

And with that, Benji left him. A metallic clunk sounded in his absence and Noah didn't bother to check the door. He knew he had been locked in. Groaning, he got up and explored the small space. Or at least what there was to explore. Within a few minutes he had seen the extent of the room. He stepped to the small sink in the corner, doing his best to rinse the remains of The Society headquarters out of his hair and feel normal again. Human.

It was a feeble attempt. Gripping the sides of the sink, he watched the dirty water slowly drain down the porcelain bowl, thoughts of olive skin pebbled under his touch, palms splayed across soft curves. Light refracting off mesmerizing green eyes. He squeezed his eyes shut, gripping the sink tighter as he willed the thoughts away.

Fuck, it would've been easier if he had never approached her. Because in that moment, when he reached out to her in that dark hallway several weeks ago, his entire life changed trajectory. Because in that moment, locked away in a maritime prison, all alone with his thoughts, instead of thinking up a plan to escape or take down the obvious threats blooming up around him, he was thinking about her. About a night in a cave lost to the reckless abandon of her body and her mind and that dangerous, little mouth. And then he left her.

He looked up, catching a horrifying glimpse of his own reflection in a small mirror mounted on the wall above the sink. Unable to hold his own gaze, he looked away and caught a black strap in the space beneath the bed. He walked over, yanking on it to reveal a small duffel bag. Nothing he recognized as his own so he glanced to the door once more before throwing the bag on his bed. He sat down next to it and unzipped the bag to reveal the contents. Within he found clothes, his clothes. A random assortment taken from his packed bags back in his apartment. A chill ran through him as he dug deeper. A spark of hope dared to burn in his heart as he pulled each article of clothing from the bag. Maybe they had put his phone in there. As the bag grew emptier, his heart sank. Nothing. Nothing but pieces of fabric.

From his apartment.

His brows furrowed. Someone would have had to go into his apartment to pack this bag. They would have known where he lived. How to get past the doorman. They had planned to take him. With a t-shirt held in his hand, he scowled at the door. But Benji hadn't known Noah would be in that storage room when he came to get him. Benji didn't seem to know what had happened outside of this boat.

With his brows knit together, Noah gathered all the clothes back into the bag and threw it against the metal wall opposite him. It fell to the floor in an unceremonious thump.

He laid back into the uncomfortable bed, throwing an arm over his eyes to block out the perpetual light shining from the bulb above and crashed once more into the delusions of his mind. Dreams he dared to experience, to wish for, to hope for in this pit of despair.

Flowers in bloom on the rooftop garden of McMillan Hall. Bees floating around the spring blossom of wildflowers. Sunlight warming his skin, warming the freckled skin of the woman next to him. Her emerald eyes radiating in the amber glow of the setting sun. Her smile wrinkling her freckled nose.

He held that imagined warmth in his heart as he closed his eyes against the sunlight, a ghost of a smile pulling on his lips.

An hour later, Benji came back with a sandwich and glass bottle of water. When his knocks had awoken Noah, he was disappointed to see the glare of sunlight in his dreams had been nothing more than that lonely bulb overhead. He ate quickly, in silence while his brother watched, and then he escorted him down a repeat of the same old hallways to a wet room lined with five shower stalls on one side and five bathroom stalls on the other.

"I'll give you like fifteen minutes. If you need me, I'll be right outside the door," Benji said to him through the open metal door. Noah nodded. A stack of towels sat on a cart with a basket attached. Noah had grabbed a fresh set of clothes before leaving his room. Once in a stall, stripped bare, he turned the water as high as it could go. The spray cascaded down him, scorching his skin. The murky liquid drained off him and with it, the tears that he allowed to spill in that moment.

CHAPTER THREE
IZZY

Water grew heavy in Izzy's eyes as Barry followed her through the heaps of rock and debris that once made up the glorious arched stone entrance into the St. Louis Public Library. Gold plated iron work with a repeating fleur de lis design laid bent under a cream stone pillar the size of a luxury sedan. What she knew of the library was lore through photographs and stories as the public funds that supported it were quickly redirected to vampire infrastructure as more and more of the city's elite took to cure all that ailed their feeble mortal bodies. And thus the power of words were overshadowed by the thirst for blood and immortality.

"Oh my God," Barry breathed out, flashing his Incredible Hulk themed flashlight to the teetering ceiling, the hand painted design flaking from the exposure and destruction. A name like STEDMAN etched into the stone like an ominous prayer against the ruins.

She peered back at the suspicious curiosity sparkling in his dark brown eyes and smiled, remembering her own first-time walking into the library. A moment of sheer chaos and yet she still possessed that same sense of wonder at the abandoned opulence of it all. A tumble of thoughts tormented after the memory. Of Vahagn. Of Noah. Of her previous life. She shook them all away and instead focused on trudging further into the dark space.

"Come on. Lando said they only had enough explosives to plant in the front. It should start to clear out the deeper we go and I think the room I'm looking for is somewhere near the back anyway." She had given him a brief run down on the way over about seeing a photo that might help with her research but didn't elaborate that said research was nothing funded by the university or approved by Beechum.

They weaved their way through the destruction. The destruction at her command. She had been a monster before she even turned.

Vahagn had died for nothing.

That dangerous thought slithered back into her mind. The first month after her entire world upended that thought had been a near constant reminder of how fucked up her entire life had become. A continual stab to her broken heart. Slowly, it had drifted, morphed into a silent murmur in the back of her mind, tucked away in the floorboards of her consciousness. It all became easier to forget with the copious amounts of weed and alcohol she drowned herself in every night.

"Izzy! Watch your step!"

She stopped abruptly, inches from a drop-off down the jagged remains of some stairs awaiting her. Her hand gripped a still standing pillar next to her as oxygen heaved in and out of her lungs. She turned, wide eyed, to see Barry straddling a large, crumbled statue behind her, attempting to make his way to her. The inky abyss the stairs disappeared into would've been a death spill.

Or would it have been? How immortal was she? She drifted to the edge again, staring into those shadows as her chest continued to expand and contract. The darkness called to her. Beckoned her to see how far she could push the life she been given. A gift still left unopened really. Untested. Unknown.

A hand gripped her arm and she whirled to face Barry, his frantic eyes searching her face.

"Jesus, are you alright? That was close. It was like you were in a trance and just walking straight for a deep dive into literal hell." He peered down the stairs and back at her, gulping. "This place kinda gives me the creeps in this state. Like images of the sunken Titanic. I'm just waiting for a dead socialite to come floating by."

She laughed and pulled out of his grasp, catching his hand to squeeze it. "No worries, Barry. I'll protect you from the undead aristocrats."

"Oh, thank God," he exhaled, shoulders visibly relaxing. "Where do we go from here? This place is a maze."

He was right. Even from her brief time there with Noah, she had been overwhelmed. The architectural wonder that was the Central Library of the St. Louis Public Library system was a behemoth. It spanned an entire city block and housed over four million books. Protests broke out the day its doors were suddenly shuttered. The local government took a "here are the rules, deal with it" approach though leaving many with their heads hung low in defeat. A few of the more outspoken community leaders disappeared shortly after word got out about how the library funds had been reallocated to the bloody pits of local night club owners and for shuttling "patrons" from the subsidized housing communities.

"I think…we need to go this way," she said, pointing in

the direction of what looked like a small, relatively unscathed hallway. They had to be near the edge of the destruction.

Except as they walked through the hallway it revealed itself to not be one at all, but an elongated doorway opening into a magnificent great room. The ceiling stood regal, two stories above them with coffered tiles, gilded with images of owls and fleur de lis. Magnificent chandeliers laid in elegant piles of crystalline rubble on the once polished marble floor. Arched windows spanned two-thirds of the height, their glass shattered across the space, as if a great force blew them about like glitter in the wind. She swallowed hard.

"Ho-ly fuuuuuuuck," Barry sang out from behind her, twirling in pirouettes across the floor, leaping over the obstacles of destruction in his path. Part of her was tempted to join him. This room invited a sort of childlike desire to dance and frolic.

Another part of her felt nauseous observing the devastation she had caused.

You're supposed to be seeing this with Noah. That tormenting thought crept in, stealing any sense of joy she might have felt in that moment. The smile that had started to etch on her face as she watched Barry disappear.

She snapped her fingers at him, heading to the other end of the room, toward another, real, hallway. She was pretty sure they needed to make their way down…

"Hey, wait a second," Barry called, before skipping through a heavy wooden door.

Fucking great, he was wandering. They didn't have time for adventures.

Rushing in after him, she said, "Barry, we're supposed to stick toget—" Annoyance became a regrettable coating on her tongue as her words suddenly stopped. Instead, she crashed into his stationary form a few feet into the room and another annoyed retort started to form when a sick sensation raised the hair on her arms.

"What a lovely little surprise," a strangely familiar, British voice purred from across the room.

⚜

Her glower shifted from Barry to the skull tattooed on the neck of the man across the room, a toothpick between his teeth as he smirked from beneath that awful tweed pageboy cap. When he saw the recognition dawn on her, his smile grew into a wicked line.

"I don't remember scheduling a rendezvous with you here, but I'm glad to see you brought us a snack," the man said, pushing off the table and stalking toward them. Izzy stepped forward, pushing Barry behind her. Then she growled like a fucking animal at the approaching man, startling herself in the process. God damn it all, what was wrong with her?

"Why do you always have a way of being where I am?" she seethed through clenched teeth, one fang pressing painfully into her bottom lip.

The man laughed. "I believe some would call that fate, lovey."

She snarled and stepped toward him again. This stopped him in his pursuit, one eyebrow quirked. So not as big and bad as he portrayed. She took another step forward and watched him tense.

"Haven't you heard? Fate doesn't exist anymore. Not when it can be bought. So, all this is another example of some creep invading the privacy of an unsuspecting woman. Why are you following me, huh? Did Charlie put you up to this? Emilien?" She hated that those were the names rolling off her tongue. Those were the men keeping tabs on her. Sure, Lando still held a watchful eye over her comings and goings, but that was mostly out of fear…of her. Not for her. She knew he had considered asking her to leave the building after her attack on Gio that fall but he hadn't hammered that last nail in her coffin. For what reason, she couldn't figure out. All she knew was every resident had reinforced locks and several more cameras had been installed in the building. Specifically in her hallway. Pointed at her door.

The toothpick in the man's mouth snapped in half. "I am no one's *dog*. I go where I please."

"Well, great. Then go." She took another step toward him. This time he didn't move, not even a flinch. Fuck, maybe she overestimated her hand.

"Why are *you* here? Seems a strange place to go on a date," the man said, eyes flicking to Barry by the doorway. He had been silent this whole time, a mouse hoping the cat won't notice him in the corner as she heard his heartbeat fluttering at maximum speed.

Of course, that was until this man suggested they were on a date together. "Oh, please! Like I would have allowed a date to drag my happy little ass through a pile of rubble for a quickie between the statues of old men. I'm into some freaky shit but I've also seen the reruns of 60 Minutes. I will not be a victim," Barry chimed. Izzy smirked. Never one to miss a chance for a quality sound bite that Bartholomew, even in the midst of a very bad situation.

She did a quick scan of the room, taking in the wooden details on the ceiling and the rows of shelves along the walls. Her eyes widened as a door in the corner came into focus. The black and white photo from her computer screen flashed in her mind. It couldn't be…

She looked up into the black orbs for eyes on the skull tattooed on the man's neck. He had stepped within her space while she was taking in the room, merely inches from her. She didn't move but her pulse raced.

His words tickled her ear as he leaned forward and whispered, "Something caught your eye?"

Her gaze shifted to his icy grey eyes and she tensed. Not because malice reflected back at her. Not even an ounce of contempt crinkled the edges of his eyes. No, he seemed to…understand what she had seen.

"Why are you really here, Izzy?" He asked, studying her with such an intensity it sent a chill down her spine that crawled across the rest of her skeletory system

"Nothing. We were just going," she said, stepping back out of his space. His jaw tensed at her apprehension. She backed toward Barry, taking a mental image of this room as she did. She would need to come back. Alone. And apparently after checking The Society calendar of creeper events.

Once both her and Barry were back into the great hall they had come in from, they finally turned their backs and started jogging across the room. But not before that accented voice bounced off the walls after them, "Be sure to be on the right side of your next battle, Isabella. I would hate to see something happen to that pretty little face of yours."

CHAPTER FOUR
NOAH

A knock sounded on his door a few minutes after he had found a small semblance of comfort in his bed. Before he could respond, the door creaked open and Benji peeked his head around it, a wild excitement in his eyes.

"Come on, Noh. Adette wants to have dinner with you."

Noah groaned. "What time is it?"

Benji pushed his way into the room, grabbing the discarded duffel bag from a few days ago off the ground. Something metal hit the floor. Benji knelt to pick it up, studied it a moment before tossing it to Noah so he could continue riffling through his things.

"What's that?" Benji asked as he pulled out a fresh shirt and a pair of jeans.

Noah grabbed the small pendant on a golden chain and his heart stopped. It was Izzy's. She had been wearing it that day in the warehouse. It had been around her neck as they sprinted to their salvation. As he was tackled and taken. Brought back to this boat.

"Noah, here." Benji shoved the clothing toward him, oblivious to the panic leaving Noah immobile.

He looked at his brother, still holding out his clothing, and knew he couldn't ask the question pounding on his chest.

Where is she?

Tossing the clothes on the bed, Benji walked over and slumped into the small chair. "Get changed and we can go meet her."

Where is she?

Noah stared at him, eyes unblinking. "Who?"

Benji looked up from cleaning the dirt out from under his fingernails, brows knitted together. "Adette, Noah. I literally just told you. Get dressed, we're running late."

Noah held the pendant in his hand as he went through the motions of removing his dirty clothes from his shift that day, too tired earlier to bother taking them off.

Where is she?

Pulling the clean black shirt over his naked torso, he asked instead, "What time is it, Benji?"

Benji looked him up and down, eyes a little wild. Too wild. "I don't know, Noah. Does it matter? We're on a boat."

Noah nodded his head, trying to understand why knowing the time would change anything. He was, in fact, on a boat. A boat full of secrets. Secrets that could tell him something important like where the fuck Izzy was.

He slipped the jeans on, pocketing the necklace, before he pulled on the black sneakers given to him with the rest of his kitchen uniform. He stood there, arms outstretched as he faced his brother.

"Am I worthy enough to meet her highness, now?" he joked, despite the underlying thundering of his heart. That necklace felt like a bright orange brand in his pocket as he thought once again, *Where is she?*

Benji scowled at him. "Don't be like that, Noah. It's not like that."

Noah let his arms drop. "Then what is it like, Benji?" His patience had started to wear thin.

It didn't matter though because Benji ignored him, instead pulling the door open. "Come on, we're late."

Benji led him down some new yet similar hallways toward the back of the barge. When there was nowhere else to go, he started up a narrow set of spiral stairs and Noah followed. They climbed in silence and emerged underneath a clear night sky on a raised, flat deck. The space had been secluded from rest of the bustle on the boat beneath them with a short metal wall. A sheet of clear glass made the back railing, offering a view into the slow, churning wake behind them. Noah chanced a glance up at the twinkling stars above before studying the man and woman stationed at the railing, heads bent in deep discussion.

At the sound of Benji's approaching footsteps, the woman turned. Adette Dumas looked healthier somehow since having a dagger plunged into her heart. That would've been a fatal blow for any mortal. He should have witnessed her death that day. Instead, she stood smiling in front of him, the dagger with the flowers etched into the blade stuck into the belt around her waist, and he couldn't help wondering what god he had pissed off in a past life to be in the midst of another vindictive vampire.

"Noah." His name rolled off her tongue with that devastating French accent. He rolled his shoulders as she continued. "*Bon chance*[2], it's so good to see you," she cooed as she strode toward them, pulling Noah into an embrace. Though slight, smaller than him in every way, her inhuman strength could be felt in the way she wrapped her arms around him. Noah stiffened, his heart rate throbbing in his neck. She dug her nails into his back before releasing him, stepping back to look him up and down. She tsked at Benji.

"Have you not shown him all the amenities, Bennie? He seems so stressed." She pouted as she studied him more. Noah flashed a glance to Benji to see if the ridiculous nickname would affect him. He hated any interpretation of his name beyond Benji. Noah had even seen him punch a man at a bar for calling him Ben. Albeit, it was after a few shots and used in condescension during a poker game. But still, *Bennie?*

And yet, the look of admiration shined bright on Benji's face. It didn't match the man Noah knew like the back of his own hand. Or thought he knew. Noah's reality had been crashing around him since waking up on this boat.

Benji rubbed the back of his neck and said, "*Désolé*[3], Adette. Time got away from me and I didn't get a chance to properly show Noah around sooner."

Noah couldn't stop the smirk that pulled on the edges of his lips. He looked up to the constellations above, attempting to hide it. The sight brought him back to a rooftop in a city far away, lying next to a woman who had leaned on him on her worst day. Sought comfort in him. *Trusted him.* He grew pale and looked back at Adette. She watched him with an intense curiosity that set the hair on his neck on end.

"Are you amused by us, Noah? *Je t'amuse*[4]?" she asked, tilting her head in a predatory way as she waited for his response.

Noah clenched his fists then let them relax before he answered. "It is a bit amusing to hear my brother speak French in such a polite tone. Most of the real French we learned growing up were the swear words." He gave her another smirk for good measure.

Adette's eyes twinkled with amusement as she turned to Benji. "Is that so? *C'est bête*[5], you never told me this, Bennie."

Benji gave her a sheepish grin then glared sideways at Noah. No longer able to take the friendly exchange of this all, Noah blurted out, "So, are we here to make jokes or is there a reason I'm on this boat?"

The man at the railing finally turned, bright orange hair whipping in the breeze as his light eyes narrowed on Noah from behind wire-rimmed glasses, shoulders visibly stiffened from his outburst. Definitely not a bodyguard, with his thin frame and academic look yet Noah knew too well what the so-called cure could do to a person like him. The strength it could coax out of their genetics.

Noah could feel the heat of rage radiating off Benji next to him, no doubt fuming over his impropriety in the presence of their "honored" company. Adette's eyes shifted from the man with the orange hair to Benji and then settled on Noah. Her words came out as a cool breeze, cutting through the autumn bite in the air. "You mean, is there a reason we rescued you?"

Noah blanched. "Rescued?" he asked, his voice rising to a level that caused Benji to clench a fist. Noah glanced down at it then up at his brother's face, into the murderous rage creasing the lines there. Noah looked away, biting his lip as a battle waged in his mind, trying desperately to reconcile the brother he had mourned with the one standing beside him. A stranger. An untrustworthy advisory. An enemy.

In that moment, Noah longed for Izzy's sharp tongue and undying loyalty.

Do you think she still trusts you, too? The thought broke through the tension, cooling the anger stirring within, replacing it with an anguish that cut deeper. Adette's voice waded through the despair.

"*Oui*, Noah. We rescued you from The Society. From that gang, *quel était leur nom*[6], the one with that woman." Disgust coated her words as she rubbed her chest. The same spot where Izzy's dagger had found its mark to no avail.

Noah glared at her. "Who said I needed to be rescued? And what qualifies you to do the rescuing? How did you even know I was there?"

Sharp, blue eyes snapped to meet his and she dropped her hand, clicking her tongue. The group followed as she turned toward a table set around the glow of lanterns near the edge of the windowed railing. Plates were set atop a bright white tablecloth. Flames flickered in the breeze in the extra lanterns set in the middle of the table. The walls extended up higher in this area, keeping a small fire within a stone chimney crackling next to the table to provide warmth.

It was all, frankly, a bit much.

"So many questions, so soon. Come, let us dine together. Get to know each other. Maybe you'll find I am not *l'ennemi*[7] you seek." Benji and the man with flame colored hair took their seats at each side of Adette, staring directly at each other as she stood at the head of the table, watching Noah. Waiting for him to move.

He contemplated his options, glancing to the murky water beyond the railing. Could he survive the jump? The swim? The wild waters of the Mississippi at night and the subsequent hypothermia?

Could he make it back to St. Louis if he survived?

As if she could read the spiral of his thoughts, he turned to see Adette's gaze focused on him. Daring him to make his move. Strike once to capture the queen and strike hard or suffer the consequences.

He sighed and walked to the remaining open seat at the end of the table opposite Adette. Once he sat down, she snapped her fingers and sat down herself. A sudden flurry of movement came out from the stairwell behind him, like a hive of bees, as people emerged dressed in black similar to his kitchen uniform and carrying silver trays. Each wore thick mitts and kept a solemn, indifferent look on their face. Noah caught the eye of the woman he had seen before in the hallway, the one with the brown wavy hair and green eyes. A shade he thought so similar to Izzy's. In the dark they seemed wrong though, missing the electric mischief that lit up the world around her and sparked a fire in his heart.

He hadn't realized he had been staring until he watched a blush tint the woman's pale cheeks and he looked away as she made her way toward him. She took her time setting the silver tray down in front of him all the while he studied her, unable to take his eyes off her. Unable to stop comparing her to the one he had left behind. The woman was shorter, more petite. Her hair was an ordinary shade of brown, not the intoxicating wine red strands of Izzy's. Her lips lacked that sly tilt that made Noah yearn to know every one of her thoughts.

Benji coughed and Noah snapped back into the present, shaking his head. He needed to focus. The lid had been removed from the silver tray and in front of him was a colorful array of braised root vegetables and a blackened piece of fish. *Touching.* He quirked a brow toward Adette. She smiled.

"Ah, *oui*, to your liking, *n'est-ce pas*[8]? I haven't been in New Orleans long but I do enjoy the flavors of the city. So different from the French food, or even the British food, I've grown accustom to all these years. *N'es pas d'accord*[9], Henry?" she purred, her tone taking on the jubilant role of hostess for the deranged dinner party before her. The Mad Hatter would be impressed. Noah sympathized with Alice in that moment, wondering how he had so easily fallen down his own rabbit hole.

"*Oui*, Adi," Henry, the man with the orange hair, said. He had a British accent that had Noah eying him suspiciously as he took a bite of food. The freshness of it all alarmed him, rattling him off his game for a moment as he took another bite. And then another. When did he last have fresh food? All his meals had been served to him cold, tasting of the time spent away from when it had been prepared. But this…this was spectacular.

Adette chuckled from her seat at the other end of the table, eyes sparkling as she watched him. He slowed his chewing, looking up at her.

"*C'est bon, non*[10]? We set up an incredible *hydroponiques* system in several of the storage containers on the boat. And our chef, *mon dieu*[11], he's a genius," she gushed, her accent getting heavier as her eyes glazed over. She reached for the deep red drink in front of her and that's when Noah noticed how it differed from the wine set before everyone else. Thicker, a deeper shade of red, almost black in the evening light.

He swallowed hard, set his fork down and assessed her. "So, you've built a whole community on a barge? Why?"

Her gaze hardened at his words. "Oh, you misunderstand, Noah. The barge is just our mode of transportation. It allows us to be mobile, able to get to where we are most needed." She gestured to him, as if he had needed her, beckoned her to come rip him out of the life he had started to enjoy. "But what we've done is rebuild, starting with your beloved city New Orleans. Emilien left it in such disarray when he scampered off with his tail between his legs, running to that wretched city in the North. Henry and I worked together to clean up his mess. Like we've been doing for the past twenty years." She stared adoringly at the man in the glasses next to her, squeezing his hand. He looked at her with the same adoration painted across Benji's face every time Adette spoke to him.

Noah glanced down to their connected hands. "For the past twenty years?"

Adette let go of Henry's hand and they both glanced to their plates, shifting in their seats. "*Oui*. Henry worked…closely with Emil at Oxford. We've known each other for quite some time. When Emilien came to me with his cure," she glanced to Henry. He gave her a gentle nod of his head. "I was…hesitant. We ended up separating shortly after and my illness started to rapidly advance. It was Henry who helped convince me to reconsider. That there was some good to come from this." She turned to Henry and gave him a soft smile. Benji watched them with an intensity that unsettled Noah.

Noah reached for the glass of wine in front of him, taking several gulps as her words sunk in.

"We worked tirelessly to develop a way to make the *disease* Emilien unleashed on the world into something truly good," she added, returning her gaze to Noah.

His eyebrows crunched together. "And how's that?"

She feigned a look of shyness that was only half believable. "Oh, *dieu*, it is such complicated and boring science talk. Too much for this beautiful evening. Even I get sleepy when Henry is talking sometimes." She laughed, overly cheerful, and the rest of the men at the table chuckled in support. Except for Noah.

"Enlighten me. Color me intrigued," he said, shifting back in his seat, wine glass held in his hand.

Benji shot daggers down the table at him but Noah kept

his focus on Adette. Watching her every movement. Her every reaction. A vein throbbed in her forehead but her smile remained.

"Maybe another evening. It is getting late and I know you'll want to get cleaned up and some proper sleep before your first real shift with the crew tomorrow." She glanced over at Benji and nodded. His brother stood, setting his fork and napkin down on the plate of unfinished food in front of him. Noah took the hint and did the same before Benji had the chance to drag him out of his chair.

The brothers made their way over to the stairwell and as Noah went to take his first step down the metal grated stairs, Adette's voice called out from the table.

"I do look forward to working with you, Noah Broussard."

Noah stepped down into the warm belly of the beast, relishing the rise in temperature as her words chilled him straight to the bone.

❖

"What the fuck was that, Noah?" Benji exclaimed as soon as the door to his room was shut.

They had made a brief stop at the laundry room on their way back to grab a fresh set of Noah's black kitchen uniform and some clean towels. Each were thrown onto his bed as Benji began pacing around the tiny space. Noah settled into the small chair to give him room, running a hair through his hair.

"How have you become so disrespectful in such a short amount of time?" Benji chastised. "I mean, who were you even hanging out with in St. Louis? Heathens?"

Noah miffed, dropping his hand to stare at his brother in disbelief. "Heathens, Benji? Really?"

UNWILLENDE HÆTHENS GÆDRIAN GIFANGAN[12]

The text flashed into Noah's mind and he gripped the armrest of the chair.

Benji stopped his pacing and turned to Noah, lips tightly pursed together as he glanced to his hands and scowled. "Yes, heathens. You talked to her like she was a criminal. Like she has done something wrong!"

His outburst snapped Noah back into the room and the disappointed look on his brother's face. God, his fucking brother.

His words danced off his tongue like drops from an icicle. "She kidnapped me, Benji. She had someone tackle me, drug me, and then tie me to a chair in a supply closet on a fucking barge that is now heading toward the one place we attempted to blow up because it was so rampant with corruption and coercion. So, yes, I have my *apprehensions* about her motives. Don't you?" His voice steadily rose with each word and he looked down to realize he stood less than a foot from his brother. His *fucking* brother.

Benji glanced over his shoulder at the closed door and looked back to Noah, searing him with the outrage flaming through his hazel eyes.

"No, Noah. I don't. You haven't seen New Orleans and what she has done there. The city is thriving, even better than before this whole shit storm started."

Noah scoffed. Like it had ever been good for them, two orphans bouncing through the system until Benji decided the streets were a more stable environment for them both. He wrapped both his hands around the back of his neck and stared up at the yellow ceiling. He shook his head and breathed out a hollow laugh. When he looked back at his brother, really took him in, there was no denying their shared blood. They had the same build and skin tone. The same hazel eyes with that golden-copper tinge. The illusion the colors created when focused on something unsettled even the toughest in their ranks. Especially in malice. But Noah was used to that disapproving look. It was nostalgic for him. It felt like warm summer nights and sneaking into abandoned buildings.

"What's your motive, Benji? Why are you here?" Noah asked, letting the fight leave his body on an exhale.

The shift startled Benji and he balked, taking a step back and glaring. "What do you mean 'my motive'? It's the same wish everyone from our city wants: freedom. For our people, for our community. This isn't about *me*."

Noah's eyes widened. "It isn't? Then why are you *here*, on this glorified ark? Did you even know I would be in St. Louis?" He gestured to the metal room, a distorted Polaroid of the past.

Benji's glare turned murderous and Noah's hand clenched into a fist. He felt his own pulse quicken, his shoulders square, his muscle tense in anticipation for the punch he was certain to receive.

Benji let out a sharp exhale, and damn him, if Noah didn't flinch in response. His brother didn't notice though as he looked away, releasing his fists. "I thought you would've been happy to see me, Noh. To see our goal didn't die with me in that building. But instead, you're asking me to justify why I would support the improvement of our home in a time when there seems to be no good coming out of the world." His brother turned around, cracking the seal on the crank door and taking a step out. Before he disappeared down the endless maze of hallways, he turned his head to Noah and said, "I'm glad you found your things. In case you still thought this was a kidnapping."

Then he slipped out the room, slamming the door shut behind him and spinning the wheel.

Noah's mind whirled from their interaction. He had no real memories of his parents, just fuzzy images that slowly morphed into abstract watercolors as he aged. But Benji had been older than him, had known their parents before they left them. *Just like he abandoned you.* He slumped into the creaky bed and sighed. His thoughts spun between Benji and his family and his circumstances and Izzy. *Izzy.* His whole life had been one colossal fuck up. He couldn't even properly romance a woman without watching her entire life go up in flames, the ashes scattering in the storm of him.

He was a curse.

He is the sickness and the cure.

Adette's words drifted back into his mind. What had she meant? It must have been Henry she was talking to while he was tied to a chair like a fucking criminal. But there had been another voice. A concerned voice.

Worry festered in his chest. Everything about this boat felt wrong, despite everyone's ministrations that all was fine and well in the world with Adette there to save them. But the whole arrangement was off. He could've sworn as Benji led him out of his "not prison" he had seen people in lab coats walking down a nearby hall.

He stood, walked toward his door. He hadn't heard the lock latch when Benji left. He could leave. He could get out now. He could make it back to St. Louis. To Izzy. To his home…

As if the boat could hear his thoughts, it groaned and he snapped out of it. Running a hand through his hair, he readied himself for another restless night of sleep. His hands went to his pockets and he found the metal of the necklace in one, heated from its proximity to his body. He pulled it out, studying it in his palm. The chain had been broken but the fat cross with Latin printed on it glistened in the dim light. ROMA had been stamped into the back beneath a picture of a man.

He needed to leave. He couldn't stay here, he knew that much. But he couldn't afford to make any mistakes again. He couldn't get distracted. Fisting the necklace, he shoved it under his pillow and sank into the spring laden bed.

✢

CHAPTER FIVE
IZZY

The ice clinking the sides of her glass set her into a mindless reminiscence of what their Friday nights used to look like; Vahagn across from her, smiling as he teased her about her unruly hair, Charlie sulking at the end of the table, Lando leading them through another story about the "old country" and his time spent stealing cars while he worked at a local pizzeria.

She grimaced as the bourbon burned down her throat, only serving to heighten the memories. Focus returned to her vision and with it, a distinct shade of steely blue eyes set on her. Charlie. Always fucking Charlie. She averted her eyes and took another big gulp, swallowing down her disdain for everything that represented her new life.

"Isabella, *mi bella*, why the long face? Has the *primavera*[13] not been to your satisfaction? The sunshine has been nice, no?" Lando grimaced as soon as the words left his mouth, hidden behind a swift sip of his drink. A sharp glare shot his way but not from her. What had Charlie acting so goddamn protective?

The glowing filaments from the Edison bulbs above her reflected in the inky night beyond the picture window, illuminating the empty seat across from her. She glanced to Lando.

"No, Lando. It has not been to my satisfaction. But it's okay. I'll figure it out."

Smoke billowed in front of the old man as he glanced warily between her and Charlie. He leaned forward, absentmindedly tapping the greying ash at the end of his cigar, nodding his head as if he understood her predicament. The fact he even tried to pretend a sense of normalcy still existed between them during their weekly meetings was insane. Any time a hint of her new "lifestyle" crept into the discussion, he quickly changed the subject. Like he could barely stomach being in the room with her. His insistence they continue this tradition was damn near morbid.

Coward, she thought. Her gut had told her to never fully trust him and god damn it if it hadn't been right. He had known about Charlie, about his involvement with The Society. Hell, he used it, gathering "invaluable" information about the gangs movements in the city from his traitor second. She could never bring herself to ask if he knew about Vahagn before it happened. She couldn't trust herself with what she would do with that knowledge.

Charlie cleared his throat. "What hasn't been to your satisfaction, Iz?"

Oh fucking hell. Someone gag her. Who let him stir the pot? A callous smile crept onto her face, morphed by her inner torment. She let out a long exhale before setting down her glass with a clunk, vintage crystal be damned.

"Gee, Charlie, where do we begin? How about with how I can't actually enjoy the sun or the warmth or the prospect of a decent fucking tan this year? Or that I have to latch onto my ex-boyfriend's neck every other day so I don't turn into a crazy version of Bloody fucking Mary?" Lando choked on his smoke, coughing next her. She flickered a glance to him, studied the way his heart rate quickened as his lungs spasmed. But her tirade had begun and she was going to see it through, even if she ended up homeless by the end of it.

"Or! How about how everywhere I turn in this god forsaken city I run into that British pub goblin that tried to murder me over a stupid fucking book last year?" The rest of her bourbon momentarily drowned out her thirst as she tossed the glass back. She scanned the bar behind Lando, looking for another bottle. No way this would be a one glass kind of night.

As she stood to make her selection, Charlie cut in from down the table, "What do you mean, 'British pub goblin'?"

She eyed her options, hand dancing between a vintage bottle of Blanton's and her favorite, Bulliet Ten Year. A tall bottle with an eagle on it caught her eye in the back of the shelf and she pulled it toward her in delight. Eagle Rare had just the bite she needed on her lips tonight. She could feel Charlie's growing impatient with her from across the room as she took her time adding another ice cube and a dash of walnut bitters into her glass. On second thought, she threw a dried orange into the mix. Why not be indulgent with her likely final visit to this penthouse?

"I mean," she said, as she pulled the top off the Eagle Rare, "that asshole with the pretentious Peaky Blinders tweed cap was hanging around where Barry and I went for lunch today." The men in this room didn't need to know they were at the library or what they were doing there. No one did as far as she was concerned. All bridges to her thoughts and schemes had burned to the ground six months ago, an ashen grey pile of dust along with the rest of the city. A dusty bottle of Stagg caught her eye as she went to pour the Eagle Rare. She set the bottle down and reached for the stout bottle with antlers etched on the front. *Vahagn's favorite*. An echo of a tear sprang to her eye as she poured herself a double and went back to her seat.

Charlie set a glacial stare upon her, watching her as she sipped the golden liquid, ignoring how similar it was to the shade of Noah's eyes in the evening light. A warmth she hadn't found in that room since he left. She scowled at Charlie.

"What do you want, Valentini?" she barked.

"Where the hell were you that Callum would be hanging around?"

"Callum? Is that his name? God, that's forgettable. And unfortunate. How did a man named Callum find himself in a vampiric crime syndicate?"

"Same as the rest of them, he was a graduate assistant in Emilien's lab. Where were you?" Charlie pressed, the persistent bastard.

She grinned and took another sip. No wonder Vahagn loved this stuff. It was smooth. "The location doesn't matter. He was there and I did not appreciate it."

He narrowed his blue eyes on her, staring for a beat. To her surprise, Lando's cigar had burnt to an ashen nub on the end as he simply observed them. She rubbed her arms and shifted in her seat.

"Fine, be mysterious. But there has been some…discontent since what happened this fall, so at least try to be careful if you run into any of those guys around the city, okay?" Charlie said, taking on the role of caring male figure again. It was starting to make her itch.

The thick amber swirled lazily with the slow melting ice cube in her glass and she studied it. Got lost in it, the two liquids fighting each other until the inevitable occurred and they became one.

"Yeah, yeah, yeah. I've been hearing that for, shit, like seven years now? It clearly hasn't worked so can I suggest a new tactic?" She scanned the empty table, noting the number of empty rattan backed vintage seats. It wasn't just The Society dealing with discontent in their leadership. Lando's contribution to the destruction of the library and the rumors he might have been in the know about Vahagn's death circled around his ranks like piranhas on a hunt. As a result, his numbers had seen a steady decline.

Where do unemployed gangsters go to find work? She would have to ask Gio the next time she saw her. If she ever saw her again. Or if the woman ever talked to her again. Lando's daughter had disappeared after the holidays, apparently something big going on overseas that she had to be there for full time. Plus the last time they had spoken to each other, Izzy had attempted to rip her throat open. So there was that.

Charlie's jaw tightened. But it was Lando who spoke through his cloud of smoke. "There still hasn't been a resolution with the Frenchman?"

Izzy rolled her eyes and went back to studying the world beyond the windows, with its secrets lurking in the night. It was one thing to be damned to an eternal life and a whole other thing to suddenly be included in the business discussions of a failing mob.

Charlie glanced at her before saying, "No. Dumas is still waffling between going after his wife or moving forward with his plans here."

That clipped her attention. "His plans?" she asked.

Lando answered. "He wants to replicate his 'success' in New Orleans. Apparently his investor had a six month plan for the Gateway to the West that the vampire has surpassed."

Vampire. The word had started to acquire an offensive connotation in her mind. Like she was no longer human. Just a monster. To be fair, it didn't feel wrong.

She wrinkled her nose at Lando and glanced down at Charlie, sitting with his hands clasped in front of him, staring out the window in thought. Had he always been this contemplative? He had been different since that fall, like his traitorous ways were catching up to him, even forced upon him as they had been. A speck of sympathy floated through her and she felt disgusted, taking a long draw on her drink.

"So what? He's behind schedule. It happens. But what do you mean like New Orleans?" she asked, remembering Noah's description of the Crescent City and how it had turned into a southern hellscape.

This time Charlie spoke, his voice husky, "Exactly what you're thinking. Give the elite the immortality they crave, even if they have to finance it, and make the rest of the community fodder for their every indulgence."

And St. Louis was the right kind of corrupt for that plan to actually work. She hoped its citizens could continue the fight against it, for a little while longer at least. But a future like that felt imminent with their leaders taking the bait.

"What's stopping him? In either scenario?"

Charlie sighed, leaning back against his chair. The wood creaked under his weight. "After the explosion and subsequent fall out this past fall, loyalties have faltered. A lot of the guys in The Society aren't sure if Emilien is fit to lead them. And he hasn't made an effort to convince them otherwise with his inability to act. It's like the shock of seeing Adette has consumed him."

Lando sat, smoking his cigar and nodding as if Charlie's word were all old news to him. She studied the older man. How deep were his ties with The Society? Did they know the deception he played with them? Were they playing one against him?

She turned back to Charlie. "And what do The Society members want?"

He assessed her with something like pride as he said, "A great majority want to ready an army to go after Adette. I mean, she walked into the city, into the warehouse, took one of their most valuable soldiers, and left."

Izzy stiffened. "Most valuable soldier? Noah didn't even want to be in The Society. He was only in because of his brother and then ran away when he died."

Charlie tilted his head, eyes glittering a violent shade of blue. "Is that what he told you?"

Fury went through her like a violent wave and she pushed back from the table. She had humored them all enough for the night. As she turned to exit the room and the god forsaken penthouse, Charlie's footsteps pounded behind her.

"Izzy, wait," he said, hand brushing her arm.

She pulled out of his grasp and stopped, hand on the thick metal handle of the ornate door. She studied the carved design of wolves, the pack stalking through the woods. On a hunt.

He sighed, running a hand through his black hair. "I'll talk to Callum. In the meantime, probably don't go to the old library. It might be a new meeting place for them while they are figuring out the hierarchy in the organization."

She nodded her head once, heart pounding. *How had he known?* "Is that it?" she asked calmly.

He let out another sigh. "Yeah, that's it." Resignation softened his words.

She couldn't find a reason to care as she pulled the door open and slipped into the dark hallway.

Her apartment welcomed her with a haunting of memories. Vahagn sprawled on the couch, eating her cache of snacks and hogging the good controller for the video games. The one he didn't drop into a pitcher of margaritas one Christmas. Noah in the kitchen, cooking and cleaning. Smiling, the softest dimple creasing his cheek. The night of the dinner party a lifetime ago with Gio and Barry laughing hysterically at Vahagn's expense.

The happy warm glow of these memories morphed into passionate screaming matches with Charlie, the emotions of which always led to them fucking on her couch, her counter, her bed.

She slammed the door shut and all these thoughts went up in smoke, revealing the cold, dark space before her. She stalked toward the collection of liquor bottles lined up on her kitchen peninsula. Not bothering with a cup, she grabbed the tequila and dragged her feet toward her closet, kicking off her shoes as she went. Collapsing onto the floor in the corner of the tight space, she worked the loose floorboard up and rifled through the collection of items within. It had been a month after Noah disappeared when she noticed the random box of items sitting outside the building across the street. Normally she would've left it alone but her curiosity got the best of her. When she walked up and saw the vintage Saints sweatshirt sitting on top, she grabbed the whole thing and brought it upstairs to her apartment. That night devolved into sloppy crying into a bottle of bourbon as she pulled out the meager remnants of Noah's life. All of which lived under her floorboards with the rest of her secrets. She pushed the sweatshirt aside to reach the linen wrapped package deep within.

Freeing the book from its protective sleeve, she leaned back against the wall and propped it open on her knees. Her vision as a vampire had improved to a frighteningly good level as she sat in the dim lighting of her closet floor and read every ornate, decorative word in front of her without even a squint.

The script within The Ramblings had drove her mad those first few weeks after Noah's disappearance. He had been the one who could decipher the text. She had worked hard in his absence to learn but only made marginal progress, mostly with the words she could sound out. The rest was gibberish. Even the best translators online were of no help. She took a swig of tequila and flipped lazily through the pages. A note fluttered to the floor and she hastily picked it up. The creased edges were worn from the hundreds of times she had pulled it out, reading and re-reading Noah's tight scrolling script.

Izzy—

His handwriting tore at her heart and she took another gulp of liquor. Where *had* he gone? Was it by choice? Charlie made it sound like he knew he would be taken. But he couldn't have known.

But why would he leave you this note then?

She shook her head and took another swallow of the amber agave liquid in the bottle. Reaching into her pocket, she pulled out her phone, clicking through to her text messages. Specifically, to the ones between her and Noah. Her finger hovered over their last conversation to each other.

Then before she realized what she was doing she typed out a new message.

IZZY

> Please tell me you can see this and you're alright and you didn't leave me on purpose because I could really use you right now.

She stared at the screen, thumb posed precariously over the Send button. Another healthy gulp of tequila slid down her throat, a drop spilling out the corner of her mouth. The screen continued to taunt her as the droplet rolled down her chin.

"Fuck," she said, deleting the message and rubbing the liquor away. She glanced out the frosted window to her right, the moonlight barely illuminating beyond it. Scoffing, she looked back to her phone and turned the thing off. No one would be reaching out at that hour anyway. Not anymore.

Pressing her back into the brick wall behind her, she took another drink. Only a quarter of the bottle remained. She stared into the frosty deep blue light from her window, drinking until her thoughts turned to black, her vision along with it.

⚜

The streets were dustier than she remembered them being, though it had been a while since she had been to that part of the city. Her heels clicked over the cobblestones beneath her. She halted, scanning the streets. Actually, she wasn't sure she had ever been there.

The arch loomed behind her and she desperately tried to get her bearings but the streets were all wrong. The curbs were masoned stone, not the modern concrete she knew. The cars rumbling over the stones were old, classics. Even the signs looked like original vintages, the hand-painted letters beautifully scripted across the brick walls of buildings.

She groaned and press her palms into her eyes. Another dream. At least it wasn't one of her awful memories but how long would she be stuck in her own psyche this time around?

A pull like a string around her rib cage guided her down the road. She turned a corner and shining in bright, neon letters, like a beacon, was THAXTON'S.

She couldn't recall the place from her time, her version of St. Louis. Still she pushed through the door, taking a double take at her reflection in the glass door. Clad in a short, flapper style dress and strappy heels, she looked like a long-haired version of Clara Bow. She tried to stay in the shadows as she slinked in, spotting an empty booth in the corner with a view of the whole room. A band played on a raised, polished stage, a respectable smooth jazz melody at home in any modern-day elevator. Several people sat at small tables, in close conversation or watching the men play as they drank clear or white liquids. The occasional cloud of cigar smoke plumed into the air.

A waitress walked over. "What are you having, sweet cheeks?" she asked.

"Oh, um, bourbon. Neat, please."

The woman shushed her, looking around nervously. In a panicked voice she said, "Ma'am, we are not that type of establishment."

Izzy barked out a laugh. "Is this not a bar?" She gestured to the counter where a man, who looked very much like a bartender, stood cleaning glasses. But then she examined the glass shelves behind him. The empty glass shelves.

The waitress straightened, dusting the front of her apron in a huff. "We are a music hall. Nothing more. You may have water or milk or any rendition of those options. That's it."

Izzy sighed. "Water is fine." The woman scurried away.

She had ended up in prohibition. What a terrible fucking way for her subconscious to tell her to sober up.

A glass of water, neat, was placed in front of her a few moments later. The woman hurried off before Izzy could even say thank you. She took a sip and scanned the crowd. Everyone seemed ordinary. Nothing of significance.

Why had her mind brought her here? And how could she get out?

Just as she contemplated climbing to the top of the building to throw herself off it in an attempt to wake up from the drolling boredom of her dreamscape, the bell above the door rang out across the space. Her curiosity sparked, she leaned over the edge of the wall around her table, catching a view of the man who walked in. He wore a dark cap and well-tailored suit, all in black tweed. His shoes shined in the golden glow from the sconces on the walls, setting a dim ambiance on the space. His dark eyes scanned the room, stopping when they landed on Izzy. He ran his eyes down the length of her exposed legs and back up, smirking when he met her gaze again. Her eyes widened and she shrunk back, taking a couple of panting breaths before she got a grip with herself. This was a fucking dream. One with a fun, new twist stalking across the room. She assessed him as he strode past the bartender, giving the man a nod. The bartender nodded in return, threw his towel over his shoulder, and turned around, assessing the empty shelves.

The man in black walked into a dark hallway at the back of the room. As he approached a door to his left, he met Izzy's gaze one last time, before disappearing within.

"Intriguing," she whispered to herself as she worked her way out of the booth and walked toward the door. It looked like nothing special. Just a door. It could be anything, a closet, a bathroom. Yet, she reached for the handle and turned it.

A hand grasped her shoulder from behind and she whirled to see the fanged smile of the bartender before her, his golden eyes aflame as he drawled, "Let's not open doors we can't see the other side of, sweetie."

Her eyes opened to the soft blue glow from the twilight shining into her closet. Wincing at the crick in her neck, she looked around, studying her surroundings. Back to reality, with the empty tequila bottle resting atop Noah's sweatshirt and The Ramblings haphazardly shoved back into its plastic.

Groaning, she ran her hands down her face, rubbing roughly on her skin. Maybe she would stop drinking if it was going to lead to these awful cliffhanger dreams. She pulled her hands away from her face, ready to get up and go to bed, when she noticed a mark on the back of her hand. A stamp. A capital T. Her heart rate sped up as she rubbed at it and watched it disappear.

CHAPTER SIX
NOAH

The next morning, Noah jerked awake to the sound of the wheel screeching open on his door. He shot up, fists raised to fight, chest heaving. Benji strode in, caught a glimpse of Noah's defense and threw his own hands up in surrender, flashing a goofy smile.

"Still see you're trained well, that's good. But unnecessary now. Come on, I'm going to take you down and introduce you to the staff." Benji tossed Noah his uniform before adding, "Get dressed. You have five minutes."

The adrenaline slowly released its grip on Noah's heart rate as he ran a hand through his hair. *Fuck.*

"What time is it?" Noah groaned, peeling off the shirt he had slept in.

Benji rolled his eyes so dramatically, his neck had to follow. "Does it matter? Just get dressed, you're already late."

"And whose fault is that?" Noah grumbled under his breath as he stood, pulling the black drawstring pants on over his boxers. It was the same uniform the workers delivering their food last night wore. The same one he had been wearing alone in the kitchen, washing dishes with no one else around but Benji sitting by the door on guard. The black on black ensemble seemed to stand out against the rest of the crew he had seen. A dark shadow among their brighter, army green or khaki sets.

"The kitchen staff starts the earliest but they also get the most breaks throughout the day. Honestly, it's a pretty good group of people. It won't be bad." Noah couldn't tell if Benji was trying to convince him or himself.

Once Noah had his black sneakers slipped on, he said, "Show me the way, keeper."

Benji narrowed his hazel eyes on him but didn't deign a response. Instead, he pulled the door open and started walking down the hall, assuming Noah would follow. Noah sighed and stepped out of the room to do just that.

As they walked, he scanned the walls, trying to take note of the names on the small, discreet metal plates attached to various doors. A few simply said, "Authorized Personnel Only". Making mental notes of the scarce landmarks, a rusty pipe on the ceiling at the intersection, a light bulb off center like it had been hit with a bat, a handle painted blue instead of the typical moldy yellow. The color and its abundance around the boat sent him closer and closer to the edge of insanity every day.

Benji took a sudden left turn and Noah nearly blew past him as he committed the broken chip of glass in a door window to memory. They stepped down into the large, open galley kitchen. The small staff of five stopped their content chorus of murmurings and banging pots as soon as they entered. All eyes settled on Noah and desperately, he wished he could disappear. A pair of soft emerald eyes caught his own as he searched for a place to hide. He held her gaze for a moment, seeing fiery red curls and freckles that didn't exist on the woman before him. A faint blush tinted her porcelain skin and he looked away, meeting the eye of the larger man walking toward them

That's not Izzy, you dipshit, his mind shouted at him. Not her. Not here.

The man stopped in front of them, a burly guy with grey hair, a grey beard, and a large belly. Each of his large hands were decorated in stacks of various rings and he stuck one out toward Noah. Noah shook it, the man nearly breaking a bone in the process. "JEFE" was inked into the man's knuckles, along with a pale yellow flower in full bloom on top.

"Noh, this is Sancho. He's in charge down here," Benji said as Sancho released his death grip on Noah. He hid his grimace as feeling rushed back to his hand in pinpricks.

"Nice to meet you, Sancho," Noah drawled.

"Ah, another *chico del pantano*," Sancho said, grinning wide.

"Swamp boy," Benji translated, smiling and elbowing Noah in the ribs.

Noah nodded his head. It certainly sounded better in Spanish.

The man, the *jefe*[14], began pointing to the rest of the crew. "*Pantano*[15], this is Nigel, Rory, Gilbert, Hannah, and Nadia." The last name, Nadia, fell on the woman with the green eyes.

Not Izzy is what he told himself when their eyes met again. He frowned and looked back to Sancho.

"Everyone who starts out in this kitchen cleans dishes, as you've been doing and much to the relief of ol' Gilbert over there. So, that's where you'll be today." A silver serpent wrapped around the finger pointing to the large basin sink in the back of the room. The water rushed steadily by outside the window next to the sink, the sky an ink black that didn't signify if it was night or morning. Disorientation had been an understatement on the boat. Which way was up, what time was it, what's the difference between right or wrong. But he felt an itch to know what constituted as a day here. Like some truth laid in that simple knowledge as he studied the blackness of the world outside a second longer.

Everyone had given him a grunt or a nod as he worked his way to the sink. Only Nadia had stopped him, pressed a small, light touch to his arm as he passed, squeaking out a "Hi." A deep crimson blush flooded her face when he looked at her and she turned back to her work, kneading several pillows of dough.

Noah settled into his work quietly, letting his mind get lost in the repetitive cleaning as dishes were dropped into the dirty basin throughout his shift. Before he could think to check out the window and figure out a time, a big hand clapped on his shoulder and he nearly collapsed under the weight of it.

"Time for a break, *Pantanoso*. We eat in here," Sancho announced, turning away from Noah before he could acknowledge him. Noah quickly washed his hands, drying them on the towel swung over his shoulder as he approached the stainless steel island in the middle of the space. Stools had been dragged up and everyone sat around, chattering as he slipped into the empty space between Nadia and Gilbert.

Against his nature, Noah spoke to the man on his left. "Hi, I'm Noah." The man responded with a grunt.

Nadia spoke instead. "Nice to meet you, Noah. I'm Nadia. Ignore Gilbert—he hasn't been happy a day in his life." She flashed him a smile, faint tinge of pink tinting her cheeks as she did.

Noah offered her a polite smile in response. "It's nice to meet you, too," he drawled, putting a hand out for her to shake. Her hand felt frail in his own.

Nothing like Izzy's. He wanted to growl at his own thoughts. For all he knew, Izzy thought of him as the enemy. At the very least, she had to hate him for abandoning her. He couldn't spend the rest of his life comparing every woman with fucking green eyes to her.

But can't you?

"So, you know Benji, then?" Nadia asked, an eager curiosity as she watched him.

Noah nodded as he chewed his sandwich. It was simple and yet, exquisite. Grilled chicken, with actual grill markers and everything, smothered in a delectable barbecue sauce, topped with shredded cabbage and sandwiched between the bread Nadia had shaped into beautiful loaves that morning. It was still warm beneath his hands.

Swallowing the bite in his mouth, he responded, "Yes. He's my brother, actually." He didn't sense a need to lie about that. But the shock on Nadia's face had him second guessing his decision to divulge such personal information.

"Really?" she mused, her expression turning contemplative. "He never mentioned you."

This sent Noah's mind reeling. Why would Benji not mention him? Why had they come to St. Louis then, if no one was expecting to find him? Before he could fall deeper down the rabbit hole opening in his mind, Sancho interrupted his thoughts.

"How's it taste, *Pantanoso?*" The nickname appeared to be sticking around.

"*Muy delicioso,* thanks for cooking it," he directed his appreciation to the table. He was given grunts and glares in response. The only person to offer him an ounce of a friendliness was Nadia.

"So, tell us about St. Louis, my friend," Sancho

followed up.

Noah tilted his head. "Weren't y'all there?"

Nadia glanced to her hands clasped together on the stainless steel counter. "We weren't allowed off the boat. Most of us weren't, actually."

Sancho cleared his throat pointedly at her and she blushed, seeming to shrink further into herself. Noah studied the two, and the rest of the crew before letting out a long exhale, filing that nugget of information to unpack later when he avoided sleep by staring at his ceiling, trying to figure this place out.

"What's there to tell, then? It's chaotic. Everyone for themselves. But it had a sense that was how it operated before…" Before all the world went to Hell in a *panier*[16].

Sancho huffed out an agreement, Nadia's shoulders relaxing as the older man murmured something along the lines of "cursed city" and went back to eating.

Noah deigned to ask the question dancing on his tongue, studying the bits of cabbage and barbecue drops on his plate as he said, "How's New Orleans?"

Everyone froze. It was for a nanosecond, imperceivable, but it was a collective movement and set the alarm bells blaring in his mind.

Sancho glanced around the table before saying, "It's much improved. Probably a completely different city from the one you left."

If only he knew, Noah thought, taking another bite of his sandwich, chewing slower this time. The ingredients turned to dust in his mouth and he had to chase it down with a couple deep gulps of water.

They all continued to eat in silence for a while after that. Once everyone finished their meal, plates were placed in the dirty basin and Noah's work began again.

By the time dinner for the kitchen crew came and went, Noah wanted nothing more than to collapse onto his horrible bed and fall into a fast, dreamless sleep.

✦

Unfortunately, sleep didn't come fast or dreamless for Noah. Instead, he laid on top of the scratchy canvas blankets, staring at the ceiling and it's peeling layers of paint. He had known moments of incredible peace in the weeks leading up to his arrival on this floating metal asylum. He had felt a semblance of home. Of caring. Of affection. Of…

He groaned and rubbed his hands over his face. It didn't help as the only image to meet his eyes when they closed were emerald pools of fire, a freckled nose scrunched in a laughter that enveloped his every sense, the softness of her skin beneath his touch, how the goosebumps raised beneath it.

His eyes flew open. He couldn't do this tonight.

He climbed out of bed and paced the small space, remembering his conversations that day. That moment when he brought up New Orleans. It had been off. Benji spoke like the Crescent City shined with the eternal light of the moon itself since the arrival of the Antisociété. But every single person in that room tonight froze at his mention of the city. And the way Adette spoke to him, like she did him a favor by kidnapping him.

As if the thought of what happened to him struck like a lightning bolt, he sat back down on the bed, mouth open in shock. Tears sprung to the edges of his eyes. He had been *kidnapped*. Again, for fuck's sake. And not just kidnapped, fully taken away from everything he knew without an ounce of hope that he could make his way back.

He huffed out a cold laugh as he looked to the black

duffel on the floor across from him. "They even thought to pack me a bag, how lovely," he murmured, running a hand over his face.

Then he froze.

Slowly, he reached a trembling hand under his pillow. Fingers met the cool metal and he pulled out the golden cross with its broken chain.

He held it in his palm, a slight tremble as he studied it.

And a new question worked its way to the forefront of his mind.

What happened to Izzy?

❖

Every day became a monotonous cycle of washing and drying dishes, broken up only by surprisingly incredible meals from Sancho and the rest of the kitchen crew, and mildly prying questions from Nadia. Noah decided he had revealed too much on that first day so resorted to vague or misdirecting answers to suffice her. Assessing her goal in her endless questioning had caused the uncomfortable feeling in the pit of his stomach to grow.

Yet he had more pressing issues at hand. After the initial first few days, Benji became too busy to come release Noah from his prison so his door lock fell under his own control, as well as his ability to move about the boat. It was not without a multitude of eyes on him but Noah took to walking the halls of the barge in his free time. That is how he discovered the quieter times on the boat early in the morning, before his shift in the kitchen began. When vampires and humans alike found a common ground to rest—each before the sun came out, for very different reasons.

This is when the real adventures began, taking note of each turn, every important labeled doorway, or passageway that appeared off limits. He had slowly been making his way toward the front of the barge where he had been kept prisoner. That section seemed closed off from the general population, far fewer black and green uniforms, like Benji wore when not decked out in black battle gear, and more white lab coats and beige scrubs. He needed to know the boat's secrets before her left.

There was a clear distinction between job roles and their perceived importance within the organization as well. Kitchen staff ranked right at the bottom alongside the janitorial staff. Every single person above them sneered at their black, boxy uniforms with the elastic waistbands. Orders were barked at them and requests were made in haste, as if their time was inconsequential.

It all set Noah's blood on fire. How could *this* be better than what Emilien had been doing with The Society?

A week came and went as they meandered down the Mississippi. Within that time, Noah had a general idea for the layout of the boat and its inner workings. In fact, he had made it to almost every section except his prison quarters. He remembered some more rooms glimpsed briefly down a hall when Benji had escorted him out of that dingy supply closet but the closer he got to them, the more turned around he became.

That morning, he awoke determined to change that. He slipped out of his room, dressed in the all black uniform of his lower class crew member rank. It allowed him the ability to blend into the darkness as well as the subconscious of anyone who might walk by him.

All was quiet in those early moments, nothing but the gentle groan of the massive boat through the mighty Mississippi.

Until he turned a corner into a dark hallway and felt the hair on the back of his neck immediately stand up. *Someone was nearby.* He could feel it. He kept pace, moving like he normally did through the halls, contemplative but with a purpose. Like he belonged there, even when no one else was in sight.

Everything was cool.

Everything was casual.

Everything was fucked when he heard a soft, feminine voice coo behind him, "You're up early."

Noah whirled around and, in the darkness, the woman ran into his chest with a huff. Instinctively, he reached out to stabilize her and his heart sank when he met her bright green eyes glowing in the dim light from the exposed bulbs dotting the other end of the corridor.

"Nadia," he ground out. His tone bit through the thick air. Of all people he thought might run into him on this mission, it hadn't been her. Still, it could've been worse. Noah had prepared to use any means necessary to avoid being thrown back into that makeshift prison cell.

"Are you lost?" Nadia squeaked out. She stood close to him, her chest brushing his stomach with every breath she took. She was so much shorter than Izzy. He took a step back.

"Um." Fucking hell, this had thrown him. He pulled a hand through his hair, glancing around their surroundings. "Potentially."

Nadia stepped forward, pushing past him to stare down the hall to the ominous light shining beyond. "Or did you mean to come this way?" When she turned back to him, an air of mischief shone in her eyes.

Noah rubbed the back of his neck. It wasn't like he *distrusted* Nadia. But he didn't know her either. He had no reason to trust her, or anyone on the barge for that matter. Hell, he had been strapped to a chair as their prisoner just over a week ago. And when they arrived in New Orleans, would he be offered a semblance of freedom like he had now? Or was this all a temporary reprieve?

The uncertainty coursing through him dissipated as he swallowed it down and in his absence of a response, she filled in her own. "I can help you."

"That's unnecessary." The words rushed out of him.

She ignored him and continued down the hall, saying over her shoulder, "It's really no trouble. Besides," she tossed him a wry grin. "It might look a little less suspicious if you're not alone."

Noah ran a hand through his dark brown hair again, watching as her form slowly blended into the darkness. She had a point. Being alone, as a previous-possibly-still prisoner of The Antisociété, likely didn't paint a warm, fuzzy feeling in the hearts of anyone who might happen upon him in what felt like a restricted part of the boat. On the other hand, he had noticed the way she had looked at him. Blushing whenever their eyes met. Finding an excuse to touch him. To talk to him. He didn't want her thinking this was anything more. It couldn't be anything more. Not when…

Her footsteps were faint as she neared the end of the hall.

"Fine," he said, jogging to catch up. In the dim light of the caged bulbs along the next hall, her smile radiated up at him, that typical pink tinting her cheeks.

"Great, we need to go right." And with that, she turned down the hall, beckoning him to follow.

A new part of the boat opened up around him, one he had only theorized the shape of after a quick glimpse during his moment of emotional despair. But as they walked, the entire layout of the boat shifted. The once narrow corridors built to make efficient use of the space expanded into pristine, clean lines. Space to move and not bump into anyone along the way. And along the walls were large observation windows, peering into dark rooms behind heavy metal doors with actual handles. No submarine style cranks or chipping yellow paint to be seen.

Noah squinted as they passed, trying to catch a view within one of the rooms but Nadia hurried down the hall.

"We need to be quick. Everyone will be waking up soon," she said. Her footsteps padded softly along the metal flooring and he did his best to mimic the sound. At the end of the hall of windows, she stopped.

"I've never been beyond here but I know you were kept in a room somewhere down to the right and the laboratories are to the left a ways."

Noah's gaze narrowed on her. "Laboratories?" Why would they need laboratories on a barge?

Her lips parted as if about to answer him when the soft click of a door closing echoed from the corridor to their left. They scurried back down the row of windows, turning into the dark, narrow hall they had come from right as voices filled the silence they had just occupied.

"It's all in French, I can't understand it," she whispered. He placed a hand over her mouth, her cheeks growing warm beneath his touch as he silenced her.

"*Les essais ne se déroulent pas comme elle l'avait prévu. Je ne suis pas tout à fait sûre...*[17]" The voices drifted off as they passed the junction they had just stood at and vanished down the hall still left unexplored.

Noah turned, releasing his grip on her face. "We should head back."

Nadia nodded and said, "Yes, people will be waking up soon and our shift starts in about an hour."

They walked back in silence, pausing outside a door Noah didn't recognize. "Well, this is me. I need to change before duty and…" Noah started to move past her, heading toward his own quarters to comb over everything they had discovered when she called out in a rush, "Same time tomorrow?"

Noah stopped, turning to tell her no, but she had already slipped into her room, the door closing softly behind her.

CHAPTER SEVEN
IZZY

Sweat flew through the air as Izzy twirled, swinging the broad sword in her hands around before slamming it into the straw dummy Lando had strung from the ceiling. The weight of the blade pulled her toward the makeshift man. Kicking it square in its scarecrow looking chest, she flipped over backward, landing gracefully into a crouch, the sword held out to the side, ready for defense. Not a tremble in sight. For a moment, pride coursed through her. She had been working on that landing for weeks, finally able to control her super human capabilities enough to not land on her ass or nearly break her neck.

Vampire capabilities. The thought immediately sobered her and she stood up, shoulders slumped as the blade dragged across the floor.

A low whistle and slow clap sounded from the door and she had her sword pointed in the direction in an instant, nostrils flared, breathing in that citrus scent she knew was *him.*

"And here I was, about to give you a compliment," Charlie said as he ducked under the sparring ring ropes and walked toward her. She tilted her chin up and raised the sword to align with his jugular. He stepped within an inch of the blade and raised a brow.

"But I see we aren't in the mood for compliments today." He lifted a hand, flicking the blade with his middle finger as a sly smirk formed on his lips. Her teeth ground together when his steely blue eyes met her own. "Would you rather spar?"

Rolling her eyes, she dropped the blade with a scoff and started to walk away. "I'm done," she announced.

"We can go to first blood," he tempted her.

She stopped her retreat, turning slowly on her heel to face him. Annoyance brimmed the edges of her words as she spoke, "I'm not sure what sort of masochism you're into these days, but I don't want to be a part of it."

He flashed a smile at her, running a hand through his thick, black hair. It had grown out some over the past few months and the tousled, shiny waves nearly fell to his shoulders. Vahagn would've hated it.

Vahagn. A vice tightened around her heart at the thought of him and she let out a soft exhale, grimacing as she broke her gaze from Charlie to try to compose herself. Her breaths shook slightly as she breathed in and out. When she looked back at him, he let out a deep sigh, his eyes thoughtful.

"It's not for me," he said, the words soft. Kind. She fucking hated them.

She stared at the floor, nose scrunched as she thought on it. She'd been training at night, let in under the constant watchful eye of Lando's unfortunate lackey of the day that pulled the third shift. Which meant she had been training alone for a good portion of it. Lando could barely look at her, seeing the monster at its finest, the cool finesse in the fluidity and strength at which she moved. It would be nice to practice that move on a living body...

She sighed and motioned for him to go get a weapon.

"You still gonna to use that broad sword, King Arthur?" he joked as he walked over to the wooden work table set up with practice weapons. There were better, stronger weapons in a hidden room in the office. Most on the table were made of hard wood or cheap, dull metal.

She scowled at his broad back as his hands roved over the menagerie, making his selection. She swung the sword around with one hand, testing her grip. "Yes, I am, thank you. It's my new favorite."

"I know," he murmured. His spine straightened and she watched as he reached for a plain wooden pole arm hanging on the wall behind the table. The stupid, boyish smile he had on his face as he turned caused her own lips to twitch upward for a second.

She frowned at her body's reaction to his joy and said, "Seriously? How are you supposed to draw blood with a glorified stick?"

He winked at her. "Guess you'll have to find out."

And before she could think of a retort, he swung the long wooden staff directly at her midsection. Her eyes widened but her reflexes kicked in, moving faster in her new body as her wrists raised, tilting the broadsword down to block. He pulled back only to advance again, swinging the staff overhead before cutting down diagonally, aiming for her opposite shoulder. The bastard had gotten crafty in their time apart from partnering in the ring. She swung her sword over in an arc, knocking the wooden pole to the floor in the process. Their weapons locked and gazes met. His look of adoration filled her with warmth for a brief moment before he flew over her sword, using the leverage from the pole to launch himself upward. Once on his feet behind her, he whirled, swinging the staff with one arm straight into her back. She let out an "oomph" before stumbling forward.

All air left her body and panic flooded through her as her lungs seized, refusing to do anything, take anything. She gasped, groaned and sputtered, grasping the sword harder as she bent over, trying, desperately trying to take in a breath.

Charlie swore under his breath, taking a step toward her. He extended a hand and groveled, "Iz, are you okay? I'm so sorry, I thought you would've saw that com—" His words were interrupted as she heaved the sword around, fighting hard against the protest in her body as the pain burned an endless hole in her chest. Through gritted teeth, she raised the blade, dropping it gently onto his shoulder. The cool metal kissed the soft flesh of his tattooed neck. Her vision speckled with black spots and a flash of a memory crossed her mind. Another man, another blade, another neck she made bleed to prove a point.

Charlie's eyes widened, his breaths coming in quicker, and she watched the vein in his neck pulse once, twice. Her lungs came back to life in time for her to scream as she pulled the sword down, leaving behind the smallest of cuts on Charlie's neck. Nothing fatal. Nothing that wouldn't heal in a couple days. Nothing to leave a scar.

The sword clunked to the ground, too heavy to clatter, and she leaned forward, resting her elbows on her knees as she gulped in the precious air she had been deprived of for so long. Charlie came up beside her and placed a tentative hand on her back. Her muscles relented under the pressure, too exhausted to fight him off.

Once her breathing returned to normal, she stood and his hand dropped to his side. She glanced at him and he gave her a smug smile. "You won." He turned his head to the side to show her the thin line of blood along his jawline. Saliva pooled in her mouth.

She glared at him, turning away from the sight. "Why do you look so happy about being sliced?" she asked as she bent to pick up her sword.

He shrugged, swinging the pole arm around in the air. "I like bearing witness to your successes, that's all."

Her eyes narrowed further as she walked over to the table to drop the broadsword with the rest of the weapons. Charlie followed, pole arm swinging acrobatically through the air.

"You really only came up here to bother me?" she asked, irritated. He looked too…happy.

He ran a hand through his dampened hair as he used the other to prop the pole back into place on the wall. "Actually, no. I need to talk to you."

Her eyes widened and she took a step back. "About what?"

He didn't immediately answer her. Instead, he sauntered over to the cool down station, pulling a fluffy towel out of the warming machine. She followed, her ire growing as she nabbed her water from its spot outside the sparring ring ropes. The place was empty, this was her alone time, and here he was, *being* in it.

He sat down on the matted floor with a groan and she flopped down across from him. "Getting too old to be flipping around like a young thug?" she jested.

"Har har, very funny," he replied, rubbing a spot on his shoulder. She studied the movement. Who was this guy? The Charlie she knew, had fallen in love with, had been cocky, arrogant. The textbook personality of a mafia boss's second in command. The Charlie she learned him to truly be was an unapologetic, controlling asshole. The Charlie sitting before her? He seemed relatable. Likable. What had changed?

Killing your best friend, for starters, her subconscious reminded her. Nausea roiled through her. And rage.

"Please temper whatever thoughts have you currently snarling at me." He gestured to her facial expression as he pressed his feet together, knees sticking out like the wings of a butterfly as he pressed his elbows into his thighs. "Do your cool down, Ciampi. You're not immune to sore muscles just because you get to live forever now," he said through a groaning sigh.

She kept her eyes on him as she pulled her legs out from underneath herself and straightened them, leaning forward to feel the pull deep in her muscles. A heavy sigh escaped her.

He seemed pleased when their eyes connected. Then he looked away before saying, "Emilien has been asking questions."

She stiffened, wincing as her hamstring seized up with the sudden tension.

Charlie frowned as he watched her, shifting so his left leg straightened while his right remained bent. "Quite frankly, so has Lando. They both want to know what's going on in your mind. What your plans are?"

She sat up, skin on her forehead wrinkling. "My plans? What do you mean, my plans? I don't have any plans."

He pulled his knees up, draping his arms over them. The delicate vine of green leaves and pink blooms intertwined in a dangerous dance with the black snake weaving between them. Her eyes narrowed on the snakes head, the slits for eyes staring back at her.

"Your plans. For the past six months, you have been mostly holed up in your apartment. You no longer come to the gym in the morning, you show up late to family dinner or completely sloshed, you are barely going to work…"

"Hey! Beechum approved me to work from home and

during off hours, as needed," she bit back.

His tone shifted. "Yeah, and how much of that is truly needed? You have access to a blacked out SUV that could take you to and from campus without even stepping a booted toe into the sun. And it's not like you instantly turn to dust in it, Iz. You would have to walk naked across campus to really feel it."

She rose to her feet, the blood rushing to her face as she shouted, "And how would you know?" Her cool down be damned. Seems Charlie had come to fight after all.

He balked, letting his hands drop to his sides as he stared at her, on the edge of disbelief and annoyance. "I would know, Izzy, because I've been working for them for the better part of the past year! But that's my business, my career choice. When was the last time you talked to Barry?" He stood up and crossed his arms, broadening his chest in the process. She scowled.

"Just the other day," she sniped, mirroring his stance.

His eyes glanced down to her crossed arms and he tilted his head, sarcasm radiating off him before he even spoke. "Oh really? And how's his new boyfriend doing?"

Izzy opened her mouth to speak then closed it. Stunned. Barry had a boyfriend? Since when?

Since you've been wallowing in the disappearance of yours.

But Noah hadn't been her boyfriend. He had hardly been more than a stranger. A stranger who arrived right before her entire world fell to absolute shit and conveniently disappeared afterward, leaving her to pick up the pieces. Alone. She couldn't forget that little truth.

"I…didn't…" she started to say.

Charlie moved, stepping forward to place a tentative hand on her cheek. She backed out of the touch, water threatening to spill over her eyelids.

"I know," he said, earnestly. "I know it's all a lot right now. I get it. But these guys," he motioned to the giant room around them. "They don't get it. The way they see it, you're an asset. But you need to decide if or how you want to be that for them."

Her expression turned murderous as she looked into his ocean eyes and growled, "I don't want to be anything to anyone. Not here. Not anymore."

Charlie sighed, running a hand through his long, black hair. He studied his reflection in the mirror next to them before facing her and saying, "Then fake it."

Her eyes widened. "Fake it? What is this, a joke to you?"

He shrugged. "Join them. Both of them. Play their games. Keep your friends close and all that."

She pressed her lips together. "What good would that do me?"

"It might help you get what you want," he said, a tinge of sorrow on his beautiful face. It had, unfortunately, not scarred when she had kneed him in the face that past fall.

"And what would you know about what I want?" she snorted, irritation returning to her words. How dare he act like he knows her, understands her. Just because she used him as a living Capri Sun didn't mean he had a clue what she was thinking, wishing, hoping would happen.

He rubbed at the ink on his forearm, one side of his lips tilting up it a grimace. He shook his head slightly and met her gaze. "Because I see how you look for him in every room you're in, even when you know he won't be there. Even when it's just you and me."

If she could set fires with her gaze, Charlie Valentini

would be a raging inferno.

"How dare you psychoanalyze me, Charlie." She shoved past him toward the door, snatching her bag off the floor. She hadn't bothered with a locker anymore. Who would dare steal from her? Turning to face him, she let the full weight of her wrath bleed through her words. "Just because I tolerate your presence enough to drain you of your own life force, doesn't make us friends. It doesn't even make us friendly. So stop pretending you know what I want. Or who I am. Or what I am." She heaved out a heavy, rushed sigh, looking away, catching a glimpse of her enraged reflection in the mirror.

What was she?

She scowled, turning to walk through the door but not before barking, "And don't give me your fucked up advice either."

She burst out of Lando's penthouse, startling the guards on duty. They eyed her warily as she shouted, "Fuck," before storming down the hall back to her apartment. Where she would be alone. Just how she liked it. How she preferred it.

❖

CHAPTER EIGHT
NOAH

The next night, Nadia appeared as soon as he turned around from gently closing his door.

"We can't go there tonight," she said by way of greeting.

Noah gave her a puzzled look. "Why not?"

Her eyes danced over him and then she started off toward the other end of the boat, the opposite direction he felt determined to investigate before he left this godforsaken barge. He hurried after her, frustrated, and grabbed her arm, whirling her around to face him. A trace of fear shone in her eyes and immediately he dropped his grasp, stepping out of her space. She stared at the spot where he had touched her while he spoke.

"I already know that way extensively. Why can't we go toward the front?" He glanced around, unsure if anyone might be listening in the shadows.

She refused to make eye contact with him and simply said, "We can't. But there is something I want to show you."

Noah sighed. "I don't have time to waste, Nadia."

"Then you're better served coming with me than getting

92

yourself caught," she snapped back. His eyes narrowed on the halo of soft brown waves around her face. What wasn't she telling him?

She didn't give him a chance to question her further though as she turned on her heel and headed toward the back of the boat. Noah followed, reluctant to abandon his plan when he felt so close to getting answers. Yet, there were unanswered questions following her might answer too.

They wove through the narrow hallways, only the occasional dim light mounted on the wall to keep them out of complete darkness. After a few turns, Noah started to recognize where they were going. If there was something important Nadia needed to show him, he would follow along. For now.

When she started climbing the stairs to the upper deck where Adette had invited him to dinner, Noah reached for her hand to stop her.

"There's nothing for me to see up there," he said, turning to walk away. It had been a total waste of a night and they didn't have many left. New Orleans was three, maybe four nights away, if his calculations were right. Once they got there, he had no idea how his life would be changed yet again.

"Wait! I promise it's worth it," she pleaded from the middle of the stairs, gripping the railing.

He stopped and let out a deep exhale.

Still an idiot, his subconscious reminded him as he turned around and motioned for her to continue climbing.

His footsteps were soft on the metal spiral staircase and when they rose from the dark depths of the barge, he jolted at the bright full moon illuminating the sky. His movements slowed as he gazed up at the stars, at the sky painted in a deep indigo as the faint light of day peeked out on the horizon, threatening to chase away the long night of winter. A shiver ran through him as the chilly air hit his exposed skin but he couldn't remove his eyes from the sky. The muddy river water of the Mississippi reflected a deep midnight blue beneath them as they skated over it.

"Where are we?" Noah whispered, scanning the shoreline. Between the bigger cities with their distinguishing landmarks like the Arch in St. Louis or the Hernando de Soto Bridge in Memphis, the landscape remained relatively the same. An infinite dense tree line etched the edges of the expanse of river water.

"Just passed Natchez, Mississippi last night. We should be in New Orleans in the next few days."

Noah nodded, happy to hear confirmation of his earlier thoughts on their pace. He scanned the sky, searching for a specific constellation among the sea of them. The bright stars of Pegasus in their square orientation caught his eye and he shifted his gaze down and to the left of the mythical flying horse.

Inconspicuous, just a bunch of scattered shining dots in the sky, yet they connected to make the constellation known as Pisces. He let a small smile on his face as he studied the astrology written in the stars. It was a Babylonian tale that saw it as two fish tied together. The Romans took it further, tying the story to Venus and Cupid, the mother and son turning themselves into fish and tying themselves together with a ribbon to escape the wrath of the monster Typhon.

The thought had Noah's smile faltering, a small tug on his own heart. He stole his gaze from the ether and looked to the grey metal beneath his feet, running a hand roughly through his hair. When he looked up, Nadia watched him, a curiosity on her face. Her lips parted as if about to say something and he glanced once more upward, to that thin tether between two hearts, and said, "I think we should head back."

A sudden wave of exhaustion roiled through him and he had no will to stay up there. No will to look to the stars and dream of sharing that view with another. No will to play mind games to get answers to questions he wasn't even sure how to ask. Not now. Not while his heart clenched in a death grip and his lungs fought to do their one job and take in oxygen.

Nadia roved an assessing look over him then nodded her head. "Okay. I'm going to stay out here a little longer…but same time tomorrow?"

He met her gaze, a hope twinkling in her eyes. Bile rose in his throat as he forced a half smile and said, "Yep, same time tomorrow."

Her returning beam ripped his chest open, spilling his guts to the black water below them. He hated himself for what he was doing. Hated who he became in the presence of these people in pursuit of preservation.

But he needed answers. And as he weaved his way back to his quarters, a path he knew by heart, he studied his marks, finding a moment of solace in the surety of his footsteps. Where he could move quicker. Where he needed to slow down, to blend in as others congregated between shifts. Where he could slip into the darkness. Into the back of other's minds.

It all came to a crescendo as he stepped into his room, his breaths coming in faster and faster. He slammed the door shut, spinning the wheel closed in one go as he turned around, pressing his back against the meager offering of wall. Sliding to the floor, his panic coursed through him. He had no control over it. Over his life. It was all a vicious wave he had to ride out. His mind whirled through the images and scenarios that sought to pull him deeper and deeper into the inky abyss of turbulent waters within him.

One thought remained on a loop, pressing hot tears

against his eyelids as he stared into the flickering light bulb above.

You left her and now you're all alone.

❖

The nagging feeling Nadia knew more than she was letting on pressed on Noah's psyche as he made his way to the kitchen that morning. Once his panic attack had subsided, he collapsed onto the bed and into a dreamless sleep. He awoke to the noise of others readying about outside his quarters, meaning he was walking in late.

When he stepped into the galley, her eyes were the first ones on him, inquisitive and all knowing.

Sancho gave him a stern look and he mumbled out his apologies as he went to the back of the kitchen and got to work on the pile of dishes waiting for him. As he washed, he stole glances over his shoulder. Watching her knead and shape loaves, as if he could catch a glimpse of the secrets she hid behind that pretty face.

"We can't go that way tonight."

He should have pushed her further, found out *why* they were relegated to the back of the boat. And how she knew. Instead, he had invited her into his plans. His stomach sank as dread kicked in with the thought. He was using her and yet he had relinquished some trust to her by bringing her in. Regret felt like a palpable layer over his skin.

The knife he had been scrubbing slipped from his grip, splashing into the soapy, warm water with a clang that broke him from his thoughts.

"Noah, you ready to eat, *mi hermano pantano*[18]?" Sancho called, tearing his focus.

He nodded his head and glanced over to the deep brown gaze of the big man. A faint tattoo of a teardrop creased under his eye as he studied Noah warily. Noah dried his hands on his towel, giving the older man a cool smile as he threw the cloth over his shoulder and slinked into his space between Gilbert and Nadia. Gilbert grunted his greeting and tore into the crusty chunk of bread before him.

Rory had told Noah that was just the way Gilbert spoke to others.

"On account of half his tongue being torn out and all." When the wiry man noticed Noah's blanched expression, he continued in a hushed tone. "Yeah, craziest story. He picked up some woman at a bar, a beauty with blonde hair and the body to match, if you know what I'm saying. Anyway, one thing led to another and another and next thing you know he's in bed with her, topless and all, and she just clamped her fangs down on his tongue and ripped it out." Rory shuddered and walked away, leaving Noah to the nightmare images he left behind. Nadia filled in the rest of the puzzle for him. Gilbert Gallifreh had been a big time business owner in the French Quarter, managing the most prominent boutique hotels and inns. He could, and did, get any woman he wanted. He could close any deal over one simple business dinner.

And now? He only spoke to Nadia and Sancho. Everything else was communicated through a series of grunts and head movements.

"Hi, stranger," Nadia said as Noah eased into his stool. He gave her a curt nod and she seemed taken aback by his unfriendly manner. She leaned forward, pressing her fingers into the exposed flesh of his forearm, her touch cool. "Have I done something to offend you?" she whispered.

Gilbert glanced between them and shuffled his stool further down the table, turning his body away to attempt to give them privacy. Noah's gaze tore from Nadia's fingers and the scorching sensation of her touch to the man's movements.

He steeled himself to meet her eyes. "No," he pulled his arm out of her grasp and cleared his throat, shifting in his seat. "No, just tired. I haven't exactly had the most relaxing couple of weeks." Or months, if he was being honest with himself. Hell, years, if he really wanted to get into it.

Nadia studied him, her gaze burnishing as it shifted over every feature of his face, causing a faint tingling in his chest. He rubbed at his chest and she followed the movement as she spoke in earnest, "Well, we will be at port in about a day and a half. Hopefully once you've established a routine and gotten settled, you'll get the rest you deserve." She picked off a chunk of her bread and popped it into her mouth with a smile.

Noah stopped chewing, the birria consommé soaked crust turning to acid in his mouth. That didn't give him much time to figure out what exactly was going on in the metal confines of the barge. Or plan for his escape once he got out.

He felt Nadia's green gaze on him and he returned to eating, taking a drink of water to cover up his lapse in function. As he drank, he studied her over the edge of his cup. Flecks of yellow and brown darkened the shade of green in her eyes, making them more hazel.

Nothing like Izzy's.

He shifted his gaze to the ceiling and set his glass back down before returning to eating.

So, tonight. His last chance would be tonight.

"Yeah, maybe it'll be better once we're back home." He let the lie roll off his tongue, swallowing the sour taste it left as a smile broke across Nadia's inquisitive stare. She kept eating and chatting with the rest of the group as if nothing had changed.

⚜

It was reckless, sneaking out early in the morning on

one of their last days on the water, but Noah had been backed into a corner. No semblance of an opportunity waited for him in New Orleans. It was his last chance to get answers, with everything in reach.

At least that's what he told himself as he slipped out of his quarters, dressed head to toe in his black uniform.

He followed the maze of turns down the narrow hallways, remembering a sign here and a flickering light bulb there to direct him back to that hall of windows. His heart rate quickened as he stepped into the hollow way, his footsteps echoing back to him. He grimaced and tightened his core, lightening his step. He needed stealth. When Nadia was with him, he felt protected. As if they were caught, she could convince whoever it was to trust them. *Trust him.* Alone, he was nothing more than a suspicion fell true.

A door creaked down the way and he ducked into one of the empty windowed rooms, thanking whatever higher power cared to listen that it had been left unlocked. He remained crouched behind the door as lazy footsteps passed by. He didn't even chance a breath, his knees screaming at him from their hyper-extended position. When the hallway fell silent again, he stood slowly, the cartilage crunching in protest after the extended time in agony. As he shook his legs out, he took in the room around him. Even in the dark, the walls shined with a stark white coat of glossy paint. Stainless steel cabinets and counters lined one wall and in the middle of the room, a large stainless steel table stood sentry. Large enough for a body. He gulped as he eyed the drain in the middle of the floor and turned to head back out the door when more footsteps padded toward him. He ducked back down beneath the window.

Several voices joined the footsteps and he listened hard to hear where they went. Down the hall he had come from. Likely shift changes. Noah waited a little while longer, his knees in horrendous revolt as he tried to steady his breathing. This was his only chance and he needed these answers before he left. There was something off about The Antisociété and he couldn't waste this opportunity hiding in a sterile surgical room.

As the silence droned on, vibrating around him, he decided to take his chance. Pulling the door to the observation room open, he checked each direction for anymore signs of life before dashing down the hallway. To the right was his holding cell. To the left, the laboratories Nadia mentioned. He didn't allow himself to think, just acted as he slipped down the hall to his left. He had no where to hide under the bright, steady lights running the length of the space so he opened the first room whose handle gave to his pressure.

Fortunately, the room was empty. Feeling the clock on his luck running out, he began scanning the shelves to his right, taking stock of what looked like any other laboratory he had been in during his undergrad. White counters, white cabinets, glassware hanging from pegboard hooks, machines humming and clicking in the background. Fluorescent lighting set the entire room into a cold, lifeless aura. The deeper he stepped into the room, the less grabbed his attention. Nothing stuck out. It was all just bottles of ethers, reagents and micro-pipettes lining shelves. He ran a rough hand through his hair.

Fucking hell, what was he supposed to be finding? He spun in a slow circle in place, hand tugging his hair slightly as his eyes darted over everything. Searching, hoping, for *something*. He felt his despair bubble within, creeping to an overwhelming state when he spotted it. A large refrigerator tucked into the back corner. He quickly ran over to it, pulling open the door with a loud sucking sound.

Stored in perfect, neat little rows were hundreds of vials of thick, red liquid. Blood. Noah's vision widened as he studied them. Each shelf had a date written in scratchy handwriting, all from within the past few weeks. He grabbed one of the small glass jars from the top shelf, the most recent selection. From the week he had been taken, if his memory served him well. He ran his thumb over the printed label.

N.B. -/+

His brows furrowed. Was this…his? When would they have taken his blood?

Fuck, it could've been at any point between them drugging him and waking up to see his own dead brother alive and well, standing before him like not a day had gone by between seeing each other. How would he have even noticed a needle hole amongst the rest of the cuts and bruises marring his body? His split lower lip had only recently started to heal properly, a nice scar dimpling the middle.

Not allowing himself time to fall in the panic circling him, the smell of fresh blood trickling into the water to alert all the sharks in his mind, he pocketed the vial and continued to scan the shelves. Almost every label had the markers -/-, the occasional +/-. His was the only -/+ he could see in front of him. He started to lean down, searching some of the older dates when the door to the room slowly creaked open. He froze.

"Working late, Henry? I didn't think Adette would let you." Noah didn't recognize the British man who spoke.

Instead, he pressed himself further into the fridge, offering an apathetic grunt in response. He held his breath, squeezing the vial to the point he felt certain it would explode, painting his hand in bright red. Marking him as the traitor among their midst. Again.

The man at the door laughed and said, "Well, I just needed to grab my notes. I'll see you tomorrow though?"

Noah let out another stifled grunt. This seemed to suffice as communication as the door slammed shut. A loud exhale escaped his lips as he dropped his head.

Feeling the remnants of his opportunity slip away, he put the other two random vials he had grabbed into his pocket, scanned the contents one last time, longing for more time, and made his way back to the door. Pressing an ear to it, he listened for anymore footsteps or voices. When he felt certain he could slip down the hall without worry, he pulled the door open and started with a purpose along the corridor. Taking one last glance in the direction of his initial prison, he took the sharp right turn into the hallway of windows and ran square into the chest of his own brother.

CHAPTER NINE
IZZY

I said, 'Bring the tomes about the *high* Middle Ages,' not the entire era," Dr. Beechum barked at the freshman standing before him. The stack of books in the kid's arm had to weigh nearly as much as he did and with the added trembling occurring, the whole scene teetered on the edge of precarious.

The professor grabbed an extra thick volume from the top and the boy sighed. Izzy eyed the four-inch spine in Beechum's hand and raised a brow. She had walked directly to the archives library, hood still up from her trek across campus to forgo a drawn out explanation of her whereabouts to Barry. No one gave her a second glance on that overcast, misty day with her hood pulled over her face, the plait of her rich red hair her only distinguishing characteristic under all the black.

Beechum flipped through the pages of the book he held, sighing heavily. "See, this isn't even about the Middle Ages. This is early Modern times at best. Ah, Ms. Ciampi! Just the person I need to talk to," he called out to her, plunking the giant book back on top of the stack. The boy's feeble arms shook, the stack wobbled, and then a second later, fell to the floor in a heap of bound paper and leather covers. The freshman fell to his knees, apologizing profusely as he attempted to restack the collection, books slipping from his grip. The professor sneered down at him as he stepped over the mess and walked toward Izzy.

When he approached, his hand reached for her elbow, pointing toward the hallway that led back to his office. She pulled out of his grasp, a glare hidden beneath her hood, as she walked herself in the direction she, unfortunately, knew too well from her many meetings to remind her of her shortcomings to the institution.

Beechum tucked his hand into his pocket and followed alongside her. "Have you seen Mr. Broussard? You two knew each other, correct? I figured he might have gone back home to visit during the holidays but that was months ago. It's not like him to be so…capricious."

Izzy's heart stopped beating at the mention of Noah but she managed to breathe out, "No, Professor. I haven't heard from him." It wasn't a lie as much as it hurt to say it out loud.

The professor hummed an irritated tune as he pushed open his office door. Izzy allowed him to get seated while she stood at the threshold, fighting her conflicting instincts. Leave the door open, *like you're trained to do*, or close it? What was the worst that could happen to her? She was the most dangerous thing in the room after all.

She swallowed, leaving the door open as she shuffled stiffly into the seat opposite the mahogany desk, pulling her hood down as she sat. Vahagn had to be smiling somewhere at her decision.

"Did you just want to ask me about No…Mr. Broussard? Or was there another reason you pulled me into your office?" She grimaced at the tone she took with him but at this point in her damned life, fuck it.

Dr. Beechum's eyes narrowed on her and it set a flame of ire through her veins. *Does he even realize how easily I could snap his neck right now?*

"No, actually, I was going to bring you in on a special project. We've received a request for a materials summary: all the information we have about the Middle Ages, specifically the reign of Charlemagne and the subsequent fall out."

Izzy's vision blurred and her breathing caught in her throat. Surely, this was a coincidence?

Papers were shuffled on Dr. Beechum's desk, the man looking for something as he spoke, "I recall last fall you had taken up a bit of an interest in the topic, what with you receiving that journal in the post. Did you ever catalog that article? I'm sure it might be of great interest in this project. The requester is asking for a rather quick turnaround: one week. The quicker, the better, of course. Would you be able to get that completed? Bartholomew might be able to assist you, though…" the professor looked up from his papers with a look of disgust, "his expertise might not be *exactly* what they are looking for…"

The words barely registered in Izzy's mind as her thoughts whirled. Someone was asking questions about the Middle Ages, about Charlemagne. This could not be a coincidence. Nobody submitted requests anymore. If they did, it was for more information about the World Wars that everyone seemed to have a hard on for or to treat the university like a genealogy center for their boring family background. Anything earlier than the early waves of immigration was just frivolous, irrelevant. Left for the art collectors and antiquities dealers working for their "elite" clientèle.

"Ms. Ciampi? Would you be able to work on this request? I know you've been on a reduced work plan since the loss of your cousin but that was months ago. Surely you're ready to do something more." Dr. Beechum assessed her over the top of his frameless glasses, disdain radiating off him.

Right, her cousin. Vahagn. That was the story Barry had spun to explain her extended absence that fall after everything went to hell. Died tragically in a freak gas line explosion near the old library.

Izzy gulped, her heart rate on an erratic rhythm that had her seeing specks of black in her vision. Just a coincidence, easily explained by someone being curious. That's all. She didn't own the copyright on the subject after all.

"Ms. Ciampi? Are you alright?" Beechum's harsh words pulled her out of her downward spiral. She blinked rapidly and looked to the scowl on the professor's face.

"Um, yes," she cleared her throat before continuing. "Yes, I can work on this project." She started to gather her things, eyes glazed over. It was an unnecessary movement, she hadn't released the death grip on her bag since she sat down. She stood quickly and hurried to the door, chastising herself for how quick she moved. How *inhuman* she must have looked flashing to the door. Before she stepped into the hallway though, she turned and asked, "Who is the requester? Anyone I might know?"

Dr. Beechum pursed his lips and said, "Doubtful," as he flipped through the papers on his desk again. His eyes lit up when he found the page and he concentrated as he said, "A Dr. Callum Kimble. Some charming young British man. He mentioned something about putting together a special surprise for his mother and father. I guess they are something of aficionados on Charlemagne."

Izzy's vision turned red and she left his office without another word, slamming his door shut behind her. *Callum.*

"Ms. Ciampi! Please! Some decorum!" The professor yelled from his seat at his desk, glaring at her through the windowed door. Ignoring him, she rushed back down the hall, weaving around the bookshelves and tables in the main area of the library. She rounded a corner and pushed past the boy with his recovered stack of books. Every last one fell atop the table in front of him as a choked sob escaped his lips. But she didn't fucking care. She kept her pace, slamming her body through the door at the entrance to speed down the stairs in a personal record. God, she fucking hated that too.

Only once she was on the sidewalk out front did she stop, hissing at the sunlight hitting her skin, filtered through the blanket of clouds in the sky. She flipped her hood back over her head and instead of heading down to their basement laboratory, she climbed the decorative stone steps to the little rooftop garden. No one was out there, with the smell of ozone thick in the air. She pressed herself into the corner next to the building, the area shaded from the meager light with a small bench next to a bird bath. Sitting down, she leaned her head back against the brick walk behind her and sighed.

What fucking game was Emilien playing at? Was this his way of making her reveal her "plan" to him? Had Charlie known about this? Lando?

"Fuck," she whispered as she pressed her skull further into the rough stone behind her, squeezing her eyes shut. Noah and her had barely made any progress in transcribing and understanding The Ramblings that fall. Even with his vague notes and half-finished theories, she had no idea what the journal offered in the grand scheme of the shit storm she found herself in.

And what would he think of her now? As one of them. Would he know how it happened to her? Did he already know?

Was it all just another piece of the puzzle he was in on? Turn the poor, unsuspecting girl into a vampire and vanish from existence.

She squeezed her eyes tighter before opening them to the dreary day before her. She had no idea how it had happened and there was no way Noah would either. He would've told her if he knew. Something in her told her that much was true. But the Dumases? Secrets flowed thicker than blood between those two. And sending Emilien's lackey in to investigate the middle ages, like some twisted mind fuck puzzle?

She sat up and reached into her back pocket for her phone. Maybe that's exactly what he was doing.

She opened her search engine and typed in "Emilien Dumas, research". Several articles and advertisements popped up, toting the innovative new cure and the many financing options available so everyone could live "Happily ever after with the love of your life!". Someone would have to sign their entire immortal life away ten fold to be able to afford it.

She filtered the results down to the time before the cure. A different world entirely. A few articles popped up—one in French and another from the Oxford Medical Sciences website. She clicked on the Oxford one, a dull ache behind her eyes dreading the thought of reading French that early.

> **WELCOME DR. EMILIEN DUMAS TO THE INFECTIOUS DISEASE TEAM!**

The picture below the heading was of a slightly younger looking version of the man she knew, with his model level looks and charm radiating off him as he beamed at the camera. His arm was around another man, with unruly bright orange hair and a pair of wire framed glasses, his lips turned sideways into a sheepish grin.

> Emilien Dumas and Henry Holt join forces in the Hugh Magnus Research Laboratory in Oxford, England.

Izzy backed out of the article and scrolled down the rest of the results. Everything else was in French, mostly mentions of awards received and grants gifted throughout undergraduate and graduate studies. She switched to the images and clicked on one halfway down the page of Emilien next to a woman in a mid-length white dress, its full skirt and satin material glowing despite the picture being taken at night. The twinkling lights of the Eiffel Tower glimmered behind them. Izzy zoomed in on the smiling couple, each beaming at the other with such love and passion it sent a stab through her heart.

Tears pricked the back of her eyes and she quickly turned off the screen and shoved the phone back into her pocket. Nothing made sense and all she had were more questions than answers.

Fine, she would entertain Emilien's twisted form of communication. But not without her own bit of research as well. Play the game, just like Charlie suggested.

She stood, scowling at the picturesque little garden before her, birds and bees dancing from wildflower to wildflower without a care for the ominous weather looming above. She didn't know why she came up here anymore. It fed into some masochistic part of her, the part that longed to steal herself away to this garden, sit amongst everything it offered, and feel…alive.

❖

"Ms. Ciampi, you know you can't access the restricted area," the old woman crooned from the middle of her circular desk, not even deigning to look up from her computer screen.

Izzy huffed out an exasperated sigh. "I have a deadline, what am I supposed to do?"

"Make an appointment like the rest of the faculty and *staff* do." Her eerie beady eyes peered up at her from the tops of her glasses.

Izzy's nostrils flared. The woman was an absolute menace to society. Fuck the criminals, someone needed to be investigating the shape and size of the stick up her ass.

"Fine. Do I need an *appointment* to utilize the rest of the archives?"

The woman rolled her eyes, actually rolled her eyes, wrinkles tugging as she did. Speaking through a sigh, she said, "Of course not. How long have you been at this university?"

"Too fucking long," Izzy murmured as she picked her leather bag off the floor and made her way to the back of the library, toward the dark, caged restricted section. She set up shop at a nearby desk and parked herself in a seat facing the metal enclosure. Iron bars kept the ancient and rare tomes within safe from the unsupervised hands of the faculty and *staff*. Izzy ground her teeth, tapping her fingers on the table in front of her. She could see the fucking books.

She froze, glancing around the empty space. There were no rules against looking at the restricted section, so long as she stayed on her side of the barrier. Right? It would make her scheduled appointment more efficient if she knew where exactly to begin her search.

An echo of a smile crept onto her face as she got up, eyes trained on the trapped books before her. She gripped the rough, cool grey rungs and scanned the multitude of spines along shelves and tables within. There were many first editions of old, timeless works like Walt Whitman's Leaves of Grass and bibles dating back to the early fifteen-hundreds. All useless for her endeavor. She read the various titles and materials as she walked a little down the edge of the cage, trying to get a better view of the items within the dark room. The restricted area had been built into several adjoined alcoves underneath quiet study rooms above, accessible by the side stairwell along the wall and only with an appointment, of course.

Toward the back of the alcove, nearly out of sight, a series of smaller books snagged her attention. They were similar in size to The Ramblings resting haphazardly in her floorboard at home. A small ping of guilt hit her as she eyed the way these tomes were displayed on a velvet topped table, each with protective plastic sleeves over their covers. She vowed to treat the priceless article in her possession with a bit more care going forward. If only because she knew Noah would want her too.

She frowned and returned her focus to the small texts. It was impossible to make out any sort of title from where she stood but still she pressed her face into the harsh metal, squinting to try to get a better look. Most of them looked newer than The Ramblings, leather bound but without the warped edges or discolored pages typical of a journal from the fucking medieval times.

She sighed and looked to the floor. Her endeavor was hopeless.

The lock to the restricted area caught her eye. All she had to do was take another step to the right and it would be directly in front of her. Beckoning her.

She closed the gap and knelt down to study it. Nothing fancy, and actually pretty fucking ancient. And therefore, easy to pick. She glanced around her to the empty tables and shelves of books. No one was around. It wasn't like she was going to take any of the books. She just needed to peruse the options. Maybe take a couple pictures. She reached a hand into her hair and fished out a bobby pin. A cluster of curls fell into her face and she tucked them behind her ear as she pressed the pin into the keyhole. Black metal scraped against antique cogs as she felt around for the release pin.

"Can I help you find anything?" A wavering young voice sounded from behind her. She froze. Then, discreetly pulling her bobby pin from the lock hole, turned her torso around to see Beechum's new freshman assistant watching her suspiciously, the look bordering on fear and confusion. She could take him, easily. Her mouth salivated as she watched a vein pulse in his neck, felt his heartbeat across the space between them, listened to his breaths, rising and falling nervously.

No! What was she thinking? She couldn't murder everyone who inconvenienced her lately, holy shit. She tore her eyes from his neck and glanced to a light hanging from the ceiling above his head, giving him a tight lipped smile.

"No, thanks. I was just…tying my shoe." She glanced to her shoes to double check they actually had laces that would warrant needing tying. Black combat boots. She gave herself a smug grin. Genius.

The boy gave her one more curious once over, eyes cataloging her body in a way that had a faint blush creeping into his cheeks. Averting his gaze, he disappeared without another word, bustling back through the maze of shelves away from her.

She closed her eyes and groaned, leaning against the bars behind her. Hopeless. The whole thing was hopeless.

"I can confirm, that is not the best place to be groaning and moaning. I swear that metal splinter is still embedded in my spine," Barry said. She popped one eye open to see him standing before her, one hand rubbing his back with a frown as the other held a small stack of vintage magazines. She didn't want to know what was inside them. Or what purpose they were about to serve.

She had made that mistake once at his home. It was enough.

"I feel like I no longer know how to be a researcher, Bear," she said, pushing off the metal bar and making her way back to her abandoned table. Barry's gaze softened as he slipped into the leather seat across from her, setting his nudies down on the table like they were the latest prints of Good Housekeeping. Her cheeks heated when her eyes inevitably fell to the cover model holding an eagle feather over his junk. A futile effort though, it covered nothing.

"Izzy, you're a perfectly acceptable researcher in the eyes of Washington University and a phenomenal one in my own eyes. You've also just had a colossally fucked up past six months. You are allowed to the feel like everything isn't going your way because, to be honest, it hasn't been."

His warm brown gaze touched something deep in her and somehow his words were exactly what she needed to hear. She reached across the table and squeezed his hand.

"Everything sucks, Bear," she whispered, tears threatening to spill at the confession.

He squeezed her hand back and offered a gentle smile. "It does. It really fucking sucks," he replied.

She laughed a little and pulled her hand back to wipe away at the moisture that had spilled over. "Thanks. I know I haven't been the best friend lately. I'm sorry about that."

He flitted a hand at her and pulled the copy of *Crotch* toward him, flipping through the pages. "Oh, don't worry about me. I'm incredibly understanding for a self-righteous individual. Now, what did Beechum do this time to make you second guess yourself?"

She groaned again and dropped her forehead onto her crossed arms on the table.

"Oof, that bad? Hold on," he rustled through the stack of magazines. She looked up in time to see his eyes light up as he let out a husky laugh before pushing the copy across the table to her. "You need Mr. January 1965. It was their Scandinavian edition." He winked at her and she gingerly pulled the magazine over, leaning back. Sure enough, a naked man standing in a snow packed forest endowed the cover of *Nude Living* from 1965. Only a flap of animal hide kept him from being fully on display. He was drilling a hole into a tree. For what purpose, she didn't really care as she leafed through to the centerfold. Her eyes widened as she turned the booklet sideways and the pages unfolded.

"Oh," she breathed out.

"Oh, yes," Barry cooed.

A blush started to creep up her neck and she quickly folded the pages back together, slapped it closed, and pushed the magazine back across the table to him.

"Naked men can't solve my problems unless they can magically research and summarize hundreds of years of historical texts in a week."

Barry ogled the center fold himself before neatly placing it back with the rest of his stack and said, "You got a research request?"

"Yes, it's the first one I've had assigned directly to me. I normally only get asked to consult with them. It's not exactly in our job duties to help out the history department but I think I'm on thin ice with Beechum." She left out the details of exactly who and what she was volunteered to research. The layers of her issues were too deep to bury Barry in.

"Yeah, he had me do one last fall. It was coincidentally after that box of Polaroid nudes ended up shipped to his house instead of campus. God, he was pissed." Barry giggled to himself and Izzy joined in. The professor had dropped the box off the following morning and went into a fifteen minute monologue on propriety and respect. The whole time, a naked Santa peered up at all them from the box.

Izzy stopped laughing. "Wait, what? Who did you do a request for last year? I don't remember this."

"Oh, it was for some lady and her son. They were very secretive, only communicated through email but I guess they were doing some sort of genealogy thing, tracking their family line all the way back to the middle ages or something crazy like that. It was so boring, I erased it all from my memory the moment I submitted my report. What are you supposed to be researching? And one week? That's insane."

Izzy stared at him before pulling her phone out. "Is there some sort of article out about the middle ages? Seems really popular lately." She tried to sound cool as she typed in 'genealogy, middle ages, Wash U'. All their reports were open records, archived in a dusty corner of the website that saw maybe ten clicks a year.

There it was. Bartholomew Flores. A family study of genealogy. Most of the recent names were redacted, of course. But as she scrolled through the report, one name caught her eye. *Charlemagne.*

She stood. If Barry had answered her, she didn't hear as she pulled her bag over her shoulder and started weaving her way through the shelves to the exit. The librarian scowled at her from her island at the circular desk. Barry called out her name. But she didn't stop.

It's just a coincidence, she told herself as she pushed out of the library and started down the stairs.

"You never could put it together," Adette's disappointed voice rattled in her mind.

CHAPTER TEN
IZZY

The silence suffocated as Izzy climbed the stairs to the archives library. Her footfalls were as quiet as she could manage in the echoing space. She tripped over a step and cursed as her sneakers squeaked in the darkness. Dressed head to toe in all black, she blended well with the night sky. The moon waned and the clouds held that ever present threat of rain at the end of April, both helping to conceal her in the emptiness of night.

As long as she could keep fucking quiet. At the top landing, she paused to raise her hands up behind her head, gulping in deep lungfuls of air. Even in her immortal form, those stairs were incessant. She stared at the solid door to the library as her heart rate returned to normal. Less than normal but that fact always made her feel a little queasy when she thought too long about it. She needed to focus anyway, she didn't have all night. Dropping her hands to her sides, she winced at the slapping sound they made before walking up to the door, pulling a key from her pocket. She tried the handle, silently praying this would be easier than she imagined, but of course, the door was locked.

The key had been in the box with Noah's things on the

street. And really, she was doing the university a service by picking it up, what with the WU stamped on the bronze metal.

Keeping it? That was just an unfortunate side effect of acute emotional trauma and a general attitude of "who fucking cares". She wasn't even sure it would unlock the archives but she had a hunch. And she had done worse on far less.

Her hunch was confirmed when the key slid effortlessly into the keyhole and turned. A hum of satisfaction slipped out her lips before she painstakingly pulled the door toward her, praying to whatever entity would listen that maintenance had recently oiled the hinges. Dr. Beechum was anal enough to request such a service. He probably drove all the campus staff up a wall and out a fucking window with his requests.

Which brought her to her current endeavor. Breaking into the archives at night to do her job, which was actually not really her job but more of a seemingly meaningless task handed off to her to remind her of her place within the university, and more so, within a gang of immortal nerds drunk on power. Little did the poor professor know the bigger picture she would be uncovering with this undertaking.

If she could finish in a week.

One week. May fifth. Cinco de Mayo. Barry's big party. The first time she would be around that many people since Vahagn. So many beating hearts.

Her mind would not leave her alone.

Which was precisely why she didn't notice someone coming up the stairs until she pulled the door shut behind her only to have it stopped by a broad tattooed hand, the Billiken Blue of his class ring flashing in the emergency lights of the archives. She jolted, her heart rate elevating in record time, primed for an attack before she squinted and recognized that hand.

"Jesus fucking Christ, Charlie. Get in here before someone sees your giant ass out there. You look like a criminal," she growled.

The tall man stepped in, blue eyes glinting in the faint light. He gave her a half smile, as he leaned against the closed door behind him. "Technically, they wouldn't be wrong. Besides…what would you call sneaking into the library after hours? What could you possibly be researching that requires no one be present to witness it?" A single thick brow quirked as his Neanderthal brain worked through the possibilities.

"Ancient voodoo for ex-flings that won't leave you alone. Results are supposed to be permanent," she hissed, turning on her heel, not letting the man meat obstacle stop her. It was her one chance to get into the restricted area.

His footsteps hurried after her, all mirth lost in his voice as he said, "Ex-fling? That's all we were in your eyes? A fling?"

She weaved through the shelves, throwing a glare over her shoulder at him. Despite the darkness, his blue eyes blazed at her defiance. A satisfied smirk touched her lips and she turned her head, continuing her pursuit. "Fine. It was more than a fling but hardly love."

"For one of us," he murmured under his breath.

She stopped walking and rotated to face him. "Not this conversation again?"

He stopped as well, running a frustrated hand down his face. "No, fuck, you weren't supposed to hear that. That's not what I'm trying to do. Or say. Shit. I just…" He sat on the table behind him, eyes searching the row of books around them. "Is this really the time?"

She looked around the empty space. No alarms were blazing, no video streams recording, Beechum too paranoid

Russians were watching him as fodder to fall asleep to. She cocked her hip onto the large shelf next to her. "I don't foresee another opportunity for you to have my unadulterated attention, so go on."

He smiled and shook his head. He studied the windows above, the mist leaving droplets on the glass outside. His gaze remained upward as he spoke, voice gravelly, "I know what I did was fucked up. I know I was in the wrong more than I was in the right and I'm not going to excuse it away, blame it on my own fucked up reasons." His gaze finally met hers, a drowning pool. "But I did love you." A look if disappointment flashed over him and he stood abruptly. "And I probably always will, a little bit I think. But you know I let that love consume me. I let it mutate into something terrible and I didn't realize it until it was too late and I couldn't control it."

Was this the conversation Barry had been begging her to have with him? Because it was ruining her life. A emotive storm of anger and despair churned in her and she turned away, calculating her path again. "I don't forgive you, Charlie. You fucking killed Vahagn," she spit the words out, unable to remember how to get to the restricted section. Fuck.

He stepped up next to her, a pained look on his face as she flinched away. "I know you won't believe me, but that was one of the worst fucking days of my life. I had no other choice. He refused to join The Society and they would've torn him apart. Eaten him alive." She swallowed the bile that rose in her throat at the thought, looking to the floor as she fought back tears. She just needed to remember how to get to the restricted area so she could run away from their conversation. Charlie pulled a hand through his hair. "When he made his decision, I couldn't watch that happen to him. He deserved better. Fuck, he deserved better than anything I ever gave him." He rubbed a shaky hand over the sleeve of his leather jacket and when she glanced sideways, she saw the silver shimmer on the edges of his eyes. "I was in too deep at that point to let him go. I had already lost Noah and Emilien was pissed."

The fury surged through her as her gaze flashed to him. "You could've not fucking killed him, Charlie!" Her voice rose and she steadied it, looking away as she rattled out a whisper. "He was all I had."

"And if I could've killed myself to spare him, I would've!" He bit out in reply. His fists clenched and he let out a shaky laugh. "You know what, this wasn't the time for this conversation. Lead the way."

She blanched, turning to him. A twisted resolve ran through her. Hadn't those been the words she had wanted him to say this whole time? Why did they feel so wrong in her ears?

He rubbed the back of his neck, closing his eyes as he tilted his head back. The firecracker vine inked there, trailing up behind his ear. His eyes opened and he looked sideways at her. Something in her gaze must have prompted him to say, "I never deserved you." Her stomach dropped. He sighed, dropping his hand and looking to the floor, hands in the pockets of his jacket. "I never deserved him either. I didn't deserve to be the one that walked away that day. And it fucking haunts me every night and every morning when I see my empty apartment." He let out a sardonic snort. "I am so close to burying a fucking bullet in my mouth every single day." He let out a shaky breath and she stared at him as everything he said, confessed, roiled through her.

Leaning against the bookshelf behind her, she blinked a few times before saying, "Fuck, Charlie. Why didn't you say something?"

He snorted and stood up straight, taking an aimless step down the aisle. "Where are we going in this library?"

She glanced over her shoulder to the caged alcoves within sight. Her mission so close yet felt minuscule compared to the weight he had been carrying. "Why didn't you say something?"

His eyes followed her line of sight and he started toward them, brushing past her. She was frozen. Why hadn't he said something? Everything he said processed for several more seconds before she jogged to catch up. She placed a hand on his arm and he stopped, looking back at her, pain crinkling the edges of his crystalline eyes.

"Charlie, why didn't you say something to me? Or anyone?"

Her heart cracked for the despair she saw in his face. She recognized it. She saw it every morning in her own mirror.

"Because I don't need your pity. That would be the last fucking straw, I think." He pulled his arm out of her grasp and approached the edge of the metal bars, inspecting the ancient lock. She shuffled up to him, her mind reeling. None of this had been on her agenda for the evening. Get in, get books, get out. She tried her best to compartmentalize it all for another time and focus on the task at hand.

"So, are you going to tell me why you're breaking into a library? Don't you work here?" He looked around the space as she pulled out her lock pick kit. It had been her grandfather's, brought over from Italy and found in his possessions after he passed. She never asked why he had it. Never got the chance.

"We are breaking in because apparently the wait time to get an appointment into this particular section is minimum three weeks and your boss is requesting a research summary in one." That had been the fine print not mentioned to her by the craggy, old witch. Another detail found in the hidden spaces of the Wash U website.

"Which one?" Charlie said, as he glanced back to her. Watching her six. How annoyingly generous of him.

She pressed two thin metal tools into the keyhole, brows scrunching as she asked, "Which one what?"

"Which boss?"

"Emilien, of course. Why would Lando put in a research request about the middle ages when he could just ask me?"

"Why didn't Emilien?"

The lock clicked once, and her tongue stuck out the corner of her lips as she pressed, pressed, pressed, then a second, more satisfying click sounded. She huffed out an exhale, turning to him. She wiped the back of her hand over her brow and said, "What?"

He pushed the door open, and she stepped in as he said, "Why didn't Emilien just ask you about the research? Why the official process?"

"I don't fucking know, Charlie. He was your boss first. Hell, I hardly even interact with him enough to call him more than a villainous acquaintance." She beelined to the table of journals she had scoped out earlier that day. One with a fleur de lis etched into the leather cover caught her eyes and she gently opened it, sighing when the words were in an English she could understand. She placed it back into its plastic bag and into the backpack she had brought along. Charlie picked up another journal and she pulled it from his grasp, scowling. He held his hands up and looked around the space.

"If you would come to a meeting more than once every couple months, you might be able to formulate a better plan, you know?" he mused, not looking at her as he watched the main entrance through a small hole between the rows of shelves. She glanced up at him and then back to the books, moving on from the journals on the velveteen table to scan the spines on the shelves near it.

"A better plan? For what?" she asked, keeping her eyes on the tomes.

"Your plan to go get Noah."

She stopped scanning and looked at him. Their eyes met and a muscle feathered in his jaw before he looked back to the doorway across the library, squinting as if to get a better view.

"It might be," she mused, turning back to the books. To be honest, it's not like the thought hadn't crossed her mind. But so had several other irrational and ridiculous ones over the few months since he had left her. Her hand stopped over a spine with BUSCH stamped into the leather and the famous insignia above it. Her hand traced the eagle, a flash of The Ramblings and Charlemagne's crest popping into memory. Another flash and the memory shift to golden eyes crinkled on the edges in a smile. Grimacing, she grabbed the book, placing it into her heavy bag. She had to stop or she wouldn't be able to carry all them back to her apartment.

"Well, come to a meeting. See what you find out while you're there. Talk has been…interesting as of late," he said, pushing off the table he had leaned against as she made her way out of the restricted area.

As she clicked the lock back into place, she said, "Fine, I'll come if you promise to come talk to me, or Lando, or someone when things get bad, okay?"

She watched him swallow. "I have actually been talking to Barry," he said, eyes still on the exit.

She laughed, "I'm sorry, what?"

He gave her a lopsided grin and said, "Yeah. He grows

incredible weed in that insane little greenhouse he calls an apartment. I hit him up one night when shit got really bad and I just needed to…forget everything. He took one look at me, let me in, and we got to talking. The next thing I knew, I was lying on his floor, sobbing like a fucking child as he fed me these pretzel marshmallow chocolate chip cookies while I told him everything."

"Wow," Izzy said, as they stepped back out onto the landing, the humidity hitting them like a wall. Beechum would stroke out if he knew what she had in her backpack They descended the stairs in silence, making certain no one heard or saw them. She took the time to imagine it, Charlie, in all his brawn and tattooed skin, sobbing on Barry's floor. Barry's pink shag rugged floor.

What would Charlie have said to him? He said "everything". Izzy knew most of his back story, his reasons for leaving university, and his father's legacy, to join a crime syndicate. But if she was being honest, she had only half listened to those conversations as she raked her nails across his chiseled abs, tracing the twin inked bouquets sprouting from beneath his waistband.

Once on the street level, Charlie chuckled, looking at her expression. "Yeah, it was a pretty unbelievable experience. Like some sort of fucked up therapy session. Anyway, I see him about once a week or so. Much less sobbing now but it's been nice to have someone to talk to." He scanned the streets, checking all the dark corridors and alleyways as they walked back to their building.

That must be how Charlie had known about Barry's new boyfriend. Fuck, she had been an awful friend.

They walked in silence as she ruminated on how completely different her excursion had ended up being than how she had planned it. Once the building was in sight, she stopped and said, "I'm sorry, Charlie. I'm not sorry that bad shit happened to you after everything you've done. But I am sorry for treating you like…"

"A glorified boxed wine?" he said, amusement twinkling in his ocean eyes as he grinned at her.

She rolled her eyes. "Yes. It was rude of me. Even as much as I hated you, it wasn't right."

His grin widened. "Hated, huh?"

She narrowed her eyes and pushed past him, continuing their journey home. "Whatever, Charlie."

His laugh warmed her heart a smidge as he jogged to match her stride.

As he typed the code into the security system, he asked, "Hey, what are you doing Friday?"

She tilted her head at him but he didn't notice, his focus on the keypad as his finger hovered over the last number.

"Well, Barry's party is the next night so nothing. Why?"

He pressed the last number and the door clicked, allowing him to pull it open for her. They were welcomed by a wall of cool, dry air fighting back the blanket of humidity outside. Izzy made her way to the stairwell, Charlie toward the door into the first floor apartments where majority of the crew lived.

She stopped at the junction of the doors, looking over at him as he did the same, waiting for an answer. He ran a hand through his long black hair and he looked…nervous. Charlie Valentini looked nervous. That never happened.

"There is some place I wanted to show you. I think you might like it."

"Where is it?" she winced at the tone in her question. His behavior had unsettled her, she couldn't function.

"It's downtown so we will have to drive. We can take the Alfa," he replied.

She studied him. She hadn't driven her grandfather's Alfa Romeo in…a while. At least a year. "I'll have to check on it, I haven't driven it in a while. But…sure. Why not?" Why not. He had given her a complex that night, she almost didn't believe it was her voice as the words spilled out. But they were out now and Charlie was smiling and she kind of liked seeing him happy.

"Great. Awesome. And don't worry about the car, I've been keeping up with the maintenance on it and taking it for drives every now and then to make sure its in working order."

Before she could respond to that additional world rattling news, he turned and headed through the door and down the hallway to his apartment.

Reeling, she pushed into the stairwell and pulled out her phone. No new messages. No missed calls.

She opened that familiar text chain. The one she had viewed hundreds of times over the last six months. No new messages had been sent or received in that time. She started typing.

IZZY

> Send help. Charlie is being nice? And sincere? And it's throwing me off.

I need you here. She didn't type that last bit. Instead, she stared at the message drafted, the blinking bar beckoning her to press Send.

She let out a long exhale and deleted the entire thing before pushing into her hallway and heading back to her apartment. Her home. At least it used to feel that way.

CHAPTER ELEVEN
NOAH

The disapproval in Benji's gaze shot through to Noah's soul, setting the hair on the back of his neck on end. Someone shifted from beside Benji and Noah broke their stare down long enough to catch round, green eyes staring up at him. Nadia. He glared at the woman before turning back to his brother's wrath.

"Are you fucking kidding me, Noah?" Benji's words came out stern though barely above a whisper. A familiar disappointment radiated off him, coated his words.

"I'm just out for a walk before my shift," Noah lied, crossing his arms and setting his jaw.

Black flecked golden eyes narrowed on him and Benji said, "I knew you couldn't be trusted. I kept thinking, 'He's changed, he's trustworthy now.' You almost had me convinced too." Benji pulled something out of his back pocket, shaking his head, a wry grin on his face. He held up a phone. Noah's phone. "I was on my way to give this back to you before we got to NOLA."

Noah's heart clenched, his hand lifting toward the phone without thinking. Benji snatched it out of his reach and handed it off to Nadia.

"Now, I have to put you back in restraints. Fuck, Noah," Benji exclaimed, running a rough hand through his blonde curls, setting them wild. Their one distinguishing characteristic. Where Noah had dark auburn waves that bordered on black, Benji's were tighter, sandy blonde curls.

"Fuck!" Benji shouted and Noah flinched. His brother pinched the bridge of his nose with one hand and waved the other at him. "Put your arms out and stand wide."

How many times had they had to stand like that after getting caught by the authorities in a hair brained idea of Benji's? His heart broke as he watch his brother morph into the despotic figure.

Noah slowly did as his brother told him, never taking his eyes off his face, the anger pulsating in his temple. "Do you want me to strip too?" Noah seethed as his brother ran his hands along his arms and torso.

Benji's gaze turned murderous. "I want you to be fucking dependable, Noh." His hands roved over Noah's pockets and Noah tensed, remembering the necklace in there, tucked away every day like a fragile hope for luck. Benji reached inside and pulled out the vials instead, holding them to Noah in disbelief. Noah's shoulders relaxed.

"Un-goddamn-believable. Are you going to embarrass me further by making me restrain you or can you willingly go to the holding cell?"

Noah's teeth protested as he clenched them tighter and said, "I can walk on my own accord." He held his brother's gaze, just for a moment. A moment longer than he would have ever dared before. Fury ignited in his brother's eyes at the defiance.

Benji looked at the vials again, shaking his head, before handing them off to Nadia as well. "Take these back to the lab and get a hold of Henry so he knows they've been tampered with. I'll meet with Adette about what to do with him."

Turning to Noah, he said, "Come on. You've put a real shit show into our plans for today. On the last fucking day. Fuck, Noh." Noah could hardly listen to his brother's disappointment any longer and started toward the makeshift cell he knew all too well.

When it was just him and Benji in the hallway, walking side by side, Noah asked, "Why the vials? What do the symbols mean?"

Benji glanced sideways at his brother, letting out a long exhale. "I don't know, Noah. It doesn't matter. What Adette and Henry are doing is *good*. Once you see home, you'll understand. You'll come around." His last words were more to himself, dusted with a sort of hope. It tugged on Noah's heart. It had always been them. Noah and Benji against the world that wanted nothing to do with them. But that was when they were broken little orphans living off the streets. They could make their own choices now. Define what their future could look like.

Benji stopped outside a rusted metal door with a chipped white sign. MAINTENANCE was printed in bold, black letters across it.

"Come on. Let's make this as painless as possible." Benji sounded tired, the lines under his eyes more pronounced in the faint lighting. He unlocked the door with a key on a ring in his pocket.

Noah kept silent as he sat down, back in the uncomfortable metal chair bolted to the floor in the middle of the room. He remained silent as Benji tied the rough rope around his wrists. He didn't even grimace as the fibers bit into a burn mark he had received on his wrist from a hot pan in the kitchen.

"I'll leave your ankles free, but the chair is bolted to the floor so don't try getting up or you'll fuck your back," Benji said, standing and dusting his hands off on his moss colored cargo pants. He didn't look at Noah, instead glanced around the oddly wet room. Noah studied his brother in the cavernous light. Those fine lines had set into the corners of his eyes. There were scars along his arms, some Noah knew and some were new. They snaked up and disappeared into his dark grey t-shirt. He still held his strength, but had lost some of the bulk that had made him a star on the football field in high school. That was…until he found The Society and dropped out.

Benji clapped his hands together and turned toward the door. He paused at the threshold, turning his head like he had something else to say. A moment passed, the only sounds filling the space the steady hum of the engines, interrupted by an intermittent clang of a chain against metal from the grate above. Benji glanced to the rusty bars above, brows furrowing slightly, and then pushed out the door without a word. A couple seconds later, Noah heard the click of the lock and slumped in his chair.

❖

Their arrival into New Orleans felt celebratory with the barge abuzz with activity. But Noah missed it all. He only knew through the snippets he heard through the grate. Their late night arrival lost on him as he had been hooded and dragged from his cell into a vehicle. Fifteen minutes in a car and they ushered him out, the cool, damp air hitting him feeling familiar and foreign all at once. Hands dragged him in a door and told him to "mind his footing" as they descended a flight of stairs. The air shifted, turned musty and damp and cooler still. Once they had thrown him into another chair, his hood was removed. He scanned the concrete walls, the tiny window near the ceiling with it's metal bars over it.

The sagging cot shoved into a corner and another goddamn flickering light.

They undid his ropes and for a moment, a fleeting second, he thought maybe he could fight his way out of here. But what was the point? Where would he go? This city was damned and all his hope along with it.

The door locked and the weight of loneliness fell over him.

For the first week, no one came to talk to him. No one came to see him. No one did anything but drop off a meager meal on a metal tray twice a day.

The second week, nurses arrived while he slept, strapped him down in his bed, and took several more vials of his blood. The bruise on the inside of his elbow grew and morphed as the days passed.

By the third week, more brutish men arrived with Adette in tow. Henry stood at the doorway while the group gathered around him, bound once more in the chair. She asked him a string of questions.

"What is Emilien's plan?"

"Why were you in the laboratory?"

"What do you know about our work here?"

"What does Emilien know about our work here?"

"Who is Isabella Ciampi?"

That last question stung but Noah remained stoic. He didn't have any answers for them and thus, didn't respond. He had no fucking clue what any of these people were doing and that was the worst part of it all. He didn't know which side of the fence to stand on.

When the fourth week rolled around, Adette and Henry stopped visiting with their slew of unanswered questions. Instead, they sent Benji. Benji, who *knew* Noah. He knew Noah wouldn't talk. Benji walked in every day dragging a chair in from the hallway and sat down, one ankle propped on his knee, as he stared at Noah. For hours, they sat like that, not saying a single word. Just staring into the near mirror image of themselves.

It drove Noah insane.

But what could he say? To his brother, or anyone else for that matter.

When the new year rolled around, Benji walked in and finally spoke to Noah.

"Happy New Year. Get up. You're moving in with me."

Noah stood from the creaky cot, confused by his brothers presence in his room, by his brother talking to him, by the words he was saying.

"Move in with you?" Noah croaked, rubbing the crick in his neck.

"Yeah, I have a small suite upstairs. It'll be tight but there are two bedrooms. I'm on babysitting duty with you, indefinitely. I think it's a mistake but…" Benji's lips pursed, clearly unhappy with the situation.

"Will this be the stage where you guys start water boarding me?" Noah asked as he followed Benji out of the door and took in the narrow, dimly lit hallway for the first time. A cellar of sorts, lined with more cavernous rooms, most without doors. The walls were an old mustardy color, similar to the shade painted on the metal walls of the boat. The air held the smell of old smoke and must.

To Noah's surprise, Benji cracked a half-sided grin.

"Nah, just more dish washing. I'll get a break during the day when I drop you off in the mornings. Sancho will keep an eye on your ass until after dinner. Then I'm stuck with you again until it all starts over in the morning."

"Sounds exhilarating," Noah mused. They climbed the concrete stairs at the end of the hall and the sunlight pouring in from above had Noah squinting, holding a hand up to shade his eyes.

"Yeah, well, hopefully if you can see what we've built here, you'll finally understand all the good in everything we are doing," Benji said, a slight edge on his words. "At least, that's the theory sold to me."

Noah turned to study his brother as they climbed the last few stairs. They had lost so many years already. Years of their childhood gone, forced to grow up and take care of each other. Years in service to others. The past couple years without each other. On the landing, he grabbed his brother's arm, turning him to face him. "Look, Benji, I'm sorry for disappointing you. I just want…answers. I have been in the dark." *For a while.* Noah let the confession out to his brother, offering a slice of himself. His white flag.

His brother gave him a stiff smile and Noah turned around, taking in the new hallway with its polished floors reflecting the cheerier yellow walls. Gilded rope details edged the tall ceiling that was supported by golden columns. As they walked around the corner, Noah's jaw dropped.

"Are we in The Roosevelt?" he asked, staring up at the carved gilt tiles on the ceiling. A tear-drop chandelier hung in the middle of the grand space, illuminating the bronze stature of a beautiful woman holding a scepter underneath it.

Both Benji and Noah had worked as bellhops there one summer to earn extra cash to buy new skateboards. They were fired after being caught swimming naked with some guest's daughters one evening, using their key cards to sneak in after hours.

Benji smiled up at the chandelier and said, "The very one." He turned that smile on Noah and Noah felt the sides of his own mouth curve up in response. Benji turned toward the stairs on their right. "Come on. Let's get you cleaned up, you smell terrible. And then we will head to dinner."

Noah squinted out the window, recognizing the orange haze in the air as afternoon drifted down around them. An afternoon on a brand new year and Noah was right back in the very place he thought he would never be in again. On top of all that, he was there with the brother he thought died the last time he was there. Memories of the streets marred his vision, the golden hour shifting to the haze of fire and smoke in the air, debris blurring his vision, screams and cries drowning out the crackle of flames scorching the buildings, the bodies…

He swallowed and turned to his brother, already halfway up the stairs and looking down at him expectantly. A tight smile beckoned him on and Noah felt that familiar pit in his stomach open up as he climbed.

❖

The months blurred together as Noah settled into his routine of being dropped off in the kitchens during the day like a school child. When the rush of dinner ended, Benji would pick him up and drag him along to the various meetings held throughout the elegant hotel. His own room in the suite had been stripped of any of the finer details, just a bed and a dresser stocked with a couple t-shirts, athletic shorts, and enough uniforms to make it through the week before needing to do laundry.

It was luxury neither him nor Benji had seen in their over three decades on Earth.

True to his warnings, Noah was never let alone. Only at night, lying sleepless on his plush bed, did he find a moment to sit with his own thoughts. Often that time was spent cycling through all the conversations overheard or details deciphered during that day.

Benji's meetings had been boring at best until Noah picked up on the code his brother and the group of tactical clad groupies used in his presence. While he sat, feigning ignorance, he memorized their words and phrases.

From what he could gather, there was an issue with this *"recours"*, as it was referred to as, the so-called fix to the vampirism plaguing the world. Something about supply not meeting the demand and how they planned to enact an alternate pathway. The details of which remained a mystery, their conversations growing more and more vague as his presence wore on. He was alone, once again, while surrounded by people at a near constant rate.

As they walked back into the suite after another borderline useless meeting, Noah made his way to his room, ready to crash on his bed and let sleep drown out the roaring emptiness hollowing out all his emotions. Every inch of him had grown numb.

Which is why when Benji stopped him before Noah disappeared into his room, he responded by freezing.

"You...wanna hangout for a bit?"

Yes. No. More than anything in the world. Why the fuck haven't you reached out sooner? Why have you treated me like a criminal?

All his thoughts whirled in his mind as his hand hovered over the door handle. Taking a deep breath, he turned slowly around to look at his brother.

"What did you have in mind?" Noah asked, heart pounding for the first time in months.

The grin on his brother's face lit up the room.

"Come on, you'll love this," Benji said, turning back

around to the front door. Noah took a tentative step toward him and when Benji noticed he hadn't immediately followed, turned, beckoning him on.

"Seriously Noah, we will be late. Let's go!"

Noah paused, his mind at war with itself. Follow his brother to some unknown, undisclosed location or spend the evening wallowing in his own desolation, trying to decode more secrets…

The door closed as Benji disappeared out into the hallway. Noah held his breath. The moment the latch clicked into place, Benji opened it again and looked at Noah.

"Noh, what's wrong?" Benji asked, stepping back into the suite with his brows furrowed. He stood in front of Noah and grasped his biceps firmly.

Noah shook his head, unable to look at his brother. "I just…can't remember the last time we hung out," he choked out.

He hated himself for being vulnerable in front of Benji, for showing his cards. But Benji had been his everything, his family, his best friend, his mentor. His savior. And over the last few months, he had no one and so many thoughts he waded through every single night, feeling every ounce of sanity slowly trickle away each day.

Before he knew what was happening, Benji pulled Noah into a hug and, despite himself, tears flowed from Noah's eyes as he wrapped his own arms around his brother.

"I've missed you, brother," Benji said into his ear, squeezing him tighter, on the verge of snapping Noah's collarbone. He used to do that when they were kids, a way to remind Noah he was the younger and smaller brother. Now, it was more of a comfort, being held that tight, feeling his brother's heart beat against his own chest. Too soon, Benji stepped back, tears glistening the edges of his own golden eyes.

"Listen, there will be a bunch of other guys there tonight, so if you don't want to go, I get it. You can stay here," Benji said, searching Noah's face.

Noah shook his head and ran a hand through his hair, using the other to pull the sleeve of his black t-shirt up to dry his face. "No, no, let's go. It'll be fun. I hope."

A sly grin spread across Benji's face and he said, "Oh, it'll definitely be that."

The climb to the rooftop was a startling challenge after months of doing nothing more than walking from one location to the next. If Benji had a workout routine, Noah hadn't been privy to it and besides some basic calisthenics in the darkness of his room every night, Noah's fitness regime had seen a sharp decline, specifically in his cardio. He vowed to remedy that as he drank in the air at the top of the stairs.

The poolside deck unlocked some deep seeded memories. Taller buildings once marred the skyline, blocking the views of the giant river snaking around the city. All that remained of those stone giants were the remnants of rubble from explosions still ringing in Noah's ear, planted in an attempt to overthrow The Society and their plans to turn the city into a vampire hellscape. Instead, the plan had ruined Noah's life and sent them to another city to devastate.

With the newly established panoramic view of the city, the setting sun cast the aqua blue pool aglow against the deep purple and orange hues splashed across the sky. Noah paused, gaping at the sky and the lights strung across the patio space. There were people in the pool, despite the late April chill in the air. If memory served him correct, it was a heated pool but he still couldn't imagine wanting to jump in. Sixty degrees was still sweatshirt and jeans weather. Most of the other people were seated around the deck, engaged in little groups, talking or playing cards. Others were tucked away in more secluded areas, curtains drawn, and noises ranging from innocent giggles to passionate moans drifted out occasionally. Noah blanched and kept pace after his brother.

Benji walked up to a group seated at a round table, plastic chips thrown into the middle with handfuls of cards in front of everyone. A stack sat in the middle. Noah and Benji stood off to the side, watching the game being played. A couple people laid down their hands, letting out exasperated sighs or taking frustrated sips from their glasses. The others made trades, putting cards from their hand into the middle pile and taking replacements from another stack next to the chips. Once everyone settled with their picks, the person to the left of the dealer began, placing down a card. A ten of hearts. The next person threw down a king of hearts, a smug smirk on their face. The person to their left cursed and threw down a six of spades. When it got back to the dealer, he started chuckling. Laying down an ace of hearts, the entire table erupted in groans and outrage as he gathered up all the chips, marking him as the winner that round.

A couple of the players stood up, abandoning their seats for ones at the bar.

"Mind if we join?" Benji asked, walking out of the darkness and into the light cast from the bulbs strung above the table. The dealer looked up and his face brightened upon seeing Benji peering down at him.

"Absolutely, Benji. I've always got a spot for you," the man said, winking at his brother. Noah's eyes narrowed on the dealer. When the man caught him looking, his smile faded.

Benji didn't seem to notice as he turned to Noah and

gestured for him to sit down, across from the man watching him with uncertainty. Noah returned the look as he slipped in his chair, the air growing thicker between them. The man was well built, brown eyes sparkling against his deep umber skin as he glowered at Noah. He had seen him a few times in the meetings he had sat in on. Though obviously strong, Noah thought he could take him. Easily, if necessary. And the way he looked at his brother, it might be necessary.

Benji broke the tension. "Noah, meet Malik Dupart. Malik, this is my younger brother, Noah."

"Yeah, I know of him," Malik said, keeping an eye on Noah as he passed the cards around the table. Once five cards laid in front of everyone, he stacked the rest next to a tower of chips in front of him. "You know the rules of *bourré?*"

Noah smirked, looking at his hand. A mix of high and low cards were there, in various suits. He pulled out two and passed them to Malik to exchange. "Yeah, I think I remember the rules," Noah said, meeting Malik's gaze as the man passed him two new cards.

"Good," Malik said. "Then let's say we up the ante. Everyone pull out something worth our time."

Noah swallowed, his smirk falling. He had nothing on him except that golden cross necklace. There was no way he was parting with that. Everything else he ever held of importance was likely gone, forgotten in a city far away. Like him.

Benji broke his spiraling panic by laying a hand on his arm and giving him a sideways smile. He placed two five dollar bills on the table. "I've got you, brother," Benji said to Noah, winking.

Noah turned his attention to see Malik watching the interaction, a look of adoration and infuriation battling on his face. He had a small piercing in one eyebrow and it moved side to side as he went from scrunching his brows to raising them.

Once everyone had laid something down in the pot, mostly money and the occasional piece of jewelry, a plastic token was laid out to symbolize the first round and the game began. A scrawny man next to Malik laid down a card and turns went in silence for the first round. The scrawny man won, the token in front of him to mark it.

Malik broke the silence during the next round. "So, Noah, how was St. Louis?"

The air stilled. Right to it, then.

Noah examined the cards being laid down by the other players. The trump was an eight of diamonds—a fairly easy card to beat.

"It's a haughty little river city, not too different from this one," Noah answered, studying his own cards. The queen and ace of diamonds in front of him occasionally flashing to the emerald, freckled smile conjured by mentions of St. Louis. He could play the higher card but where was the fun in that. He laid down his queen.

Malik's gaze held on him as Benji sorted through his cards, tongue sticking out the corner of his mouth.

"I heard it's rife with vampire now. The whole city's run by them and it's gone more corrupt than it was before the immortal damnation."

"So, no different than what it was like here? Or I guess, what it's still like," Noah said, coolly. Benji laid down a four of diamonds, giving a wary side glance between the two men. Malik remained silent as he studied his cards, glancing up at the pile once before laying down a two of clubs. Noah smiled and gathered up his winning token.

"A lot has changed since you were here last, Noh,"

Benji said as they tossed their cards back to Malik to shuffle. Cards flicked across the table, occasionally slapped down by an impatient hand.

"How so, Benji? I don't get to see much of it," Noah pressed, trying his best to keep the edge out of this voice. He didn't want to ruin this time with his brother. Not when he had finally started to treat him like something more than a disappointment or threat.

Benji opened his mouth to speak but Malik cut in, "Why don't we take you out to see for yourself then?"

Benji shot the man a look that could've sparked a wildfire. Noah watched the two engage in a staring battle that rivaled one's he had witnessed between Izzy and Barry. His breath caught and he looked away.

"I would love that," Noah interjected, peering down at his cards and focusing on maintaining a normal breathing cadence.

Malik smirked. "Great, Benji and I will get something planned."

Noah focused on the game. By the end of the night, Malik ended up winning, promising to Benji he would find a way to make up his loss to him. As they stood to leave, Noah stepped off to the side of the stairwell landing, leaning against the concrete ledge as he watched his brother have a close conversation with Malik. When they started laughing at something, Benji laid a hand on Malik's arm and Noah looked away, up to the night sky. It was clear and the stars were on full display. Being this close to the ocean, each one was vibrant, speckling the darkness with light. Pisces had disappeared months ago, but another constellation, the Hydra, had come into view in its wake, the long line of stars twisting and turning.

The Hydra, the monster Hercules managed to slay even

after watching two heads grow back in place of the one he cut off. He found victory, not by brawn or brute force, but by wit. His killing blow involved cutting it down and burning the wound before it could heal. Cauterizing the problem at the source. Noah's grip tightened on the ledge, his teeth groaning as he ground them together.

CHAPTER TWELVE
IZZY

The thick pages of the heavy tome on life in the middles ages hit the linen covers of her bed with soft thump and Izzy laid back on top of the plush pillow behind her.

Nothing. There had been nothing new in that ungodly giant book. In The Ramblings, Noah had pinpointed the word for "tainted blood" and she spent the last four hours scouring the text for even a mention of the phrase. The closest she had come was a mention of tainted wine at a wedding, an entirely different bad time than the one she experienced at that moment.

She let out a heavy sigh and felt that new familiar empty ache of hunger. The desire for blood waned constant in the back of her mind but she tried to limit herself to only feed when it truly felt necessary. Unbearable. Gnawing into her every thought. Her mind wandered to the feel of the warm drink sliding down her throat, coating her tongue, wishing she had invited Charlie up for a quick snack.

She groaned. The last thing she needed was a man in her bed. Not when she had begun thinking of them as snacks. And not when the waters between them were as muddied as they were with Charlie.

His words in the library had hit a mark though. As much as she hated everything Charlie had done and the monster he had become over the past year, she didn't actually want him to die. At least not anymore. It had dawned on her reluctantly when he talked about taking his own life.

And Barry had known the entire time, not saying anything. Just his vague mentions that she needed to talk to Charlie. *"Hear him out, at the very least."*

Her palms pressed into her eyes as her thoughts ventured to Noah. In less than a year, her entire life had gone to absolute hell. Loneliness weighed heavy on her chest as she pictured him running behind her in that underground garage, one minute there and the next…gone.

"This is fucking ridiculous," she said, throwing her hands to her side and ending her personal pity party. She reached down the bed for her leather bookbag, pulling it closer to sift through the contents. As she aimed to pull out another journal like The Ramblings, her eyes snagged on the emblem next to it. A tingle shot up her fingers and she pulled the thick book out.

The leather bound cover had been embossed in gold foil on the front, an eagle flying through a capital A. Hop leaves and cones intertwined around the edge to create a border. There was no title but none was needed. The city had been built by the merger of two immigrant families and the brewing industry they brought with them. St. Louis was, and always had been, steeped in tradition. The tradition of millionaires making corrupt decisions that impacted the community at large, but steeped nonetheless.

Flipping the book open, the pages fell to a section on prohibition. Remembering her weird dream, she stopped, studying the text, reading it aloud to fill the silence weighing down around her. "Despite the downfall of their competitors, the Anheuser-Busch family found a way to flourish in a time when their number one product was suddenly deemed illegal. When tragedy befell the last local competitor, the Lemp family, Anheuser-Busch rose to the occasion, growing and thriving in the subsequent years."

She studied that word: *tragedy*. Not allowing her thoughts to wonder about on her own tragic life, she flipped through the book looking for more about the Lemp family. She knew little about them and less about what had happened to them. The only other mention of them was a picture in the acknowledgments wishing condolences to the family.

The mansion in the photo was familiar, a relic on the south side of the city rumored to be haunted but at that point, what abandoned building wasn't full of monsters lurking within? She returned to the first page that mentioned the family, studying the photo of the two men standing next to each other in an ornate board room, shaking hands. One man smiled an electric grin, the kind that sold cars or vacuum cleaners. The other frowned at the camera, out of place next to the man with his well-tailored suit and combed hair. The caption read:

> Adolphus Busch welcomes Adam Lemp to tour the new Anheuser-Busch brewing and bottling facility.

She turned the page, hoping for more information about the two men in the photo. But it was nothing but more uplifting propaganda.

> Anheuser-Busch survived the years of prohibition by selling the raw ingredients for beer making, a legal loophole, and a special elixir for vitality made exclusively for premier customers of the company.

Her phone vibrated next to her and she startled. Had to be Barry. They had a staff meeting the next day and he was preparing his pitch to Dr. Beechum about getting an undergraduate assistant for their lab. *Since I've been absent*, she reminded herself.

She shook her head, trying to garner some positivity for him and unlocked her phone.

CHARLIE

> Hey, sorry for dumping all my issues on you today. I appreciate you listening, despite everything.

Her eyes widened as she read the text three more times. Who the fuck was this guy and what did he do with the easily hateable version of Charlie Valentini she knew? That one she could navigate, understand. This was too…unpredictable.

Tossing her phone off to the side, she pulled her laptop in front of her. She needed to focus. To research. To get her life back to *normal*.

❖

Two hours later, she found herself knee deep in conspiratorial forums and amateur blogs dedicated to the history of brewing, specifically lagering of beer, the pinnacle of German immigrant success in the industry.

Turned out, the Lemp family got their start as one of the first brewers in the city to make the slow-fermented beer. But Adam Lemp's real innovative practice was his utilization of the cave systems beneath the city.

"Noah would be fangirling so hard right now," she mumbled to herself as she scanned the pictures on the black background website with it's neon green font. She squinted, trying to focus so she could relay all this information to him when she saw him again. Though he likely already knew all about the topic. He probably fell asleep reciting the names of every brewer who set their barrels in those caves.

She froze. *When she would see Noah again.* She didn't see how she would ever see him again. Fuck, he had left *her*. Not the other way around.

She shook her head, turning her focus back to the hard hitting sleuth journalism on her screen. Prohibition, according to the author, had been a real turning point for the Anheuser-Busch family. They sat around their elixir funded fires while their competitors dropped, falling under the rushing water of the times.

Izzy yawned, stretching her back as she scanned her empty apartment. This had all been a lot of history, even for an anthropologist. Looking for a distraction, she pulled her phone to her and unlocked the screen. It immediately popped to the text from Charlie. Falling back into her pillows, she stared at the screen. At the apology from Charlie. Unease billowed in her stomach and she backed out of that screen, pulling up instead one that hurt even worse to look at. The one that hadn't seen a new message in months.

IZZY

> Did you know about the Lemp family and their obsession with caves, too? Are you related to them by chance?

Her finger hovered, once again, over the Send button. What would be the harm in sending it really? If he wanted to reach out, he would have.

Unless he couldn't.

She huffed out a breath, shaking the thought away. This was getting ridiculous. She could send a text message. She could do it. No harm, no foul, or whatever Vahagn used to say.

But how would Noah respond if *that* was her first communication to him after all this time? She scowled at her phone, thumb moving back off to the side. He had *left her.* And there had been no text or call to let her know he was okay or still fucking alive or wanted her to care or to come get him. Nothing.

That nothing had seeped into the empty spaces of her apartment, of her soul. She drowned under the weight of her brand new reality and she felt *nothing*.

She locked her phone screen, throwing it to the foot of the bed and let that lie go with it.

She felt *everything* without him. In that last moment they were together, she saw a inkling of hope. Of a future for them, as they raced out of that crumbling building. Of a person she wanted to spend the rest of her life with.

The tears came hot, scorching a path down her cheeks, staining the linen beneath her.

❖

A constant drip splashed next to her face again and again. Groaning as her eyes peeled open, she pressed a hand into the hard rock next to her head. Another drop fell, wetting the back of it and she jerked away in surprise, the cold water clinging to her skin.

She looked around, easing her way to standing. The air felt stagnant, an acrid bread smell hanging on the edges of the earthen must. The walls were craggy, grey stones with hallways leading to her right and left. A few wooden barrels sat sideways on the floor, foam oozing from the seams.

She blinked at the immersive dream, then rolled her eyes. Like she needed another experience to make her question her own reality. A torch burned on the wall opposite her and she reached for it, gripping the harsh rope wrapped handle with a sick drop in her stomach. It all felt real. Too real. She pushed the flame to her right then her left, checking for what, she wasn't exactly sure. She had no idea where she was or the greater purpose of her being there, let alone which direction her subconscious wanted her to go.

Through a series of irrational superstitious thoughts, she stepped down the path to her left. A few paces down, a loud shout echoed down the chamber behind her. She jumped, nearly dropping the warm torch in her hand. More words were yelled and throwing caution to the wind in the matrix of her mind, she ventured toward the commotion.

"Du weißt nicht, wovon du sprichst[19]!" A man's voice rang out, bouncing off the walls in an acoustic surround sound. Izzy continued down the narrowing hallway, her brain repeating the man's words as she tried, pathetically, to translate the German. A year in university her freshman year was not going to help now.

"Was ist dann in dem Elixier[20], Adolphus?" Another voice responded, also male but tenser. *Adolphus.* She remembered that name from her research. The man who started the Anheuser-Busch empire. And the elixir. But what did that have to do with anything? From what she could figure out online, it was just some bullshit tonic a bunch of rich people were influenced into paying a small fortune for and in turn, the sales floated the brewer during a time of no brewing.

Walking through what was no more than a wide crack, she stepped out into a spacious cave room filled with rows upon rows of barrels. Two men stood in the middle, circling each other like wolves in the throe of battle. She squinted her eyes, trying to see in the dimly lit space. She set her torch down so as not to draw any attention to her as she worked her way along the rough, rock edge of the room, searching for a better angle. When she stopped, she recognized one of the men from the pictures. Adolphus Busch.

And everything she knew about the man vanished as she watched him lunge at the other, sinking his teeth into his neck.

"Oh my god," Izzy whispered, her heart thundering in her chest.

In the next breath, the man ripped the other's throat out, letting his lifeless body slump to the ground in a heap. Blood streamed down Adolphus's face. His teeth, no, his *fangs* shone bright in the flickering light from the torches on the walls. A rock hit the cave wall to her left, from the hallway she'd come in, catching her attention. She peered into the darkness, into her escape route. And her heart rate quickened as two glowing eyes stared back.

Quickly turning back to the slaughter below, her fear grew as she studied the man standing there, blood smeared down his front. At the monster he had become. That she had become.

Then he met her gaze and she woke up, screaming.

CHAPTER THIRTEEN
NOAH

Noah propelled out of the darkness of his dream, sitting up in his bed to the indigo tinged twilight of early morning outside his window. His heart rate steadied. It had been a long while since his dreams were something different from the usual loop of crumbling walls, burning lungs, and screams drowning out his own.

An eerie chill burrowed into his bones as he rubbed a rough hand over his face, throwing the covers off himself. He made his way out the door to the shared bathroom, grabbing his towel from its hook as he went.

The hot water blasted against his skin, deepening the warm tone of it. He emerged from the steamy room a while later to the smell of coffee from the little drip machine in their kitchenette. Benji peered on over a mug from his spot on the couch.

"Morning," Benji said. Noah kept pace on his way back to his room, grunting in response. "Can we talk?" his brother added.

Noah shut the door behind him, hanging his towel so he could get dressed into his black kitchen uniform. His heart pounded. Why was he so nervous to talk to his brother? He pulled on a fresh set of socks when a single knock sounded on his door. He froze, then set his socks down and watched the door. There were no locks. A convenient little detail about his room. Benji's room had locks.

"Noh, I know you heard me. You have freakishly good hearing for someone who played in a band," Benji's voice filtered through the door.

The doorknob turned before Noah finished saying, "Come in."

Benji smiled down at him and Noah returned it with a tight lipped grin. His pulse throbbed in his temple. His brother sat down next to him on the small bench at the end of the bed. The newest piece of furniture bestowed upon him. Earned for his cooperation.

"I enjoyed hanging out last night," Benji said.

Noah rubbed the back of his neck as he let out a sigh. "Yeah, it was fun. Been a while since I've played *bourré*."

Benji laughed. "Well, you've still got it, old man."

Noah let out a breathy laugh.

"Look, I know Malik comes off as…a lot. But he's just viciously protective. He grew up in Algiers and you remember how hard The Society hit that area when they first arrived."

Noah nodded, his smile souring and his stomach with it. How could he forget? The early stages of the transformation meant bloodthirsty vampires with little to no control. Emilien had picked a community he deemed expendable. It had been a bloodbath, bodies thrown haphazard in back alleys and along the banks of the river in such frequency the Mississippi developed a slight red tinge around the bend.

"It's okay, I get it. So, how long?" Noah asked.

Benji gave him a tentative smile and knowing look. "Not long after the explosions. He had been my liaison with Adette, meeting in empty buildings or dark cemeteries. The Society was always so freaked out about stepping into cemeteries. Like they would burst into flames if they did." His brother chuckled, rubbing at the straw-colored stubble under his chin. "Once I was officially in with The Antisociété, we ended up spending even more time together in meetings and such." Benji's smile widened and the rest went without saying.

Noah couldn't help his thoughts venturing to Izzy, sitting on her couch with The Ramblings splayed out between them. A soft smile tugged at the edges of his lips and he had to glance away from his brother.

Benji studied him for a moment, pressing his lips together before saying, "Anyway, Malik was serious about taking you out tonight. It's Cinco de Mayo in a couple days and you know how the city gets before any big party."

Noah smiled, looking to his hands where they hung between his legs. He glanced up at the clock. He needed to leave soon or he would be late. He stood and Benji followed as he made his way out of the bedroom toward the front door. Benji had been alleviated of his escorting duties recently and it had vastly improved his mood.

Noah pulled on his black sneakers while Benji spoke. "Just…think about it, Noh. Malik wants to get to know you and I think you'll be impressed with the city, how things have changed. Improved."

Noah let out a long exhale. "Okay."

"Okay?" Benji asked.

"Yeah, okay, Benji. I'll go out with y'all tonight." He turned to give a small smile to his brother over his shoulder. Benji beamed.

"Okay! We can leave after dinner," Benji said, setting his mug down on the kitchenette counter and pulling out his phone. His fingers flew across the keys as Noah pulled the door open.

And despite himself, Noah felt a bubble of excitement as he walked down the hallway to the stairs.

❖

The first difference Noah made note of outside the gilded walls of The Roosevelt were the reinstatement of the streetcars. Or rather, how they no longer traveled along the rails in the middle of the road packed full of drugged and dazed humans, fresh puncture wounds dotting their necks and arms, eyes glazed over with skin a sick pallor that haunted his nightmares. No, the people aboard these streetcars were *alive*. It unnerved him.

The hotel sat a few blocks from their destination on Bourbon Street, so they chose to walk, another key difference he noted. People were walking. Outside. At night. They passed the derelict remains of the Museum of Death with its blown out windows and boarded up door. Once an eclectic tourist attraction, in the age of the vampire it had served as a depot for those looking to indulge in their vampire kink. The Society men, and women, were happy to yield to the desires of well-paying customers, and they got a willing snack out of the deal as well.

Noah happily planted the bombs that tore that place down.

Yet, he couldn't take his eyes off the building as they walked past, the rest of the group laughing at something Benji said. Their group consisted of Noah, Benji, Malik, Nadia, another woman Nadia introduced as her roommate Shonna, and the lanky guy from the bourré table the night before. When Noah tore his eyes from the abandoned building, it was Nadia's he met as she watched him for a moment, a faint blush tinting her fair skin. His lips thinned. They hadn't talked since she had led Benji to him during that last night on the barge and he had nothing to say to her. Her friend whispered something in her ear and she broke her gaze from Noah, turning to Shonna and giggling.

God, he really hoped he didn't end up regretting his decision to come out that night. Benji had extended the olive branch and Noah needed, wanted, to reconnect with his brother, not set the twig on fire. Their dynamic had been completely off since St. Louis. Since Noah had been taken as a prisoner. Since his brother ended up not being dead after all.

Retelling the story to Izzy had opened Noah's eyes to how his brother had used him while they were both in The Society. The seed had been planted and from that day forward, it flourished as more and more of the truth unveiled around him.

The group continued straight down Dauphine Street and Noah's brows scrunched.

"Are we going to The Gold Mine?" Noah asked his brother. The Gold Mine Saloon sat on a sleazy little corner and catered to the mortal members of The Society, the few there were. Or rather had been. The owner paid a hefty fee to keep the vampires out of his establishment unless absolutely necessary. Emilien had agreed and set it up as a "safe place" for the humans in his organization to meet with community members, selling them on the idea of giving their life force away to the legion of rich, immortal assholes taking over the city.

Malik scoffed and Benji barked out a laugh, the lanky guy snickering behind them.

"That place burned to the ground after a group of humans threw Molotov cocktails at it a few months ago," Benji said, smiling something cruel to Malik.

Noah felt his face pale slightly. What had happened here that had *humans* fighting…and winning on the streets? When he had left the city, they were all being gathered up like cattle in those streets on their way to the slaughterhouse.

"No, we are heading to Potions!" Nadia chimed in from the front of the group.

Noah stopped. "You can't be serious?"

Benji's eyes twinkled as he turned to Noah, smiling. "Dead serious."

"Fuck," Noah murmured, instantly regretting his decision to come out. No good ever came from stepping foot into Potions. The speakeasy had been the very first secret establishment the vampires had taken over. It was password protected and already had a vampire theme, even before the immortals graced the crescent city with their presence. The change had been seamless. The massacres of women within? Less so.

"I'm telling you, Noah, the city has changed," Benji called out, not looking behind him as he spoke. "Trust us." Only Malik turned around, brown daggers drawing fine lines over Noah's body as the man assessed him.

Noah's gaze passed over Malik's shoulders and his steps slowed.

A crowd emerged ahead of them. A crowd. His heart rate quickened and his breathing caught up to match. As the setting sun cast its amber glow across the vibrant city, the street lights kicked on, startling him. Try as he willed to catch up with the rest of the group as they pressed into the heart of the French Quarter, Bourbon Street, Noah's feet refused to move quicker. Only when he watched Benji and Malik disappear into the throng of people, genuine none-blood-sucking people, did his feet find pace. The group emerged on the other side and in front of the bright red building of the Boutique du Vampyre.

"One sec," Nadia said, as she slipped into the store. Noah gave Benji a questioning look.

"She's just getting the password for today. They keep it tight-lipped, as you can imagine why," Benji said, gesturing to the crowds building behind them.

A few minutes later, Nadia emerged with a smirk on her face and they all followed her back down the road, into the drove of people that seemed to have multiplied in the short time they stood outside the boutique. She led them around the corner and into a garden courtyard. A few people sat around, sipping on colorful drinks and smoking sweet smelling cigars underneath the golden glow of the twinkle lights above. Noah eyed them all, taking note of a couple laughing together at a small table. The woman reached over, grazing the man's bare arm, and Noah's skin tingled. He looked away to Nadia as she approached a man dressed in all black, smoking a cigarette off in a dark corner by a small green door with an Employees Only sign on it.

"The constellations converge on a night like this, don't you agree?" she whispered to the man. A corner of his mouth tipped up as he glanced to the overcast sky above and then to the group. His eyes lingered on Noah for a moment and Noah held his gaze. Then the man looked back to Nadia and said, "Couldn't ask for a better night to view the stars." He pushed the door in, beckoning the group to follow him as he made his way up a tight staircase lined with cast iron railings.

"Enjoy your night," the man said directly to Nadia, giving her a wink and a once over before he disappeared back into the darkness down the stairs. She turned to Shonna and the two women burst into a fit of giggles. Noah felt Malik's eyes on him as their group ushered into the bar but he ignored it, focusing on taking in the space before him.

It was intimate, with comfortable velvet couches and plush sofas spread about. Doors at the back of the room opened out onto a balcony overlooking the street below. A set of double doors sat closed across from the bar. If memory served him correctly, Noah knew those opened into the private rooms that had once been available for rent when the business catered to a more bloodthirsty clientèle. But as far as Noah could tell, there was not a single vampire in their midst. Just a few small groups like their own, gathered in conversation under the piped in jazz music from the speakers placed around the room. The acoustics were surprisingly good, something all the bars in the city battled since the architecture originated before the age of amplification and electric guitars.

Noah glanced at the stage in the corner of the room, the single chair placed on it, then turned to sink into the leather barrel chair across from Malik and Benji pressed comfortably together on a love seat near the empty fireplace. They had a decent view of the eventual entertainment but enough space away so they could still hold a conversation with each other. Nadia, Shonna and the other guy sat in close discussion together on a sofa that completed the circle of space their group occupied.

Malik stood, bending down to whisper something in Benji's ear. His brothers eyes lit up and Noah watched his nose, that familiar nose, crinkle with a smile up at the other man. He watched as the normally hardened expression on Malik's face softened, warming at the sight of his brother so happy. So in love. Then Malik turned to Noah and the warmth vanished beneath a thick layer of frost.

"What will you be having?" Malik asked.

"Bourbon, on the rocks, please," Noah said. Benji eyed him curiously as Malik nodded and turned to the rest of their group. Benji's lips parted, about to say something, when both their attention was stolen by a woman emerging from the double doors, a crimson silk robe edged in fur trailing behind her. The "Restricted" sign on the door caught his eye before the three-inch strappy heels the woman walked out on. Her robe split as she stepped onto the stage, revealing a swath of smooth, brown skin. Noah's eyes widened and he turned to his brother. Benji sat back against the cushions of the couch, a smug smile on his face as he watched the woman get settled on the stage before glancing to his brother with a tilt of his head.

"Don't tell me St. Louis, of all places, scandalized you, Noh," Benji quipped. Noah swallowed and glanced back to the woman. The main lights of the bar dimmed and a purple glow shined on the stage as she adjusted the position of the chair. Turning her back to the crowd, she looked over her shoulder, catching Noah's gaze with a smirk before nodding once to the bartender.

The music that had been playing stopped and then was replaced by a long, drawling trumpet. The woman swayed her hips in time to the slow rhythm. When the drumbeats started hitting in the song, she dropped the robe, letting it pool at her feet like a puddle of blood. She bent forward, her ass on full display in the high cut black lace bodysuit she wore. Noah felt his cheeks heat, imagined who he wished he were watching in that moment, and tried to look away when a small tattoo on her left butt cheek caught his attention. He squinted, trying to make out the shape as the lights flashed between purple and red. Then she turned and their eyes met. Her body twisted and writhed in time to the classic jazz ensemble. He held her gaze, just for a moment, before turning back to his brother.

Benji sat with his arms resting on his knees, studying the woman's movements like there would be an exam after the show. The music shifted to a jazzy rendition of a popular pop song. With Noah's attention gone, the woman focused in on Benji, sauntering off the stage and toward him. She stopped in front of him and continued her dance. He leaned back, drinking her in. He only looked away when Malik arrived back with their drinks, handing a bubbling glass to Benji. The man set his own bright red drink down on the side table next to his seat, glancing at the woman as he roughly passed Noah his bourbon. The amber liquid sloshed over the edge because Noah had a clear view of the tattoo again as the woman whirled around, rolling her hips in Benji's face. She smirked at Noah from over her bare shoulder.

His grip tightened around his glass, nearly letting it slip and fall to the floor with the condensation.

Because tattooed on the ass of that beautiful woman was a golden fucking fleur de lis.

⚜

After the song ended, the woman placed a kiss on Benji's cheek and a hand on Malik's before returning to her throne on stage. A new song played and she continued her show. Noah's jaw ached under his clenched teeth and he downed his bourbon in one fiery gulp before standing.

As he passed Benji on his way to the outdoor balcony, he said, "I need some air." Benji, deep in a conversation with Malik, waved a hand at him in acknowledgment and that's all the approval Noah needed. Hell, he didn't even need it. The room had become suffocating as his mind whirled.

The Society was gone.

The city was free. Of them, at least.

Tattoos were permanent.

That woman couldn't remove hers anymore than he could remove his.

Still…

A gnawing sensation sank into his stomach and he gulped in a deep breath of the muggy air as he emerged onto the empty balcony. The entertainment inside did an excellent job of keeping the patrons preoccupied while he had a melt down. He paced around the corner of the balcony, disappearing from sight in case anyone were to follow him, and leaned against the wrought iron railing, peering up at the night sky. It had turned cloudier, a terrible fucking night to watch the constellations like the bouncer had suggested, but the moon still held an audience, the ever present beacon it was. He sighed, closing his eyes briefly as he tried to focus on his inhales and exhales, feeling the moisture from the air coat his throat.

A giggle sounded behind him and broke his concentration. He turned to see movement in the window of one of the private rooms behind him. The curtains were drawn but a sliver left the couple within exposed. A tall paler skinned man with bright white hair unbuttoned his collared shirt. His tie was already loose around his neck as his eyes bore into the woman leaning back on the bed, her red lacy lingerie in stark contrast to the white sheets. The man looked to be not much older than Noah, despite his hair color, and Noah couldn't seem to tear his eyes away as he leaned in to say something to the woman that had her head tilting back, laughing as her golden curls bounced down her back.

Noah smirked and started to turn away when something in the man's returning smile caught his eye. As the man's gaze narrowed on the exposed skin of the woman, Noah took a step closer. When the man's stare turned predatory, stripping his shirt away and ripping his neck tie over his head with a snarl, Noah's heart rate quickened. And with fangs bared, the man stalked toward the woman on the bed while everything in Noah screamed at him to run to the window and bang on the glass. To make it all stop.

Then a small hand grabbed his arm and the world narrowed back into that moment.

"There you are! I was wondering where you ran off to." Nadia smiled up at him as he turned. She threw a questioning glance at the window but from her angle, it appeared to be covered.

Noah looked back into that room. Into the blackened gaze of the man as he sat straddling the woman, his teeth sank deep into her neck. Noah took in a sharp inhale, looking away once more. The movement caught Nadia's attention and she began to peer over into his view of the room. He dared one last glance to see the curtains had been drawn fully, leaving the couple to their private matters more effectively.

"I…I just needed some air," he croaked out.

Nadia's smile widened as she looked back up at him. "Me too. That dancer is good but it was getting steamy in there." She fanned herself with the front of her over sized t-shirt, looking down at the revelers in the street below. She approached the rail then looked over her shoulder at him where he stood frozen in place, his heart beating erratic. She patted the space next to her.

Act fucking normal, Noah.

Rubbing the back of his neck, he stepped up to the railing, keeping a good foot of space from her. She glanced at the emptiness between them with a pout.

"I always loved the liveliness of this street," she sighed, eyes twinkling down in wonder at the illuminated, raucous street below.

I always hated it, he thought. They had come down here

as teenagers, him and Benji, begging for money from drunk tourists and occasionally, stealing it from them as well. No fond memories could be found on those streets.

A breathy laugh escaped her lips. "You know its crazy to think we were both living in this city and never saw each other until now."

His brows furrowed at her words and he tilted his head to study her profile. As she watched the people below singing and dancing along the neon lined street, he examined the features of their difference. Where his tawny brown skin filled in the missing pieces of his ancestry, her pale skin, silky caramel brown hair, and petite features suggested she came from the upper echelons of the city. Her experience of New Orleans would've been a heady contrast from the one he and Benji grew up in. Where her pristine neighborhood likely hid behind a ten foot tall iron gate topped with spikes, his had those bars over his windows and doors. Of course she loved the liveliness of the party below. She never had to experience it for what it truly was: a desperate attempt for many to stay afloat.

When he went to look away, he noticed she had scooted closer to him. His back straightened, about to step away when she placed a small hand on his arm, gasping as she pointed to the marching band making its way through the throng of people. A squeal escaped her lips and he cringed.

"Oh, I love this song! Dance with me?" she asked, turning to face him. She didn't give him a chance to decline as she pulled his hands off the railing and placed them on her hips. He raised them to her waist and she frowned. Her small hands slipped up his chest and around his neck. His gaze shifted to the beadboard ceiling above, nostrils flaring as he stiffly stepped side to side as she swayed to the music.

"Oh, come on, I know you can dance better than that. I've heard the stories," she teased, squeezing his neck.

His jaw tightened and he made no attempt to improve his movements. "That was a different time." *A different person.*

The music faded as the band disappeared further down the street and Noah moved to step out of her reach. Instead of creating space between them though, she followed suit placing her hands on his chest until his back pressed hard against the brick facade of the building. His eyes narrowed on her.

"Well, maybe you can start to see how times haven't changed too much since then," she purred, eying his lips. He reached for her wrists to push her away and she lifted onto her toes and kissed him. He froze. When she persisted, pressing her lips harder against his, he pushed her back.

She stumbled backward, fingers pressed over her mouth as a nervous giggle escaped her plump lips. A step toward him was all he yielded before pushing off the wall and briskly turning the corner to disappear back inside the bar.

"Noah!" He heard her call his name but he didn't stop. He didn't stop as he stepped into the dimly lit room, the dancing woman, now topless on her chair, hanging upside down with her legs spread. They opened and closed in time to the music blaring through the surround sound. Noah's teeth groaned at the pressure his jaw placed on them. He didn't stop, even as Benji saw his face. He didn't stop, even as his brother said his name, those similar toned golden eyes glancing to the balcony door. To Nadia standing in the threshold, the colorful flashing lights of the show illuminating the silver streams falling down her cheeks. He didn't stop as Benji's face furrowed into a frown. He was at the top of the stairwell, and though that disapproval on his brothers face nagged at him, beckoned for him to stay, to yield, to bend to his will, he descended into the dark.

Nadia had been right, he thought as he sprinted down the stairs. Times hadn't changed here. It was the same bullshit under a new guise. The bouncer startled as Noah yanked open the door and stormed into the courtyard. He was back on the streets in seconds, heading toward the only place he felt might hold peace for him: the St. Louis Cemetery No. 1. Ironic. Fitting.

Noah heard the footsteps as his brother approached but he didn't slow his pace. Benji caught up and matched his stride as they walked in silence. The crowds pressed into them, the smells overwhelmed him, the sounds deafened him, his mind spun. Noah slipped into a dark alley and immediately leaned over behind a dumpster and vomited. Flashes of fangs and blood and the feel of Nadia's lips on his and how it erased the last lips he'd felt there and scorching green eyes throbbed behind his closed eyes. He heaved once more, spitting before he stood up and continued down the alleyway.

"Hey, Noh, come on. Hey, wait a second!" Benji said, jogging up and placing a broad hand on Noah's shoulder. Noah stopped, his skin burning beneath his brother's touch. He cast a stony look down the alley, watching the few party goers pass by on the outer street he was headed toward.

Benji stepped in front of him, concern etched on the details of his face. His dark specked eyes searched Noah's and Noah looked away. He heard his brother sigh then turn on his heel and continue walking. Noah followed slowly.

"I assume we are headed toward the cemetery," Benji said. When Noah didn't answer, his brother looked over his shoulder and Noah gave him a single nod. His brother grinned. "Of course we are. You always had a sick fascination with that place." Benji slowed his pace until Noah walked in line next to him.

"So, are you going to tell me what happened? Nadia seemed pretty upset," Benji said as they stepped back out onto the less crowded street.

Noah barked out a sharp laugh. "I imagine she would be after kissing me without consent and me reacting by walking away."

They passed under the busy road overhead, the tall mausoleum style tombs visible ahead. Benji's face hardened. "I don't understand, she always says you're flirting with her. I figured you guys were an inevitable thing."

Noah glared sidelong at his brother. "That's insane, Benji. I'm not here to be paired off like some sick version of The Bachelor."

Benji shrugged, running a hand through his golden curls as Noah opened the wrought iron gate into the cemetery. "Just because the world has gone a bit to shit doesn't mean you have to be completely miserable, you know Noah."

Noah let out another hollow laugh, the sound reverberating off the stone structures around them as he began pacing. "Yeah, it's still a bit shit around here, isn't it Benji?"

Benji froze, shoulders broad and spine straight. "What do you mean, Noah? The city has changed. The people are free. It's vibrant and alive again! So much good has happened here, how can you still not see it?"

Noah opened his mouth to speak, to tell his brother what he saw at the bar. About how nothing had changed. Then he remembered all the times his brother had trusted him since they had reunited. Not once. He had been nothing more than a prisoner the entire time. If something happened in this city, Noah wasn't convinced Benji wouldn't think he was somehow guilty at the same time.

"Nothing," Noah said, rubbing both hands over his face. He was tired, so fucking tired.

He felt Benji studying him for a long moment. Then he saw the toes of his leather boots in front of him and as Noah pulled his hands away, Benji wrapped his thick arms around him, squeezing him into a quick hug. Two pats on the back, that's all, and then he was released. Noah missed the touch the moment it disappeared. He missed human touch. How long had it been since he felt human touch? The other night had been the first time since St. Louis. Since Izzy.

His stomach roiled as they walked quietly through the cemetery. As they exited, Benji slipped into his usual self, giving a play by play account of the dancer's performance. Noah listened in silence the entire trek back to the hotel, all the way to the door into his room.

"Noh?" Benji's voice stopped him. He turned to face his brother. "I'm really sorry it didn't work out with Nadia." His brother gave him a soft smile that turned his insides to oil.

Noah nodded, returning with a tight lipped smile as he pushed into his room, closing the door behind him.

✦

CHAPTER FOURTEEN
IZZY

For the first time in over six months, Izzy found herself enjoying a Friday family dinner. Charlie kept eying her suspiciously from his station at the opposite end of the table from Lando, raising a thick brow every time a smile cracked through the perpetual scowl she had adorned over the last several months.

"Tomorrow is *quinto do maggio*[21]?" Lando asked, a glass almost to his lips.

"*Cinco de mayo*, Lando," Izzy corrected, smiling at him. "But yes, it is."

Lando rolled his eyes and took a sip. "*Se non è zuppa, è pan bagnato*. Tomorrow, Bartholomew will be coming to have a big party on the roof then, yes?"

Izzy pressed her lips together to not laugh at the Italian expression. *If it's not soup, it's wet bread.*

"Yes, he will be here early to set and do some last minute cooking. He said he would arrive around five but everyone will be coming at seven."

Lando nodded his head slowly, rubbing his chin. His

other hand twisted his bourbon glass in slow circles on the oak table. Then his expression shifted and Izzy tensed. "And, *ditemi*[22], how are they getting home again?" He directed his words to Charlie, cutting Izzy out of the conversation.

Charlie cleared his throat and focused his gaze off her for once to look at his boss. "For those not staying camped out on your roof or in a few volunteered spare bedrooms, we have a group of men shuttling everyone doorstep to doorstep, sir."

"*Molto bene*[23]," Lando said, taking another sip of his amber beverage.

Izzy glanced out at the night sky through the near floor to ceiling windows framing the dining area where they all sat. The turbulent weather of the Midwest decided to bless them all with clear skies and cool weather for the celebration, and she couldn't wait to see those constellations from the expanse of the rooftop.

The strong pull on her heart took her breath and she blinked away, eyes boring into the grain of the table as she quietly pulled herself out of the panic ripping through her. Memories of the last night she had sat on that rooftop. After Vahagn's death. Stargazing next to Noah. Before she knew just how fucked up everything could get.

Tears pressed into the back of her eyes but her breathing steadied as she looked back to the men at the table. Charlie gave her a look of concern, offering her a soft smile and an inquisitive tilt of his head. She shook her head minutely and turned back to Lando, Charlie's words ringing in the back of her mind.

Fake it.

"Do you…need anything from me tomorrow?" she asked tentatively.

This time Lando froze, his glass pressed to his lips. His gaze shifted to her, for the first time that evening she realized, and skepticism crinkled the edges when they met. Her stomach churned. He gave her a tight smile.

"*Mia bella*, Isabella. It's unnecessary. Just enjoy your time tomorrow, yes? Besides, Charlie is plenty capable of all the duties I've assigned him." The old man gave a wary look to Charlie.

A soft knock interrupted the peace and with it came several members of the Campi di Fragole crew for the more formal business side of the meeting. She normally avoided it, finding a convenient excuse to leave early or arrive late to avoid the whole affair. Tonight, she planned to stay. To fake it, like Charlie suggested.

Until a short, curvy woman with dark wavy hair walked in, slipping into the seat across from her. Into Vahagn's seat.

"*Buona sera figlia*[24], Gio," Lando cooed to the woman. His daughter. Izzy swallowed dryly. The woman whose throat she had tried to rip out that previous fall. Whose blood she had first wanted to drain. Whose steady pulse she could hear pumping against her arteries across the table from her.

"*Buona sera,*" Gio replied, the words dripping like venom as she stared at Izzy across the table, golden lights glowing in her warm brown eyes. Where Lando feared the immortals, Gio absolutely despised them. And Izzy sat in their home as enemy number one.

Izzy's vision blurred and her throat tightened under the narrowed gaze of the other woman. The woman she had thought of like an older sister. How quickly adoration can shift to abhorrence when the monster within comes to light.

Trying to swallow against the dry socket in her throat, Izzy stood and mumbled to Lando, "I'm gonna go," before slipping out the front door and racing back to her apartment.

✤

With her feet curled underneath her, back pressed into the corner where her bookshelf met the giant industrial wall of windows, Izzy sat with the Busch family history book propped open on her bed. Her laptop sat beside her, the illuminating blue glow lighting the notebook on her lap with names and dates jotted down. It had been a couple hours since she'd left Lando's, kicking herself for thinking she could just fake it. That was the last time she took advice from Charlie. What the fuck did he even know anyway?

Three soft knocks sounded on her front door. She rolled her eyes. The devil himself wouldn't have better timing than the man on the other side of her front door.

"Come in, you know it's unlocked," she called out, not looking up from the page she was on.

The door opened gently and Charlie peered in, sharp blue eyes finding her on the bed before he stepped forward, closing the door behind him. He toed off his boots and made for the foot of her bed, sitting down with one knee tucked so he could face her.

"Since when do you keep your front door unlocked at night?" he asked.

She didn't tear her eyes away from the pages before her. "People change, Charlie."

There was a long pause before he sighed, "We don't have to go tonight. If you're busy."

She looked up at him, brow scrunched and head tilted. "What are you talking about?"

His expression wavered a moment and he looked down at the bedding beneath him, running a hand over the dark linen. A small smile cracked his lips and he looked up at her. "Another night then." He gave the bed one last rough rub. Blood stained the whites of his eyes, dulling the blue some, and she knew Lando must have broken out his secret stash of California's finest. Izzy's eyes narrowed. Charlie hadn't smoked with Lando or his crew in months.

Apparently he's been smoking with Barry and replacing you as his best friend because you can't be bothered to leave your home.

She shook the thought away and then her eyes widened. "Oh! You were going to take me to that place tonight?"

He had already made his way to the door, bent over to pull his boots back on. He stopped, straightening to look at her.

"Yeah, but really, we can go another night. It's not going anywhere and you seem busy," he said, the soft lines of his features wavering as sorrow slipped through the cracks.

"No, no, no, let's go," she threw her notebook on top of the book, pushing her laptop aside so she could climb out of bed. "I need to get out of this apartment. This building. Just...uh," she motioned to the shorts and oversized t-shirt she had slipped into. "Give me like five minutes to change." She walked into her closet before calling out through the open door, "How am I supposed to dress?" She stuck her head out the door to eye his black slacks and black button up, a gold chain peeking through the open few top buttons.

A soft smile stretched across his face, a slight dimple appearing in his right cheek. "Whatever you wear will be perfect."

She grimaced. "Awesome. Super helpful male response. Make it eight minutes to warm up my lady brain so I can read your mind a little and pick out an outfit to match this Goodfellas special you've got going on." She motioned to his ensemble and he let out a throaty chuckle.

"Yeah, okay. Eight minutes, Ciampi. But not a second more," he said, flashing a bright smile her way before she disappeared into her closet.

For a moment, it felt like going back in time, the banter and smiles as they got ready to go out together. Before it had gone to hell with jealousy and controlling behaviors and screaming matches ending in slamming doors. For a moment, she remembered the man in her apartment with fondness, not hate.

She waltzed out of her closet exactly seven minutes and forty-five seconds later clad in a black wide-leg jumpsuit, held up by thin silky straps and a deep, plunging neckline. At the last minute, she pulled a skintight Gothic black lace t-shirt over the top.

Charlie sucked in a breath as she emerged but quickly averted his eyes, glancing at her door. He cleared his throat. "Ready then, slow poke?"

Her fingers pressed into the soft material of his sleeve as she leaned on him to pull on a pair of colorful wedge heels. "Hey now, let the record show I was faster than my allotted time."

He openly assessed her before giving her a wink. "You could've done that in five minutes."

She released his arm, giving him a tight smile. "Come on, let's go to this mysterious special place already. Maybe I'll find better company there."

His gaze clouded a moment. "Maybe," he said softly as he pulled her door open, holding it for her.

❖

Charlie pulled a familiar set of keys out of his pocket as they exited the stairs into the parking garage beneath the building. The metal keychain in the shape of Italy, with its red, white, and green colors of the flag inlaid within, glinted off the bright flood lights above. All the residents' keys were left at the front desk under the watchful eye of Larry. Another safety feature Izzy endeared in the beginning but felt the overbearing weight of suddenly. They walked past several rows of blacked out SUVs and various sports cars that would be illegal for street driving if anyone cared about such a thing anymore. Halfway up the last aisle on that level, parked between a Maserati Veyron and an ostentatious gold Ferrari Laferrari, was the candy apple red 1959 Alfa Romeo Giulia of her childhood. It was laughably smaller than the sports cars sandwiching it and yet Izzy couldn't take her eyes off it.

"You cleaned it?" she said, running her fingertips along the sleek side of it.

Charlie looked up as he manually unlocked the door, his black hair falling forward over his bright blue eyes. He gave her a small smile. "Yeah, of course."

Izzy marveled at her Nonno's car, even as she heard the passenger door unlock. She hadn't been down to see it since driving it over the day she moved into the building and maybe one drunken night she barely remembered where she showed it, and the backseat, to Charlie.

He stepped out of the vehicle and made the short walk around the front, reaching in front of her to open the door. She looked up at him in bewilderment and he quirked a brow. "Unless you want to drive…?"

"Why?" she asked in lieu of an answer.

He stood there, door open, frozen in a moment where he hadn't expected what she would say. Dark eyelashes dusted his cheeks as he blinked a few times then gave her that half smile that hinted at a dimple in his cheek, looking away to the Laferrari. "I just remembered all the stories you told me about your grandparents and this vehicle was mentioned in at least half of them. But you never came down or drove it and I didn't want the next time you did for it to be…"

"In disrepair," she breathed out, running a shaky hand over the roof. Not even a speck of dirt came off. Tears burned at the back of her eyes. Even the leather within looked pristine.

"I don't think you would've ever let her get that far." His soft words floated around her.

But I did…if it hadn't been for you.

She turned to face him, fanning her eyes slightly. "How do you know she's a she?"

He chuckled, running a tattooed hand through his black hair. "Nothing this beautiful should be insulted by being called a man."

Her eyes widened and mouth dropped open slightly and she started looking around the parking garage with scrunched brows. His spine stiffened and his hand reached down for the blade tucked in his boot.

"What? What is it?" he hissed, scanning the space methodically, a violent edge radiating through his voice.

She finished her visual circuit then looked him up and down. His broad chest heaved as his blue eyes danced from her to the rows of cars. His fingers kept opening and closing around the hilt of the knife. His knees were bent and Izzy thought she spotted the beginnings of sweat at his brow. And she burst out laughing. Instantly she became the sole focus of his intense stare as it narrowed, the knife lowering with it.

"You're laughing at me," he growled.

Izzy caught her breath, wiping the tears that finally sprang free from her eyes. "No, no, of course not. I was just looking for the real Charlie. Someone replaced him with this non-misogynistic, sweethcart doppelganger and I'm concerned about what happened to the asshole version." She gave him a wink as she slid into the passenger seat. Might as well let the poor man drive after she nearly gave him a heart attack. He shut her door with the softest amount of force required and she breathed in the new car smell of the interior, so different from the baked in cannoli smell from that one Christmas her Nonna had left them in the trunk…until the following Easter. She pressed her hand into the soft leather of the dashboard, watching him walk around the front, shaking his head before looking up at the ceiling, as if asking for a prayer of patience. She smiled to herself and focused on the rest of the car, including the infamous backseat.

He slipped into the driver's seat, putting the dagger back into his boot as he studied her. Then he put the key in, turning the engine over with a roar. A couple taps on the gas had the throaty sound reverberating through the seats.

"Just promise me," Charlie halfway yelled over the sounds of the engine rumbling. "Only do that again tonight if there's actually a threat? I can't have you edging me with danger all night long."

"But that just takes away all the fun," she said with a wink.

He turned his head to give her a sly smile as he tossed the car into gear and peeled out of the spot. They slowed to take the curb exiting the garage, pulling out onto the barren street. He revved the engine a few times. Their eyes met. For a moment she let herself get lost in those azure pools, in the happiness she saw dancing through them. He flashed her a bright, crooked smile and the next thing she knew, her back was pressed into the seat behind her and she peeled her eyes off him to watch the city she loved flash by in a blur.

Charlie took the long way around to get to the highway, the fun way with all its tight twists and turns, but then once they were on the open road, he let the engine go. Wind whipped around the cab through their cracked windows and Izzy couldn't help but laugh as her curls were tossed into absolute chaos. She rolled her window down some more and let her hand out, feeling the force of the world as it slid through her fingers. It was heady, that rush of air, the familiar streets and the speed as they headed toward the river, the arch aglow against the night sky. It had remained lit despite the darkening of the street lights below. Nobody wanted anyone on a private jet to accidentally crash into the thing in their newly monopolized airspace.

They eased off the highway, zooming past the derelict baseball stadium. Once the athletes within found a path to immortality within their means, their desire to entertain millions plummeted. The only sports still around were those that were never paid enough to begin with to afford the cure. And their respective games had been bastardized, abominations of what they once were in order to entertain the bloodthirsty desires of their new captive audience.

Izzy had been distracted by downtown, taking in all the ways it had changed since she had last ventured into the belly of the city, so when the engine suddenly cut off, she jumped. She looked around to see they were parked in another garage.

Charlie chuckled softly. "Come on, jumpy. Let's get you inside before you have me stabbing at shadows." He started to make his way around the car to open her door but she didn't give him the opportunity.

"I can get my own door, you're well aware," she snipped at him as she emerged from the vehicle.

His jaw clenched. "Too aware, yes."

They stared at each other for several seconds. Then she stepped forward, slipping an arm around his elbow. He glanced down at the connection and gave a soft, sad smile.

They walked in silence, stepping out into a dark alley. For a moment, her heart thundered in her chest as panic rose, remnants of a life come and gone. When the darkness should be feared. Charlie didn't seem to notice as he led her around the corner. Izzy tripped over her own feet and Charlie turned, catching her other arm and straightening her. His ocean eyes searched her.

"You okay?"

She shook out of his grip, glancing at the building behind him as she rubbed her arm. "Yeah, yeah. It's just…The Thaxton. I saw it doing some research and it…just took me by surprise, that's all."

A smile cracked Charlie's worried expression. "Well, I can't wait to hear all about this research because that's exactly where we are going."

Her eyes widened. "No shit?"

He shook his head, grabbing her hand and leading her on down the empty street. "Yes, shit. Now let's get there before you freak me out anymore and I change my mind about this entire evening."

They approached the metal door, different from the reflective glass in her dream, and she flinched when a slim peep hole opened, a pair of hazel eyes peering out. The hard expression settled on Izzy for a few seconds before they glanced to Charlie, crinkling on the edges.

"Mr. Valentini! Back again! And with a guest! Come in, come in," the male voice echoed through the small opening. The peep hole slid back into place and the sound of metal parts clanking against each other reverberated out onto the quiet street. The hinges groaned as the heavy door was pushed out toward them.

"Now, Mr. Valentini, you know the rules," the short man in a black fedora said to Charlie, eying Izzy sideways. The spats on his shoes matched his rat pack accent. "She's your responsibility." A bigger man stood off in the shadows, only the occasional light catching his eyes made him visible. And his pulse. The steady *thump, thump, thump* in Izzy's ears. A strong pulse. A heavy pulse.

"I'll take my chances with her," Charlie said.

Izzy snapped her gaze away from the statue in the dark, wiping the drool away from the corner of her mouth. She glared at Charlie but followed his lead as he stepped through thick, burgundy velvet curtains.

She gasped and Charlie gave her an inquisitive look over his shoulder. It was just like her dream. The small stage, where a band atop it played smooth jazz. A few couples sat around small round tables. A thrum of beating hearts filled her eardrums, drowning out the band as her focus took in the familiar space. A bartender stood illuminated by the bar lights with bottles upon bottles lining the glass shelves behind them. Her eyes snagged on the door in the back, the one from her dream, and she started to drift toward it when Charlie's hand settled on her waist, guiding her toward an ascending set of stairs on the other wall.

"We will sit upstairs tonight. It's a bit…quieter," he whispered into her ear. She wound around the wide marble spiral staircase, Charlie always a step behind. It opened into a private balcony overlooking the stage and crowd below. She leaned against the railing, taking in the intricate art deco molding and the sun inspired mosaic in the middle of the ceiling.

She heard Charlie talk to a waiter behind her before he sidled up next to her.

"It's beautiful, Charlie," she sighed as she studied the history written in the details on the walls. The lives lived here.

"Yeah, it is," Charlie said. She glanced sideways to see him looking at her before turning his focus up to the mosaic as well. They stood there together for a few minutes before the waiter could be heard behind them setting down their drinks. Izzy could almost smell the blood coursing through the woman's veins and was happy for the distraction on the table. They each eased into a plush leather chair, disappearing from the view of the patrons below. It all felt incredibly intimate. Too intimate. Izzy reached for the drink before her, taking a hefty gulp. Surprised by the thick feel in her mouth, she nearly spit it out, a small crimson dribble running down her chin. She caught it as she looked at Charlie, a question in her eyes. The taste on her tongue set her on fire, every nerve ending humming.

Charlie watched her over the top of his own wine glass, the rim pressed against his lips as he grinned. "You like it?"

She nodded, taking another more reasonable sip. "What is it?" She tried to sound cool even as everything in her felt *alive*.

"A special cocktail they make here. I thought you might like it," he said, taking a sip of his own drink. "Seeing as its base is a mix of wine and blood."

Izzy choked, coughing as she set her glass down on the table, looking at it like it was poisonous. She turned her horrified look onto him and the bastard chuckled.

"Relax, Iz. They cater to all clientèle here. There is a mutual understanding that when you pass through that door, the only blood you can consume comes in a glass. And it's sustainably sourced from blood banks that pay a generous rate and require testing before donation. So, please, enjoy yourself," he finished, gesturing to her glass as he raised his own.

She sat, dumbfounded for several seconds as his words seeped in. Mindlessly, she raised her glass, gently knocking it against his before taking another sip. It felt sinful how good it tasted. Better than anything she'd had so far. Albeit, all she'd done is either drink Charlie's blood or the lifeless, cold, congealing blood bags Lando graciously had delivered to her apartment every week. A generosity centered on keeping her at bay so her neighbors didn't start to look appetizing.

Leaning back, she let the warmth from the wine envelope her, spreading through her body and relaxing her muscles. It even calmed her constantly anxious thoughts. Why had she been so nervous about coming here?

"So, tell me about your research," Charlie said, watching the lights dance behind the band below.

Research? Oh, right. Her "research" on Thaxton. A.K.A. her wild fucking dream.

"Oh, um, well, it was more of a glorified version of using a search engine. But it seemed like the original speakeasy was in the basement?" she lied, smoothly.

Charlie nodded his head and looked to her. "You would be correct. It was originally built as a Kodak retail building of all things but the mob bought it out and ran a speakeasy in the space beneath during prohibition."

Well, that was even more than she knew so she nodded her head, taking another sip of her delectable drink. They watched the band play for a bit.

"How did you find this place?" Izzy finally asked as the band took a short break below.

Charlie turned toward her, studying her through the candle light of the lantern burning on the small table between them. He cleared his throat, glancing away before he spoke. "This is where Lando would have me meet with Emilien. Sort of a common ground for all the gangs in the area, the respectable ones at least. Eduardo, the man at the front door, doesn't take anyone's shit so it's neutral territory. Unless you want to find yourself sunk into an eddy in the Mississippi. He's a little old school if you can tell."

Izzy watched him as he ran a nervous hand over the polished wood grain of the table. His heartbeat stayed steady the entire time he spoke. *Thump, thump, thump.*

"Why are you being so honest with me?" she asked, breaking out of the lull from the metronome in his chest.

He tilted his head, giving her a sad, half grin. "What do I have to gain by lying to you? Hell, what do I even have to lose by telling you the truth? Might as well give you a fair hand."

Because it was all a game. Deep down, the entire shitty situation was just an orchestrated game of cat and mouse between two egotistic, power hungry men leading armies…for what end?

The fury must have started to creep onto her facial expression because Charlie reached across the table and squeezed her clenched fist, "Hey, come back to me."

She blinked and the red edges of her vision dissipated.

He smiled. "There she is."

She pulled her hand out of his grasp and took another sip of her drink, glancing to the golden sconces on the wall behind him.

"So then, why bring me here?" she asked, studying the artwork along the wall.

He set his glass down. "I know what it feels like to be isolated. And then to further isolate yourself because of it. When it becomes more comfortable than the alternative. I wanted to remind you what it felt like to live. To be on the other side of the door for once."

She held his gaze as he spoke, letting every last word he said hit her fully. It was the most caring moment she had ever experienced from him. Scratch that. This was the caring *version* of

Charlie Valentini her brain had washed away from her memories, replaced with the rage bestowed upon her. Her grip tightened on her glass.

"What did you mean by suggesting I need to fake it with Emilien and Lando?" she asked, an edge touching the tone in her voice. She pursed her lips and took another sip of her drink.

His own expression hardened and he sat back in his chair, letting out a quick breath. "At first, when I joined Lando's crew, I was young and cocky and thought I had found an easy hack for life. I got paid a fuck ton of money and all I had to do was take care of the scum in this city. Then I started moving up the ranks. Getting jobs that were more…intense. The stress of it all started to weigh on me. Vahagn," he choked over the name. "Vahagn and I would talk about it but eventually I think it just got to be too much for both of us to carry each other's burden. That's when I snapped. That…night, with you. With us. I went to Lando's afterward. He had been talking about this big plan he had in the works that he wanted me in on. And I felt reckless and ashamed and like I needed to risk something, risk myself so maybe I could wash all those feelings away. When he laid out the plan to me, I walked into it willingly, expecting to be eaten alive. Instead, I was welcomed into a second gang when really all I wanted to do was die."

Izzy let him speak, keeping her eyes narrowed on him. Narrowed on his heart rate. The steady thrum. The unwavering honesty. She didn't know whether to smack him or hug him in that moment.

He huffed out a long sigh and looked her in the eye, icy steel to her forest green. "This is all to say, I had to fake it. On both fronts. I had to give them what I thought they wanted because men like Lando and Emilien expect nothing less than full loyalty to their missions. But, Izzy," his gaze softened on her.

"Don't sacrifice yourself in the process. Don't make the mistakes I made." His throat bobbed and her vision reddened again.

"I'll never be like you," she snarled.

His face fell, a deep sorrow etched into the details of his handsome face. He seemed older in that moment. A ghost of the confident gangster who had caught her as she fell on that first night they met.

"That's all I can ask for now," he said quietly, downing the rest of his wine in a single gulp. Her glass had been empty for a while. He stood, pushing his hands into the pockets of his pants. "You want to stay or take us home?"

Her expression lightened a bit as he tossed her the keys. "You'll let me drive home?"

"It is your car." He gave her another sad, sideways smile as she felt her own lips tug upwards. She peered down on the metal in her hands, the lights of the bar glinting off them.

CHAPTER FIFTEEN
IZZY

I'm gonna…" Izzy said, gesturing to the restrooms down the hallway as they stepped back onto the main floor.

Charlie gave her a quick nod and headed toward the bar. She hurried down the hall and right past the restroom, her sights set on the inconspicuous door from her dream. She had to know. Taking a deep breath, she reached for the handle. *It was just a dream*, she told herself. Just a mysterious, incredibly vivid dream, and the last time she had one it ended with her on a wild goose chase deciphering crumbs of information from an ancient book. Information that had required the help of one missing Noah Broussard.

She shook her head, letting the thought slip away in the process, despite the crease in her brow. He wasn't there. He had left her. She had to do this on her own. Her eyes narrowed on the handle, tongue grazing the edge of her fang as she grabbed it, giving the bronze metal a twist and pull.

Nothing happened.

"Fuck," she swore under her breath. She glanced over her shoulder, down the empty hallway before she twisted the

185

handle again, harder. The door groaned against the added pressure of her strength but still, it didn't budge. She huffed out an exasperated sigh and let go, rubbing her red hand on her pants. In defeat, she slipped into the bathroom to run cool water over her skin before she emerged again, heading toward the bar.

As she scanned the crowd looking for Charlie's familiar dark hair, tatted neck and bright blue eyes, visible even in the dim lighting of the room, her gaze snagged on the tall man standing in front of him. That pageboy hat set her blood to an instant boil and she bared her fangs as she stalked toward him. Charlie glanced over the man's shoulder at her, his eyes widening into depthless pools before his lips moved. *Callum* turned, flashing a cocky ass grin at her when their eyes met.

"Good evening, love. Fancy running into you here. I wouldn't have expected it, all things considered." He turned back to Charlie as his words rolled off his undulating British accent.

"And what the fuck is that supposed to mean?" Izzy growled, stopping a step within his personal space. He turned back to her, his silver eyes roving over her before a sly smirk tilted one side of his lips up.

He leaned down, his breath tickling her ear as he spoke. "It means you're not welcome here by our boss. Not until you learn how to play nice and start getting us some answers."

The hair on the back of her neck stood up as he leaned back. Before he fully left her space though, he planted a quick kiss on her neck. Nausea and rage roiled through her and before he fully straightened, she felt the crunch of his orbital bone as it shattered beneath her fist. Satisfaction washed away her rage and she smiled as she followed with a cross hook with her left. The pop as her other fist met his nose was a symphony to her magnificent new hearing.

"You fucking bitch!" Callum's words were muffled behind his hands as he tried, and failed, to quell the flow of crimson from his face.

Izzy watched in awe, transfixed by the beauty of watching a man like Callum succumbed to nothing more than a *winging idiot*. Then she felt her body being hauled backward, toward the exit. Yet she remained entranced, watching the blood take on a new color as it seeped into the wool tweed of the pretentious asshole's vest. She grinned, imagining the nightmare of a time he would have removing that stain.

The humid air on the street brought her back to reality, lightning skirting across the sky as a thunderstorm threatened to open a down pour at any moment.

"What the fuck was that, Izzy?" Charlie growled, tossing her backward so he could look her in the eye. His own widened when he caught sight of her, the rage, the thirst, the *hunger*. She never looked at herself when she fed, rarely did she even glance at a mirror. She could barely handle the monster staring back, let alone see what it looked like when it was released.

"Did you *see* what he did to me?" she hissed back at him, gesturing toward the door and the filth of a man within.

Charlie ran a rough hand through his black hair. He paced down the sidewalk some before leaning against the brick facade to pull a cigarette out of his breast pocket. She hadn't seen him smoke in…forever. He put the unlit cigarette in his mouth, leaning his head back as he closed his eyes and sucked hard on the roll of tobacco.

She tentatively followed, leaning up against the wall next to him. Bumping her shoulder to his, she held her hand out. He cracked an eye open, his lips quirking up slightly as he removed the non-existent smoke and passed it to her. She pretended to take her own drag while he spoke. "No, I didn't see what he did. He, you, move too fucking quick for me to even comprehend you've moved at all. One minute you were talking and the next he was spouting blood all over the place from that nasty left hook of yours." He rubbed his jaw, wincing at the memory of her throwing one at him during their sparring the other evening.

Izzy let out a shaky exhale, passing the unlit cigarette back to him. "Really? You didn't see him whisper in my ear? Or kiss me on the neck?"

The cigarette fell to the ground. "He did what?" he grumbled, pushing off the wall and stalking back toward the door. She reached for his arm, stopping him.

"Just leave it, Charlie. I don't need you to fight my battles. I never have," she said, quietly. She released her hold on him and started back toward the alley to the parking garage. The air crackled with the smell of ozone and another flash of lightning illuminated the street. She felt him next to her a moment later, matching her stride.

They walked in silence until he pulled open the driver's side door for her. Before she could slip into the leather bucket seat though, he stepped in front of her. She looked up, the heady rush of the alcohol and the blood and the fight pushing her to get lost in the way the dim lighting made his eyes look like sapphires. He studied her face, reaching a hand up. She flinched and he froze, a look of shame crossing over him. Her expression softened and she swallowed as he moved his shaky hand up to push a loose wine red curl behind her ear. His fingers dragged lightly down her jaw, his eyes glancing to her parted lips and goddamn, where did they get that wine because she did the same.

Only the moment she did, she saw swollen lips, a deep cut down the middle, bruises marring the jawline of another man.

And when she looked up, it was into golden orbs set ablaze against the gentle expression of someone else. Someone not there. Someone *gone*. Her face paled. She stepped back, bumping into the roof line of the car. Then she ducked under Charlie's arm and fled the parking garage.

❖

After nearly breaking her ankles three blocks later, she slowed to a walk before slipping into the dark doorway of a boarded up business to catch her breath. That's where she stood when the sky opened up a second later, drenching the city street in a wall of hot water.

"Not even a refreshing shower, huh," she mumbled to herself. She fished her phone out of the small wrist clutch she had brought with her that evening.

Five missed calls and a dozen text message notifications filled her screen.

CHARLIE

Izzy where are you?

Izzy come back

I'm sorry

I fucked up

I'm going to drive around a bit please let me know when you see these or where you are or if you got home

Izzy sucked her teeth, about to put her phone away when she glanced out to the street just as a giant chunk of ice hit the pavement. Hopefully Charlie would be smart enough to pull the Giulia into a garage instead of driving around in that storm. Blowing out a breath, she leaned against the wall behind her, staring at the illuminated phone screen.

The text message thread was pulled up before she realized what she was doing.

IZZY

I miss you

Without hesitation, she pressed Send and let her head drop back against the rough grey stone behind her, squeezing her eyes shut.

When silence pressed against her senses several minutes later and the humidity hit a limit beyond her comprehension, she opened them. Unlocking her phone screen, she looked at the message she had sent. And groaned. She had *sent* the fucking message. Of all messages.

And even worse, it had gone through. There went her theory his phone was at the bottom of a bunch of rubble in a demolished warehouse or lost in the muddy silt of the Mississippi river.

Which meant he had gone willing. Her chest tightened. He had planned this entire fucking fiasco and she had been nothing more than a pawn in the game. A piece of the fucked up puzzle, one she still didn't know her purpose in. But he had known it, used it, and fucked her over for it.

"Fuck," she screamed through clenched teeth.

A car rumbled up to the curb. A candy apple 1959 Alfa Romeo Giulia. Charlie stepped out of the driver's seat looking frazzled and...pissed.

"Get in," he demanded.

"Abso-fucking-lutely not. You're such an asshole, Charlie," she bit out, disdain coursing through her blood and her words.

"Yeah, I fucking know, Izzy. But I would rather you make *me* walk home than watch you do it, so get in," he barked back, walking to the other side of the car and opening the door.

"I am not in danger on these streets anymore. I *am* the threat. I could snap your neck right where you stand and feel *nothing*," she seethed. His eyes were violent pools of blue as he stared back at her.

Then he stepped into her space, just a couple inches shy of being domineering. "Then fucking do it, Izzy. God knows I've wanted you to for the past six months." Though his words were a whisper, they brushed against her lips and through her body, causing her to shudder.

Moments passed as they stood there, glaring at each other. Daring the other to move. To act. To react.

Eventually she broke her stare, shoving her shoulder into him as she walked to the driver's side of the car.

"Get in the car, you piece of shit," she barked, sliding into her seat. As she adjusted her mirrors, he simply stood there, looking up at the rotting plywood of the storefront. Izzy revved the engine impatiently but he didn't budge. She was seconds from pressing the horn when he turned, his face ashen. Without a word, he slipped into the passenger seat, staring blankly ahead.

She tossed the car into gear but not before taking one more glance at the business she had sheltered beneath.

VALENTINI & SONS LAW

Her gaze shifted to the melancholy etched into those beautiful lines on his face. She shifted a couple more times before the stone buildings towering around them were nothing more than a blur and the only thing either of them could hear was the roar of the engine.

CHAPTER SIXTEEN
NOAH

Last order of business is security for tonight's celebrations in the Quarter. You know the cops aren't shit in this town and Adette wants to make sure we are handling our city and our citizens accordingly," Benji commanded to the group, all eyes on him. Another meeting where Noah sat there, eyes glazed over, absorbing every single detail without flinching or showing a shred of interest. That was until his brother's words registered in his mind. He straightened, assessing the only family he had left on that planet.

Malik stood up beside Benji, placing a comforting hand on his brother's back before he began listing names and locations. Noah glowered at the man before taking note of the people around the room. He should have known something was up when he walked in and barely had to try to hide in the crowd. It seemed as if every crew member was in attendance. Even Sancho and Nadia stood in the back of the room with the rest of the kitchen crew.

"Noah, Benji, Nadia, and myself, we will be stationed in the thick of it outside Big Easy, so if you need us, you know where to find us," Malik said, nodding to the group before pocketing his phone he had read the lists from and sitting back down.

Big Easy, the rowdiest bar on the shit side of the Mississippi, right at the corner where Bourbon Street met St. Louis Street. Fucking poetic.

"Keep your wits about you," Benji shouted to the restless group as murmurs started to fill the small room. "But don't forget to enjoy yourselves. It's Cinco de Mayo in the Crescent City. *Laissez les bon temps rouler!*" *Let the good times roll.* The last line caused the room to erupt into hoots and hollers. Noah watched his brother the entire time as he laughed at something Malik whispered in his ear, grasping the other man's arm to steady himself.

The hair on the back of Noah's neck stood up and when he glanced to the corner the kitchen staff occupied, his gaze met the dull green shade of Nadia's. His eyes narrowed and yet her response was to tilt her head in innocence and give him a soft smile. An icy shiver rolled down his spine. They all worked their way out of The Roosevelt and onto the humid streets of New Orleans.

"This place really hasn't changed, huh, Noh?" Benji asked, elbowing him as they walked through the throng of people already beginning to crowd the streets. They had eaten an early dinner and Noah realized it was in order to get out there before the crowds got too thick to even travel from the hotel. Trumpets blared their jazzy tunes as the masses ebbed and flowed around them, going in and out of the bars peppering Bourbon Street.

"It's hard to believe it if I'm being honest," Noah admitted as he shouldered past a drunk guy humming along to the song the marching band in the middle of the street played. His voice rocked on the edge of being a yell over the commotion and it was all quickly becoming sensory overload. The last time he had seen this many people on these streets, the sounds ringing in his ears had been screams of terror and pain. The pulse in his chest quickened as those sounds echoed in his memories. Nadia glanced back at him, giving him a once over before pressing on into the crowd. They stopped outside the bright neon red sign of Big Easy's Daiquiris.

"Okay, Malik and I will stand out here. You and Nadia go across the street, outside Fat Catz," Benji yelled over the piped in jazz music from inside the bar behind them.

"Incoming!" A man yelled as he shoved another out the door and into the street, where he proceeded to vomit into the storm drain.

"Fucking hell," Noah cursed, leaving his brother and his partner behind as he made his way over to his station outside the adjacent bar. Fat Catz clientèle made Big Easy's look juvenile as he watched a man damn near having a full-blown *menage a trois* right next to the entrance.

A permanent scowl fixed to Noah's face as he stood sentry on the curb outside the bar by himself. A few minutes later the shock of an ice cold drink against his arm had him whirling around, ready to throw someone on the ground. Nadia stepped back and smiled up at him before handing him a plastic cup filled with a frothy beverage.

"Benji said you were a lager guy and you were probably gonna want something to deal with the children on the streets tonight," she said, flashing him another smile.

An inaudible mumbled of thanks escaped his lips as he took the beer from her, being careful not to touch her hand in the process. If she noticed, she didn't act like it and instead sidled up into the space next to him, scanning the crowd absentmindedly and bouncing to the music. By that point in the evening, the menagerie of brass and drum beats on different tempos from the music filtering out of the bars and the performers on the streets had set a dull ache in the back of his skull.

He pinched the bridge of his nose, closed his eyes briefly before taking a few gulps of the cold beer. It went down smooth and in that moment, he was glad for the beverage.

They stood in silence for three more beers, Nadia always running to a get a refill inside Fat Catz when his cup started to get empty.

On the arrival of the fourth beer, he gave her a smile he immediately regretted. She blushed and stepped closer to him.

"Look, I need to apologize for last night. I was…out of line and just really misinterpreted your signals," she blurted out.

Noah glanced sideways at her as she spoke, her words directed toward the crowds around them. Her blush deepened to a scarlet red when she turned to finally look up at him. Her green eyes blurred to a specific shade of emerald that had him sucking in a breath and looking away. He let it out before he spoke. "It's fine. I just…I'm not looking for that right now."

She nodded her head slowly, pressing her lips to her cup. God, why did he feel like an ass for turning down a girl who all but threw herself at him without consent? He downed the rest of his beer and watched her do the same. Regret coated his mouth. He needed to stop, to slow down, to *think*. When Nadia made to go back into the bar for another round, he grabbed her wrist like the idiot he was and pulled her into his space.

"Dance with me," he drawled, not believing that was his own voice as the words came out.

She placed her other hand on his shoulder as he shifted his hold to take her hand. He twirled them out into the street, and they swayed slowly as the songs all went through a lull, bands shuffling along to different streets, following the crowds.

When a loud trumpet droned out the instrumental intro to a popular club song, he twirled her away from him and then pulled her back in. She smiled up at him as their pace picked up in time to the music, their steps quickening together beneath them. A crowd began to gather around them as they whirled around the band playing in the middle of the intersection. As the song crescendo-ed and the final note hit, hanging in the air around them, Noah dipped forward, taking her with him. She squealed and he surprised himself by laughing at the sound.

✦

They were still laughing as they jogged back across the street. The crowds cheered them along and the noise started to overwhelm Noah. The dull ache of all that alcohol pulsed in his temple. He walked past their established spots outside the bar and slipped into the back alley behind the building without a word. The moment he was in the darkness the noise deafened and his pulse began to slow again. He leaned against the wall behind him, breathing deeply to catch his breath. Nadia slipped into the darkness, doing the same on the wall across from him.

He studied her and when their eyes met, he let out a nervous laugh. Why had he let her feed him with alcohol like that? She stepped forward, smiling up at him. He followed the visions he had when he looked into her green eyes and didn't even think to stop her, to tell her no. To recognize the predatory look in her eyes as she closed the distance between them. He was lost in the desire to be somewhere he wasn't, just one more time.

And he opened the door by saying, "I can't remember the last time I laughed like that." It felt innocent, a mere observation.

And yet she stepped into his bubble, slipping into the space between his outstretched legs. Her hands gripped his sides with a punishing strength before sliding up his chest and around the back of his neck. Noah's muscles tensed beneath her touch. His head spun and everything happened so quickly.

Through a moment of clarity he said, "Nadia, I—"

"Shh," she interrupted, pressing her finger against his lips. His body seized. He felt paralyzed under her touch as images of the night before flashed into his mind. Only this time when he went to shove her away, her grip tightened around his arms, pinning him against the rough stone. His stomach dropped.

"What the fu—" he said just as she pulled back, a feral smile widening across her face. Petite little fangs glinted in the dim glow of the twinkling lights strung between the buildings. Without a moment of hesitation, Noah kneed her in her side. As she doubled over, hissing in pain, he pushed her onto the wet ground and fled from the alleyway.

❖

Pushing through the throng of people, Noah's panic quickened. The sounds of cheers and music morphed into a distorted track of screams and explosions. The lights glowing above flickered until they looked like flames licking up the sides of the buildings. The heat became unbearable, pressing against him, suffocating him. Nausea roiled through him as he tried to orient himself. Faces, smiling fucking faces, blurred, swirling into a mass as he stumbled along the street, letting the crowd take him in their flow. He vaguely registered his name being called out as he stumbled onto an emptier side street. Hands grasped his arms and threw him against the orange wall of a building and Noah groaned as his head hit the hard surface.

Malik stood in front of him, arms crossed and Noah started to snarl something at the man about personal boundaries when Benji filled his vision, lightly smacking the sides of his face.

"Noah, what the fuck happened to you?" Benji's drawl came out distorted, his face blurring with Malik's. Fuck, he should not have drank so much.

All his recent memories came crashing into him and a moment of clarity seeped in as he watched his brother talking to Malik. All the pieces seemed to fit together.

Noah raised his fist and punched Benji square in the nose, feeling the fragile bone snap sideways.

"What the actual fuck, Noah?!" Benji screamed as Malik stepped around him, pinned both of Noah's arms behind his back and pressed his face into the rough brick. If he had been sober, he wouldn't have been able to be restrained. His rage burned bright. His brother had to fucking know. Yet as much as he struggled, Malik's grip held firm. The familiar zip of cable ties around his wrists sounded foreign and somehow like home alongside the melody of saxophone notes in the distance. A memory of his old life, his older brother. Malik shoved Noah forward and that's when he knew he was fucked.

There were no second or third or fourth chances coming out of that scenario.

"You fucking lied to me," Noah growled to his brother, emboldened by the prospect of nothing. It's freeing, the inevitable loss of all autonomy. Noah kept his eyes on his brother as they pushed through the crowd again, one hand holding a rag to his nose, the other gripping the front of Noah's shirt, dragging him along. Occasionally, Benji would glance back at Noah, eyebrows furrowing together. Malik pushed on Noah's shoulder, catching his brother's gaze before they pulled out of the commotion on Bourbon Street.

Neither man said anything to him as they made their way back to the hotel. No one spoke as they entered the front door, stalking across the polished marble to the back hallway behind the elevators. No one spoke as the bone jarring creak of a familiar basement cell door opened. No one spoke as they shoved Noah onto the uncomfortable, dank cot. No one said anything until Benji finally removed the rag from his face, dabbing as his nose to make sure the bleeding had been stanched.

"I had finally started to trust you, Noh." The bloody rag held in his hand as he pointed at his prone brother, unable to move with his arms bound. Noah glanced to Malik, realizing a sleeve of his t-shirt had been torn off. The same shad of faded blue as the rag clenched in Benji's fist.

Noah's eyes shuddered back to Benji as he pulled something out of his pocket.

"I was going to give this back to you tonight. I even charged the damn thing and turned it on and everything." Benji flashed the screen of his phone at him. The generic background image blinded him in the darkness, a spike of pain going through his skull. His vision adjusted and he noticed the one red alert for a text message. Noah tried to reach for the phone but the plastic cables bit into his skin and he hissed.

Benji shoved the phone back into his pocket and sighed. "Just as I suspected though. You're still stuck on St. Louis. On something, or rather, someone there." The blood on Benji's face had dried into a deep crimson, almost black. It cracked and flaked off as he spoke. "Instead of seeing all the good here, the *mission* here, you're just sitting around, pretending. Like I wouldn't notice. Like I'm not your fucking brother! What were you going to do? Run away? Where?" Benji's laughter cause Noah to flinch.

Malik leaned into Benji's space to whisper something in his ear. A cruel smile spread across his brother's face and Noah watched him nod his head enthusiastically.

Both men turned on their heels and walked out of the door without another word. It screeched closed, the lock clunking into place.

They left him there, tied up like a hog, and still fucking drunk. And stuck on an internal loop of what that message had to say. Or what Izzy would think when he didn't reply.

✦

CHAPTER SEVENTEEN
IZZY

The next morning Izzy sat at her kitchen counter, sipping her coffee and casually flipping through the *Busch Family Legacy*. Ignoring the books for her "research request", she had instead spent the last few days reading the tome cover to cover. The words blurred together, nearly memorized by then and yet…something about it still caused a tingle in her chest. She felt uneasy each time she touched the pages like a shift in the temperature. She had to quickly flip away from any images of Adolphus Busch, the founding father of the empire, the sinister depth in his stare burning her skin. Huffing out a sigh, she closed the book and peered through the crack in her black out curtains to the daylight beyond.

Emilien had explained the sensitivity to sunlight logic to her on one of the few times she deigned to meet with him early on. A pseudo "Welcome to vampirism" symposium. Something about rapid regeneration of cells and increased bodily performance caused the damage from ultraviolet rays to be quick and intense. Or however the fuck he had described it. All she knew was it fucking depressed her to have an apartment with a wall made entirely of giant windows only to have them covered during the daylight hours. Night became a decadent moment when she got to pull back those fabric hangings and stare up into the sky for several minutes, drinking in the vastness of the world. Allowing it to shrink her problems into perspective.

Except last night. Charlie remained silent on the entire ride home . When she parked the Giulia back into her designated spot, he pushed out the passenger door and marched up the stairs before she was even unbuckled.

She shook her head at the memory, the scowl on his face, the dull tone to his vibrant eyes, and took another sip of coffee. The caffeine buzzed like lightning through her veins. Another side effect of her new persona, albeit a fun one at least. Though drugs had a short life span in her body, quickly metabolized and flushed out, that first moment of consumption felt like pure ecstasy.

The only thing that surpassed it all were those moments when she got to sink her fangs into someone else's flesh, drinking down the warm blood from within, letting it caress her tongue, coat the inside of her mouth, life vibrating through her...

"Jesus Christ," she swore as coffee splashed onto the counter, a few drops landing on the cover of the priceless family fluff piece she had stolen from the university. She quickly set her mug down far away from the book and rushed into the kitchen to grab a towel. She rummaged through the space beneath the sink when a knock from her front door sounded across the apartment. Moving to sit up, she smacked her head on the deep sink basin.

"Fuck me," she swore again.

"Izzy? Are you okay? What are you doing in there? Or rather...who?" Barry's voice called out from behind the door.

She crawled out from under the sink, rubbing the back

of her head as she stood. "Come on in, it's unlocked," she called out as she jogged back to the book, praying she hadn't been too long to cause irreparable damage. She began frantically blotting the cover as the front door opened. Barry shuffled in underneath several tote bags of supplies, kicking the door shut behind him. He deposited his goods down on her white leather couch and walked over to her.

"Since when do you not lock your door?" he asked, curiously eying her desperate attempts at saving the book that should not be in her possession.

She skirted the question. "Do you think this is noticeable?" She held the book up where four drops of brown stains had spread across the burgundy cover.

Barry grimaced. "It's not *great* if I'm being honest with you. Where did you find that thing anyway?" He grabbed the book and began flipping through the pages.

She cleaned the rest of the coffee up off the counter and went into the kitchen to toss her rag next to the sink. As she started making Barry a mug of coffee, the machine humming in the background, she said casually, "Oh, um, the restricted area."

Barry let out a throaty laugh. "No, you didn't. You can't take anything home from there. Beechum barely lets you touch half the books in there…" His jovial tone dropped as his gaze shifted back to the book, deep brown eyes widening in horror. "Isabella Giorgina Ciampi!" he exclaimed as he furiously but gently placed the book back on the counter and gestured the sign of the cross three times.

She turned to him, his mug in her hand as she scowled. "That is not my middle name."

"And you're not supposed to *steal* books from the university!"

"I had to Barry! Beechum wants this report done next week and I've got nothing but a full blown distraction in the form of *that* book! Did you know there were several other German brewing families in this city but only the Busch family managed to survive, and thrive, while all the others failed?"

Barry pinched the bridge of his nose. "I cannot deal with this today." He walked over to his pile of stuff on the couch, rummaging through the bags.

Izzy grabbed the book and placed it back on her bookshelf, away from any more errant liquids. When she turned back around, Barry had stopped rummaging and looked around the dark space of her apartment suspiciously.

"Is it weird?" he asked, his tone shifting as he pulled out some miniature piñatas. He liked to fill them with little canisters of pre-rolls and single servings of his homemade edibles. The only requirement to play was everyone had to hit them with one of the tiny souvenir baseball bats he had procured from the stadium before it fully shut down.

Izzy sat cross legged on her bed, watching him pull out the decorations and sort them into piles. She folded her arms across her stomach and looked at the dark window hangings.

"It's like…I blacked out. That day, or night, or whatever. Which I did, apparently. Lando called the doctor and everything. They moved me back into my room but I didn't wake up until three days later. And then it all just…changed. Rapidly. I mean, I had fucking fangs. I still have fucking fangs." Her tongue slid over them as she spoke, the feeling still foreign to her.

Barry had stopped unpacking and sorting and had climbed up onto her counter, perched there while she spoke. His expression so soft she felt a hard pit form in her chest. She wasn't sure why she had never told him this story. In a way, it made it all seem too real. Made it too real what she was: a monster. But with him here, watching her, nodding his head as she spoke, that warmth in his eyes, she started to see why it had been so easy for Charlie to open up to him.

"Anyway," she shrugged. "at the end of the day, becoming a monster is like the least of the shitty things that have happened recently."

Barry jumped off her counter and walked over, sitting on the floor in front of her and grabbing her hands in his own. "Oh, Izzy. You're not a monster. You didn't ask for this. Hell, you don't even know how this happened."

She met his gaze and felt his eyes rove over her features.

"Do you?" he asked, tilting his head.

She sighed and went into her closet, pulling open the floorboard and fishing out The Ramblings. She came back out and onto her bed, opening the book to the final page where all of Noah's notes were tucked in. She handed them over to Barry.

"I keep reading and re-reading these and I *think* Noah figured it out or had a theory or something. Obviously not about me, I don't think, but something in this journal. And it's like…right there in front of my face but I just can't grasp it." *And I really wish he was here to help me figure it out.*

Barry's brows furrowed as he read Noah's wispy script.

"When did he write these?"

Izzy shrugged, "I don't know, sometime last fall. I kept the book in my closet and he was always with me when I had it pulled out."

He handed the stacks of notes back to her and she shoved them into the ancient journal, slipping it back into its protective sleeve.

"Well, we don't have to figure it out tonight, or next

week even. Right now, we have *got* to get this pork butt in the oven and the *pozole* simmering," he said, squeezing her hands.

She smiled at him and nodded. She wanted to know what happened to her, how it happened. *Why* it had happened but he was right. She didn't need to know tonight. She just needed to live. They grabbed the bags with the food ingredients and she glanced over her shoulder one more time to the book on the shelf, that eerie tingle in her chest rising, before they headed out the door to Lando's penthouse.

❖

Lando's men ushered them in, saying the boss man would "be around" and that they were instructed to "make themselves at home". A task easier said than done. Since the fall when Lando made it known he was not only aware of Charlie's transgressions with The Society but had been in on the scheme, their relationship had been rocky. Her new taste for blood became a further wedge.

"Smells *delizioso*," the old Italian man said as he emerged an hour later from the dark hallway into the open concept living room, making his way into the gourmet kitchen.

Izzy looked him up and down before nodding her agreement with a hum.

Silence filled the space and soon the sound of the *pozole* simmering away on the stove became a deafening cacophony.

Barry looked between the two of them, neither making eye contact with the other or really anything in particular. Izzy moved to the counter to ready the salsa and do something, anything, with her hands.

Barry cleared his throat. "So, Landy, where's the good chianti hiding?" His words broke the stagnant tension in the air like a rusty ax.

Lando looked up, gave the other man a nod of his head then opened the wine fridge beneath the ebony stone of the island.

"No, I already checked there. I mean, the *good* stuff. The stuff I know you make Gio ship back in cases," Barry insisted with a wink.

Lando let out a soft chuckle. "How do you know about my secret stash?"

Barry stirred the soup in the pot. "I have my sources of information." Izzy had her back turned to their interaction as she gathered the ingredients and started chopping, her ears always turned toward the men.

"Ah, well, with that *certezza*[25] I guess I cannot lie," Lando chuckled as he disappeared back down the hallway. Izzy followed his back as it disappeared. He emerged a few minutes later with a bottle wrapped in straw, no label.

"This comes from a private vineyard in my hometown. They have used the same recipes and techniques for over five hundred years." He set the bottle down and looked around for a corker. Izzy reached into the drawer below her, fishing one out and handing it to him. Their eyes met briefly. The wrinkles creasing around his brown eyes seemed deeper. She looked away, back to her task.

Lando spoke as he twisted the metal into the cork. "The *vinaio*[26] is old school, working under the *sistema di baratto*[27]. Every year, in order to be on the list for the following year, you have to commit to providing a good the wine maker and his family will need."

"I've heard of this wine," Izzy chimed in, not looking up from dicing a tomato. She felt Lando's gaze sear into her. "*La famiglia di mio Nonno*[28], they provided their largest hog every year for a case."

When she looked over her shoulder, Lando's gaze had softened like it always did when she used his native tongue. She gave him a tentative, closed lip smile.

Barry watched them for a moment before he asked, "So, what is the Denalo annual offering then?"

Lando looked at him, his gaze hardening. "Protection."

Barry and Izzy exchanged a look as the old man walked to the bar. She shrugged. The details of Lando's overseas syndicate remained a mystery, even to Charlie. The only person who knew anything was Gio and she kept her secrets as close as the blood pumping through her veins.

Lando returned with three glasses, pouring a healthy amount of the burgundy liquid into each. He passed one to Barry and set one down on the edge of the island nearest to Izzy. She walked over and picked it up. He raised his own.

"*Morte ai francesi*[29]," he said, fixing his gaze on Izzy.

"*Viva Puebla*[30]!" Barry sang, clinking his glass with Lando's before draining the entire thing. Izzy laughed, smiling at the normalcy of Barry being, well, Barry. When she turned back to Lando, something in his gaze caused her smile to falter. It was...fear.

Fuck, her fangs. He was afraid of *her*.

Cautiously, she extended her glass to his. He tapped it without taking his eyes off her, even as she raised her own to her lips. The intimidating stare followed the liquid as she took a sip, trailing over the column of her throat. He tore his eyes away and took his own sip with a grimace.

"Alright, I'll leave you *bambini*[31] to finish in peace, yeah?" the older man said as he stood up off his stool and disappeared back into the inky abyss of the hallway.

Izzy watched him until he melted into the shadows, and

though she could no longer see him, she could feel him watching her.

❧

CHAPTER EIGHTEEN
IZZY

The party had been going on for nearly two hours and even more people were appearing from the stairwell. Izzy had started the evening helping Barry with organizing the different tables of games, each with its own custom cocktail to go with it. When she started walking around trying to serve the other guests though, he shooed her away, forcibly telling her to enjoy herself.

"Your energy as a hostess is very off-putting and it's making the salsa taste weird," he said with all the tender love and care he could muster.

And with a wink from her friend, she took her *cantarito* in its clay cup and ventured to the sidelines of the thick crowd. A prick of concern for the infrastructure of the roof with all these people on it flashed through her as she sank down onto the circular outdoor bed underneath its tangle of golden twinkling lights.

As soon as she felt the cool fabric beneath her, a heavy weight of loneliness fell over her. Memories flooded in, the familiarity of the space throwing her to the past, to the last time they had celebrated on that rooftop. A celebration of life, gone before anyone thought to consider a goodbye. Her eyes stung and she scanned the crowd, looking at the happy smiles and tried to absorb the sound of their laughter, tried to steal an ounce of their joy.

Her moistening eyes landed on Charlie, hunched over in conversation with Barry and another man she realized must be his new boyfriend. The one she had yet to meet. Hadn't even known about. She reminded herself to go say hi later. When she felt less heavy. Less of a burden. She took several long gulps of her drink when Charlie caught her eye. He held her gaze as he said something to Barry. Her friend turned to see her and smiled, nodding his head knowingly to Charlie. He broke away from the two men, weaving his way toward her, azure eyes never leaving her own.

How had her life gotten so fucked she looked forward to talking to the man who single handedly ruined it?

Charlie stopped in front of her, looking down at her with a sad sincerity in his eyes.

"I'm sorry, Izzy. I truly am." *Getting right to it then.* She looked at him, at his fidgeting hands, then patted the space next to her. His exhale visibly relaxed his shoulders as he sat down. A cup of clear liquid cradled in between his broad hands and she raised a brow at him. He let out a nervous laugh.

"I've been finding my own success being an ass lately. I didn't think I needed any extra help tonight," he said, taking a sip of his water.

"How noble of you," she murmured, taking another gulp of her fruity, alcoholic drink. They observed the party goers in silence. Gangsters with nearly every visible piece of skin covered in ink stood among the elderly residents of the building, as well as members of Barry's immediate *and* extended family. She recognized a few staff members from the university, the "cool ones" as Barry put it.

After a few minutes, Charlie sighed. "This is the strangest party I've ever been to."

Izzy snorted out a laugh, smiling into her clay pot. "You never came to one of the cheese sandwich parties Vahagn and I used to throw then."

He chuckled, looking down at his half full glass before glancing over at her, a twinkle in his eyes. "No, somehow my invitation to those never arrived."

She let herself get lost in those crystalline pools for a second before turning back to observe the crowd. "Oh well, that's your loss. The goal was to make the most outrageous cheese sandwich imaginable. It'll never be the same without Vahagn though. He would order his cheese like months in advance. One year, he made his own bread and potato chips, went the whole nine yards. Then he sandwiched it all together with this insanely smooth Havarti straight from some monastery in Denmark."

"Potatoes chips and cheese...as a sandwich?" Charlie quirked a brow at her.

She turned to him, nodding in earnest. "Oh yes. This is why you were never invited. You can't see the genius of a cheese sandwich party." She held his gaze as she took another sip. His eyes softened and then a sorrow washed over him and he glanced away.

"You know, I'll never be able to apologize for what I did to him." His voice had quieted and he swallowed hard. "I'll never be able to forgive myself. This life...it just gets so fucked so quickly, before you can even start to see what is unfolding beneath your own making. I didn't...I hadn't realized how far off course I had gone in life until last night...until I stood beneath the entrance to my father's building." His gaze had drifted to the ground as he spoke, rolling his empty cup between his hands.

"You're right," she said, watching as he flinched. "I won't forgive you. I can't forgive the things you've done, Charlie. To me, to Vahagn, or even to…" She let her words trail off before she said his name aloud. "I hate you, God, I hate you so much for everything you've done. But deep down, I know there were some moments when it wasn't all shit."

He glanced up at her, hard lines etched into the corners of his eyes and along his forehead. "No, please. Don't. Don't try to pretend I was ever anything good for you."

She studied him for a moment, at a crossroad of reconciling the Charlie who had unapologetically ruined everything she loved with the one sitting before her, willingly standing on the stake for his mistakes.

"Okay then. I won't." She turned back to the crowd, taking a long sip of her drink, tapping the bottom of the pot to get every last drop. "But at present, you're one of the closest things I have to a friend, if one were to look at a four-course meal as a friend that is. So, I'll temporarily move past your transgressions."

She looked sidelong at him, a half smirk pulling on her lips.

"A four-course meal, huh? That good?" he joked, a wicked smirk on his face. It disappeared when she jabbed him in between his ribs.

"Don't test my limits," she said, setting her empty clay pot on the ground.

"Yeah, it has been a while. Are you doing okay?" The sincerity in his voice broke something in her.

"I'm…" *Unwell? Depressed? Coming apart at the seams as I listen to the pulse of every single human on this rooftop, smelling the intoxicating scents of so…many…different…blood types?*

Charlie scanned her face, his lips pursing. The scar in his brow furrowed and he squeezed her knee before standing up, offering her his hand.

"Come on," he said simply.

She tilted her head at him. "Where to?"

"Well, unless you want to drink me dry in front of a crowd, and what the Cinco de Mayo spectacle that would be, I think you would prefer a private spot for your Michelin star meal."

She rolled her eyes but took his hand in hers and stood. "Okay, let's not get ahead of ourselves. Mom and pop at best. Definitely served on Styrofoam plates."

His laugh softened the tension in her. It felt easy to head down the stairs and slip into one of Lando's guest bedrooms, locking the door behind them.

⚜

"So, you and Charlie disappeared before I could introduce you to Oscar," Barry pouted from behind his wine glass full of water on her couch.

Izzy flipped through the Busch family manifesto on her counter, humming at the tingle of warm blood on her lips. After Charlie insisted she feed for more than her standard couple of minutes, she slipped out of the party and went back to her apartment to change into comfy clothes. She had been reading, sipping on a red wine night cap, a delicious chaser to her blood dessert, when Barry stumbled in. He had showered and changed into his pajamas before collapsing onto her couch. The water was from her.

"Where did Oscar run off to anyway? I thought you would be staying with him," she asked, looking up from the text on the pages in front of her. She didn't even need to look down to

214

recite what it said. *Adolphus Busch, born July 10, 1893 in Mainz-Kastel, Wiesbaden, Germany, emigrated to the United States in 1857…* She had started to feel like Dr. Beechum, an insufferable known-it-all.

"He has to work security early in the morning and didn't want me to get woken up by him," he replied, swaying on his way over to her. As he slipped into the seat next to her, she picked the book up, eying his glass warily before taking it away.

"Psh, you mean he didn't want you keeping him up all night long," she joked, raising a brow at him.

He snorted out a laugh, very unbecoming of him. "That too. Find anything interesting or useful in that book?"

She sighed, running her hand down the page opened before her. "No. I've read everything in it and besides some glorified Busch family propaganda, there is nothing useful in here."

Barry grabbed the book out of her chest and slapped it closed, placing it on the counter.

"Hey!" she argued, reaching for it. He slapped her hand away.

"We need to talk about you and Charlie."

Fuck me. "What's there to talk about, Barry?" she sniped, folding her arms across her chest.

He turned to her, placing a hand on her arm as a serious look fell over his features. "Look, I'm not saying you should forgive him. Hell, I don't fully forgive him for anything he has done but…you might find he understands your situation more than you know."

Sudden, uncontrollable anger pulsed behind her eyes. "And what would you know about my *situation*?" Everything came out a growl as she sat up straighter.

Barry's eyes widened as he pulled his hand away. "I mean the situation where you've suddenly become a pawn between two warring gangs against your adamant desires to be nothing to neither of them."

Her eyes narrowed on him as a snarl escaped her lips. She felt his pulse throb across the space between them. "How fucking *dare* you pretend to even understand what I've been going through. While I've had my literal world ripped apart in sixteen ways from Sunday, you've been growing your research and planning parties and finding fucking love in the actual hellscape that is the world today!" Her voice grew louder with each word and it wasn't until he stood at her door that Izzy realized he had stood up and backed his way to it while she spoke. Even worse, she had stalked him the entire way there.

His deep tan skin glistened with sweat, tears brimming his eyes as he pulled the door open.

"You're right, Izzy," he sniffled, stumbling out of the threshold. "I don't understand but I've been trying. I've been here for you, for whenever you were ready to talk. But clearly, that's not tonight."

And with that, he slammed her door shut, leaving her alone to regret everything about her life once again.

❖

Thirty minutes later, a soft knock sounded on her door before it popped open gently.

"Iz, are you in here?"

She groaned her greeting from her seat on the kitchen floor, tequila bottle still in one hand, an unlit joint in the other. She had planned to light it and smoke the whole fucking thing so she could spin into a vortex of numbness and forget everything about the past two days. But then she couldn't find a lighter and turns out being immortal still didn't make her able to start a fucking flame with her hands. So, she settled for an emotional support bottle instead.

Charlie stepped into the threshold of the room, searching at eye level before his gaze drifted down to where she sat. He pressed a hand to the floor as he eased himself down, keeping plenty of space between them. She leaned her head back against the cabinet doors and closed her eyes.

"He ran to you?"

Charlie chuckled softly. "Where else was he supposed to go? The shuttles ended a while ago and I think he secretly has always wanted to sleep in my bed."

"Oh, there's no secret about that. But you're the missing part in that if you're in my kitchen right now."

She cracked an eye open to see his smile falter. "Yeah, well, I had more important places to be."

"You don't have to do this you know."

He tilted his head. "Do what?"

She sighed, opening her eyes and looking directly at him. "Atone. We all fucking get it. You fucked up and you hate yourself for it."

His chest flinched and his shoulders tensed at her words. A grimace pulled on his lips as he studied a tile on the floor. "I know. But you'll be happy to know I'm not here for me. I'm here for you."

This time she laughed, the hoarse, raspy sound vile to her own ears. "And what are you going to do? Bat your beautiful blue eyes and wish the shame away?"

He studied her for a moment and she shifted under the scrutiny. "No. I'm just here to listen. I can talk as well, if you want, but I know how you feel about the things I have to say."

She let her stare narrow on his own. "And what do you have to say that I haven't heard on repeat for the past six months,

Charlie? That this is not my fault? That Vahagn would've wanted me to move on? To live? Well, guess what? I am living. Forever. I can't fucking stop it. And not only do I get to live forever, but I get to do it as a fucking monster." She took a long pull on the tequila bottle, slamming the glass down hard on the tile. A hairline crack spread up from the base of the bottle.

Charlie swiftly crawled across the floor and grabbed the bottle from her. She glared at him. He glared back and stood.

"I'm not taking it away, just finding a better container," he reassured her as he reached for a stainless steel bottle inside her cupboard. He emptied the contents of the broken bottle into the steel one and handed it back before sitting down next to her.

She took a tentative swig and passed it to him. He held it in his hands.

"You're not a monster, Izzy. But I know what it's like to feel like one. Fuck, I feel like one every day. I can't even escape the mistakes I've made in life. Every where I turn, there they are. There you are." He rolled the bottle between his hands, as if contemplating taking a drink.

"Charlie, I…" She swallowed, composing her words in her mind, letting her bitter anger and sadness subside. "I wanted to love you, you know. I did, for a time. But it all became too much. You became too much. Then you became violent on top of it and I didn't deserve that. No one does. So, when you went to kiss me yesterday, I panicked. I cannot go back. Truly. We can be complicated friends at best. But never again. The water is too muddy."

He nodded his head, letting out a shaky breath. He turned to look at her, a rim of silver setting his bright blue eyes ablaze. The flower inked on his throat bobbed as he swallowed. Studying her face, he said softly, "Okay. Complicated friends."

She gave him a half smile and leaned her head back against the cabinet, closing her eyes again.

"What am I going to do with Barry?" she asked, squeezing her eyes shut tighter as her head throbbed.

"Talk to him," he sighed. "He's surprisingly understanding. I also think he uses people's secrets in some sort of skincare routine? His pores are absolutely flawless."

Izzy giggled. "Oh, you do not want to know his actual skincare routine."

His voice rose as he asked, "What do you mean?" and she opened her eyes to see his eyes grow wider and wider as his imagination worked overtime.

She laughed out loud, breathing heavily. "No, I'm not going to ruin your life with that information." She stood on wobbly legs and stumbled out of the kitchen. She felt Charlie's presence behind her as she made her way to the couch and crashed into a seat.

"No, Izzy, I do need to know. My mind is reeling," he pleaded as she leaned her head back, closing her eyes to stop the room from spinning. She reached a hand out, feeling through the air until she found his face and petted it.

"Shh, time for sleep now," she whispered, shifting around to put her legs across his lap, snuggling her face into the corner of the couch. She opened one eye to see him with his hands hovering over her, as if trying to find the least offensive place to put them.

"Charlie, just relax. I will bite if I hate anything you do," she said through a yawn. The warmth of his hands radiated through her knee and shin and she huffed out a laugh.

Sleep ebbed and flowed through her consciousness. Before darkness descended fully over her, she head him whisper,

"You'll always be my biggest regret."

CHAPTER NINETEEN
IZZY

The next morning, Izzy woke with a start, the movement shooting a lightning bolt of pain through her skull. Wincing, she squinted her eyes open, rubbing the sleep away with a groan. Charlie sat stoic in his spot, head slumped to the side, resting on a throw pillow. His facial features had softened in his sleep and for a moment, she remembered the man she thought she had loved. Quietly, she pried her legs out from under the heavy weight of his arms and padded into the kitchen.

Not daring to rouse the coffee machine's minstrel song, she pulled her emergency jug of cold brew from her fridge and made a quick drink before settling down at the kitchen counter. For a few sips, she watched Charlie sleep, her heart pained, thinking of the number of mornings when it had been Vahagn in that spot. Blinking back the threat of tears, she focused on her bookshelf instead. On that foreign relic sitting on her shelf. She shuffled over to it, pulling it free from its temporary holding station in her collection. With the meager light peeking through the crack in the curtain, she lifted the familiar pages open. Absentmindedly, she flipped through them as if they were the newest edition of a magazine, sipping her drink. Lando's gardener had recently harvested a fresh batch of strawberries and used the tops to make her a delicious syrup for her lattes.

Two of the pages stuck together and she frowned. She didn't think her coffee incident from the day before would've soaked through. She set her glass down far from the book and steadily started peeling the pages apart. It was one thing to steal the book, but another one entirely if she ruined it. After several quiet yet panicked minutes, they came apart. In the dim light, a shadow cast over the pages as she studied them for damage. Her eye caught on the seam. Hidden along the space between the pages was a flap. Using her nail, she pried it out. No, not a flap. The whole page opened into a pocket. She sat up, one hand under her chin as she studied the book. She *thought* the pages had been unusually heavy but reasoned a family like the Busch's spared no expense in publishing their puffed up history.

Another piece of parchment stuck out from within the pocket but she had no way of loosening it without tearing the page entirely. And then Dr. Beechum would really murder her and her entire deranged side quest would be for naught. Her chair scraped against the floor as she leapt from her seat then froze. Charlie shifted a little, moving the pillow onto the armrest of the couch and propping his legs up in the space she had abandoned. Being much more mindful of the volume at which she existed, she snuck into her bathroom and rummaged around in a drawer until she found it.

"Aha," she whispered in triumph as she held up a pair of silver tweezers. On quick, quiet feet, she ran back to the seat. The process of releasing the page from its home was painstaking. Starting from the top, she had to grip and pull the paper a millimeter at a time, moving down the page as she went. In fifteen minutes, barely a quarter of the page stuck out of its impossible paper sandwich.

"What are you doing?" Charlie's gruff, sleep-ladened voice sounded from directly over her shoulder and she jumped.

"Fuck, Charlie, I almost ripped the damn thing!" She scowled up at him. He gave her a lopsided smile and blinked sleepily before heading into the kitchen.

The coffee machine purred, excited for the attention it adored, and Charlie turned around, leaning against the counter. "So, what are you doing?"

She glanced down at the book before her, birthing a page like a fucking hippo.

"I...think I found something. I know I found something. I don't know what it is but I'm trying to get it out to figure that out."

Charlie turned as the machine beeped its tune and walked over, taking a couple small sips of the hot liquid before setting his mug down next to her glass. He pulled the book toward his space.

"Hey, I was—"

He held up a hand, examining the pages in front of him like a safe he was trying to crack. After several minutes, he pulled in three spots and the entire page came loose. He held it over his head as she reached for it.

"What do you say?" he asked, a wicked smirk on his face.

"You're a glorified blood bag," she said sweetly.

He shook his head and handed her the page, then settled into the seat next to her, grabbing his coffee from its confinement. He motioned to the page. "Go on, read it to the class."

She scanned the contents on the parchment in her hands and her eyes widened. "Holy fuck…"

Taking a sip, he rolled his eyes then said, "I highly doubt it says that…" His brows narrowed as he leaned over her shoulder. Setting his mug down, he went to reach for the page again but she swatted him away.

"It says," She glowered at him as he sat back in his seat, picking his mug back up. "'Despite rumors, the Lemp family was the first German family to bring the process of cave lagering to the brew scene in St. Louis. Shortly after the Anheuser and Busch family merger, tragedy befell the Lemp family and lasted for decades until the brewery and the mansion were abandoned.'" Izzy flipped the page over and gasped, dropping it. It floated to the counter, landing atop the page in the book. A page she hadn't realized had been a large portrait of Adolphus Busch himself. And the page that landed next to it was a portrait of one Adam Lemp.

The man whose neck she had watched get ripped from his body in her dream.

Charlie opened his mouth to speak when his phone vibrated from its spot on the coffee table, the sound reverberating off a metal pin in the chest and filling the room with a high-pitched buzz.

He studied her face for a moment longer before cursing and pushing off the counter. He picked his phone up by the third ring.

"Yes?" he growled into the phone. Izzy saw him nod along to whatever the person on the other end said through her periphery but her focus had been fixated on the images of the two men. Something about Adolphus seemed familiar too but she couldn't seem to place it. She ran her fingers across each of the pictures and startled when Charlie said her name.

"Izzy, we need to go. Emilien wants to meet at the house in fifteen." He gathered up his things and ran a hand through his unruly black hair.

Her face scrunched as she finally tore her vision from the book. "We?"

Charlie stepped into the bathroom and she watched through the open door as he splashed his face a few times. He spoke into her sink, hands gripping the stone counter. "Yes. We. Specifically, you and me. I don't know who else will be there, but he was adamant you come with me. So, let's go." He walked back into the living room after drying off his face. He pulled his keys off one of the bent forks and spoons her Nonna had made into hooks when they were newly immigrated, unable to afford a proper key hook.

Izzy looked down at her pajamas, the baggy, torn up clothes and rushed to her closet. Walking out a minute later in an oversized t-shirt and jeans, they exited her apartment to make their way to the parking garage.

Charlie unlocked the passenger door for her. It had been easier for Larry to dig up the Alfa's keys since it had been recently driven than going to the back room for Charlie's set. Izzy dropped into the seat as he paced around the front of the vehicle and slid into the driver's seat. Izzy had only been to "the house" once, where she got incredibly drunk on St. Germain and champagne then proceeded to cuss Emilien out in French. Something along the lines of how he compensated for his small dick by taking over the world with a half-baked cure to immortality. Either way, he hadn't invited her back and she hadn't wanted to go anyway. Joining The Society felt more out of necessity than desire when she had woke up blood thirsty, scared, and alone, so fucking alone, over six months ago. She hadn't known where to go, *who* to go to…then she remembered the stories Noah shared about the explosions in New Orleans. Emilien had survived that. And despite it all, despite how much she hoped he hadn't survived their attack, she felt he had. And he would have all the answers she needed. As long as she was willing to bend to his will.

She leaned her head against the window, feeling Charlie's gaze on her before he shifted into gear. The city blurred by as they sped down the streets, a new thrum of anxiety building in her chest the closer and closer they got to the infamous house.

CHAPTER TWENTY
IZZY

The "house" Emilien procured after the warehouse explosion looked closer to a castle, complete with a fountain out front feeding into a large canal that required a bridge to get across. Once a museum for St. Louis University several blocks from Izzy's apartment, the mansion had been gifted to the immortal scientist and his legion in their dire time of need by the university president. The rumor was the president had developed a recent taste for blood as well.

The Romanesque-style home occupied a secluded edge of campus, off the road enough to require anyone coming in to approach by foot. A convenient advantage for The Society. Two reddish stone towers speared the clear blue sky before them as they stepped out of the car and began the short trek to the front door.

"Did he say why he wanted to see us?" Izzy said from beneath the wide brimmed hat she had found in the car, gesturing between them before absently reaching for her empty neckline. She tugged on the hem of her shirt, the fabric itching against her skin.

Charlie studied her movements and a muscle in his jaw clenched. "No, he just said *'depêche-toi'*." His irritated voice hit her before his words did. He had become increasingly annoyed the closer the car got to campus.

"And that meant 'drag that wretched girl along too'?" Izzy asked, gaze focused down on the pristine pavement beneath her feet. If she thought Wash U was pretentious, this institution took it to a whole new level.

Charlie scowled at her. "No, it means hurry up. So, hurry up." He picked up his pace and she shuffled up to match it.

"I know what it means," she grumbled.

He studied her out of the corner of his eye. The house loomed before them. Izzy chanced a glance up to the contemplative stone faces on the corbels. They stared back in perpetual silent judgment. Her gaze shifted over to Charlie and his ire softened a fraction.

"Just…try not to bite anyone's head off, okay?" he pleaded as they cut along the slim walkway to the entrance.

She gave him a vicious grin, fangs making an appearance and all, even as her heartbeat deafened her own ears. "Me? I only have a taste for troubled bad boys, not heartbroken Frenchmen. No blood will be shed unwillingly today." She followed her bravado with a wink.

A smirk cracked the chiseled composure on his face and he shook his head. His voice grew serious again when he spoke. "I mean it. Getting a call at random without any details and a firm request to *depêche-toi*[32] spells disaster in my world. Something has gone wrong. Tread carefully. Please."

They stepped underneath the tan columns up to the immaculate wooden door. Charlie turned to her, his hand twitching at his side before it curled into a fist. His blue eyes bounced between her emerald ones and he whispered, "Please," once more with enough conviction to pierce her soul.

She nodded. Without breaking their stare, he reached up and knocked three times on the door. A second later, it opened and Callum peered out, a sneer on his face. His hat had been removed and to Izzy's surprise, he actually looked less intimidating without it. Just like a young man, albeit one suspended in a moment in time. But he could easily fit in with any of the students on campus.

Izzy's eyes narrowed on him. Is that how Emilien had done it? Corrupted the young, impressionable minds of his pupils into an *idea* of forever. All for the clout of approval from their professor? A man self-absorbed in his own research? Disgust filled her veins with acid.

Callum flashed a sultry smirk at her, spilling the acid from her blood into the back of her throat. "Morning, love. Ready for round two? I usually like to wait until the second or third date before we get rough, but you seem willing to jump right in, so let's." His accent made the words come out ten times more vile as he cracked his knuckles.

"Over your dead body," she replied, shoving past him into the house. Despite its current company, the space evoked a sense of warmth and comfort with its exposed beams, solid mahogany details, and detailed stained glass windows. Izzy would have dreamed of living in a house like this as a kid, running in and out of the secret rooms, sliding down the long balustrade.

Her imagined giggles shrank to screams as Callum brushed up behind her. Goosebumps sprang up across her body as he leaned in and whispered in her ear. "Don't reveal all your kinks to me at once. Let's play a little harder to get." He cut ahead of her before she could elbow him in the nose. Again. She knew it had to still be tender, even if it was healed.

"We are meeting in the conservatory," Callum

announced, leading them through the house. Izzy imagined how it would feel to slice his throat open and watch the blood paint the pristine rug beneath their feet in a crimson bath.

Charlie's hand on her arm snapped her back and she unclenched her fists.

"Thanks," she mumbled. Being back in it, in this world and with him, it all felt surreal. The monster within her clawed, gnawing at her soul. Wanting to escape. To be set free.

"Just, be cool, okay?" Charlie whispered low enough for only her to hear. He kept his gaze trained on the back of Callum's head as they journeyed into the darkening depths of the extravagant home. Izzy studied the lines on Charlie's face as they hardened the closer they got to the conservatory. All Izzy knew about the room, and the house itself, came from a brief section in her high school history class. The conservatory had been tucked away from view, a secret oasis. Only rumors existed for its use, the most popular being satanic rituals on Full Moons and orgies with the socialites of the city.

Callum stepped aside as they approached a doorway. Charlie darted in front of her, walking in first. She gave another glare to Callum as she passed. He responded by licking his lips, biting the lower one with a fang. Fucking prick.

Disgusted, she pushed into the circular room and froze. It was a room of windows. The entire space looked like a shrine to the sun, wooden "beams" radiating out from a central point on the ceiling while every outer wall consisted of a tall pane of glass. Blackout curtains were drawn closed over each, casting the space into an eerie glow from the light leaking in from the edges of the dark fabric. Where the sunlight persisted. She swallowed.

"Isabella, so nice of you to join us finally, *oui?*" Emilien cooed from a leather chair placed furthest from the door. Her spine straightened at the breathy sound of his French accent, the nonchalant command he held in his simple words. "Will you be waging a war on my ego today?" he added, smirking as he lifted a glass of scarlet liquid to his lips and took a sip.

"It wasn't planned but time will tell." Her words rattled a bit as she scanned the room full of mostly men, a few women, all with murder in their eyes, setting the dormant human in her on high alert. Was that a natural, leftover feeling? Were they innately aware of how feeble she felt? Prey unaware as the predator stalked in the tall grass?

Did any of them have a nagging sense of humanity? Or had it disappeared with all the years they had spent leaning into the monster within.

Would that happen to her?

"Izzy," Charlie urged next to her. She held his hand in her own, the grip teetering on bone crushing. His worried eyes scanned her then motioned to Emilien. The beautiful Frenchman had stood up, hand gesturing to the empty chairs in front of him. He quirked a brow when Izzy looked at him.

"Please, *s'asseoir*[33]," he said, a deadly smile creasing his face. A face she remembered in anguish as her dagger pierced the heart of his beloved wife. Ex wife? Surely there was a statue of limitations on marriages believed to be ended by fake death?

Charlie and Callum stepped up to two of the empty chairs while Izzy stood frozen. Could she run? How far would she get? She had been neglecting her cardio work some, but her new body could take a beating. But against honed vampires?

An audible exhale escaped her lips and she stalked toward a third empty seat, sinking into the smooth leather. Once seated, the rest of the men standing followed suit.

"Well, I imagine you all are dying to know why I've

called you here," Emilien said, toying with them, his words dangling in front of them.

No one answered. Izzy itched to shift in her seat, to look away but she held her gaze on him.

"Ah, we will need to become friendlier than this, *mes amis*. We are about to go on a trip together," he continued, leaning back into his seat and pressing his fingertips together

Izzy frowned. But it was Callum who spoke, a harsh growl filtered through his Manchester accent.

"What the fuck do you mean a trip?" His tone startled Izzy as she turned wide-eyed at the man. Charlie's ocean eyes danced between the two men, shifting in his own seat, calculating the situation. She could feel his heartbeat, smell his blood as his temperature rose.

Death incarnate stared back at Callum. Emilien's words frosted the edges of the room as he spoke, a frown on his face. "If you're not going to play along then I guess I shall *au fait*[34]." He clicked his tongue and the rest of the room shuffled out, leaving the four of them to stare at each other. Well, three of them. One pulled a fucking cigarette from his pocket and lit it. Clove. Izzy bit back her scoff as the spicy cloud plumed from Emilien's lips.

Once the door to the room shut, he continued. "It appears my beloved Adette has taken refuge in our old hometown, *Les Grande* [35]. We sent a scout to follow her when she disappeared from the rubble and destruction created by a certain fiery redhead and her elusive boyfriend." Emilien's sharp gaze flickered to Izzy in something she could interpret as disdain. "They ported in New Orleans a few months ago. The scout returned last week with as much information as they could gather. And I believe it's time we pay her a visit, don't you agree?"

Charlie chimed in next, stealing Emilien's attention just

as his gaze branded into Izzy's skin. She released a breath and looked to Charlie. A storm of emotions waged on his features and came out as anger when he spoke.

"You're telling me you've been tailing your wife this whole time? And what information have you gathered? Why do we need to go down there? How do you want me to explain this to Lando?"

An icy fury exuded from Emilien as he turned his focus on Charlie. "Why do you need to know this information? Make up a story. You're a *tres bien*[36] storyteller." A feral grin slid across the man's face.

Charlie stood, running a hand through his hair. Callum stiffened, his hand sliding to his side.

"Seven months ago, you believed she was dead. Hell, twenty years ago, you believed she was dead. Then she just arrives out of thin air and you want us to go waltz into her living room without any information or even a plan."

Emilien rose. Physically, Charlie loomed over Emilien. But there was an animalistic danger about Emilien that seemed to dwarf Charlie a notch. Emilien stalked toward him, stopping inches from his face. When he spoke, no one else could hear the words he said, but the blood drained from Charlie's face. When Emilien turned his back to Charlie and walked back to his seat, Charlie glanced to Izzy before sinking stiffly back into his seat. Callum relaxed, removing his hand from his side.

With his back still to them, Emilien took a sip of his drink, the liquid leaving a thick film along the edge of the clear glass. "Like I said, we will be going on a trip. Pack light. We leave tonight." He snapped his fingers and at that, the door to the conservatory opened. A hand pulled Izzy from her chair and ushered her to the exit. She looked around in panic to see the same happening to Charlie. Callum remained seated, a scowl on his face as he watched the back of his boss.

CHAPTER TWENTY-ONE
IZZY

"Can you drop me at Barry's place?" Izzy asked Charlie as they slipped back into the Alfa, chewing her bottom lip.

His lips tightened and he looked sideways at her. "You can't tell him where we are going. And we don't know how long we will be gone."

She rolled her eyes and glared at him, leaning back into the leather seat. "Thanks, Captain Obvious. This isn't my first time dealing with *gang secrets*."

He remained quiet, the only sound filling the space between him the purr of the engine and the quick pauses when he shifted gears. When the road they needed to turn right down to head back home came and went, she smirked knowingly out the window.

Barry lived on the other side of the park, closer to campus. His building looked straight out of a Victorian historical fiction with its whitewashed stone entrance and grand mahogany arched door. His apartment held a mid-century bohemian charm, *trés approprié*[37] for him. The best part of the whole space was the balcony overlooking the park across the street, the arch in the far distance. Many drunken sunsets had been spent on that balcony. The memories choked her a bit and she discreetly dabbed at her eyes. Where had those days gone?

Charlie pulled up the curb. Before she stepped out, she turned to him and said, "I can walk home. It's not that far."

Keeping his blue eyes fixed ahead, he said, "I'll wait."

She studied his profile. The set in his jaw sent a chill down her spine. This man took everything from her. Her happiness, her sense of safety in her own home, *her best friend.* How could she forget all of that?

"How chivalrous, but really, it's fine. It'll be nice to get some fresh air before I'm stuck traveling with a bunch of men." She shuddered at the thought.

Steely conviction froze her when he turned his head, meeting her gaze, silencing anymore jokes on her tongue. "I'll wait, Izzy." His eyes flickered to the rear view mirror before settling back on her.

As she rose out of the car, she swallowed, glancing behind them to see the black sedan with its blacked out windows parked five car lengths down the near empty street. The engine radiated a shimmery heat.

Fuck, okay. She stepped up to the door of the building and with a shaky hand, pressed the buzzer for Barry's place.

"Yesssss?" Barry's voice cooed through the intercom.

"Hi Bear, can I come up?"

There was a long pause where she considered the possibility of him saying no and her sulking back to the car, tail between her legs. She deserved it, if he did. Wouldn't even argue it. Instead, the door buzzed and she pulled it open, not letting the opportunity pass her by. Chancing a glance over her shoulder, she spotted Charlie, sitting in the Alfa, his gaze fixed on the rear view mirror. On the car behind him.

Izzy stepped into the stairwell, wanting the ten-story climb to contemplate how she would broach her apology to Barry.

Hi, I know I yelled at you and stalked you like a starving wolf in pursuit of a plump sow but also I'm about to leave with a gang of vampires and my ex-boyfriend and I don't know how long I'll be gone or if I'll even be coming back and all I want to do is scream and cry and run far far far away.

Satisfied that none of that would make the final cut, she stepped onto the landing and stood there a moment longer. Her lungs strained as she inhaled deeply, willing her heart rate and breathing to return to normal.

Yet composure felt completely out of her grasp. Letting out a frustrated sigh, she pushed through the wooden door out of the stairwell and walked the twenty feet to Barry's front door. She didn't even get a chance to knock before it opened and a burly man started to step out.

"Oh! Um, hi? I'm Izzy," she said, awkwardly sticking her hand out.

The man smiled at her but as soon as he went to take her hand and speak, Barry called loudly from behind the door.

"No! Not now! You can meet him on a different day! Go!"

The man gave her a sheepish grin and a shrug before he gently pushed passed her. He did whisper, "It's nice to meet you," to her as he squeezed by before disappearing down the hall.

Barry pulled the door open fully and motioned for Izzy to come in. Various silk scarves covered the lamp shades and hung in decorative strings along the walls. Eclectic artwork popped off against the white paint. Whimsy wooden designs had been pressed into the walls, accentuating lines and corners while sleek modern furniture filled the rest of the space. A giant jute rug in the middle of the living space completed the look. All Barry.

Izzy stepped in tentatively and then followed after Barry as he made his way into the kitchen.

"Want a drink?" he asked, holding up the golden pineapple shaker in his hand.

"Um, sure. Thank you." She winced at the cordial tone in her voice. "I mean, no. I can't stay. Charlie is waiting outside."

Barry stopped slicing a lime and turned, his dark brow raised. "Go on." His arms folded across his chest as he studied her.

Izzy's hand reached up to the hollow at her throat, feeling nothing where a golden cross used to lay. Her heart sank as her pulse fluttered. She pulled her hand away and frantically rotated the black ring on her thumb instead. "I'm sorry," she eked out.

Barry's head tilted. "That's it?"

She looked up at him and saw the hurt in his eyes. It broke her. "I'm really sorry, Barry. My life has been…a fucking disaster since this past fall. I can't think straight. I clearly can't act right. I don't even know myself anymore and I just feel so fucking alone." Her voice cracked a little on that last word and she had to look away from him again, her lower lip trembling.

"But you're not."

She looked back at him, his brows furrowed as the tears still threatened. "Huh?"

The crease between his brow deepened. "You're not alone. You haven't been alone this entire time. Hell, you're not even alone now. I have been here. I have always been here. And I know Charlie is pretty low on your list, and for good reason, but he's been there for you too. You have to understand how deep his regret runs by now." He looked at the floor, his voice getting quiet before he continued on. "He was going to leave last fall. Escape somewhere he couldn't be found. But he didn't want to leave you alone in the hands of both Lando and Emilien."

Izzy blinked away her tears and shook her head. "What are you saying, Barry?"

Barry took a step toward her, squeezing her hand. "He's been there, looking out for you, from the start of all this. He came to me, as sort of a last ditch effort to talk to someone I think. He was torn between ending it all or disappearing into the night. But then he realized that without Vahagn or Noah, you would be in that building with no one watching your back. Keeping *your safety* number one priority."

"But…I…I." She hadn't realized. All those times of giving Charlie nothing but the worst of her and he had taken it, focused solely on keeping her best interests in mind. She choked a little. "I don't deserve that, Barry. Fuck, last night I was…" She looked out the window. He gripped her hand tighter.

"Izzy, I know this hasn't been easy for you. And yeah, I got a little scared last night and ran off to Charlie because of it. But here you are. Because nothing as small as you wanting to rip my throat from my magnificent neck will stop me from loving you."

A choked sob escaped her lips and she flung herself into him. He stumbled back but wrapped his arms around her regardless, holding her tight for several moments while her tears stained his silk shirt. When she pulled back, keeping him in her arms, she said quietly, "You might stop when you hear what I'm about to say." She felt him stiffen under her grasp and she stepped back. "I'm leaving."

He stepped back, hand to his chest, clutching at pearls he never had. "What do you mean, leaving?"

"I can't say. I don't know how long I'll be gone either. But can you—?"

"Flourish a glorious tale to excuse your prolonged departure from the evil lair in which we work so the dictator of our department doesn't fire your ass once and for all? Absolutely. Fortunately for you, it is summer break and he's about to go on his three-week long golf sabbatical."

She beamed at him. "How fortunate, indeed."

He hesitated, studying her smile. Her fangs. Then he smiled and pulled her back into his embrace. She heard the steady thrum of his heartbeat. "I'm going to miss you, wherever you are going. And whatever you're doing, please stay safe and stay slay, okay?"

She nodded her head quickly into his shoulder. "Of course," she whispered.

He held her as she backed away, heading toward the door. Just before their grasp broke, he said, "Come back to me, Izzy."

She smiled over her shoulder, heading for the stairs. "Always, Bear."

❖

Back at her apartment, she slipped into her closet, digging out her leather bag. She tossed in a couple t-shirts and pants, breathing easier after her talk with Barry. She danced a little, checking and rechecking how many pairs of underwear she would need. She stopped when she looked at her usual sleep attire, running her hands over the faded, threadbare t-shirts. Her hand grazed the worn, soft cotton of a black sweatshirt. Pulling it from its own spot on the shelf, the garment unfolded, revealing the golden fleur de lis emblem on the front. The soft fabric brushed her cheek as she pressed her face into it, breathing deeply. Layered beneath the familiar scents of her own home a faint hint of smoke and bourbon clung to the fabric. She opened her eyes, willing her hands to fold it up and put it back on the shelf. Except her hands stuffed it into her bag.

Sitting on the floor of her closet, she scanned the small space before walking out to the main room of the apartment. Spotting her cup on the counter, she went to put it in the sink for future Izzy to worry about when she caught the image of Adolphus Busch on the table. Her skin prickled as she looked to Adam Lemp next to him. Slamming the book shut, and trapping the extra page within, she wrapped the sweatshirt around it and shoved it in her bag. A knock sounded on her door just before it popped open softly. Charlie swore under his breath.

"What's your problem?" she asked, frowning at his immediate scowl.

"You don't need to go from one extreme to the other. You could just lock your door," he said, exasperatedly checking all the locks still worked.

She rolled her eyes. "You do remember your kind, and you specifically, is why I locked it the way I did to begin with, right? I figure now, I'm the bigger threat," she replied dryly as she scanned her apartment, making sure she wasn't forgetting anything necessary. Clothes? Check. Book? Check. Fangs? Check. She stared longingly at her coffee machine before turning around, eyes roving over her comfy bed and the wall of bookshelves behind it.

"Duly noted," Charlie said, stiffening by her harsh words. "Are you ready to go?"

Her eyes caught on the flash of metallic light and she walked over to the shelf. "Almost," she replied, reaching for the handle of a perfectly balanced blade. The black Z etched into the steel felt like a void against the spotless chrome beneath it. Eyes glanced to the shelves until she found the custom thigh sheath to go with it. Strapping it around her leg, she placed the dagger in with a satisfying *schwing*. She turned to Charlie and nodded her head once.

"Okay, let's go. We are meeting downstairs," Charlie said, holding her door open for her. He watched her as she locked at least one of the deadbolts, pleased when she stuck the key in her bag.

On the street, they waited in silence as the sun shifted, slowly painting the sky into shades of orange, pink, and purple. They could see the black Escalade approaching from several blocks away, the only vehicle daring to be on the road at that hour.

"Are you ready?" Charlie asked, eyes trained on the nearing vehicle.

"Not even in the slightest," Izzy admitted on an exhale, adjusting the strap on her shoulder. Even with her mood lifted from her meeting with Barry, she had a persistent sense of dread watching the vehicle come closer and closer.

His blue eyes met hers briefly before he refocused on the vehicle a couple blocks away. "Just remember to keep your emotions in check and always be watching, listening. I couldn't gather any more information and neither could Callum after our meeting. So be prepared for anything."

Callum? She opened her mouth to ask what he had to do with *them* when the SUV pulled up to the curb and a man dressed in black stepped out of the passenger door, opening the door behind him. Izzy peered into the luxurious space.

Rather than the standard rows of seating, plush benches lined around the back of the vehicle with ambient overhead recessed lighting. A half wall with a retractable window separated the back from the driver and each section of the backseat had the same capabilities to split it up. Emilien sat against the very back corner behind the driver, Callum along the outer bench to his right.

"Bonsoir mes belles compagnes[38]. Let us get the show on the road, as you say." Emilien's smile slid like ice down her spine as she stepped up into the vehicle, sitting with her back to the driver. Her eyes remained trained on the biggest threat. Charlie climbed in next to her, setting his backpack at his feet. She flinched as the door slammed shut. When the man climbed back into the passenger seat, the vehicle lurched forward, pitching Izzy toward Emilien.

"Calm down, *mon amore*[39], it's going to be a long drive. You'll pull something if you remain that tense the entire way," Emilien sneered, leaning back in his seat and closing his eyes.

Her brows furrowed as she pulled the strap of her bag off her shoulder and set in at her feet. "We're driving all the way there?"

"*Oui,*" Emilien replied, bored. His eyes remained closed.

"And that's going to be safe?" Charlie growled, leaning forward.

Emilien popped one eye open before leaning forward with a sigh. He rested his elbows on his knees and looked straight at Charlie as he spoke, "I'll remind you I own the world. I can come and go wherever I please. However I please. We need *l'effet de surprise*[40], which means getting there quickly, which means taking the roads. Alas," he leaned back again, hands spread wide before resting behind his head. His eyes closed once more. "the vehicle. Now, get comfortable. It will be slightly longer as we navigate around some of the worst parts of the path."

Izzy sank back into her seat, the dread in the pit of her stomach deepening. When communities found their government leaders taking money to fund their dreams of living forever, things like road maintenance and repair fell to the wayside. Why bother fixing the roads of the common folk when you could take a private jet or helicopter? As they exited the city, Izzy watched the tall skyscrapers vanish, replaced by growing fields, many abandoned, allowed to go back to the feral order of nature. Panic roiled through her, her heart rate increasing. She couldn't recall the last time she had left the city. All she knew of the world outside her little bubble were the horror stories Vahagn or Charlie would comment on. Roads made dangerous not just by the deteriorating terrain but also by the unorthodox tolls set up by angry men who had found themselves out of jobs as their local governments collapsed.

Even with Emilien's assurance, Izzy felt bile rise in her throat as she stared out the window. The multi-paned window. The bullet proof window.

✦

CHAPTER TWENTY-TWO
NOAH

His hands remained tied behind his back the remainder of the night. When the morning rays broke through the feeble window in its reckless pursuit of his sanity, Noah could barely feel his fingers. But fuck, could he feel his head. He didn't bother with attempting to get up, knowing the movement would bring nothing but pain.

Someone came in and released his restraints a time later. They tossed a piece of crusty bread and a glass of water on the floor before they left. The ice pick wedged into his skull kept him quiet as he sat up, rolling his shoulders forward then backward. A sickening crack radiated from his right side and he winced. Pulling the small heel of bread from the floor to his mouth fatigued his tired muscles. Only his desperation for water willed him to lift that heavy burden of a cup to his lips. He finished it in three gulps. Without thinking, he tossed the glass against the concrete wall of his cell and watched it shatter into a million shimmering pieces.

He stared at the pieces, his fuzzy memories of the night before roiling through him. Drinking outside Fat Catz, like an idiot.

Dancing in the street with Nadia, like an idiot. Catching his breath in the alley. Letting her follow. Letting her come toward him. Her fangs. Nadia with fangs. *Nadia had fangs.*

"Fuck," he swore. Nausea rolled through him and he focused on the sharpest shard of glass against the wall. How was he supposed to escape this? When Benji had walked into his cell that first day on the barge, he thought, for a blissful moment, he had been saved. He could *finally* stop running. But then it became abundantly clear Benji sold into the Antisociété rhetoric. His brother, his only family, once again in the talons of a French psychopath.

Only this time it didn't feel like a ruse. Joining The Society initially had been an attempt to save their city, their home. This? This felt real. This felt like a mission Benji was actually willing to die for.

And where did that leave Noah? He scanned his surroundings, cobwebs dusting the corners of the concrete room, a persistent musty smell tickling the back of his throat. He closed his eyes. Surely, they didn't mean to keep him a prisoner forever. At some point, it would just be easier to kill him.

The door opened on a bone splitting creak and a bulky, unfamiliar man stepped in.

"You sober?" he growled, his words like a jack hammer on Noah's skull. "By that grimace, I'll say yes. Come on. You've got fifteen minutes to clean up before boss lady wants to meet with you."

Noah eyed the man warily but stood up, allowing himself to be ushered out of the door and back up the stairs to the front door of Benji's suite. The man pushed around Noah and knocked once on the door, turning back to face him. The door immediately opened and Noah stared face to face with his brother.

The reddish-purple half moons under his eyes and swollen cheeks could be felt in the phantom of pain tingling across Noah's knuckles. He clenched them.

"I'll take it from here," Benji drawled slowly, an unfamiliar coolness in his tone.

The man left, heading for the elevators. Benji and Noah stood there a moment longer, staring at each other. Their nearly matching eyes locked on the other's next move. Noah tried to reconcile the brother before him with the one who broke into cars when they were younger so they didn't have to sleep on the ground in parks or in the cemeteries.

Benji took a step backward, opening the door wider and motioning for Noah to come in. He did and made a beeline for the bathroom, heeding the man's warning about Adette's impending arrival. A few minutes after he stepped into the shower, relishing the hot water against his skin, Benji's voice drifted in from the hollow cavern of the bathroom.

"I know you're apprehensive, and for good reason, but can you promise to just hear her out this time? I don't want to lose my brother. Not again."

Noah froze, his soapy hands around his neck. Without responding, he began rubbing his hands furiously over his face. A moment later the door clicked shut. Noah shut the water off, quickly drying with the plush white towels of the luxury hotel and then got to work brushing the acrid taste of sour beer out of his mouth. He stared at his frosted reflection in the mirror. His shower had been quick, enough to feel semi-human again, so only half of the mirror was coated in steam. Blurred ink reflected back across his chest, the fleur de lis on one side, a smoky cloud across to the shrimp on the other. The shrimp he got done with Benji in the chair next to him. It was a play on the shrimp po'boy. New Orleans through and through, they were the poor boys of the bayou. But at least they were always together. Until that fateful day over a year ago, when it all went up in literal smoke.

Noah spit into the sink, splashing cold water on his face. Gripping the edges of the sink, he looked up and met his own golden gaze for the first time in months. Dark purple circles pooled under his eyes, the creases along the edges of his mouth deepened. He looked his age for once in his life. Wiping his face dry, he wrapped the towel around his waist and walked out into his room. It looked untouched since yesterday. Almost like none of it had happened.

Except it did. And he had to decide today what he planned to do. How he could escape this. Or if he decided to accept his fate once and for all, forgetting everything he had left behind. His life in St. Louis. The brother he knew as a kid. Moving on and adopting a new life, a new persona.

He reached into the pocket of his jeans from the night before, finding the small golden charm on the broken chain within, the metal warming beneath his touch. It was the last real thing he had in this world. The last thing he trusted.

⚜

Five minutes later, a knock sounded from the front door. It ricocheted across the common area and into his room. He looked up from his perch on the edge of his bed. Taking a deep breath, he walked out into the spacious room. Adette sat on the couch, already comfortable while Benji worked in the kitchen, the sound of ice clinking against glass filling the silence.

"Noah, how lovely to see you. Please, come take a seat," Adette cooed, a saccharine smile on her face. Noah walked slowly to the armchair facing the couch and sat down. A man with a perpetual scowl stood behind it, eyes trained on the back of

Noah's skull. The skin on his neck itched but he didn't dare reach up to scratch it.

Benji shuffled into the room with what looked like a glass of tea with a slice of lemon stuck into the lip. Where the fuck were they getting lemons from?

"Thank you so much, Benny," Adette said, smiling up at him as she took the glass. There was an awkward silence and then Benji finally took the hint.

"Right, I need to go check in with the others about their new schedules and finish putting together the plans," Benji said, clapping his hands together then shifting from one foot to the other, deciding which direction to turn. Once he finally made his way to the door, he grabbed his keys off the counter and pulled it open. He paused in the threshold, looking back at them, his gaze bouncing between Noah and Adette before he nodded his head firmly and left. A moment passed after the lock clicked into place and then Adette spoke, her tone growing more serious.

"I understand you had a rather dramatic evening." She took a sip of her tea, trying to hide her grimace as she set it down. Noah smirked. Sweet tea was an acquired taste. Benji's sweet tea required a signature of intent to become diabetic.

Noah cleared his throat. "Something like that."

Adette hummed, studying the walls around the room before she turned her assessment on him. "You don't agree with our mission?"

Noah tilted his head at her. "I don't think I understand your mission, to be frank."

Another moment, another assessment of him before she spoke. He felt uneasy under her constant scrutiny but remained stoic. A flash of fangs caught his eye as she opened her mouth to speak. "I know it's hard to believe, but when Emilien came to me with his so-called cure all those years ago, I balked at the idea. It seemed reckless, like *se prendre pour dieu*[41]." Her features turned angry and she collected herself a moment before she continued more calmly. "When I refused, he went off in a fury, teaming up with a very powerful, very bad man. That's when my dear Henry came to me. He and Emil had been working together on this project, and he had similar concerns. We decided then we needed to continue the research. To find a better way."

Noah's eyes narrowed. He leaned forward, resting his elbows on his knees. The man behind him tensed. "And why are you telling me all of this?"

Adette's smile on him faltered a fraction. "I'm telling you this to help you understand. We are trying to right the wrong my husband unleashed on this world. He released a monster, *un fléau*[42], onto this world. You saw the streets last night, *non*? Is it not like it once was? Before? Vibrant? Alive?"

Noah considered her words. Despite the glaring issue of blood thirsty creeps still lurking in the dark hollows of the city, the community was more alive and *laissez faire*[43] than he had seen in years. Still...

"But what about what I've seen? What happened to me last night?" He dared to ask these questions, his heart a heavy drum beat against his chest.

Adette's gaze turned a murderous shade of crystalline blue. "*De quoi parlez-vous*[44]?"

"*Je parle des suceurs de sang qui sont encore parmi nous*[45]," Noah replied. Surprise washed over Adette and her wide eyes flickered to the man behind him. A mask quickly settled over her features, hiding the obvious shock he just witnessed.

"I'm giving you another chance because I believe you'll be a valuable asset to our organization. Benny has told stories of your skills while working for my husband. But don't take it lightly. Eyes will be on you every day, even more than they have been. *Tu marches sur un fil*[46]." At that, she stood, motioning to the door with her head. The man behind Noah brushed the back of his chair as he made his way to the exit with her.

Stopping as the man held the door open, she turned back to where Noah still sat, and said, "Be mindful of your place here. I would hate to take all this away from you." She raised a hand to the extravagant suite. And with that, she left, the following silence sucking the life out of the room.

Noah made his way to the door on silent feet and peered out the peep hole. Sure enough, a man stood across the hall, eyes trained on the door Noah leaned into. One of the man's hands rested on his hip, a gun in a holster beneath it.

A knock sounded on the door ten minutes after Adette left. The man from across the hall, gun still holstered at his hip, told Noah to get ready for morning kitchen duty. Taking his time to slip into the black uniform, he stared at his reflection in the big mirror covering the wall by the closet in his room. He hadn't looked at it much. Ignored it mostly. Now he studied his expression. Studied himself. And then hardened into the man he had been all that time with The Society. Stoic. Silent. Someone to fade into the shadows until needed. He sighed. Somehow, he always found himself needed.

Shaking his dark brown hair, the soft waves brushing the edges of his jaw, he headed toward the door, attempting to smooth the pillowy mess down with a hand. As soon as he walked through the door, he bumped into the man on guard.

"I'll escort you," the man gruffed.

Noah nodded and started toward the stairwell.

"Oy! We'll take the elevator. My knees didn't sign up for babysitting young deviants."

Noah couldn't help the grin on his face as he turned around and followed the man toward the elevator bay instead.

Squeezing into the tight space, he assessed the man. He stood a head shorter and a couple more stouter than him yet the "Don't fuck with me" demeanor came across loud and clear.

"Heard you punched your own brother," the man filled the silence matter of fact. Noah met his eyes briefly before looking back at his own reflection on the elevator door.

"Well, he must have been a right twat to deserve a smack down from his own little brother. Don't lose that spirit," the man grumbled. Noah couldn't decide by his tone if it was meant to be encouragement or chastising.

The bell dinged and the doors opened to the first floor in all its shiny opulence. Noah steered them left toward the kitchen and staff rooms.

"Sancho will be in charge of you while you're working. I'll be by to pick you up later. Stay out of trouble in the meantime, will ya? Sancho may look all cute and cuddly but I've seen him choke out a cobra with his bare hands. Something like that sticks with ya."

Noah nodded along as the man spoke and couldn't help the smile breaking his facade again. He thought for a moment to ask the man his name but he was determined to forget everything about this place. He needed nothing to make him second guess his plan to leave.

The man and Sancho gave each other a firm, single handshake as Noah shuffled into the kitchen, his head hung low as he made his way back to the sinks. All eyes burned into his back as he passed the empty space Nadia would've stood, rolling and shaping dough. He didn't bother with niceties, just got to work washing the pile waiting for him.

⚜

That night Noah crashed into a dreamless sleep, pulled into the dark depths of slumber.

The next morning as he pulled on a fresh black uniform, Benji knocked on his bedroom door.

"Come in," Noah called out, slipping the rough cotton shirt overhead.

Benji stepped in, rubbing a hand against the back of his neck. He crossed the room and perched on the edge of the bed as Noah pulled a brush through his hair. The length of it made him look unpredictable. Unruly. He barely recognized the man staring back at him.

A man with a mission.

And that's exactly what he had. His mind had been made up, plans set, a path mapped out in his head. He would leave tonight and never look back. On The Antisociété, his brother, any of it.

"You're going to be with me later today. We have some special guests coming in and Adette needs us to ready some rooms next door at Hotel Maison for them. So, around lunch, I'll grab you and we will head over. Sound good to you?"

Noah's hand froze as he gripped the hem of his shirt, trying to find the least itchy way to let it lay.

"What special guests?" This was a variable he hadn't accounted for but he could adjust.

Benji waved a dismissive hand and stood up, walking out the door. "It doesn't matter. Happens a lot around here. The investors like to see the success story. Just be ready for me after lunch, okay?"

Noah turned to his brother, his gaze stoic. "Okay."

In the kitchen, the gossip buzzed in the air, electrifying everything it touched. Everyone silenced the moment Noah stepped into the space. However, the information was either too good or the energy too palpable for them to remain silent for long.

"We've been asked to double the supply."

"I hear he looks like a model."

"At his age? No way! Even if…"

"Silencio! Por favor[47]!" Sancho shouted across the room, quieting everyone. Noah remained on task, washing, rinsing, drying, repeat. He felt the lethal gaze of the older man on him.

The tension in the kitchen stifled any conversation the rest of the morning. Once lunch was served, Noah could hardly sit still at the prospect of leaving, if not just to escape the atmosphere of the kitchen. The reprieve to be passed from one keeper to the next when Benji arrived, even if Malik was in tow, had every muscle in Noah's shoulders relax.

They all walked outside, into the suffocating heat with the sunshine blinding overhead, and down the street to the hotel. Malik cleared his throat and asked Benji, "How many did they say?"

Benji looked sideways at Noah before he turned his head to Malik and said, "Six, five will need extras. We'll put them all on the top floor and a group of guards below, working in rotation."

Noah kept his gaze trained forward. The walk to Hotel Maison Pierre Lafitte was a short one and soon they stood underneath the balcony overlooking the street. The golden oak doors with their black tinted windows loomed before them. Malik fished a set of keys from his pocket and unlocked the door on the right. Noah quirked a brow at him and Benji commented, "All part of The Antisociété, brother."

Like that cleared anything up.

The space had been more modernized than The Roosevelt with its white walls accented by sections of the original red brick and sharp black details.

"Malik, you double check the first floor rooms. I know a few men live here permanently but there will be others with them. Noah and I will head upstairs and work on prepping the guest rooms." Benji turned, heading for the carpeted stairs. Noah caught Malik's gaze, a threat laid bare within his brown eyes. They held each other's stare for a moment, words spoken in volumes without saying a thing. Then Noah scoffed and followed his brother up the stairs.

In the white hallway, Benji gestured to their left and they made their way to the end of the hall, through a door that matched all the rest except for the black **#1** painted on the front. Beyond the small entryway, the room opened up into an apartment type suite, complete with a sleek living room with full wall to ceiling windows looking out to the street below. Ferns swayed on the nonexistent breeze outside them. The ceiling rose another floor to a loft above, a spiral staircase leading the way next to the kitchen.

"Go ahead and start taking the sheets off the furniture and stick them in the hamper. We will take them down to be cleaned when we are done."

Noah started in the living room as he watched his brother make his way into the small kitchenette. He pulled the sheet off the couch in a plume of dust as Benji bent down. The steady hum of a refrigerator purred throughout the space. With a satisfied nod, Benji disappeared into a door underneath the loft, the faint sounds of water splashing. Noah moved about the living room, pulling sheets and tossing them on the floor. He made his way up the stairs, hoping to find a hamper and maybe even a duster.

With no luck finding either, and the bed clean underneath the sheet that had been thrown over it as well, he headed back downstairs to ask Benji about the hamper.

His brother squatted in front of the fridge, checking a thermostat within the appliance. Noah slowed his steps downward as he watched Benji pull his phone out and press it to his ear.

"Yeah, in apartment one on the second floor. It's not cooling. Yeah, I know, but just in case, right? I know they have an extra with them but for all five? Okay. Okay. Yeah, I'll check the unused rooms." Benji pocketed the phone just as Noah stepped down onto the main floor of the apartment, allowing his steps to be heard. Benji looked up and smiled.

"All good?"

"Yeah but do we have a duster? This place is covered in the stuff," Noah said.

Benji laughed and pulled his phone back out, typing something as he said, "You were always the cleaner of the family. I'll have Malik bring us up a cart. We will need it anyway."

Noah nodded his head then gestured to the fridge. "Want me to look at it?"

Benji looked up from his phone to follow his gesture. His smile faltered. "Oh. No. That's unnecessary. We will just trade it out with another one. Don't want people to have lukewarm drinks in this heat, right?" He flashed a bright smile at him.

Noah kept his face unchanged as he replied, "Yeah, the worst."

Benji dusted his hands off on his jeans and walked to the front door. "Come on, the other rooms are smaller. We can get started on them until Malik gets here with more supplies."

The rest of the rooms were standard hotel size, single rooms with a bathroom, queen bed, and a small refrigerator in the corner of each. Every one was plugged in and checked for temperature as Noah stripped sheets off beds and checked the bathrooms were stocked. Malik arrived as they stepped out of their third room with a cart that had a large hamper on it and, thankfully, a feather duster.

As Malik locked the front door behind them later that afternoon, Noah dared to ask, "So, when will these special guests be arriving?"

Benji and Malik exchanged a look before his brother said with a shrug, "Later this evening, early morning. Don't worry about it."

CHAPTER TWENTY-THREE
IZZY

The world disappeared into inky black through the tinted windows of the SUV as they sped along the barren highways. Interstate travel was rare as it stood but overnight travel was damn near unheard of, even as the thing to be feared in the night.

Emilien almost immediately fell asleep once they had exited the city limits, his legs propped up on the side bench in front of him. Callum, Charlie, and Izzy shared brief glances, shifting uncomfortably in their seats while a remarkably calm look befell the monstrous man. Charlie leaned his head back against the glass panel behind them, staring through the extended moon roof above. Izzy took one more look at Emilien before peering out the window to her right. She could just make out the outlines of the trees, slightly darker than the night sky behind them.

A couple hours passed before the window separating the driver from the rest of them rolled down, startling Charlie.

"We're nearing Memphis," the man in the passenger seat said, turning around to look at Emilien. When he didn't stir,

Callum reached a booted foot across the vehicle and kicked his leg. Emilien awoke with a start, hissing his fangs at Callum. Callum looked indifferent as he gestured forward.

The man repeated himself.

Emilien nodded. "Be on guard. Latest reports didn't mention any checkpoints but you never know what you might encounter. If you see something, don't stop. The car can take it."

Izzy sat up a little straighter. Checkpoints? Charlie spoke before she could ask what was on her mind. "What exactly should we be preparing to encounter in Memphis?"

Emilien waved a hand at him and propped his legs back up, closing his eyes again. "Just wannabe rival gangs and such. Nothing major."

Charlie balked. "Nothing major? Last I heard, Memphis made St. Louis look like a wedding destination."

Emilien opened one eye, then sat up with a sigh, focusing his attention on Charlie. "Charlie, Charlie, Charlie. *Tu t'inquiètes trop*[48]. The only reason I brought you along is because you keep that troublesome woman next to you in check. And you serve as an emergency snack. Leave the worrying to those in charge here, *oui*?" A fanged sneered cross his shadowed face, darkness playing with the lines of his face.

Charlie challenged the man's stare a moment longer before asking, "And what other cities do we not need to worry about when we pass through them?"

Emilien leaned back again, not bothering to prop his legs up this time. "We may have some interactions in Jackson but our biggest threat lies in New Orleans."

"What's in New Orleans exactly?" Izzy dared to ask. All she knew about the city was the secondhand information from Lando after the riots nearly two years ago and how haunted Noah seemed by them. The riots he had helped plan, with his brother, to take down the very man sitting across from her. The failed attempt to end this once and for all.

Emilien's predatory gaze shifted to her and she felt it hit her skin like a wall of pin pricks. "My wife has taken it upon herself to clean up the city. So, I want to see what she has done," he sneered.

The car began to slow. As Izzy and Charlie both shifted to peer out the front windshield, the driver floored it, sending them both to the floor. But not before they saw the horde of people running toward the vehicle.

No. Not people.

Vampires.

"What the fuck is that?" Izzy screamed as she pulled herself back into her seat, Charlie doing the same next to her. They shared a horrified glance. The vehicle sped toward the group with no intent of stopping. Neither were the vampires.

As the car neared the drove, Izzy made out the appearance of one in the front. The woman's skin was gaunt, greying, and stretched across her bones in a sickening way. A few straggled clumps of hair flowed from an otherwise bald head. But it was her eyes that made Izzy stop breathing. Black pools, devoid of color, of life, seemed to stare directly into her soul. Elongated fangs protruded from the perpetual snarl on her face as she paced toward the SUV.

Izzy swallowed.

"Impact in five seconds," the driver said, calmly. He aimed for the woman and her depthless gaze. Before Izzy could even process what he meant, a loud thud hit the windshield. Izzy flinched, turning her face toward Charlie, wide eyed. Her cheeks felt wet with the tears she hadn't realized started streaming down her face.

Three more thuds hit the hood and Charlie wrapped his arms around her, trying his damnedest to block out the noise as she pressed her face into his chest, tears flooding the front of his shirt. Her fingers clawed into her neck, searching for the golden cross that wasn't there. Fangs bit into her gums.

The wreckage lasted for an eternity and yet ended after just two minutes. Charlie held her for another five. When she felt ready, she pushed against his chest. He released his grip, giving her the space she wanted. Their eyes met, his iced over, hardened by what he had seen. Izzy turned to look out the windshield but Charlie placed a hand on her cheek.

"Don't," he croaked hoarsely. Deep lines pulled taunt on the sides of his mouth. He was…rattled. He was never rattled.

"Oh, come on, Charlie. Let her see what will happen if she decides to run away. The world is desolate for a lonely vampire like her," Emilien said, a sadistic smile on his face.

Izzy turned to him. "What do you mean if I run away? I'm not beholden to you. I'm not beholden to anyone."

"You truly believe that, don't you? And where would you be without your band of mafia brothers, *non*? Or even that quirky little friend of yours? You are beholden to everyone in your life. You could not exist without them. Especially that one sitting next to you." Emilien gestured to Charlie. She glared first at Emilien and then at Charlie.

Callum chuckled from his spot near Emilien. "Easy, boss. This one has more fight than even I think I could handle."

A snarl reverberated through the backseat.

A snarl from her own lips.

She glanced at Charlie. He stared at her through wide pools of azure, a stark contrast against his ashen face. Fear radiated off him, she felt it in his pulse. Smelled it in his blood. Fuck. She swallowed, the thought sobering her. She shifted back in her seat, turning her focus away from the men in the vehicle. They still had hours until they made it to New Orleans. The landscape passed in various shades of black outside her smeared window. Her stomach roiled as she stared at the smears, remembering what, or rather who they were. She closed her eyes, knowing the answers to her stream of questions would be ignored. Yet an uncomfortable pit grew in her stomach as she remembered the woman's stare, so lifeless and cold.

The following miles passed in uneventful silence. They stopped once along the way at an abandoned rest area to relieved themselves and stretch their legs. The driver took the opportunity to openly assess Izzy so she did the same, arms crossed over her chest. He stood several inches taller than Charlie with a bald head and a gruff, dark beard. Black ink decorated the dark skin on his head. Fangs bared at him when his gaze lingered on her chest.

As she opened her mouth to string together some of her finest phrases, Charlie placed a hand on her shoulder. She whirled on him, pushing him away.

"I don't fucking need your help, Charlie," she sneered, stalking back to the vehicle as the rest of the group did the same. Emilien watched them with the door held open.

Charlie caught up to her, gripping her wrist, forcing her to spin around and face him. "Hey, hey, stop for a fucking second, Please, Izzy," he pleaded with her as she tried to rip out of his grasp.

She settled for a stern stare at him but didn't move. He released his grip and she crossed her arms again.

Charlie sighed, running a hand through his ebony hair. "Look, I know we haven't been on the best of terms for a while now but when we get to the city, we need to stick together. I don't trust a single one of those men in that vehicle and I trust that psychopath's wife even less. I don't know what he has cooking up in his demented mind, especially after Memphis, but if shit goes sideways, we need to be together so we can get out. Okay?"

She had to agree with him. Their trust in one another was fickle but a far cry stronger than the trust she had in the men behind her. Still, she paused. It meant teaming up with the man who ruined her life. Who took everything good from her.

She studied the care in his eyes. He meant his words.

"Together," she said, giving him a weak smile.

A tight one creased the edges of his mouth in response. "Together," he repeated, nodding once.

❖

A sea of lights reflecting off the muddy waters of the Mississippi greeted them as they drove into the city limits of New Orleans. Izzy stared out the window, mouth agape.

"How is this possible?" she asked in disbelief. Her nerves were on edge the entire trip and she wasn't sure if she had hallucinated the normalcy outside her windows. New Orleans should be in ruins.

Emilien scowled. "I do not know."

The driver winded through the crowded streets, taking detours where whole bands played in the middle of the street.

Emilien's scowl morphed into a hard line on his face. Callum shifted uneasy next to him, wiping his hands on his pants as he glanced to Charlie and then Izzy. Izzy chanced a glance over to Charlie. He met her with a stony expression.

Together, his eyes seemed to say.

"We're here, boss," the man in the passenger seat said.

Izzy turned back to the window and her eyes grew wide

as she took in the building before them. Awash in golden lights, "THE ROOSEVELT" was written in art deco font across the black awning. The structure towered into the sky and she pressed into the window to see the top. The door opened and she fell out with it. Catching herself, the concrete bit into the palms of her hands. She stumbled up, wiping her hands on her pants and fanning her face from the shock of oppressive wet heat.

Emilien followed her out with much more grace. He looked her up and down, sneering one fang at her. Sweat had already begun to bead down her back as Charlie and Callum appeared from around the back of the vehicle.

"I imagine they will be expecting us, but if not," Emilien's smile turned devilish as he adjusted his collar, peering up at the building above. "Prepare yourselves."

Great. What the fuck was that supposed to mean? Izzy looked to Charlie in desperate clarification and he simply shrugged. Then his hand slid up to pat the handle of the gun he had holstered in his chest harness. A serrated knife rested underneath it. Izzy placed an assuring hand on the handle of her dagger and sighed. The cool metal felt like a gentle squeeze from the person who had gifted it to her. Who she lost to these monsters. Her expression turned to stone as they followed Emilien toward the white stone steps leading to the entrance.

The hair on the back of her neck stood up right before Callum whispered, his breath tickling the back of her ear, "Murder looks good in your eyes."

She elbowed him square in the sternum without a second thought and he let out a satisfying gasp. He wheezed for several long seconds as he tried to recover. A wry smirk pulled on the corner of her lips.

"Fuck," he growled into the night air and Emilien

whirled on them, his teeth bared, eyes alight.

"Once inside, you let me handle the talking. Keep your ears and eyes open. And *l'amour de dieu*[49], don't kill each other! These rugs are expensive."

They all froze. Emilien seemed satisfied with their response to his temper flaring. Then he turned and saw them too.

Clad in black armored gear, a group appeared at the top of the steps. A small armory covered every one of them, from swords to daggers to hand guns. The only distinguishing feature between each of the figures were their macabre eyes between swathes of tight cloth over their faces. One of them, his dark brown eyes focused on Izzy, tilted his head in a menacing fashion.

"I believe they know we are here," Izzy breathed out, gulping for oxygen to prevent her from fainting.

Oblivious to any sense, Emilien straightened and beamed up at the group, taking a step forward.

"*Bonjour, mes amis*[50]. I believe my wife might be expecting me?"

Izzy stiffened at his words.

The man in the front tore his gaze from Izzy as he leaned toward his shoulder, the void where his mouth would be shifting underneath the fabric over it. A moment later, he stepped aside and a man with bright orange hair and wire framed glasses stepped out from the glass doorway.

"We thought you might be here sooner. Did you get stuck in traffic?" The man spoke with a proper British accent, unlike the gruff one Callum had. His eyes shifted over their small group, a wary smile on his face.

The smile on Emilien's face fractured for half a second then widened. "Henry, my old friend. *C'est un delice*[51], seeing you here. Long way from Oxford, *non*?" Emilien sounded breathless, his words teetering on an edge of jovial insanity. Whoever this Henry was had him rattled. The two men stared each other down. Izzy reached for Charlie's hand and he grabbed it, squeezing. The movement caught Henry's eye and seemed to shake him out of the trance he had been in.

"Please, let me invite you in for a quick drink before we show you to your rooms down the street," Henry said, stepping back and gesturing to the door. Emilien stood still for a second longer before he climbed the stairs, stalking past the line of black on each side. Callum followed at a less aggressive pace, looking each person in the eye before disappearing into the building.

Charlie glanced sideways at her, gave her hand a tight squeeze, and then led the way up the stairs. She followed a step behind him, keeping her eyes trained on the pristine stone steps beneath her. Just as she slipped within the cool, air-conditioned lobby though, her gaze shifted up and caught on a pair of golden eyes. So similar to a color that haunted her dreams every night for the past seven months. Yet slightly different. Her brows scrunched and she tripped. A hand attached to those eyes reached out, righting her.

"Be careful," he drawled and her breathing hitched. As she stared back up at him, she noticed the flecks of black and her heart sank. This wasn't Noah.

She ripped her arm out of his grasp. "I'm fine," she barked at not-Noah and rushed inside to catch up with the others.

CHAPTER TWENTY-FOUR
IZZY

Henry led them into a long room. A dark, polished bar lined one side while small round tables surrounded with leather-bound barrel chairs were placed about the other side in a *laissez faire* way. A hush filled the room as they walked in, heads once tilted in close conversation on the plush golden velvet couches tucked against the wall, turned to them. Untouched drinks left condensation on the table tops. The mosaic of black diamond and dot tiles on the polished floor reflected the black battle gear on every patron in the room. Izzy could only hear her own heartbeat, thudding deep in her chest. She tried to temper her wide-eyed gaze. She wasn't fucking prepared for this. All her time spent with Lando and his crew did not help walking into that den of vipers.

Thankfully, Charlie pulled her arm and led her into the smaller, private room next door Henry opened up for them. She passed the man with the golden eyes, next to the man with murderous brown ones, giving each a cursory glance as she followed her group in. Henry disappeared, closing the door behind him as Emilien dropped onto another plush couch in the middle of the room, spreading his legs and pulling his hands behind his head. How could one man be that cocky in a moment like this? Izzy and Charlie stood off in the corner next to a small bar cart.

Never sit down when facing an enemy, even one disguised as a friend. Vahagn's voice echoed in her mind and she sucked in a sharp breath. Charlie glanced sideways at her, his hand tightening into a fist and then releasing as Callum sank slowly into the barrel seat adjacent to them, within ear shot. The man who had driven them here and his passenger stood in opposite corners from each other, assessing different angles of the room.

"Any money on if this ends in a blood bath?" Callum said under his breath, leaning his forearms on top of his knees.

"Grow up, Callum," Charlie sighed.

Callum laughed. "Mate, I'm older than you."

The jokes ended as the sharp, steady *tap tap tap* of stiletto heels echoed across the tiled floor. Emilien sat up and as if on a second thought, pulled a hand through his hair once, twice, then brushed the front of his black button down silk shirt.

The last time Izzy saw Adette, her dagger was embedded hilt deep in the woman's chest. As she sauntered into the room, flanked by Henry and two other men in black, Izzy could not tear her eyes away from that spot on her chest. She had survived that wound. There was only one way she could've survived that. Panic coursed through Izzy and Adette's bright blue eyes shot up to meet hers, murder hardening the edges around them before she focused in on Emilien. The group stopped in front of him and the two guards pulled their balaclavas off. A mess of tightly curled golden hair to match the golden hazel eyes of the man who had caught her on the stairs had her stomach clenching. *Not Noah.* But of course it wasn't. It couldn't be. The man next to him leaned in as Not-Noah whispered something in his ear. His deep brown eyes quickly spotted Izzy and Charlie, dancing between the two of them. Izzy narrowed a sharp glare back at him. His eyes widened a fraction at her challenge.

Adette's heavy French accent interrupted their interlude. "Emil, *ça fait longtemps*[52]?"

Emilien's gaze tore through her, transfixed. "*Trop long, mon amour*[53]," he replied, the words falling out in a gasp. He cleared his throat, looking away from her before glancing back up. A soft, sad smile pulled on her red painted lips before her gaze shifted to Izzy. Hatred marred her beautiful face and Izzy stood a little taller knowing she could invoke such a sudden shift in the woman. Then she remembered the hilt of her knife sticking out of her chest again. A hard swallow worked its way down her throat.

"And I see you've brought guests. New friends?" Adette cooed.

Emilien looked back at Izzy and grimaced. "Something like that."

Adette's gaze tore through her as she looked her up and down. Raising a perfectly manicured hand, Adette snapped and Not-Noah stepped forward. She leaned back and whispered something into his ear and a faint flush tinted his bronze neck. He straightened then nodded to the other man before they both disappeared out the door.

"I had dinner prepared for you before you head to your *chambres*[54]. I figured after your travels you might be…hungry." Adette's eyes flickered to Charlie.

Izzy felt him stiffen next to her. Good. At least she wasn't the only one freaking the fuck out.

"Please follow me," Adette continued, walking toward the door. "I hope you don't mind eating inside. The heat is too much, *non*?" She turned sideways, glancing once more at Izzy before Emilien stepped forward. Adette smiled at her husband, looping her arm through his and he looked down at the touch with tormented adoration. Yet Izzy could see the happiness radiating off him in that connection. Henry stood outside the door as they exited and watched the entwined couple, awash in a medley of horror, anger, and hurt. He followed them, staring daggers into the back of Emilien's head as he laughed at something Adette said. The rest of them filed out, leaving Charlie, Izzy, and Callum standing in the room.

Callum stood, brushing his hands off on his cargo pants. "Well, looks like I lost my own bet with myself." He disappeared out the door.

Charlie waited a minute before he leaned in close to her and asked, "Are you okay?"

"Are any of us okay?" she responded, her voice on the edges of shrill terror. She stepped toward the door, following the rest of the group out. He matched her steps.

"Good point," he murmured as they passed the empty bar, all the patrons gone except the bartender watching them, drying glasses. Charlie let out an exasperated huff. "I have been in some wild scenarios and I'll be honest, I do not know how to act in this one."

Comforting, she thought as they walked through the gilded halls of the exquisite hotel. How had Adette commandeered all of this?

"Let's just...play it by ear. Fake it till we make it, right?" Izzy jabbed Charlie in the ribs playfully and a smile cracked his cold expression. But on the inside, she heard the truth. That quickened heart rate, as jumpy as the man holding it in.

The group led them into a large banquet room where one long table had been set with fine China and silverware. Bottles of wine speckled the table alongside candles blazing in the dim lighting. A man stood in the corner, a stoic statue as they all found seats. Adette sat on one end of the table and Harry on the other, keeping each other in their sights. The man in the corner stepped forward and began directing people to seats that apparently had been assigned. Izzy was pulled from Charlie and placed to the right of Henry. At least she still had a clear view of the door. Callum sat across from her, smirking. Charlie sat next to Adette, across from Emilien. Their driver and his accomplice sat down by Emilien and Charlie. The brown eyed battle-ready man from Adette's crew sank into the seat next to Izzy, leaving the one next to Callum empty.

Izzy became acutely aware that her only ally in that room was a *nervous* gangster and maybe a vampire twenty years her senior who only wanted to fuck her. Or fight her? She hadn't figured out entirely what Callum wanted and would waste no thoughts on figuring it out.

The man next to Izzy relieved himself of his heavy vest, setting it on the back of his polished mahogany seat. Izzy studied him as he removed a gun and two knives, setting both in the table in front of him. He caught her looking and gave her a tight smile.

"Never too careful though, right?" he drawled with a wink that made her shiver.

A couple more guards walked into the room and stood sentry next to its opening. The door swung open once more and Not-Noah rushed in a flurry, pulling off his vest as he made his way to the seat next to Callum. He didn't bother with putting any weapons on the table.

Izzy attempted to tear her eyes away from him but the longer she looked, the more he resembled Noah. Her heart thudded in her chest and Callum gave her a quizzical look. She shook her head, blinking a few times and taking several large gulps of water. So, this is where she would lose her mind. Would Barry understand? Did Lando foresee that this would happen? Did Emilien? What was insanity like as a vampire? Hadn't she already felt insane the entire time she had been one?

She looked up again, hoping the man had morphed into some hideous caricature of what she had seen. He didn't. If anything, the familiarity engraved deeper into her mind, never to be erased. Alarmed, she glanced down the table, seeking Charlie's gaze. For comfort? Fuck, she couldn't unpack that thought right then as her heart lurched in her chest. Charlie sat deep in conversation with Emilien and Adette. In panic, Izzy looked across the table to Callum, who had been studying her with a concerned curiosity, his chin rested on top of his intertwined fingers.

"You okay, pretty? The heat getting to you already?" he joked, a morbid twinkle in his silver-grey eyes.

God, that did not fucking help.

Henry cleared his throat just as Izzy's grip tightened around the dagger sheathed on her thigh. She snapped out of her panic, the steadily increasing static in her mind silencing to the low murmurs of conversation around them. Blood rushed back into her knuckles as she reached for her glass to take another gulp of water.

"I don't believe we have been formally introduced. I'm Henry Holt," the orange haired man said to her, a crooked grin on his face.

She glanced once more to not-Noah, her heartbeat picking up immediately then returned her focus to the older man next to her.

"Isabella, Izzy...Ciampi," she replied, handing him a clammy palm.

He took it in his own weak grip. Weak grips made her nervous. Weak grips meant men who either couldn't hold their own or underestimated her. Both of those made them dangerous if she stood in the way of what they wanted. Fucking fragile ass egos.

"Callum Kimble," Callum chimed in, heavy on the accent.

"Ah, United or City?" Henry asked Callum, his eyes lighting up behind his wire rimmed glasses as he released Izzy's hold.

Callum grinned, "United until the day I die." He winked, taking a drink of water from his glass. "However, I root for City when we aren't playing them."

Great. Another fucking conversation about sports. Many organizations had crumbled in the aftermath of the vampire revolution, specifically sports that didn't pay their players as much as they could make as personal guards or in private blood banks to the rich and powerful. Why a vampire felt the need to employ an athletic mortal to protect them? That was a different discussion, one she'd never gotten around to indulging.

"So, *Izzy*," the man to her left said and she shifted her gaze to him. He reached across the table to grab one of the bottles of wine, a red from Spain. He poured some in her glass, then the man's across the table, before he put some into his own. He picked up his glass, leaned back in his chair and studied her with humorless eyes. "What's your story?"

Her eyes narrowed and the man across the table mirrored her expression.

"You pour me a drink without my consent, don't even ask me my name, and then want to know my life story?" She scoffed. The man next to her choked, nearly spilling crimson wine onto the table as he hastily set his glass down.

Not-Noah smiled and it felt like an electric shock. "She makes a point, Malik," he said, smirking as he took a sip of his own wine. Izzy kept her glass on the table. He glanced to it then to her before he looked to the man next to her, Malik. "Might I suggest some introductions?"

Malik rolled his eyes. "Sorry if I don't find myself entertaining strange women often these days." He shifted in his seat to face her some and held his hand out. "I'm Malik. That asshole across the table is..."

"Benji," he announced enthusiastically, standing up some to reach far across the table to intercept their handshake.

Izzy didn't move. Izzy couldn't move. She couldn't breathe. *Benji.* There was no fucking way this was Noah's brother. Unless...her eyes snapped up to his, searching for answers in those gilded pools.

"Fucking hell, sit back down. You're terrifying her," Malik said, swatting Benji's hand away. But she couldn't see them. Her mind reeled. *Benji.* No wonder he looked like Noah. But...he was supposed to be dead.

"You're supposed to be dead," she whispered.

Benji's eyes twinkled as he squinted at her, tilting his head, hand still extended toward her. "What was that?"

Malik eyed her suspiciously, lips parted slightly when Adette rose, clinking a spoon against her own glass.

"*Calme, s'il te plâit*[55]." The room went silent and all eyes fell onto her beautiful face. All except Malik's. His gaze seared into Izzy's face as she looked at the woman, her mind reeling.

Would he know who she was?

How would he know who she was?

He was supposed to be dead.

"I am so happy to reunite old friends and new," she smiled down to Henry and then Emilien. "Please, raise your glass and let us toast to renewing those bonds, *oui*?"

"*Oui*," the room replied in unison.

Izzy murmured, "*Oui*," under her breath and took a large gulp of wine without clinking it with any of the raised glasses before her. The men around her eyed her warily as they touched their glasses and took sips.

"So, your name?" Malik said as Adette sat down, motioning to the guards at the door. One stuck his head out the door. A moment later people in simple black kitchen uniforms began filing in. Izzy turned her focus on Benji and Malik, her vision tunneling in on them.

"Izzy, but you already heard that," she said, gesturing to Henry. The man was deep in conversation with Callum over the merits of education in London versus Manchester and Izzy was glad she didn't have to entertain Emilien's second for the evening while her entire sense of reality fell apart around her.

"Yeah, we caught that, but tell us something fascinating. What's your greatest fear? Who was your first bully? How would you like to die?" Benji asked, the excitement in his voice raising her own blood pressure. His golden eyes shined with mischief.

"Benji, please. Let's not be morbid. How about...what do you like to do?" Malik sighed, exasperated. He took another sip of wine.

"Um, I research. I'm a researcher. Anthropology," she said, stumbling over her words. Who was she or rather, who did she want to be to these men? She glanced down the table to Charlie, still lost in conversation with Emilien and Adette. He had done a piss poor job preparing her for the politics of this life. Fuck him.

Benji's face lit up and he leaned forward, abandoning his glass. "Oh, fascinating. So, like dinosaurs and stuff?"

Izzy rolled her eyes, shifting her focus back to the men

near her and taking another sip of her wine before she knew what she was doing. Alarmed, she quickly set the glass back down. She needed to keep her wits about her. "Um, no, that's paleontology. I study human behavior, specifically cultural behavior around times of crisis or major global change."

Benji sat back in his seat, picking up his glass with a huff. "Less fascinating but still interesting. You would like my brother," he added and her heart stopped.

Malik gave Benji a look before he asked, "And St. Louis? You live there?"

"Yes," she breathed out, her gaze locked on Benji. The wait staff were a blur of black behind him. *His brother.*

"And you do so willingly?" Malik sneered, taking another sip of wine.

Izzy snapped out of her trance. "Better than a city built on a delta. Like trying to put lipstick on a pig, don't you think?"

Malik chuckled and said, "*Touché.*"

Izzy leaned back in her seat and looked up.

Straight into the familiar golden gaze that haunted her every waking and sleeping memory, a scar running down the middle of his perfect lower lip.

That time her heart truly stopped beating.

And he looked away from her, his face devoid of expression. Devoid of recognition. Devoid of anything.

That time she felt the crack rip through her chest as her heart broke.

CHAPTER TWENTY-FIVE
IZZY

The rest of dinner disappeared as she watched Noah.

Noah.

She watched as he stood in the back of the room. She watched the bored expression on his face. She watched as he cleared plates with indifference to those seated at the table. She watched as he reached in front of her. He didn't even fucking flinch when his arm brushed her shoulder as he grabbed her untouched plate of food.

Malik and Benji exchanged a look and turned their conversation to Emilien's other two men seated next to them. Occasionally Malik would glance over at Izzy, his thick black brows pinched as his eyes skated over her. But she didn't care. She could not tear her attention away from Noah.

At the end of dinner, as Noah disappeared out the door with the rest of the kitchen staff, the world around her came back into hazy focus, as if waking from a dream. The tension radiated off Emilien and Adette as they were escorted back out of The Roosevelt, Benji and Malik with their small crew as they walked down the boisterous street. A bottle of wine passed between them, laughter muffled in her ears as she watched them attempt to sing along to the jazz tunes on the street.

Izzy followed behind, numb, empty. The music sounded grey. The colors of the vibrant street muted.

He *left* her and didn't even *pretend* to not know her. She was *nothing* to him.

"Hey," Charlie said, brushing up next to her. She didn't move. He told her his evening had been spent as mediator as a heated discussion erupted between Emilien and Adette throughout dinner. He never got a chance to look up from them as heavy tension flowed from their end of the table.

One foot in front of the other. That's all she needed to do. Walk. She could walk. Charlie pinched his lips together and shoved his hands into his pocket, walking side by side in silence. The journey ended quickly and soon they were welcomed into another hotel, led up plush carpeted stairs to the second floor. Emilien didn't wait long after Malik told him his room number, striding toward the door and slamming it shut. Callum strolled to the room across from his boss, eying the man's door with pursed lips before disappearing into his own. The driver and his passenger filled the two rooms next to him. Charlie went in the door next to Emilien's and Izzy into the one next to it.

"Enjoy your stay," Benji said with a sly smirk, then threw his arm over Malik's shoulders. The two men disappeared down the hall giggling. Izzy scoffed and threw her door shut.

A plush queen-sized bed filled most of the space. There was a armchair next to the single window in the room. Izzy tossed her leather bag into it and sank to the soft carpeted floor. Tears she wanted never came. Instead, a knock sounded from the wooden door on the wall separating her room from Charlie's. She unlocked it and pulled it open from the floor. Charlie held up a bottle of wine and two plastic cups, grinning as he scanned the room. When he didn't see her right away, he frowned. Then looked down.

He moved to the edge of her bed, sitting down to face her. His frown etched lines into his forehead, the blue black of his hair shadowing them. He pulled the half-removed cork from the bottle and poured some of the crimson liquid into the cup. Izzy took the one he offered her. He drained his own small cup in three gulps and refilled it before looking to her.

"You wanna tell me what's wrong?" he asked. She stared at the end of the immaculate bed, tears threatening to brim her eyes and yet, they wouldn't.

"He was there," she whispered. Her cup rattled precariously as she held it by the rim.

Charlie's brows furrowed. "Who was there?"

Flashes of dark mahogany hair between her fingers, the tang of blood as they came together, the boom of explosions, the cloud of dust chasing her to the street, the emptiness that followed.

"Noah." His name escaped her lips like a tidal wave and with it, her heart clenched. Her grip seized and the plastic cup fell to the floor. Red splashed across the pristine ivory pile. Clutching her hand to her chest, she sat up on her knees, pulling a box of tissues down from a small dresser in a useless attempt to soak up the ever growing stain.

"Fuck," she sobbed, frantically pressing the wet glop of tissues into the floor while still clutching her heart.

Charlie bent down next to her, holding out a white towel. He must have grabbed it while she panic- cleaned.

"Thanks," she mumbled and pressed it into the spot. It wasn't great but better than her first attempt. Once the towel held nearly the same ruddy color as the floor, she sat back in defeat, letting her head fall against the door to the hallway.

A dense silence filled the air.

"What do you mean Noah was there?" Charlie asked, walking on his knees to sit next to her.

She spoke through the tears finally flowing freely down her face. "I mean, he was fucking there. With them. And I'm pretty sure that was his brother sitting by me. Talking to me. Fuck." She slammed her head back against the door and groaned in pain.

Charlie grabbed her hand, twisting himself around until he knelt in front of her. His other hand cradled the back of her head. "Hey, wow. Fuck. How did I miss that?" He shook his head and then focused back on Izzy. "Did he say anything to you?"

She squeezed her eyes tight and a sob wracked through her body. "No. That's the thing. He didn't even act like he knew me. He didn't even notice me. I was invisible to him."

"Fuck, Izzy," Charlie said, pulling her to his chest. She welcomed the comfort of his embrace, leaning into his strong muscles as she sobbed. He held her for several minutes, letting her breathing return to normal. When he pulled back, he searched her face then stood, dragging her up with him. They walked across the threshold into his room. He put her down on the edge of his bed and then left, coming back a few seconds later with the bottle of wine. Handing it to her, he sat down beside her with a sigh.

She took several long pulls from the bottle until she had to stop for a breath. She passed him the bottle and he set it on the floor.

"Are you okay? I mean, are you going to be okay? With him being here?" He studied her, reaching up to push a curl behind her ear and setting a hand behind her neck.

She looked up at him through blurry, swollen eyes and nodded. "Yeah, it's just…all these months I wondered…I thought maybe he might have planned it all, been in on it all. But a part of me thought, hoped…maybe he hadn't been. But now?" She looked into his ocean eyes. A warm pool of shades swirled within them, the steady *thump thump thump* of his heart beat calmed her. "Now, I know."

Charlie nodded, a small frown on his face as he glanced to her lips and then back to her eyes. He swallowed. She watched the motion and reached up with a hand to graze her fingers against the hard line of his throat. She followed the line of his collarbone, tracing back up the line of his jugular vein.

Before she knew what she was doing she leaned forward. He stiffened beneath her as she pressed her lips to the hollow spot of his throat. She felt him relax as he let out a breath, so she did it again. His voice vibrated against her lips as he said, "Izzy, please don't do this to me."

"Do what," she asked rhetorically as her lips traveled up his neck, placing soft kisses along the way.

"Break my heart," he whispered as she pressed her lips against his cheek. She pulled back to look him in those azure pools, letting herself get lost in them.

"Then don't let me," she purred, leaning toward him. As her lips hovered his own, she felt him release a shaky breath and for a moment she regretted it all. Regretted doing this to him, even if he had done so much worse to her. But she needed to feel *something* other than the agony Noah caused her. So, when he leaned in and their lips met, she didn't pull away. She laced her hand into his thick, black hair and pulled his mouth against her. He grabbed her waist and pulled her onto his lap. He fell into the bed with her on top of him. Their kiss deepened. Her hands roamed to the hard planes of his chest and she began unbuttoning his shirt. His grip tightened around her wrist suddenly and he pushed her up.

She hovered a foot above him, looking at him with a brow raised and a question on her lips.

"This isn't real. I can't do this if it isn't real," he breathed out through his swollen lips. She could feel his pulse through them. She wanted to feel it again. She leaned back in and he pressed her away further. She sat up and looked down at him, puzzled. He shook his head and then ran both hands down his face, groaning in despair.

Propping himself up on his elbows, he looked at her and said, "Go back to your room, Izzy."

Hurt, she climbed off him. She studied him for a moment then nodded her head. Before she turned to go back to her room though, she reached down and grabbed the half full bottle of wine off the floor. Slamming the door between their rooms shut, she sank back to the floor next to the damning stain hidden under an equally stained towel and drained the bottle.

And yet she felt *everything*.

CHAPTER TWENTY-SIX
NOAH

The stars twinkled in the steamy sky above and Noah felt like dying. His heart rate teetered on the edge of arrest. The relentless pounding began the moment he walked into that room and laid his eyes on her.

"Fuck," he cursed through his clenched jaw, hands gripping the stone wall around the rooftop of The Roosevelt. The rough rock bit into his palm. He searched the stars again, uncertain what he wanted…needed to see in them. Direction? Purpose? A fucking sign as to what he should do next?

In answer, a cloud rolled in and blocked out his view.

"Sheesh, what a fucking nightmare blunt rotation that would make," Benji drawled, appearing beside Noah. He leaned a hip against the wall, oblivious to turmoil ripping through Noah's mind.

How had everything gone *so wrong*? How could Izzy be *here*? In the depths of Adette's stronghold?

Fuck.

Benji turned around, resting his elbow on the top of the

grey stone to scan the street below. "Who would've thought The Society would be in such chaos? Phew, Adette really must have done a number to Emilien. I didn't catch enough of their conversation but it looked...intense." He huffed out a sigh but Noah barely heard him speak.

The Society. What the fuck was Izzy doing with the fucking Society? He barely registered the rest of the people in the room once their eyes met. It took everything in him to not fly across the table and rip her free from the hell they were in. It would've been both of their endings, but in that moment, he felt he could've taken down every vampire in the city to free her.

But would she have come with him?

He raised a hand to run it through his hair, but stopped midway, clenching it into a fist when he saw it start to tremble.

"Who was that girl you and Malik were talking to?" He kept his tone even despite the staccato racing in his veins.

Benji tossed him a sly smile and looked back to the city, "You saw her too? I swear every other guy and a few of the women even asked me about her on the way up here. She is alluring, if a bit dull. Not even halfway through the dinner she just went mute. But Malik and I were supposed to talk to the men sitting next to us anyway. Did you know they drove straight through Memphis to get here? Crazy. They also kept looking at that guy sitting next to Henry, like they were studying his reaction to this whole shitshow, not Emilien's. Weird dynamic." His brother shook his head.

Noah replayed the look on her face as he had looked away, watching her out of his peripheral while he tried to focus on not getting them both killed. The hurt that had shined bright in her emerald eyes. His chest clenched.

"Anyway, I wanted to talk to you about her anyway," Benji said, interrupting Noah's thoughts.

"Who?"

"Isabella Ciampi. Adette seems suspicious by her presence tonight too. We already have a kitchen crew over there now but I'm going to have you do housekeeping. You're a clean freak anyway and we need information."

Noah turned to his brother. "You want me to spy on a gang of vampires?"

Benji shifted to face him. "Like that's hardly a new role for you."

Noah's jaw tightened. "And when Emilien recognizes me? You remember we worked for him once, right?"

Benji waved a hand at him. "That's old news. Emilien didn't really want or need us. We were nothing but fodder for him. Well, at least he wanted us to be," Benji gave him a wink.

"I'm being serious, Benji. How am I supposed to just spy on them when I bring them fresh towels every day and make their beds?"

"Come on, Noh. You're so dumb for such a smart guy. Do it when they are not there. Adette is going to give them the full tour of the city. Go then," Benji's words edged with a touch of condescension.

"And what about my security detail?" Noah quipped.

Benji turned back to the pool as a couple giggles wafted from the water. "Sancho will help, he's just as anal as you, and you will still have Frank."

Noah had never bothered to learn his new shadow's name.

"Great. And I guess doing this task will help regain some of your trust in me?" Noah said, studying the rough edge of his palm.

Benji gave him an incredulous look. "Nah man, it will

help you contribute to the mission and help us take down that slimy organization, once and for all. They ruined our city. They ruined the world. We finally have a shot at giving them what they deserve, don't you see that?"

Noah gripped his hand tighter and nodded.

"Find their weakness, brother," Benji said, pushing off the wall and clapping a palm on Noah's shoulder. Noah flinched but his brother didn't see it as he strode over to the pool, already unbuttoning his shirt.

Find their weakness.

Before they found his.

He glanced down the road to the roof of the Hotel Maison and then turned around, heading straight for the stairwell.

Staring down the stairwell exhausted Noah so with a sigh, he walked over to the elevator and punched the down arrow. Long seconds passed and the bell rang. Stepping into the metal box, he stared at his reflection in the mirror along the back of the elevator. The door closed behind him and the movement made him flinch. Exhaling, he punched the floor button on the panel and ran a hand over his face as he descended.

Spy on The Society. The Society that consisted of his ex-boss, his ex-colleague, and his... He groaned, pinching the bridge of his nose hard. Fuck, why was Izzy even with them? The thought of spying on her alone made his skin crawl.

The bell dinged and Noah stepped out onto the floor, making the right-hand turn and the twenty paces to his and Benji's suite. He turned the handle, expecting it to be locked, as he fished the key out of his pocket. To his surprise, the handle gave and he slowly pushed it into the dark space. His movement triggered a light switch, brightening clinical white walls with stainless-steel cabinets and counters around him. He froze. This was not his suite.

He started to back out of the room when voices drifted down the hallway. Slipping back in, he pressed the door shut quietly and frantically searched for the light switch to manually turn them off. Keeping his ear pressed to the door, he reached a hand out toward the switch on his right. The voices grew louder. His fingertips brushed the edge and then found purchase and pressed. An audible click sounded and then the room descended into darkness just as voices floated through the space under the door.

"I'm just afraid we rushed this. Hell, it was rushed to begin with, but this seems to have taken a turn," a male voice said. Two shadows appeared in the light shining under the door. Noah held his breath and prayed there was a God out there that would keep them in the hallway.

"I hear what you're saying. The wasting is getting bad. She's exclusively on the special blend now. Can't even stomach the ordinary stuff. It's awful." Tones of empathy and disgust coated the words from the female voice responding to the man.

The footsteps shuffled away and Noah couldn't make out what the man said in reply. He waited a few more minutes to ensure the coast cleared before he let out a heavy breath.

He turned his back to the door, staring off into the darkness of the room. A special blend? He remembered the vials of blood he had stumbled upon in the barge but most of those seemed to be the same "blend" and they had plenty of them.

The only difference had been on his own vial.

Feeling his luck growing thinner by the second, Noah shook his head and slowly pulled the door open. Peeking his head out, he listened for any more voices. Silence fell across the corridor and he jogged out of the room, down the hall into the stairwell, not trusting the elevator ever again. As his footfalls set a steady, quiet rhythm, he tried to process what he had heard.

The *recours*, cure for vampirism, wasn't working. At least not in the way they had wanted. And Noah had to get out of there. Both of them.

CHAPTER TWENTY-SEVEN
IZZY

Callum knocked on her door at five forty-five in the morning, like the bastard he was.

"We need to be ready by eight-thirty," he said, first eying her mass of disheveled dark red curls and then the crimson stain on the floor. He quirked a brow at her and added, "Having fun without me again?"

"Fuck off, freak," she growled and slammed her door in his face. Ready for what? The entire drive down here had been a performance in how well Emilien could sleep in a vehicle. As far as she could tell, there was no plan beyond coming to New Orleans.

She turned her back to the door. The soft down comforter on the bed beckoned her while the door to Charlie's room and offending stain next to it filled her with a rush of embarrassment. How had she been so stupid to allow herself to fucking kiss Charlie? Charlie! The man who spent their entire pseudo-relationship controlling her every move and flying off the handle if she took one step without his knowledge. Who hit her in a fit of rage and tore out of her apartment, literally leaving her front door hanging off the hinges. Who had killed her best friend, the only person she trusted with her life.

Instead of allowing herself to crawl back into bed, she shuffled into the bathroom, leaving the lights turned off, and cranked the shower to the hottest setting possible. Standing under the liquid inferno, hands braced on the tile wall, she let it singe her skin to a bright red before turning the heat down. Her mind focused on the pain as blood throbbed against the burning flesh on her chest. It meddled with the pain of rejection she felt last night when Noah walked right into the room and pretended he had never even known her. Not even a glance. A signal he *saw* her. Nothing but stoic indifference. As if in the end, she had been nothing but a mere pawn in a game she didn't know she was playing.

A sigh rattled through her and she shut the water off. She climbed out of the stall, wrapping a towel around her hair and then around her body. That was the last of them, after Charlie sacrificed one to her desperate emergency wine cleanup. She would need to track some more down later.

Her stomach grumbled. Fuck, she was going to have to find something to eat too. Distracted by the soul-shattering revelations during dinner, she hadn't even touched her food. She was running on red wine and spite.

Quickly tossing on a large linen shirt and matching shorts, she strode out the door, hair still damp, and headed toward the stairs. Each creaked a different tune as she descended; stealth be damned. Though she didn't think it mattered much. She was pretty certain someone knew her exact whereabouts from the moment they had entered the city limits. She walked across the lobby into a large dining area, round tables scattered throughout, ready for the morning rush. In the back of the room, she saw the swinging doors and heard the clattering of a kitchen.

She pushed the door in and immediately stopped, along with a crew of five men and women. One man, heavier built with tattoos etching his hands said, "*Buenos días, señorita*[56]. Did you get lost or can we help you with something?"

She hugged her middle, shifting uncomfortably with so many pairs of eyes on her. *So many heart beats thrumming in one room.* "Um, I missed dinner last night so I just wanted to find something to eat."

The man glanced warily around the kitchen as the rest of the crew murmured to each other. "Was the supply in your room not to your satisfaction?"

Supply? Her brow furrowed. Recognizing her confusion, the man set down the towel in his hand and walked to her. "Can you show me to your room so I can check for you?"

She peered up at him and nodded, following him out the door. The stairs groaned in protest under his weight but held. He walked right up to her room, unnerving her, and unlocked the door with a key from his pocket. Izzy watched him from the threshold, hesitant to allow the door to close her in with him.

Opening the small fridge in the corner, he stepped back and motioned for her to see. Inside were bags, at least twenty, stacked and filled with a dark red liquid. Blood bags. She gulped, feeling her own blood heat in her cheeks. She met the man's eyes, the encouraging smile he had.

"Would you prefer a different method? We have a few women and men on staff who are happy to accommodate—"

Oh my God!

"No! No, I mean, that's unnecessary," she rushed out through a nervous chuckle. "This is…fine. Thank you. I didn't even think to check first."

He gave her an appraising nod and then left.

A monster. That's what she was to these people. She enjoyed eating regular food, it was still necessary. She was still alive after all, still *human*. The blood craving came from some more scientific jargon Emilien never got around to elaborating on, but she felt two different versions of hunger. But to this group, she was only a blood sucking monster and nothing more.

Sighing, she crossed the room and pulled open the fridge door, grabbing a cool bag. Long rubber straws extended from each, like a modified hospital blood bag.

Mortified, she sat on the floor and sucked. Then a thought had her stopping.

A few women and men on staff who are happy to accommodate. How many vampires were still in the city that needed to be accommodated? Losing her appetite, she stuck the bag back in the fridge and pulled back the curtains on her window. Beyond lay a small balcony with a wrought iron banister. Running her hands along the top edge of the pane, she found a small lock and handle. Undoing the clasp, she pushed and the window swung out. A wall of sticky air hit her and she knew her hair would be a giant frizz ball in seconds but she didn't care as she climbed out onto the balcony. The space was large, extending down what would be the hallway, and connecting all the rooms to this one area.

Sunrise lingering on the horizon but for now, the city sat in darkened silence, the parties long died out. Sitting on the edge, palms scraping as she wrapped her hands around the rough metal, she peered out into the twilight sky, faint stars still twinkling above.

❖

They met in the lobby at eight twenty-eight. Izzy checked her phone to make sure they were on time and to respond to Barry's live streaming messages about the intern applications he had received so far. There were two and one was someone aspiring to be a mortician.

"How lovely of you all to meet so early," Adette announced as she waltzed through the front door in a flurry of movement. She wore a flowy ivory dress that billowed behind her. Harry followed close behind, getting whipped in the face with cloth as the air shifted with the air conditioning inside. Two more men came in behind them. Malik and Benji.

Izzy went to return her attention to her phone when one more figure darkened the tinted glass.

And then in walked Noah.

They locked eyes for a fleeting moment. And yet within it her world stopped and started again. He broke their gaze to look at Benji. His brother, their similarities so striking when they stood next to each other, turned to him and whispered something. Noah nodded and turned toward the stairs. Izzy tracked his movement and before he ascended the carpeted staircase, she swore he glanced in her direction.

"Holy shit," Charlie mumbled under his breath next to her. She hadn't noticed him sidle up to her. Fuck, she needed to get her mind straight. He could've been anyone.

She shoved her phone into her pocket and quickly glanced over him. If last night bothered him, he didn't show it. Which made the whole thing even worse. Every man in her life ignored her presence in different ways.

Emilien entered from a dark hallway behind the front desk as Noah made a silent climb up the stairs. His attention was focused on his ex-wife as she approached him, leaning in to kiss him on each cheek.

"Today is a bit of a stormy day, so I apologize for the

humidity, but I think you'll be happy for the clouds." Her eyes danced from Emilien to Callum and then Charlie before they settled on Izzy. "We have our tinted vehicles outside as well. We will need to split up when we drive, but the trips will be short. In fact," she turned to Malik and Benji, the men nodding and moving to the front door, "the first trip will be on foot. I want to show you the city." She beamed at Emilien and for a moment, Izzy got lost in the look of awe on the man's face. Then it disappeared, fading into a scowl.

"Lead the way," he growled, motioning to the open doors spilling in the steamy air from outside.

Adette walked out the door, immediately flanked by a large man dressed in all black. A shadow to the incandescent aura of her. Emilien stepped up beside her, further shrouding her in darkness. The rest of the group followed out the door. Izzy chanced one last look up the empty stairs, her chest twinging as she trickled out behind Charlie. As she passed through the wall of air conditioning keeping the oppressive heat out, her gaze caught on Malik's holding the glass door open. Her heart quickened and she tossed a wide brim hat and sunglasses on before sidling up next to Charlie.

Charlie glanced up at the overcast sky and then to the group ahead of them. The streets were quiet at this hour, the revelers sleeping away until the night began again. To go out at night...

A woman ahead of them turned, her wavy brown hair flowing behind her as piercing green eyes met Izzy's. Her immediate glare caused Izzy to frown and she turned to Charlie to ask him about the rest of their group that morning when Malik appeared next to him. She felt Benji's presence on her other side before he spoke.

"So, have either of you been to NOLA before?" Benji drawled, adding an extra New Orleans flair to the question.

Charlie grinned. "Not in a way I would remember it."

Benji and Malik barked out a laugh but Izzy eyed Charlie warily. When would he have gone to New Orleans?

"My brother would know more about the connection, but does it compare to St. Louis?" Benji added. They approached an intersection and turned right. A red streetcar rang its bell as it passed, patrons sitting down or standing up. Some watching the sights go by, others engrossed in reading a book or looking at their phone. Izzy paused, watching it pass. It seemed so normal. Such an ordinary scene. Vastly different from the picture Noah had painted of the city. Of the *lie* he had served her on a golden platter.

The others in her little group stopped as she gaped at the simplicity of it all. Charlie cleared his throat and the confused heartbreak in his eyes mirrored her own. How could this be?

She cleared her throat and continued walking. "They are a bit different," she finally responded.

Benji nodded his head, studying her profile for a second before looking around the area appreciatively. It was Malik's gaze she felt burning her under the shade of her hat. She studied the buildings as they passed. A few were nothing more than piles of yellow or grey stone rubble, remnants of hand painted letters spelling out the torment that had apparently grasped this place.

Benji shocked through the silence with another question. "And what of my brother? I heard he was working at a university and you mentioned you were a researcher. You can't miss him. Looks like a less handsome version of me." He leaned over to wink up at her from under the brim of her hat before he smiled at a scowling Malik on the other side of Charlie.

The stagnant air caught in her lungs and she opened her

mouth to speak but nothing came out. Malik's gaze tightened on her, searing into her. Her fingers itched to reach up and rub her neck, to find it scorched beneath his gaze. Instead, she kept her gaze focused ahead, Charlie brushing his shoulder against her own.

"I...um, didn't see him," she lied. The words were sandpaper on her tongue. He was nothing to her. She swallowed the tears the thought threatened to loosen. "The university is surprisingly big, all things considered," she added for clarity.

Her response seemed to satiate Benji as he watched some people get off the streetcar, waving at them. She let out a sigh of relief.

Adette continued to lead them down the palm tree lined road. Their little quartet in the back walked along in silence. Laughter sounded from the larger group ahead. Izzy focused on the woman with the silky brown hair. Her head was turned, as if listening in as Izzy stumbled over her answers about St. Louis and Noah.

"Maybe you guys can swap stories later," Malik said out of nowhere.

Izzy stumbled and this time Charlie caught her. "I'm okay," she whispered, nodding her head at his concerned look. She peered up over her sunglasses to see Malik watching her, pure malice in his eyes. She held her breath.

Adette's voice broke through the tension. "Eyes up! Here is the *pièce de résistance*. Bourbon Street."

Malik's eyes tore away from Izzy's as he looked ahead to the woman in charge. Izzy straightened, catching a glance with Charlie. His eyes were soft with concern as he studied her face. She gave him a tight smile and faced the woman. She stood before them, arms spread as they approached the intersection. A band played down the road, in the middle of the street, the whines of saxophones and expressive beats of the drum filled the air. People stood around, watching. Some dancing. Everyone smiling.

"*C'est incroyable*[57]," Emilien said in awe.

Izzy couldn't help but agree. But it was Callum's vicious stare settled on his boss she studied in that moment.

❖

The tour took them on a loop down Bourbon Street and then up St. Louis Street before turning around, heading back toward the hotel.

Outside the Maison Hotel, Adette leaned in and said something to Emilien. He nodded his head and then she turned to the rest of the group. Callum kept his gaze trained on his boss.

"I have arranged for a lunch a bit outside of the city so we will take a short trip, but I promise it will be worth it." The words floated on the airy tone of her accent. Izzy tensed despite it. Outside of the city? This wasn't part of the plan. Fuck, she wasn't even sure if there was a plan. She had allowed them to charm her around the streets. They all had. Her heart raced.

Charlie reached for her hand and squeezed it. She thought about ripping it away, out of his grasp, especially as Malik watched them. But against her better judgment, her heart rate calmed with his reassuring touch. He still had her back, even after everything she had done.

"We have three cars," Adette said as the vehicles pulled up to the curb, a quiet group of valets stepping out of the vehicles and heading down the street. Nothing could be seen through the level of tint put on the windows.

Adette, Henry, and Emilien climbed into the first, her large guard climbing into the driver's seat. Callum and their drivers climbed into the second, the woman with the wavy hair climbing into the driver's seat. Which left Charlie and Izzy to continue their tenure with Malik and Benji. Malik climbed into the driver's seat. Charlie beat Benji to the passenger door and climbed in with smug ease. If Malik was startled by the tatted up Italian man grinning next to him, he didn't make it known.

Benji stepped up next to Izzy and said, "Ladies first," before pulling the door to the back seat open. She slipped into the leather bucket seat behind Malik, her eyes meeting the comforting blue of Charlie's. Benji followed and once he slammed the door shut behind him, the caravan of SUVs pulled away from the curb.

"Where exactly are we going?" Izzy asked, trepidation in her voice.

Malik studied her in the rear view mirror but it was Benji who spoke. "Laura Plantation, about an hour outside of town."

Izzy stiffened. An hour? Fucking hell, what had Emilien agreed to? "That's a heck of a drive for lunch."

Benji smiled. "But well worth it."

Charlie cut the tension by adding a new layer. "So, Benji, you worked for Emilien when he was in New Orleans?"

Izzy watched the jovial lines in Benji's face harden. "I did," was all Benji said in response.

Charlie turned to Malik. "And what about you?"

Malik shook his head. "No, I wasn't pulled into that mess, thankfully."

"But you were pulled into this one?"

Malik's grip on the steering wheel tightened. "I volunteered for a cause I felt just."

Charlie chuckled. "I suppose I can relate to that."

Malik threw him a sideways glance.

Izzy eyed Charlie, wondering about what play he was trying to make. He was versed in these types of scenarios, where every word dripped with twelve different meanings. But she couldn't decipher the purpose for building the tension in the car immediately. That seemed to be the nail in the conversational coffin though, and they rode in silence for the remaining forty-five minute drive. With their vehicles the only traffic on the road once they left the city limits, the trees blurred past, the murky green festering a growing ache in Izzy's chest.

The vehicle slowed and Izzy stirred, looking out the front windshield as they turned down a red gravel path. Oak trees grew on each side, towering over and joining limbs together to create a shady tunnel. Beyond, a large yellow house loomed, green shutters outlining the rows of windows on the first and second floor, a wrap around porch on each. A bright red gate stood open and expectant against the white picket fencing surrounding the home. The mansion, really. Charlie glanced over his shoulder at Izzy's look of wonder as they neared the home.

Benji snorted. "Yeah, everyone has the same reaction their first time pulling in here."

"Psh, first time? I have it every time. This place is insane," Malik added as he pulled the big SUV around, parking behind the second in their caravan.

Two lines furrowed between her brow as she glanced once more up at the home, the sun beam wooden carving mounted over the porch.

Sweltering, moist air flooded the vehicle as Benji opened the door, snapping her into the present. She stepped out, looking out across the property, the sunlight filtering through the Spanish moss and giant arms of the trees. For a moment, it felt like that foreign feeling of peace. Then she turned around to peer up at the house and noticed the fourth black SUV parked next to the first in their caravan, the one Emilien stood outside, holding a hand out for Adette as she stepped down.

"Are we meeting someone here?" The question set her pulse on fire as she asked it.

Benji followed her gaze and said, "Oh, that. We asked a few of the crew to come help assist with lunch and getting rooms ready."

Her brows furrowed. "Rooms?"

But Benji disappeared up the stairs into the plantation home. Malik's gaze crawled down her skin before he followed after Noah's brother. Charlie stepped out of the vehicle behind her.

"Remember your training," he whispered, sending a shiver down her spine.

The group ahead ushered them up the plank porch and into a set of double doors. Within, there was a large mahogany dining table laid out with place settings for them all. Once again, she was seated next to Malik and Benji, Charlie grouped with Callum and Emilien on the other end of the table, next to Adette.

Charlie and Callum gave each other a stare that held a conversation Izzy wasn't privy to understanding before they both turned their attention to their boss as the man stared adoringly up at his ex-wife.

"Please, sit. Make yourselves comfortable. We have a very special meal prepared for you," Adette said. As everyone lowered into their seats, a group of people filed in, an older man with a graying beard, an older woman, her hair in long braids and held back with a bandana, and a woman who appeared to be about Benji and Malik's age. Malik tensed as they entered but Benji beamed.

"Abel, Erlie! Shit, is that Willa?" Benji rose out of his chair, approaching the small group. Adette's lips thinned as she watched him but kept a smile painted on her face.

The man and woman set their platters of food on the sideboard, turning to face Benji as if in disbelief. The older woman stepped forward, putting his face between her arthritic hands.

"Benji? Is that you?" Her voice cracked but the accent held thick and strong.

Benji nodded his head underneath her touch. A tear ran down the woman's cheek as a curled hand went to her mouth, a squeak of a sob escaping from beneath it. Benji wrapped his arms around her, disappearing her from view.

Emilien cleared his throat, seeming to notice the irritation in Adette's eyes at the interruption. Benji let the woman go, quickly looking over his shoulder at his boss before turning back. He gripped the shoulders of the older man, tears glistening the edges of his sparkling brown eyes.

"Sorry to interrupt," Benji said, running a hand along the back of his neck. "I wasn't sure if you guys would still be in the area but I'm glad to see you. And even more glad it's your cooking we're about to eat." Benji grinned over his shoulder at Malik and then back at the couple before sitting down in his seat.

"As Benji suggested, the Reaux family is here to provide us with their famous Creole cooking. They are locals to the area and even had family on this plantation." The old man stiffened under Adette's words but worked quietly, uncovering the platter of food. Izzy's brows furrowed as she understood her meaning and she looked down the table to see Charlie with a similar expression on his face. The young woman with the couple, the Reauxs, followed the old man around the table, serving everyone a large spoonful of red beans and rice. Setting the empty platter back on the sideboard, he picked up the other and the young woman scooped a healthy portion of shrimp and crawfish next to the rice and beans.

Izzy inhaled the delectable smells. Her stomach growled as the spices hit her palate. She would not let the meal before her disappear before she even got a bite.

Once the man had served the last person, his wife grabbed the other empty platter. Adette raised her glass to them and everyone followed. The couple bowed, but the younger woman remained standing, watching, memorizing the face of everyone in the room. Her eyes locked on Izzy. Izzy's skin prickled as she held her glass up to her and then took a sip.

"*Bon appetit*," Adette called out to the table as the Reaux family left.

The meal passed in a communal drum of silverware on antique porcelain.

Once everyone's plates were nearly empty save for the tails and shells of shrimp and crawfish, they sat back in a comfortable silence.

A hushed conversation ensued down the table before Adette stood once more.

"I hope you all don't mind me being so forward but I would invite you all to stay this evening, enjoy the remarkable sunset this home has to offer and the sounds of nature. We've all been in the city life for *trop long, je pense*[58]."

Izzy froze, the meal in her stomach rolling uncomfortably.

Stay.

Here.

Remember your training. Instinct told her to keep her eyes, her focus on the biggest threat in the room. Her eyes roved over Benji across from her. He didn't seem remotely surprised by this news as he sucked the heads of his crawfish on his plate. Desperate, she looked down the table, her gaze catching with

Charlie's. A fire raged within his stare but the hard set of his lips told her to stay the course and not question it.

Easier fucking said than done, as her trembling hand reached for her glass, tasking a long sip to steady herself.

"Benji, please show Charlie, Callum and Izzy to their rooms. Mailk, come with me. I would like to discuss the security plans for the evening and tomorrow."

Malik nodded his head once, "Of course." He stood and followed her out of the room, Emilien and Henry in tow.

Benji stood, gesturing for them to follow. With trepidation, Izzy watched and mimicked Charlie's movements. They made their way along the porch to the stairwell outside. Sobs from behind a partially opened door caught Izzy's attention. She glanced at Benji and the rest of the group, each distracted in Benji's tour guide descriptions of the home and its history. She peered inside the door and her breath stopped.

The older woman held a tall man with dark, wavy hair, his broad shoulders and strong arms wrapped around her. Izzy's heart pounded in her chest as he looked up, only the profile of his face in view as he smiled. It was directed at the younger woman, returning the sentiment tenfold, and yet her own heart stuttered. As they moved to separate, Izzy ducked her head and hurried back to the rest of the group as they climbed the wooden stairs to the second floor. Benji continued his monologue but Charlie glanced behind him, quirking a brow at her. She shook her head.

Benji gestured Callum into the first room, Charlie into the next. As Charlie disappeared behind the shuttered wooden door, Benji opened the door next door.

"Here you are," he said with a sly smile. Then he disappeared back down the stairs.

She stepped in, eying the simply made four-poster bed

with its bright white quilt and the older style furniture around the space. A wall of windows lined the back of the room, all with curtains pulled over them. As she closed the wooden French doors they had come in through, twisting the lock shut, her eyes caught on the second door to the left, inside the room. She stepped up to it, running her hand along the wood grain. She reached for the handle, expecting a closet, only it was locked. She stepped back as if an electric shock ran from the brass handle through her hand. Charlie's room was to the right of hers. But who was to her left?

She spent the next few hours on the floor of her room, watching that door. Spiraling at the possibilities. At the outcome of their time there. At what she was supposed to do.

She heard a terse conversation from the room behind her, Charlie's room, but didn't stir. Not even as a door slammed and footsteps sounded outside her room. She stayed on the floor until she heard a knock on her door.

CHAPTER TWENTY-EIGHT
NOAH

I see someone gotcha good recently," Erlie Reaux chastised Noah, holding his chin between her thumb and forefinger. He grimaced.

"The fact I walked away with only this scar should be a sentiment to how good I am," he replied. The older woman released his chin to smack him on the shoulder but they both stood smiling at each other instead, a warmth in her cheeks he hadn't seen in forever.

"All these years and ya still can't escape a scrap, huh, Noah Broussard?" A smooth female voice sounded behind him and he couldn't help but smile wide as he turned around to face Willa Reaux. Tight curls coiled down to her shoulders and her skin a deep brown that shined with the amber glow of the setting sun. The lunch started late with the travel and lasted longer than planned with the discussion he could overhear between Adette and Emilien from the kitchen next door.

Willa walked forward and Noah pulled her into a friendly hug, squeezing her tight before releasing her. "I'll remind you the cause of every single one of those fights was something Benji said aloud when it should've just been a thought."

"Already talking about me?" They all spun to see Benji walk into the kitchen. Noah stiffened beside Willa and she gave him a confused sidelong glance before she stepped up to Benji, embracing him and then cupping his ears.

"Ya ears are warm so I guess ya senses are still working," she said with a wink, releasing his face.

"Willamette Reaux, as I live and breathe. Last time I saw you, you were a gangly little teenager whose hair seemed at war against this Louisiana humidity. Where did that girl go?"

The look Willa gave Benji raised the hair on the back of Noah's neck. "She grew up, Benji. Hit the gym, learned to throw a punch, and discovered hair gel. What went wrong with ya?" she asked, her words dusted with mirth as she ruffled his golden blonde hair, the curls going wild in the process.

He gave her a lopsided grin as he tried in vain to tamp down the mayhem on top of his head. He turned to Noah, his cheerful demeanor slipping.

"Noh, I have you staying in the room next to Isabella. They are connected, just so you know." His tone was all business.

Erlie shifted uncomfortably next to Noah and turned to Abel. The old man kept his gaze assessing Benji but his brother didn't notice. His gaze fixated on Noah, gaging his reaction.

Keeping his composure collected, Noah nodded. "Alright." What more could he say as his heart pounded heavy in his chest? His brother's eyes narrowed on him.

Willa looked between the two brothers and then stepped up to her mother, grasping her hands. "Okay ya two. Let's get home before dark. Them mosquitoes out there are real bloodsuckers this year." Her gaze shifted up to meet Noah's, concern on her face, before she turned to help her parents collect their equipment and start loading boxes.

As they were about to step out the door to leave, Erlie turned back to Noah. "Remember, son, if you need anything, we just where them skeetas bite," she whispered, leveling a look on him as she squeezed his hand.

"Yes ma'am," he said, nodding and squeezing back. Her fragile grip lingered before slipping out of his to head out the door.

When he turned back to his brother, Benji had shifted to watch the family through the open door, loading up their equipment. A smile leveled on his brother's face and he reached a hand out, grasping Noah's shoulder next to him.

"Can you believe that was Willamette Reaux? Phew, what a missed opportunity, yeah? Too bad she always preferred you."

"I'm pretty sure she preferred Sally Chilcott," Noah added.

Benji's eyes widened and he looked back out the door, watching the white van disappear in a cloud of dust down the driveway. "No way!"

Noah smiled, slapping his brother on the back. He worked the knot off his apron and tossed it on the stainless-steel counter.

"Yes way. Sancho, you can come out of hiding now. We all knew you were in there," Noah called. A rattle and then a crash sounded from the pantry and then the larger man lumbered out the wooden door.

"*Mortal pero no silencioso*[59], that's what they say," Sancho joked, dusting the flour coating the front of his black uniform.

Benji wrapped an arm around Noah's broad shoulders and steered him toward the door. "No worries, Sancho, I'll take it from here. You know where your room is?"

Sancho didn't look up from removing the white dust. "*Si, chico del pantano.*"

❧

As they stepped out onto the porch, Noah peered into the dining room and saw no one had cleared it yet. He ducked out of Benji's grasp.

"I still need to take care of this," he said to his brother. Benji waved a dismissive hand at him and disappeared up the stairs to the second floor. With the property teeming with The Society and Antisociété alike, and miles from downtown, Noah escaping or getting up to no good must have been a low threat.

He cleared the dining room, setting the dishes next to the sink to deal with the next day. He worked his way into the parlor next to it, where Adette had met with Emilien and Malik to discuss the security for their overnight stay. The overheard conversation had been painted with terse French and the awkward mediation from Malik. He sighed, picking up the empty wine and bourbon glasses when the strums of weak guitar chords cut through the silence around him.

Only one person Noah knew played that horrible.

He walked out onto the porch, chasing the horrendous sound around the corner until he saw them. A mass of wine-red curls caught his eye first and froze him in place. The strumming stopped and Benji waved him over to the clearing in the palm garden. They all sat in wooden Adirondack chairs, the ones Abel, Benji, and he had built a lifetime ago, around a fire meant more to dissuade the bugs than for warmth.

Noah took the stairs down to the grounds. When Izzy turned to see who was approaching, her fiery gaze had him tripping over a root. Everything in him screamed to turn around. He was out of his depth with this dynamic. And yet…he couldn't escape the draw of the flame. He recovered his near fall, glancing back up, his gaze settling on Malik.

While everyone watched Noah approach, Malik watched Izzy.

"Noah, please, come put these people out of their misery," Benji pleaded, beaming as he held the guitar and pick out to Noah.

Noah grabbed the instrument and sank into the empty chair beside his brother. Right across from Izzy.

"My brother is the musician in the family. He was even in a band. What was it, The Southern Hounddogs?" Benji asked, turning to his brother.

Noah held Izzy's gaze as he said, "The Whip Pets." Izzy's eyes narrowed on him, fire light dancing in those emerald pools then darkness as she looked away, taking a long sip of her bourbon. He watched her lips against the glass, the bob of her throat as she swallowed. His own mirrored the image.

"Ah, right! Well, play us some whippetry while I roll us up some of Louisiana's Finest," Benji drawled enthusiastically. He pulled out a jar of ground sage green buds and a pack of hemp papers.

Noah picked a few strings, adjusting the pegs until he got it as tuned as he could get by his rusty ear. He strummed a simple G chord. At the sound Izzy sat up. He felt her attention on him as he played through some chord progressions, but he kept his eyes on the strings and his finger placement. *Focus on what you can control, Broussard.*

"Ah, so much better, right? Well, I'm glad you guys were willing to come hang out with us. It gets a bit stuffy in those dinners, don't you think?" Benji asked.

"While being held hostage, I find it's best to take the good things as they are offered to you," Izzy chimed in, taking another sip of her bourbon. Charlie choked on his drink next to her, Noah noticing the man for the first time. The sun had set enough that only a bright orange glow filtered through the trees, the house blocking most of it. The glow of the flame bounced off her features as Noah looked up, muscle memory kicking in as he played a soft melody. Her eyes dipped to his hands and he fumbled the next note. No one noticed.

"Oh, you're not being held hostage, Isabella," Benji joked, leaning back in his seat as he held the joint to his lips and lit it. A puff of smoke enveloped him and he passed it to Malik on his right.

"What would you call driving us all the way out here to only make us stay the night then?" Charlie asked. His bright blue eyes flickered to Noah but then focused on his brother.

"We're just trying to show you what good has happened here. Maybe give you guys some ideas for when you head back to St. Louis," Malik said as he held the smoke in his lungs. He exhaled on a cough, shakily handing the joint to Izzy.

The blaze erupted in her vision as she held the tip of the roll to her lips, smoothly sucking in the smoke. She held it, and Noah's focus, for a few seconds before tilting her head back to exhale, breaking the trance he had fallen under. Fuck, he needed to get a grip. His heart pounded as he kept his rhythm on the guitar. She passed the reefer to Charlie, leveling a heated stare on him.

"I heard you spent some time there. How did you find it? In need of fixing?" Her question was directed at him and the world disappeared around them for a moment.

His song changed, shifting to something more sorrowful. "Fixing? Even if it needed fixing, I don't think anyone can just walk in and do it. Everyone seems pretty set in their ways there," Noah drawled slowly, matching the tempo of the chords thrumming beneath his fingers.

Charlie passed the joint to Noah. He stopped his song and looked at it for a moment. When he met the electric blue gaze of the man next to him, he decided to take the good being offered to him. Holding the botanical wrap between his thumb, forefinger, and middle finger, he took a deep drag, letting the smoke billow into his chest. He held it as long as he could manage and exhaled. The effort ended in a fit of coughs that had Benji and Malik laughing as Benji quickly handed a bottle of bourbon to him. After a few swigs and some tears shed, he looked across the fire to see a devilish smirk on Izzy's mouth. She raised her glass toward him and he raised the bottle in kind.

Before he could take another drink though, Malik said, "So y'all really never ran into each other in that city?"

Panic tightened Noah's grip on the bottle and he passed it back to his brother, picking the guitar back up so he had something, anything, to distract from where this conversation was going.

Charlie spoke, shaking his head and relaxing into his seat. Izzy watched him as if studying him. "Nope. I didn't see Noah until that day you guys raided The Society, taking him and throwing our plans a bit sideways."

"I came into the picture after that fruitful day. Please enlighten me. You took your brother?" Izzy asked, turning to face Benji. Malik eye narrowed on her.

Benji sat forward, passing the joint to Malik and leaning his elbows on his knees. "I wasn't actually there for any of the action. Didn't even know Noah was in the city until they said we had a new recruit on board. I walked in the room and what do you know, my own flesh and blood!" He gripped Noah's shoulder, squeezing. The motion caused Noah to slip a note in the new song he played, a jazzy blues melody.

"A new recruit?" she asked, tilting her head to the side. "And tell me, Noah, right?" Noah nodded to her, watching a wry smirk play on her thick lips through the crackling sparks of the fire. "How does New Orleans compare to St. Louis now that you've been to both?"

He watched the words leave her lips. "Incomparable," he breathed out.

Her smirk softened and his song changed again, quickening in tempo. Benji sat back in his seat, looking between the two of them before leaning in to whisper something to Malik. Both men stood and Benji wrapped an arm around Malik's waist before saying, "Enjoy your evening friends. I'm off to do exactly that."

Malik smacked Benji playfully on the chest and while his brother laughed it off, the other man leveled Noah with a look that reminded him he wasn't free. The two disappeared into the dark. There was a path they followed that Noah knew took them to a smaller house on the property, away from the main house. But close enough, if needed.

A second later, Charlie stood with a groan. "Well, I know when I'm making a crowd. Iz…if you need anything," he looked over his shoulder at Noah, "I'm right next door."

She held her eyes on Noah as she responded to Charlie tersely. "Yeah, night."

The tall man stood there for a second, as if contemplating his decision to leave, then he walked off into the blackened night around them.

Noah's song changed again; a melody that had been stuck in his head for months.

Izzy watched him play for several minutes, her chin resting on the top of her propped up knee. A war waged between them as they both stared at each other. Noah willed her to see the truth, to uncover what was going on here. Her face twisted in thought, different emotions playing across her face. The lines he had memorized shifting. Her lips pursing then relaxing. Brow scrunching together then softening. He watched every movement, held every second, pulled into the gravity of her.

The moment she spoke, he heard every note even as the words came out barely on a whisper.

"Why?"

He fumbled the chords and found himself unable to recover as his hands shook. Fuck. The flames of her engulfed him finally. He set the guitar in Benji's abandoned seat and ran a hand through his hair and down the back of his neck. He opened his mouth to speak but then straightened, looking around them. The trees echoed the songs of the crickets and cicadas, an overwhelming cacophony as he focused in on it.

How could he know they wouldn't be overheard? Sensing his trepidation, Izzy sighed and stood.

"Goodnight, Noah." The words cut like a knife through his heart as the last of the fire light chased after her until she was gone.

❖

Staring into the fire, Noah felt his pulse roar through his veins as his world tilted on its axis.

Why?

Fucking brilliant, beautiful question. Hurt and pain in that single word haunted him, relinquished his ability to move, to breathe, to think beyond the anguish and anger in her vibrant green eyes. Time passed in a flash of spiraling despair and before he knew it, the fire in front of him became nothing more than a bowl of glowing embers.

He stood on shaky legs, adjusted his mind to the new altitude, and made his way back to the main house, climbing the stairs in silence. His room was the last one on the right. Sancho slept below, next to the kitchen and the stairs.

Walking into his room, the light under the connecting room door sparked a memory.

You're staying next to Isabella, Benji had informed him.

His heart rattled as his pulse quickened. Fate granted him one last chance, to correct course. To please his feeble case to her. To let her know he hadn't left her. To give her a why. And then maybe get them the fuck out of there.

The floor creaked underfoot as he approached the carved wooden door. Running a hand through his hair, he exhaled then knocked twice, lightly as not to disturb anyone else. Enough for her to hear, to know he was there.

Footsteps padded toward the door and he saw her shadow underneath. She stood there for an agonizing moment before pulling the door open fully.

She had changed into an oversized Bayou Brothers t-shirt and a pair of crawdad boxers, items he recalled from the tourist souvenir shack down the road highlighting the local entertainment. Likely raided by Adette's crew for their surprise guests. Her soft curls were swept over her shoulder and she assessed him like...like he was a threat.

He cleared his throat. "Izzy, I..." Fuck, what was he going to say to her? He should've thought of something outside instead of staring into the fire like a madman. "I...fuck. Can we talk?"

"Are we not talking right now?" she asked, green eyes

narrowing.

He held her gaze. "You know what I mean."

She stared him down a moment longer before she stepped into his space and brushed passed, closing the door behind her. He remembered that smell, the salty brine of sweat on her skin mixed with the vanilla and spice that sparked all the wrong memories in that moment.

He turned around to see her sitting on his bed, her knees drawn up to her chest and arms wrapped around her legs. Her skin was paler than he remembered and it caused the freckles across it to stand out like stars in the midnight sky.

He walked over to the space on the bed next to her, shifting as he sat so he faced her.

He studied his hands as he spoke, "I don't even know where to begin."

Her legs dropped to the floor and she turned her body to face him. "How about starting from the moment you disappeared without a trace? Or better yet," A fury burned in her vision as she spoke. Her tone calculated, her words sure. "From the moment you started using me so you could infiltrate my home and get your hands on The Ramblings? How did you do that anyway? When did you have the time to go in and take notes? And why even leave me messages if you were just going to run off when your brother came to the rescue? I thought he was dead, you know? Was that a part of the ruse too or just a ploy to make me feel bad for you so I would sleep with you?" She looked away, her lower lip trembling slightly before she sneered, "Pathetic."

Noah's brow furrowed deeper and deeper with every word that left her mouth. Only when he sat long enough to process what she said, what she had thought all this time they had been apart, did his expression soften.

"Izzy, fuck, no." He reached a hand out to pull her chin back to face him. Silver rimmed those emeralds, piercing his heart, his soul. "That's not at all what happened. I thought Benji was dead. Fuck, when he walked into the room I was tied up in on the barge, I thought I was hallucinating. I thought, 'Great, you've been captured once again, ripped away from the woman you love, and now you're going insane because your dead brother has walked in like nothing ever happened'." He willed his hand to let go of her, his fingers where they had touched her tingling.

She searched his face, tested his features for a lie, tested him. When she seemed satisfied he told her the truth, her lips parted and eyes widened.

"You didn't work with Adette to interrupt our plan?"

"No."

"And you didn't run away with them after blowing up The Society to come back here?"

"Not at all."

"And," she choked on the words trying to escape her. "And you...love...me?" Her head tilted and her hands trembled.

"Devastatingly so."

Silver ran over the edges of her dark lashes. "Noah..."

He shook his head, looking away from her, searching the wallpaper for the words he wasn't sure he could express. When he looked back at her, a vise clenched round his pounding heart, certain it was loud enough for her to hear. "Izzy, from the moment I was ripped away from you, I've been trying to find a way back. A way back to you. But this," he motioned to the space around him, the chaos they were in the middle of, "This is deeper than we originally thought. Every time I tried to get out or get more information, Benji was right there to drag me back into a cell. This is the most freedom I've been offered in months."

Izzy lifted a hand to his cheek and he leaned into the touch, a shudder rolling through him. Her touch released the tension within him and he felt the tears wetting his cheeks with no ability to stop them. She leaned toward him, her lips hovering a breath away from his.

"And to think I wasted all this time trying to fall out of love with you," she whispered.

Noah's eyes flew open to meet hers. He reached up, taking the back of her neck in his hand, the other pulling her waist toward him, into his lap as he devoured her lips. Devoured her words, her heart and her soul, taking everything she offered him and giving it back tenfold.

They fell backward onto the bed, her legs straddling him as he worked his hands underneath her shirt, pulling the mass of fabric over her head. Stripped bare from the waist up, his eyes fluttered over her before smoothly flipping them over, pinning her to the bed with his hips. She let out a soft giggle that turned to a purr as his fingers slipped under the waistband of her boxers, pulling them over her smooth, muscular legs. She laid out before him and he cursed softly under his breath as he stood up, memorizing every curve and dip, every delectably soft spot on her body that begged for him to grip.

He ripped his shirt and pants off in record time before climbing back onto the bed, settling onto his knees and looking down at her. She openly assessed him, a hunger in her eyes that both rose his core temperature and spiked his adrenaline, tingling every nerve ending in his body. With shaking hands, he slowly roved them up her legs, pressing into the soft inner flesh of her thighs before gripping the pillowy skin of her stomach, traveling up to palm her breasts.

"You're a goddess, Z," he growled. She flashed him a

smile but his focus remained on her body. His lips devoured the constellations on her freckled skin, studying the astronomy before him. Memorizing their patterns, the way they curved along the planes of her skin. The salty sweet taste danced on his tongue as he licked his lips. Her breathless gasp held him ransom as he placed a light kiss onto her hip bone, her light olive skin shimmering as she convulsed beneath him.

"That tickles," she breathed out before moaning as he bit her lightly in the same spot.

"I'm just trying to commit this moment to memory in case I am truly hallucinating, still tied to a chair in a basement somewhere," he said against her skin as he drifted further down, holding her ass firmly.

This time when she gasped, her thighs pressed him further into her, and he consumed her with the want and the need catapulting through him, setting his body on fire. As she convulsed underneath his grip, he ravaged more and more, insatiable by the feel of her, the sound of her, the taste of her.

"Noah, please," she cried out, a giggle on the end as he flicked his tongue. Giving her one last long suck, finishing with a soft lick, he released his hold on her. Wiping his mouth with a finger, he sucked it into his lips, groaning with his eyes closed. Whatever deity wanted to end him could do so in that moment.

And one spoke in response.

"Oh fuck, that's hot," she said. When he opened his eyes, she looked at him with a ravenous curiosity that ignited everything within him. Wrapping an arm around her back, he pulled her up to him, gently kissing then nibbling on her lip.

"Are you ready?" he asked.

"Stop being chivalrous and give me what I want," she commanded.

Noah smirked before shifting his other hand between them, positioning his cock at her entrance. Wetness spilled onto him as his tip slipped in and he nearly came as the hot slickness poured down the length of him. She leaned forward and whispered in his ear, "Stop playing games with me, Noah Broussard."

Smiling, he gripped both hands on her hips as he thrust fully into her. A sharp moan escaped her lips and he crashed his own against them to silence it. He kept pace for a few more thrusts then shifted the motion back and forth, slowing the tempo, and capturing every sound she made in his mouth.

As they found a slower rhythm, their lips separated and she leaned her forehead against his shoulder, a soft, shaky "Fuck," escaping her beautiful lips.

"As you wish," he whispered, a bead of sweat rolling down his forehead as he picked the pace back up. She rolled her hips against him and ecstasy chased him as he felt her tighten around him. A groan escaped his throat and he felt her lips press against the hollow space there.

"Z, I'm..." His breathless words escaped him, his pleasure hitting its peak, about to tumble over the edge.

Just as he began moaning out, spilling himself into her, a sharp pain followed by a warming sensation flooded through him. He came harder than he had ever before, resisting the urge to yell out her name and wake the whole town.

When they both fell back sideways into the pillows, rolling onto his back and gulping for air, he lifted his hand to the throbbing spot on his neck. Feeling the hot wetness beneath his fingers, he pulled his hand away.

Shock, horror, anguish, fear—they all battled within his recently elated heart as he stared at his hand, the familiar crimson of blood on his fingers.

CHAPTER TWENTY-NINE
IZZY

The gods above and below could've buried Izzy in that moment, the taste of him on her lips her last will and testament. The feel of him in her, truly in her. Even Barry's finest cultivar couldn't touch this high. She hummed and it came out a purr.

"What...the...fuck, Izzy?" The words trembled out of Noah's delectable mouth. The mouth that had been on her skin. Another feral noise beckoned from within then her eyes snapped open. Horror and fear hardened the edges on his face that moments ago had been softened into pure pleasure. And his hand...it was red from the blood coating her tongue. She yearned to reach up and lick them clean.

Fuck! An ache formed in the pit of her stomach as she rolled off the side of the bed, quickly moving to pick up her clothes, pressing them to her front. Her body shook as tears streamed down her face. Fuck, what had she done? How could she have been so fucking reckless?

"Oh god...I'm so sorry. Fuck, I'm so sorry. I–" A

hiccup stopped her words as a sob escaped her lips. One more look at his face as he sat up, hand still pressed to his neck in disbelief, sent her running back into her room, slamming the door behind her without a thought and locking it.

She backed away from the wooden structure, hands trembling as she stared at the threshold. Tears flowed down her face as she replayed the entire scene over and over again in vivid detail, one hand reaching up to the empty space at the hollow of her throat, to everything she had lost. And continued to lose. Then she ran to the metal wastebasket next to her bed and hurled up everything in her. She heaved and sobbed until nothing else came out, collapsing onto the floor and curling into herself. Death never came willing to the monster when they most wanted it. She squeezed her eyes tight. Someone banged on the door separating the two rooms. A plea sounded from Noah on the other side and another sob wracked through her. She curled tighter, letting the pain and sorrow she had tried to keep at bay all those months flood through her, washing her in despair. She deserved it.

A second later, the front door to her room opened and Noah came in, having thrown on a shirt and a pair of shorts since she'd last seen him, naked. So beautiful. So easily broken. He knelt beside her, the sweet metallic scent of his blood washing over her, and she squeezed her eyes shut.

"Izzy. Z, please. Look at me," he said softly. He placed a tentative hand on her arm and she recoiled from his touch, the lightning feel of it too much.

"I'm so sorry, just leave me," she sniffled, pressing her face into her arms.

She heard shuffling and hoped he had taken her word, leaving her once and for all. There was no honor in loving a monster.

She allowed the idea to take root. It grew quickly, taking shape as a tall, foreboding tree, barren of leaves, of life. Just the ominous branches reaching out for her, to drag her under the soil, into the Hell she called home.

Then those branches were lifting her up. She opened her eyes and started to protest, to fight against the demon tree, but Noah gently lowered her into the bed, underneath the covers he had pulled back. She shivered, watching him with wide eyes as he tucked the blankets in around her like a child.

Without a word, he went over to the wastebasket and took it outside the room, then on a second thought, popped his head back in to say, "I'll be right back."

A minute passed.

Then two.

Her panic started to pulse, the heavy beat trying to convince her he had left again. Had finally come to his senses wherever he went and decided this was his one and true moment to escape it all, The Society, Adette, his brother, her…

Before her thoughts could plummet off the cliff in her mind, he came back into the room with a familiar looking wicker basket full of items. She glanced at its twin in her room, in the corner, meant for laundry. He locked her door behind him and set the basket on the other side of the bed. He then pulled out a thermos and poured a clear liquid into the lid.

"Just water," he said, passing the army green cup to her. She shuffled upright in the bed, taking it from him to wash away the taste of bile and blood in her mouth. She watched him as he then pulled out a bottle of amber liquid out of his magic basket.

"Bourbon to wash it all down with," he said, giving her a lopsided grin. "I took liberties in what I thought might be your poison of choice." He paused and then added, "Well, all things considered." His hand waved over his neck.

"Did you just make a joke about me sucking your blood?" She asked, irritation feathering her words.

His smile widened. "I just figured your drink of choice might have changed but we wouldn't know unless we did a fair taste test." He took a swift from the bottle before passing it to her. The liquid burned her raw throat, taking away whatever acrid taste remained in her mouth.

"And?" He asked as she passed the bottle back to him. He took another swig, keeping those golden eyes on her.

"Shut the fuck up," she growled. He snorted and then cursed, coughing.

"Fuck, that burns that way," he said, setting the bottle down on the bedside table.

She peeked over the edge of the basket. "What else do you have in your magical basket?"

"Oh, just some light reading I stumbled across recently," he said as he pulled out her leather bag and then the two parcels wrapped in linens within. She froze. He placed the basket on the floor and then climbed into the bed next to her, setting the parcels down in front of him. He began unwrapping one. It was The Ramblings. "Thought we might take a trip down memory lane before we," he unwrapped the other book. The Busch family book she had thrown in her bag when they had left St. Louis. "Delve into whatever you've been spending your clever little mind's time on lately." He looked at her with a devastating twinkle of mischief in his golden eyes.

"When did you," she began to ask, reaching for The Ramblings.

"Since when do you not lock your door?" he interrupted, flipping open the thick, familiar pages of The

Ramblings. If Dr. Beechum saw him handling it without gloves in this humidity, he would have a very visible aneurysm.

"Since I became the thing most feared in the night. Why do you have these books?" she asked more urgently. Noah's flipping through the pages stopped and he set the book down, turning to face her. She looked away to her hands clasped in her lap.

"Hey," he whispered as he placed a hand on her cheek, pressing until she looked up at him. "You're not a monster." In his short absence from her, he had cleaned up the wound on his neck, the smell softened, less intoxicating. The wound had already begun to heal, a creepy phenomenon she could never get passed. His eyes followed her gaze as it focused on his neck, on the skin stitched together so perfectly. He used his other hand to tilt her chin up. Concern and... love shined bright in his golden eyes as he said with earnest, "You are not a monster, Z."

Her lip trembled and she nodded her head. He placed a kiss on her forehead, pressing his fingers into the back of her neck, into the touch before he released her and turned back to the books.

"However, we should probably figure out how this happened to you and I figured that's exactly what you were doing with these all the way in the bayou. Unless you're not telling me something," he said, looking sideways at her as he flipped The Ramblings back open.

She rolled her eyes and leaned into his shoulder, reaching over to flip the page to his last set of notes. "No, Noah, I did not choose this life for myself."

"I didn't think so. Do you want to tell me about it?"

"About what?" She pulled the notes out of the book, scanning the familiar words she had memorized, his quick scripting strokes a comfortable sight. Could he see the number of times she had folded and unfolded them?

Noah gently pulled the notes from her grasp, sticking them back in the book and closing it. "What happened, Z? After we got separated, what happened?"

A shaky breath left her lips on a strong exhale and she gripped her hands together. He reached over, separating them so he could hold her left one in between his own.

"I tried, fuck," she blinked, staring at the ceiling before continuing, "I tried to go back into the smoke to find you. When I stood on the streets and saw you weren't there, I tried to go back. For you. But Lando pulled me away, said we needed to go. I fought him the entire way back to the penthouse. Then as he sat there, questioning me about what happened, and I just…blacked out. I don't remember anything after that. I was asleep or in a coma or something for three fucking days. Gio stood by my side, taking care of me and shooing away any unwelcome visitors. And then I woke up and it was like the world was assaulting me on every cellular level. When Gio walked back into my apartment after taking a break to grab breakfast, I attacked her. She hasn't talked to me since then. And I've been subsisting off Charlie's involuntary donations when I need them." Noah stiffened at her mention of Charlie but rubbed his thumb over her hand.

"So, you don't know how this happened?" Noah asked, chewing the bottom of his lip. Suddenly he was out of the bed and pacing the floor. Izzy watched him, one brow lowered.

"Correct. Another astute observation by the young academic protégé," Izzy said sardonically, her head tilting. Noah snorted but kept pacing, a hand on his chin as his brow furrowed in deep thought. He stopped, reaching over to grab The Ramblings from the bed. He flipped it open to the page with his notes, studying his own handwriting for a bit. The creases on his forehead deepened, his face growing taunt as he calculated. Then the book fell from his grasp, landing with a soft thud on the bed as his panicked golden eyes met her own.

$$\clubsuit$$

CHAPTER THIRTY
IZZY

We can't stay here," Noah said. He began packing the books back into her leather bag in the basket, throwing her clothes from that day at her.

Izzy sat up startled in the bed, beginning to dress. "What do you mean we can't stay here? Where else would we go? We are surrounded by vampires and disgruntled ex-lovers. Not to mention the gators outside and the mosquitoes that drink more blood than me." She threw her hands up, gesturing to the great dangerous outdoors beyond the oak door.

Noah snorted. Then a dark shadow passed over his face and he paled, stopping his packing endeavor to meet her gaze. Dread filled his expression as his lips thinned.

Izzy's grin shifted. "What is it?"

Noah shook his head. "Nothing, just a crazy thought." He finished packing things into her bag, the bottle of bourbon included, and hoisted it over his shoulder. He held a hand out to her, his face hardened with severity. "But we do need to go. Right now."

Izzy took his hand, brows furrowed as she pushed the

covers away and stood next to him. "Okay, but where to? We are miles from civilization. And most of the people here seem to be employed with Adette."

"You have no idea," Noah murmured as he walked to the door, peeking out between the wooden slats. He turned back to her, creases deepening along the edge of his golden eyes as she slipped her boots on. "But I promise, it has to be tonight. I don't know what's planned but whatever they are telling Emilien and Charlie is probably a lie."

She studied his features. "But what about your brother?"

Something shifted in Noah, turning his features harder, colder. "He can be trusted least of all. Are you ready? It'll be a bit of a hike and you will get assaulted by the insect vampires," he said, deflecting the tension as he looked her up and down.

She looked down at the linen outfit from earlier that day. "This is as good as it gets, I'm afraid."

Noah stepped forward, placing a hand on her neck. She started at the touch. How natural it felt. How she hadn't been touched like that...ever. Golden eyes searched her green ones through long lashes. "You're perfect, Z." He grinned, leaning forward to place a kiss on her forehead.

As he released his grip on her and turned toward the door, she whispered out, "Wait!"

Noah paused, hand hovering over the door handle.

Izzy sighed. "We have to get Charlie."

A storm of fury and confusion clouded over Noah as his hand flexed into a fist. He dropped his head before turning to face her. "You've got to be fucking kidding me?"

⚜

Izzy stepped out of her room and quickly tiptoed over

328

to Charlie's door. She knocked once then tried the handle. Locked. Like a smart person.

She was about to knock again when the shuffle of sheets and then feet sounded on the other side of the door. A click sounded and Charlie pulled the door open, confusion on his stupidly beautiful face. When he recognized Izzy standing before him, his demeanor shifted and a lopsided grin pressed into his pink lips.

"Needed a midnight snack?" he grumbled, his eyes barely open through the sleepy haze around him.

As she opened her mouth to respond, she felt a hard warmth behind her and then felt the vibrations of Noah's voice as he said, "She's plenty satisfied but we wanted to see if you're interested in a little escape instead?"

A smolder of hate darkened Charlie's face, snapping him awake fully as he straightened, eyes roving over Noah and then his proximity to Izzy. He took a step back and motioned for them to come in, scanning the outdoors before shutting the door.

"You know these walls are paper thin and the doors are basically shutters, right?" Charlie chastised as Noah walked in, making himself at home in the chair in the corner of the room. Izzy stood between the men, unsure how to balance the palpable tension held in the air.

"I'm plenty aware of what can and cannot be heard in these rooms. I'm also aware you were sound asleep when we were originally about to leave but your dear friend Izzy here decided you were worth stalling for." Noah motioned to the room around them. "Thus, here we are."

Charlie shifted his glare from Noah to settle a look of confusion on Izzy. "What the fuck is he talking about?"

Izzy sighed, running a hand through her knotted curls.

The humidity had been unkind to her and the activity of the night hadn't helped. She twisted the strands around her hand then tied them into a knot.

"We are, apparently, getting out of here. I want you to come with us," she said, leveling a serious look on Charlie. He snorted, about to laugh in her face when he faltered. His eyes widened.

"You're insane. You're both fucking insane," he said, pointing at each of them before running a rough hand through his raven hair. "They drove us here for a reason. We can't escape. Where would we even go?" His eyes bounced between her and Noah.

"Noah seems to think we have a place we can go, at least temporarily, until we can figure out how to get back to St. Louis," Izzy said.

Charlie ran his hand down his face, staring at the ceiling and letting a few Italian expletives escape his lips. "And then what? We go to St. Louis and pretend this was all a big nightmare? Move on with our lives? Him and I take turns contributing to your dietary needs?"

Noah started to stand but Izzy held a hand up then stepped toward Charlie, glaring.

"You know you don't have to ruin every good opinion I have about you? You could just speak to me like I'm a human fucking being and keep your shitty comments to yourself."

"But you're not a human anymore, are you, Iz? Not really," he bit back. Izzy glowered at him, her hatred renewing for the man. She didn't hear him get up behind her, didn't even know he had moved until Noah stood between her and Charlie. And then the next second his fist connected with the perfect jaw of one Charlie Valentini.

CHAPTER THIRTY-ONE
NOAH

Punching Charlie felt good. Too fucking good. Noah had to restrain himself because his left fist itched to follow with a hook to the stomach just to watch that blood pouring from his mouth hit the floor.

Violence in the form of sapphire blue eyes turned back to stare him down and Noah opened and closed his fist, ready to hit him again. Then a shock of red hair walked into view, his world focusing in on *her*.

"Jesus fucking Christ, can you two stop fighting like battering rams for five fucking seconds? The sun will rise in a few hours but even then, there is no guarantee someone isn't awake right now. And apparently, we need to go. Immediately," she urged, giving him a look he couldn't begin to decipher.

The two men held each other's gaze for a second more. Charlie scoffed and looked away, wiping his crimson coated mouth with the back of his hand.

"You're right," Noah ground out. "We need to get moving."

Charlie ran a rough hand through his raven hair. "Fuck," he growled as he threw back on the shirt and pants he had worn that day. A couple weapons were discreetly strapped onto his body a moment later and he looked between Noah and Izzy.

"So, where the fuck are we going?"

"First, somehow off this property," Noah said, adjusting the straps on Izzy's bag so it felt snug against his body. He needed to be able the maneuver the terrain.

Both Izzy and Charlie turned to him and said in unison, "What?"

"You can't honestly expect us to steal one of their vehicles and not have them hot on our heels. Hell, I can almost guarantee they have the things tracked. They have loosened my leash here tremendously, which means they think I can't escape," Noah added, taking stock of Charlie's room. It was eerily familiar. His hands tingled as he started opening a few drawers in the antique dresser.

"Well, can you?" Charlie asked, skepticism in his tone.

Not looking up as his hand skimmed the top wooden panel of each, Noah said, "I can. I spent my summers out here. What do you think teenage boys did after curfew? Stay in their rooms?" He didn't elaborate on the why he had been out there: for an inner-city program that sent kids like him and Benji out to the country to learn "valuable life lessons" in exchange for free labor. Noah shook the memory away. "Look, you're going to have to trust my lead on this. Follow me, and I'll at least get us out of here." Then derive a plan from there. He hoped.

A hand gripped his arm and he froze, turning to meet Izzy's emerald gaze.

"Tell me what you need from us and we will do it," she said, searching his eyes. He didn't know what she would see in them so he shifted his gaze to Charlie and back to her. His lips tightened and he looked back into the drawer, rummaging. His hand felt the edge of tape then the familiar etching of a small, metal item. A satisfied smirk creased his cheeks as he pulled out the item, shoving it quickly into his pocket. Benji had always made sure they were prepared for anything in those days.

"Getting off the grounds will be the hardest part, but I think we can cut through the garden we were in earlier and sneak along the wooded edge of the property. We will be exposed when we cross the main road, but there is a dense forest across the way we can travel through. We have less than a mile to go. From there..." his sentence fell off because from there, he hadn't a fucking clue what to do. He only hoped he was making a good judgment call.

Izzy nodded her head, her instant agreement warming something in his heart. They held each other's gaze for a moment, a slow smile pulling on her lips before they both shifted their gaze to Charlie.

Charlie, studying the two of them with a look between hurt and fury, looked Noah up and down, clicked his tongue against his teeth and let out a deep sigh. "Fine, lead the way, Bayou Boy," he murmured, gesturing to the door.

Noah smirked. "Keep an eye out for the gators, pretty boy." Then he proceeded to the door, pulling it open enough for him to stick his head out. The moon shined half bright in the sky, offering just enough light to see across the property. That same light would work against them until they could make it to the woods, but that was a concern he would burden himself with. He needed them to follow him. He could take care of the rest. From this vantage point, he couldn't make out any patrols on the property, but that could mean nothing in with a team of vampires working for The Antisociété.

Cursing under his breath, he pulled back into the room to nod the all clear to them both and then pulled the door open, slipping silently down the balconied hall toward the stairwell. He stopped at the top to listen below. Izzy placed a hand on his shoulder and he took a moment to familiarize himself with the reassuring touch. To sear it to his soul. Once certain there was no one lurking below, he started down the stairs, his footsteps invisible. Izzy must have followed his foot placements as they descended because he didn't hear her, only felt the tingling sensation that she was behind him. His hair stood up on the back of his neck as his body remembered that sensation from a lifetime ago. *A predator stalking its prey.*

He shook the thought away and misstepped, a low groan echoing through the thick night air. He froze. He didn't dare look behind him. The crickets continued their song and a lone owl hooted from the top of an oak, but no one came to investigate, no alarms were blaring. Yet they stood there for several heartbeats more, his own quickening as he willed himself to pick up his foot, knowing a repeat of the sound could be their ultimate demise. *Could she hear his heart?* He cursed himself, holding his breath as he lifted his foot. Thankfully, the stair remained silent as he stepped onto the stronger, *quieter* supported edge. Once they made it to the landing, he dared to let out an exhale. Slipping to the edge of the wall, darkened by the overhang of the balcony above, they slid along the building toward the porch stairs that led to the garden below. As they approached the room next to the kitchen, he paused, listening. The deep resonance of Sancho's snoring escaped the shuttered wooden door.

Under that blanket of noise from the room, they quickly paced across the porch and down the stairs, into the dark night.

They passed the banked fire from earlier, Noah throwing a longing look to the guitar still abandoned in the chair. A world where he could get lost in playing music didn't exist anymore. Not for him at least. He pressed them on, moving quickly through the maze of tall, trimmed bushes and fanning palm trees. The soft trickle of a fountain beckoned ahead, marking the halfway point. A small smile dared to pull on his lips and he caught himself. It was too early for hope. As he turned a corner within the bushes, opening up to a giant banyan tree in the middle, a grunt and a beautiful, violent curse escaped into the air behind him.

He whirled around to see Charlie lying on the ground, a boot pressed into his chest. A boot connected to Nadia, who held Izzy's hair, forcing her back against her. The moonlight glinted off the sharp blade pressed into Izzy's neck.

Through the relaxing melody of running water and insects chirping into the night, Nadia cooed, "Going somewhere, lover?"

❧

"Let her go," Noah growled, taking a step toward them. Nadia pressed the knife further into Izzy's neck. A pained gasp escaped Izzy's lips and she squeezed her eyes shut.

"You know, in a different life, maybe under different circumstances, I think we could have been friends," Izzy said, her eyes popping open to meet Noah's, a green fire burning in the filtered moonlight. "I like your style."

Nadia barked out a laugh. "And in this life, you're going to be dead."

"Nadia," Noah growled again, daring a step forward, reaching a hand toward them, toward Izzy. "Let her go, now."

Nadia pouted at him, pressing her boot further into Charlie's chest. He groaned, but didn't attempt to move, his eyes locked on the woman's hold of Izzy.

"Tell me where you're taking them and I'll reconsider ending her life here." He recognized that voice she used on him. The false confidence it pulled at within him. She sounded trustworthy, earnest. Lies.

Playing his cards as best as he could manage, he held Nadia's wild gaze and dared another step forward. Only a foot of space stood between them. She pressed the knife further into Izzy's neck, a rivet of blood streaming down as she sneered up at him. His blood, he realized. Something feral scorched within him. His eyes flicked to the fangs in Nadia's wicked mouth. Slowly, he lifted his hand and wrapped it around her wrist, never taking his eyes off her mouth, off the threat before him. When he felt her relax under his grip, he met her ravenous stare, piercing through those dull green eyes. So unlike the fire in Izzy's. She pushed Izzy to the ground and stepped toward him.

Then her lips crashed into his own and he had no time to react. The kiss was violent and rough and *wrong*. But he had to do something. Something to save *her*. To buy them time. He lifted a hand to Nadia's neck, pressing his lips into hers. She hissed at the touch, writhing her body aggressively against him in possession. He prayed Izzy saw it for what it was and slipped away into the darkness. She needed to be saved. Repulsion rolled through him as he slipped his hand into his pocket.

A soft click sounded, stopping Nadia's movements as he flicked his free wrist. As she pulled back from him, her eyes snagged, widening, as she looked to the object in his hand. A bright, silver switchblade, three golden fleur de lis engraved into the handle hidden in his grip, glittered in the meager light filtering through the tree branches. He didn't give her a chance to process it further as he slid the sharp blade across her throat, pressing into each carotid artery in his pass, severing them.

Nadia stepped back, coughing and sputtering as both her hands wrapped around her neck. Crimson liquid pooled over her fingers, bleeding out faster than her body could repair itself. Shock and anger flooded her frantic expression. She tried to step toward him but the life drained out of her too fast. He had forgotten how fast it happened as he took a step back. She stumbled then fell to her knees. A new emotion flitted across her face, one that haunted Noah with every kill he had under his belt. *Fear.* When the person recognized they were trapped in their body, on its destructive path toward the end. Nothing they did, nothing they said, could stop them falling into darkness…forever.

Once the life vanished from Nadia's eyes and the sputtering stopped, he walked forward. He wasn't religious but still sought the comfort in his ritual. He touched his fist to his head, his chest, then across to his left shoulder, stopping on his right. He bowed his head, flashes of all those faces, all that *fear*, cycling through his mind.

"Noah, we need to go," Izzy said from somewhere behind him. He heard it in her words too, that fear. He swallowed the bile in his throat, looking at his hands. They were surprisingly clean; his movements had been too swift to let the blood splatter on them. The same couldn't be said for his switchblade, hidden all those years in that drawer upstairs. The first blade Benji had gifted him during their initial summer spent out on the plantation. His protection.

Noah placed the blade next to Nadia, in the pool of blood seeping into the grass beneath her. Her lifeless eyes remained open and he reached out, closing them.

As he stood, turning to Izzy, a new weight fell between them. She studied him as he rose. She took a small step back, looking up at him like he had looked at her earlier that evening.

Because as easily as she could end him, he could do just the same to her.

CHAPTER THIRTY-TWO
NOAH

The rest of their journey across the road proved uneventful and once they were all in the wooded forest across the way, they were able to slowly carve a path through the dense foliage. Noah stole glances at Izzy but she seemed in a silent battle with Charlie as they picked their way along the imaginary trail he followed. One he had followed many times in his youth. Even with less than a mile to travel, it still took them over an hour to make it to their destination. Every snap of a twig or splash in the nearby river set his nerves further on edge. Each passing minute felt like a notch in the rope of the guillotine.

A faint glow of candlelight shined ahead of them and Noah's heart pounded as he picked up the pace. Together, they slipped out of the thick forest and across the open space to the house set along the Mississippi River. They approached the porch at the back of the house, facing the river and hiding them from the road. Noah raised his fist to knock then stopped. A speck of blood on the back of his hand caused his chest to clench. *What had he done?* A flurry of deaths by that hand flashed through his memory, his fist tightening.

Another fist lifted underneath his as he fought for a breath, softly knocking twice. He glanced sideways and saw Izzy peering into the arched window at the top of the door. Seeing her there, with him, and *alive*, reminded him to breathe. He dropped his fist, glancing behind him to catch Charlie, back turned to them and yet with one eye on Noah.

The door opened, stealing Noah's attention back to the task before him and to Willa Reaux standing there, her wild hair wrapped in a silk scarf and her gaze one of dangerous questioning.

"Noah Broussard, what are you..." Her words stopped short as her gaze shifted to Izzy next to him and Charlie standing behind, scanning the forest they had just left.

"You know how your mama said if I ever needed anything," Noah said, rubbing the back of his neck. He had trouble holding her severe gaze. The scrutiny in those deep brown pools nearly suffocated him. "I need something and I have no one else to go to with it."

Willa's brows narrowed and she held him under her watchful eye for a moment more before she stepped back, opening the door wider to welcome them in.

"This isn't going to cause any trouble for my parents, will it?" Willa asked after Charlie stepped into the room, clicking the lock shut on the door.

Noah ran a hand through his hair. "I wish I could say no, and I'll do everything in my power to make sure it doesn't, but I can't make any promises."

"Not this time then, huh?" Willa said, crossing her arms over her chest. A memory crashed through him, a younger Willa next to him, tears welling in her eyes as a boy laid on the ground, bloodied and unconscious. The last time he had needed the Reaux family to save his ass. The time who vowed to never put his problems on them again. Fuck.

Nausea flowed through him. "Not this time." He felt Izzy's gaze sear into him, no doubt catching the tension in the air as Charlie busied himself with shutting the curtains in the room.

Willa pursed her lips and nodded her head. "I'll get papa, but mama stays out of this, you understand?"

He nodded his head, swallowing.

"Good. Y'all make yourselves comfortable." She eyed them all warily, her gaze settling longer on Izzy. Then she disappeared into the darkness of the sleeping home.

Charlie slumped into a leather couch, satisfied no one had followed them or could see them. A war raged in Izzy's expression when he looked to her, standing by the back of a plush recliner.

"Don't you think it's a little dangerous pulling them into this? I mean, Adette and Emilien saw them both today at lunch, Noah. Don't you think your brother will lead them here first?" She whispered tersely, running a hand over the corduroy fabric of the chair.

Perceptive as always, she saw the hand he had dealt. The one he held onto with a gamble, desperately praying that the God he no longer believed in would listen and give his brother an ounce of a moral compass for once. Surely, he wouldn't be so callous as to throw the Reaux family, *their family*, into the burning fire of the situation they had woven themselves into. Not after everything. The bloodied boy's body popped into his mind again; Benji standing over him, Willa's face ghostly white and stained with tears, and Noah saying over and over, *"I promise, it'll be okay. I promise. I promise we'll fix this."*

"I think this is the best option we've got," Izzy

interrupted his thoughts, her gaze fusing to his skin, making him itch. He paced over to the library along the wall. An old stone fireplace filled with candles loomed over the shelves, making the room feel like home. His hands slid over the spines as he looked at the mantle. Mama Reaux never saw the need for a fireplace in Louisiana but always said "an empty hearth is an empty heart of a home". *Their home.* Noah's hand fisted.

"I think we could've cut the brake lines on all but one of those vehicles and got as far as we could get before ditching it," Charlie quipped, pulling out a dagger to clean on his t-shirt.

Izzy slipped into the big chair next to the couch, tucking a knee up as she sat back, the chair rocking slowly. Noah watched out the corner of his eye as she pulled her bottom lip between her teeth, as if lost in thought about the scenario Charlie proposed.

She shook her wild red curls. "I don't know, Charlie. I think they probably have someone watching us, beyond what is at the plantation. I mean, you saw that hotel. You saw that city. It's impressive…but something felt…off."

Noah's spine stiffened and he turned, daring to catch her eye. "What do you mean?" he asked, his hands going clammy.

She roved a tentative look over him. "I just mean, it seems too good to be true. It hasn't been that long since it was a hellscape to be a human in the city. And now? It's like it never happened. What gives?"

Noah breathed out a sigh and looked to the ceiling. "I don't exactly know but you're right. Something is off." He leveled his stare back on her. "But I'm just riding on bits and pieces of conversations I've overheard and random things I've seen." His mind wandered to the rows of vials, the ones with his initials on them. N.B. -/+. The only one different from the rest.

His words seemed to pique her interest and she leaned forward, setting her foot on the floor. "What type of conversations?" she asked.

Noah opened his mouth to fill them in on all he had overheard on the barge and in The Roosevelt, but Abel Reaux walked into the living room, scanning the late-night company warily.

The years weighed on him and Noah noted Willa's supporting arm the old man clung to. When was the last time Noah had seen him? A lifetime had passed between his days as a scraggly, tormented teen and the man he was, standing before the family he had wanted to call his own.

"Noah, what's this about?" Abel asked, eyes dancing between Izzy and Charlie. They certainly looked like intimidating figures to find sitting amongst the old novels in the middle of the night. Noah winced at the tattoo on Charlie's neck, his piercing blue eyes studying the old man like he could be a threat.

"Uh," Noah cleared his throat, "Erlie said earlier today if I needed anything, I knew where to find you. Unfortunately, I do need something. A big thing. And you know I wouldn't come here unless I had no other options. You have given me so much over the years, forgiven me for so much, pretty much saved us as kids and I'll forever be indebted to you and..."

Abel held up a hand. He turned to his daughter, giving her arm a squeeze before releasing his hold. He then leveled a determined look on Noah and shuffled toward him on unsteady legs. When he stood before him, Noah saw the strong-willed man beneath the body trying to fail him in his older years, the one that taught him to sharpen a knife, to cast a line, to always hold a door open for a woman, no matter how many times she told him she could it herself.

343

Speaking at a volume only Noah could hear, Abel said, "Noah, my boy, you could never be an imposition to us. We raised you like the son we never had and we wished…dreamed…we could give you boys the life you deserved but," silver lined the old man's eyes as the words choked him up, "but you know the world works in mysterious ways." Noah cleared his throat, his own eyes feeling hot as the older man spoke. "When we finally had the funds to take you in, we learned Benji had aged out and taken you out of the system with him. We had no way to track you down. I wish…I wish more than anything we could've been something more for you two." Noah's lower lip trembled. All these years of feeling like a torment on their lives for those five summers, wanting to be loved like the Reaux family gave so freely to them. "Let us be that now. Whatever you need, we will find a way to make it happen."

Noah's eyes flickered to Willa, her watchful eye on the two of them, before he met the old man's gaze again, nodding once. "I promise this will be the last thing I ask of you. I can't take anything more, not from you."

A rough palm laid on Noah's cheek and it sent a shudder through him as he tried to hold his composure. "Whatever it is, it's yours."

Noah held Abel's gaze, seeing the sincerity in them, the years of support and sacrifice. And that love. Fuck, he wanted to turn back time.

But there was only going forward.

"Do you still have that old john boat?"

CHAPTER THIRTY-THREE
IZZY

He killed her.

The words rolled over in Izzy's mind as she helped Charlie lower the old skiff into the murky water flowing beneath the creaking dock. The life drained out of Nadia's eyes, blood pooling around her, and Izzy's grip slipped. She apologized as Charlie held tight as his end of the boat caught the current of the Mississippi.

"You okay?" he asked as she recovered her hold on the boat, tossing in her bag as Charlie tied off his end to the dock.

She looked up, spotting Noah next to Willa on the shore, talking and nodding to each other. The woman kept a wary eye on Noah, tilting her head as she listened and responded to him.

"Yeah, just…yeah," she replied to Charlie.

He stood, dusting his hands off. Noah and Willa embraced, in that easy way of old friends who knew each other's souls. In that way that shot a punch through Izzy's gut as she glanced away. *He killed her.*

Charlie met her distant stare. "Izzy, are you okay?"

Noah jogged down the dock toward them and she gave Charlie a half smile before focusing on rolling the thick rope in her hands. "I have no other choice but to be okay at the moment, Charlie."

He let out a long sigh, raking his hand through his black hair. "It's just…that was—"

"Okay, we should be able to make it to the marina about twenty miles upriver," Noah interrupted unknowingly. "From there, we will grab whatever vehicle we find keys to or we can probably hot wire one quickly, if needed." His golden eyes roved over their work with a nod of appreciation. He held a hand out to Izzy. For a second, she saw that hand as it moved with such practiced precision, slicing into Nadia's neck. The world spun underneath her as their hands met. She studied the pained expression on his face as he helped her into the boat with its faded paint job and busted vinyl seats. Noah stood on the dock for a second, flexing his hand before he followed her in. Holding the rope that kept them to the dock, he motioned for Charlie to hop in, working on untying them.

Charlie did not move.

Izzy rolled her eyes. "Come on, Charlie. I killed that spider. I'm sure the rest of his friends saw and scrambled off."

A soft quirk of a smile played on his lips. "I think my place is here."

Izzy's heart pounded. *What?* That wasn't part of the plan, even in its scraped-together, taped-up state. "What are you talking about, Valentini? Get in the fucking boat."

He shook his head and looked back at the softly lit home, slowly coming into clearer view as night shifted to twilight. Willa stood in the back doorway, watching them. Izzy watched his throat bob as he swallowed hard. "I can't let this family get backlash for this."

Noah's hand gripped the thick rope wrapped around a large pillar, keeping the boat from being swept away with the current. "Charlie, they have a plan. They will be protected, even if Benji truly doesn't have a heart anymore and sells them out. We need to go." She heard the restrained urgency in his words, his eyes shifting warily to Izzy.

A muscle tightened in Charlie's jaw and his eyes met Izzy's as he spoke. "I was never meant to have this much time with you. To have you put up with me for this long. Let me," he choked up and tears sprang to her eyes in instant. *What was he doing?* She started to protest when he cleared his throat, holding up a hand. He squeezed his eyes shut and when he opened them, the intensity crashed through her. "Let me do this. I owe that to you."

Izzy shook her head, her heart pounding outside her body. She felt the entire scene unfold beneath her as she drifted above. If she screamed at him to stay, would he even hear her? "No, Charlie. That's not what I want." The words startled her as they tumbled out, raw and rough. But they were the truth. She no longer wanted Charlie Valentini dead. Sure, she wanted to strangle him most days. But dead? He didn't deserve that. Does the monster deserve to be put down because of what the world made them into?

Charlie let out a hollow chuckle, pulling a hand through his raven hair as a breeze kicked up from the river. "Of course, you only want me around when I'm dead set on running away." He walked forward, clapping a hand on Noah's shoulder. The fabric indented around his grip as their eyes met. "Bayou Boy, take care of our girl."

No. This wasn't what was supposed to happen. Her eyes frantically danced between them as her mind whirled. She rubbed her palms against her legs, coaxing the shake out of them. This was insane. Charlie was a goddamn idiot and clearly couldn't think straight anymore. A product of continued blood loss, maybe? In this heat, surely that would explain his inability to think straight. She started to stand up, to tell him as much, to get his ass on the fucking boat so they could leave as the sky shifted to a milky indigo. But she paused. As Charlie's hand drifted from Noah's shoulder, Noah reached up and gripped his wrist. Charlie stopped his retreat, scarred brow quirked.

Golden eyes reflected the filtered moonlight as Noah met her gaze briefly. Then he turned back to Charlie, lips thinned. "Hold on. I have…a hunch. If you're going back, I imagine you know what they're going to do to you."

Charlie's face paled as he nodded, a hard swallow working its way down his tattooed throat.

Noah hopped out of the boat, Izzy's hands gripping the sides as it rocked side to side from the movement. He tied the rope off around the metal cleat in the dock. *What the fuck were they doing?*

Izzy tried to stand, to stop this madness and get these silly men in this fucking boat before they were all used to paint the river red, but the rocking was too strong and her stomach started to follow the movement. "What the fuck, guys? Everyone get on this fucking boat before I'm drifted off into these nightmare waters alone." Her heartbeat matched her mind's frantic energy as her grip tightened around the metal.

Noah ignored her and asked instead, "Do you have a knife?"

Izzy patted her body mockingly and held up her empty hands, her core tightening to keep her steady. She hadn't had a chance to go back to her room after their morning tour and she could picture her dagger on the bedside table. Her heart sank.

Noah sighed, running a hand through his hair, an errant curl flicking into his eye.

"Here," Charlie said, holding out a short dagger from his belt.

Noah turned his focus to him. "Thanks," he murmured. Then he made a quick slice into his forearm, the smell of blood cutting through the sweet summer heat and river water in the air. A mix between a gasp and growl escaped her throat as she stood instantly, steady on her feet despite the boat's wobble. Charlie stepped back, his eyes wide on Noah.

"I know this sounds ludicrous and vile," Noah breathed out as he pressed around the wound, the crimson liquid beginning to flow. Izzy's mouth watered. "But drink my blood before you go."

Charlie looked horrified as his eyes danced between the blood streaming down Noah's arm and his face. "You're fucking with me, right?"

Noah looked grim as he shook his head. "I really wish I was. I don't know how much you'll need but better to go with more than less."

Izzy couldn't find the words to work out what was unfolding before her, couldn't find the ability to move, to stop it. *He killed her.*

Charlie met her gaze then turned back to Noah. "You are fucking serious?"

"As a heart attack."

Charlie ran a hand through his hair again, pulling slightly on the ends as he stepped forward. He grabbed Noah's wrist, staring at the cut. He swallowed and Izzy watched the movement with envy and shame. "And why am I doing this?"

Noah's gaze flicked back to Izzy before he said, "If my

theory is correct, it'll turn you into a vampire. Welcome to immortality, brother. Drink up." He pushed his arm into Charlie's grip.

A sick sort of recognition flashed over Charlie's face as his eyes bounced from Izzy to Noah and back again. Then it morphed into rage and his knuckles went white around Noah's arm. "You motherfucker. You turned her? When?"

Noah's back straightened as he stood his ground. "I…didn't mean to. I didn't know. Not until I looked back at my notes in The Ramblings, after everything I've seen and heard the past seven months, and the loose pieces started to come together. It's only a hunch, I don't even know for certain it'll work but if it does—"

"It'll cripple Emilien," Charlie said matter of fact as he dropped Noah's arm.

The world spun around Izzy. Noah's blood…turned her? But when had she drank his blood? That evening notwithstanding, the only other time she had put her mouth on him was last fall in the cave when they…

Her eyes widened. The cave when they had kissed each other like their entire lives depended on it, no regard for the injuries on Noah's body. No regard for the deep cut on his lip, the one that left the crooked white scar on his pinched lips as he looked at her. Clouds blurred the intensity of his golden eyes as his brows knit together, as if trying to read her mind.

She took a step back, collapsing into the split vinyl of the foam seat beneath her. Lines etched deep between Noah's brows as he studied her a moment longer. Then he turned back to Charlie.

"You know he's going to drain you within an inch of your life. I don't know what will happen if he consumes some of my blood, if you have enough time to turn, but I don't think it'll be good. If my blood is in your system, there's a chance—"

"This will be his demise," Izzy whispered from her seat as she clutched her chest, willing oxygen to flood in, her heart to pound instead of the stillness she felt beneath her hand.

Both men looked at her and Noah nodded.

Charlie swore, looking to the stars fading in the sky above. Izzy watched him as he paced in a circle but Noah kept his gaze on her. She chanced a look at him. Let herself search for what he wasn't telling her. Charlie hopping from one foot to the other stole her focus. He shook his shoulders out and stepped up to Noah's extended arm. The blood had already dried, the wound working to knit itself back together. He pulled his knife back out to make a fresh cut.

"Here," Izzy said, stepping off the boat on unsteady feet. "Let me." She felt him watching her. She heard his heartbeat, the quickening as she approached. Was he scared of her? His skin set her on fire as she gently grabbed his arm, studying the wound mere inches from her lips. As saliva pooled in her mouth, she felt a faint throb in her fangs. That was new. She glanced up at him, his golden eyes reassuring her with a gentle nod. Then she sank her teeth into his flesh. A tempting flow of blood pooled in her mouth and she pulled away, pressing the back of her hand to her mouth as she handed his arm off to Charlie.

She looked over her shoulder to see Charlie lean forward with a grimace and wrap his lips over the two dark holes marring Noah's forearm. And then he drank. Or tried to. The first pull gagged him and he spit it out onto the dock. He rallied after a couple more gags and latched back on, taking down several large gulps without breathing before shoving Noah's arm back at him.

The back of his shaky hand wiped over his mouth, his

lips pressed hard together as he breathed heavily through his nose. Noah let his arm drop to his side, a couple droplets of crimson splashing onto the weather worn wood as he climbed back into the boat. The engine started on a sputtering roar. Izzy watched this all happen before her, trying to calculate the misdirection in her life that allowed this fucked up series of events to unfold.

"You don't have to do this, you know," she whispered above the engine to Charlie.

His eyes softened as he dropped his hand. "I do," he replied. Then he enveloped her in his broad arms, trapping his heat against her face. She gripped his shirt, pulling it to her face as she breathed him in, that citrus scent of him. Everything felt so *wrong*. A stream of tears poured from her eyes as his hands worked in slow circles on her back.

All too soon he stiffened, his rhythmic movements stopping. He pulled back, hands on her shoulders as he studied her face, as if memorizing the lines and freckles there. She tried to do the same through the blur of tears.

His eyes glanced to the boat where Noah busied himself with imaginary tasks.

"You know he's madly in love with you, right?"

She looked over her shoulder then crinkled her nose as she looked back at Charlie. "I don't know."

He killed her. Her heart sank as that thought slipped in.

Charlie's hand rose to her cheek, brushing a rough thumb against her cheek. Then he flattened his hand against her neck and pulled her toward him to place a kiss on her forehead. "You do know. You deserve to be loved like he loves you." And just like that, he stepped back, cold chasing his absence despite the summer heat clinging to the early morning air. "Let him in, Iz." Then he turned and strode off the dock.

Izzy watched him hop off the end then disappear into the darkness of the woods. Letting out a deep sigh, she turned and climbed into the boat, wordlessly finding her place back on that busted seat. Noah untied them and kicked the boat into reverse. Once the river flowed evenly on both sides around them, he flipped it forward and they set off north. Against the current. Away from the city. Away from The Society. Away from Adette and Emilien. Away from everything.

CHAPTER THIRTY-FOUR
IZZY

The cool morning breeze filled the space between them as they sped up the river. Izzy closed her eyes, savoring the reprieve from the stifling humidity as the earthy air tickled her face. The steady hum of the motor tuned out the world and the thoughts threatening to consume her like a tidal wave. A soft smile pulled on her lips as the rhythmic motion started to lull her to the sleep stolen from her that evening.

His gruff voice broke through the silence, just above the engine. "If I knew sooner, I would've told you."

Suddenly, images flashed in her mind, her night unfolding in nightmare succession. Her eyes flew open to make it all stop, focus narrowing on him. Noah gazed ahead, hand on the steering wheel and brow furrowed. As if he could feel her looking at him, he glanced over, a shudder passing through him.

"When did you know?" She hardly recognized her own voice. It sounded sturdier than she felt.

His throat worked before he spoke, looking down at the rushing black water beneath them. "I still don't. I didn't put it all together until that moment. It's like the pieces were just floating around in my head and then they clicked when Charlie said he was going back. They are," He cleared his throat. "They are not going to be kind to him."

Izzy hummed, the sound lost to the din around them. She figured as much. Not much made Charlie Valentini look afraid and when he looked into her eyes one last time, it was fear that shone back. She stared at the black shoreline passing by, the vague shapes of trees slowly coming to life as the midnight sky lightened further. Dawn approached, whether it found you ready for a new day or not.

"And your brother?" She asked, still studying the shore.

Noah's spine stiffened out of the corner of her eye. "What about him?"

"Does he know? About your blood? I would guess his is the same." She turned to face him again, lips pressed tightly together.

"I don't know what Benji knows or thinks anymore." The words came out with a bite Izzy hadn't expected. "If he knows, he never let on to me. And if he doesn't, it's because he's too busy chasing pipe dreams."

Silence filled the air again. She didn't know what to say next. Where they stood. So much had clearly happened, to them both, in the time they had been apart. So many new questions added to the list of unknowns between them, deepening the permanence that they were still just strangers in each other's stories. And what would it take to escape the pit of unease pooling in her stomach?

The engine cut off as they slowly turned into the dark marina, a phantom hum deafening her in its wake. Water lapped against the abandoned boats tied to rows of interconnected docks.

They coasted down between yachts and fishing trawlers until they found an empty space. Noah hid the key in a small box under the driver's seat and hopped onto the wooden planks, holding the heavy rope tied to the boat. With his other hand, he reached for her. For a brief moment, their gazes connected as their hands touched. Emotions flooded her, a tsunami of uncertainty between them. That unknown threatening to consume her. She averted her eyes, looking at the marina around them. It was quiet, a ghost of what it would've been before. Early hours like that had been prime time for fishermen. The dock would have been bustling with activity. Not anymore.

Noah quickly tied the boat to the dock, double checking his knots. Then he grabbed her hand and she stumbled after as he pulled her down the dock. They weaved past rows of small john boats and skiffs similar to the one they had come in on. Noah studied each, peering down each row as they made their way closer to the shore.

He stopped suddenly at a line of big, ocean ready yachts. "Stay here," he said simply before he jogged down the wooden planks, disappearing into the dark.

Izzy stood there with nothing but the steady lap of water beneath her feet and an eerie sense of dread crawling along her skin. The weight of all her world as she knew it crashing down drowned her in the silence, grating at her peace. How long had the marina been abandoned? Her hair stood on end as the seconds pressed into minutes. She rubbed her arm, glancing up and down the rows. Shadows danced in the darkness and her heart picked up pace as her mind started to whirl.

She took a tentative step in the direction Noah had gone, her eyes constantly scanning the desolate marina around her.

A sinister scraping sound filled the air. Seconds

unfolded in heavy heartbeats as her eyes frantically searched her surroundings. Sudden flapping wings above her caused her to jump. Without hesitation, she checked the space behind her and took off at a brisk walk down the dock in search of Noah, fuck his instructions to stay put. Her gaze and attention remained on the presence she couldn't shake from behind her as she hurried, her footsteps tapping in a crescendo on the wooden planks beneath her feet. She picked her feet up to jog just before she rammed right into a hard force, propelling her backward. Her foot slipped on a wet patch and her stomach dropped as she started to fall. A million nightmares passed through her as she braced for watery impact she knew awaited her. Two strong hands gripped her arm and her waist, ripping her from that inky bath mere inches beneath her.

"Shit, Z, are you okay? I didn't see you." Noah's gentle southern drawl felt like a breath of fresh air and she breathed deep, crumpling into his chest as he lifted her up. He froze, his hands softening their grip as she pressed her body into him.

Then she remembered—the life slipping out of Nadia's eyes.

He killed her.

She stepped out of his grasp, his hands following her movement as if unable to let go. She maneuvered around him, avoiding the edges of the dock and instead keeping her eyes on him as she backed down the dock.

"Yes, um, yeah. This place is just creepy. Let's get out of here, yeah?" she replied, turning around and striding toward the direction she had come. Noah jogged to catch up to her, matching her brisk pace. When they got back to the wider main dock, she went to turn left and he grabbed her wrist, pulling her gently to the right. The touch felt like ice and fire all at once, burning her to the core. As if he felt it too, he dropped her wrist but didn't leave her side.

"This way," he murmured.

As a parking lot came into view, Izzy slowed.

"How will we know which ones have keys?"

"Like this," Noah said as he fished for something in his pocket. A moment later, a speedy looking sedan flashed its lights.

"How did you—"

He flashed her a grin over his shoulder and walked toward the black Audi. The windows were tinted a shade far from legal back in the day when cops cared about those things and the chrome still shined beneath a decent layer of dust.

"Call it a hunch," he said, as he pulled open the passenger seat and motioned for her to get in. Creamy leather seats filled the space with the smell of new car and luxury, preserved from one final detail before its owner disappeared. She dropped into the seat, placing her bag at her feet. Noah closed her door and walked around the back of the vehicle, his eyes dancing over the body as Izzy studied his movements, studied him. The man would be her demise in more ways than one and here she was, waiting for him to do it. Part of her welcomed it.

The driver door clicked open and she jumped. He slipped into the seat, his eyes roving over her in an unspoken question. A breath, a moment, a lifetime shared between them. Then he cleared his throat and focused ahead, putting the key in the ignition. It took a moment and a couple taps on the gas pedal for the engine to roar to life but as it steadied into a satisfying purr, a grin spread across his face. She followed the mischievous twinkle in his eye like a beacon in the night.

"Thankfully, they left it with a full tank so we should only have to stop once along the way. I'm going to let it run for a second while I check the trunk for any extra supplies but then we have to get out of here. I'm not sure how much of a head start Charlie bought us."

She nodded, swallowing hard against the lump in her throat. She hummed an agreement and Noah watched her, his expression unreadable. He slipped out the door, quickly checking the trunk. The closing of it a moment later rattled the empty space of the cabin before he came back to his seat.

"There is one tank of about four gallons so we won't be entirely fucked," he said plainly, slipping his seat belt across his body and putting the vehicle in reverse. As he turned to look behind him, his gaze caught on her lack of a seatbelt, eyebrows furrowing.

She shrugged and turned her expression on the side window. "Not much of a point in one anymore," she said.

He braked hard, a pause radiating between them before he shifted into drive. They pulled out of the parking lot and onto the empty main road. Noah kicked the engine up, the revs bellowing along the windy backroads as they made their way to the open interstate. Only the headlights illuminated the road in front of them, the world outside a tunnel of near darkness closing in around them.

He killed her.

The thought jolted her awake, churning her stomach as she replayed the image of Nadia's forever-life disappearing.

He killed her.

He moved so fast, almost imperceivable. She had only blinked and there he stood, blood seeping from her neck.

He killed her.

How rich would the soil be where they left her body?

"How did you do that?" Her quiet question broke the silent thrum inside the cabin.

He tore his gaze from the empty highway to give her a sideways glance. She watched him swallow hard, grip tightening around the wheel. And yet his heartbeat remained unchanged as he said solemnly, "My role within The Society was never exactly innocent."

She stared at his profile as he took a long breath, eyes glancing to the mirrors, checking on the nonexistent traffic. "I was known as a Fixer. Politics get messy as power grows and those at the top need someone to…help ease the tension."

She shifted in her seat, turning her body to face him. "So…you what? Killed people?"

His expression pained as he looked over to her, his hand twitching but staying steady on the wheel. His jaw flexed as he looked back to the road. "Among other things…yes. I was often sent to hunt and…kill anyone who threatened the mission of The Society or Emilien's role within it."

"Can you give me an example?" The question escaped her lips before she thought better to ask. To know the truth could break the fragile thread between them, that unspoken scale tipping precariously to either of their side's.

"I don't want to justify my actions to you," he said, softly, golden eyes piercing through the darkened space, stealing her breath. He offered her a way out of knowing, of damning the illusion they still held up like a veil.

"I asked. I want to know." The words felt heavy as iron as she said them.

The car slowed as he pulled them over to the shoulder. She eyed the space outside, searching for a threat but his gaze focused on her, cutting through her anxiety and pulling her in.

"In the beginning, it was mostly those he had lost control over, who couldn't handle the blood lust. They were a danger to everyone and the innocent body count was rising. It felt…justified, my work. My duty." He shook his head as if the memory still haunted him. "Once those situations started to ease, everything shifted. I was sent to spy on higher powered people, watch who they organized with," he swallowed, looking away as he said, "Get in on their good graces. Emilien was…likely still is…getting paranoid about a coup. He wanted control. He had a vision and he didn't want any obstacles in his path so I…"

"Eliminated the threat?" She didn't recognize her own voice.

His watery gaze met hers as he nodded once. She reached across the console and took his hand, giving it a light squeeze. He let out a deep exhale, squeezing her hand back before turning away, checking his mirrors, and putting the car back in motion. The monster comforted.

Only…which one?

CHAPTER THIRTY-FIVE
NOAH

Hours passed and at some point, Izzy had fallen asleep. Noah rummaged around the back, miraculously finding a blanket under the passenger seat. Further searching yielded a pair of sunglasses. He threw the blanket over her as best as he could manage at speed and set the sunglasses on the center console.

She woke up with a yawn that morphed into a hiss as the sun shined through the windows, despite the heavy coating of tint on them.

"Here," he said as he passed her the sunglasses. Their fingertips brushed as she took them from him and placed them over her eyes.

"Thanks." She yawned again and stretched her back like a cat. "Where are we?"

"About fifty miles from Memphis."

Izzy stiffened. "Oh no."

Noah's glance shifted from the road to Izzy and back again. In the last half hour or so, there had been more and more abandoned cars on the side of the road. Some of them crept into the lane and he had to really focus to avoid hitting them.

"What do you mean, 'Oh no'?"

"We can't go through Memphis," she commanded, popping open the glove compartment and rummaging through it.

"What are you looking for? And what do you mean we can't go through Memphis? It's the fastest way." They were making great time without traffic or the law to contend with but every moment spent on the road felt like a death wish.

"You don't understand. We cannot go through Memphis. Aha!" She held up a map and started unfolding it, a serious look of concentration on her face as she studied the interstates through Mississippi.

"There is no other way around Memphis, Z," he said, tapping impatiently on the steering wheel.

"Here, if you go two sixty-nine, we can skirt around the city and hit forty then take that until we can work our way back. The two sixty-nine exit should be coming up," her squinted eyes shifted from the paper to the road ahead. A big green sign popped up, listing Interstate 269 in ten miles. She pointed to the sign and looked at him. "There! Take that in ten miles."

She started folding the map up neater so it only focused on the roads that followed the big, muddy river through the middle of the country.

"Izzy, that's insane. That will take us like three hours out of the way." A bit hyperbolic but he wanted to be back in St. Louis this evening. Earlier if possible.

She reached over and gripped his arm. He glanced down to see the white-knuckle grip around his darker skin.

"Noah, something happened in Memphis. We can't go there." Her voice trembled slightly as she stared ahead.

His brows furrowed and he shifted in his seat. "What happened in Memphis?"

"I'm not really sure but it's full of," she gulped, releasing her grip on his arm. A line of red fingerprints were left behind. "Something." She turned to him. "Something…wrong."

He recognized the terror in her eyes, the same way she had looked at him in the garden with his knife dripping blood into the ground. Fuck.

"We are already pretty close to the city and I haven't seen anything. And it's daylight. Surely we will be fine. It'll take us five minutes, ten tops, to get through the city and then it'll be smooth sailing home," he reassured her.

She studied him, that fear still there, breaking his heart by the second. Slowly, she nodded but he watched as her grip shifted, pressing into the fabric of her linen pants.

Five minutes came and went and they had barely made it a quarter of the way through the city proper. Abandoned vehicles littered the highway in a dystopian nightmare, windows smashed, doors ripped off their hinges lying on the pavement like fallen leaves. A chill snaked down Noah's spine and he kept looking over at Izzy, regretting his decision to not listen to her. Her leg shook with anticipation and she gnawed on her bottom lip as her emerald eyes scanned the road from behind her sunglasses. A fang peaked out over her plump pink lip and he snapped his eyes back to the road, a tingle spreading across the back of his neck.

"So far, so good, except for having to weave around all these cars," he said, feigning confidence for the both of them. She nodded her head, gaze fixated on the world beyond the windshield.

The sign to exit for GRACELAND passed by and he let out a shaky breath. They weren't even halfway through the city. Izzy seemed to sense his impatience and clenched the fabric of her pants tighter, scanning the spaces along the side of the road.

"Fuck," she said suddenly. Noah followed her worried look out the windows, frantically searching for the alarm. "They are hiding in the shadows inside the buildings," she whispered.

Just as she said it, his eyes met the empty, callous pits of something vaguely human in the dark doorway of an abandoned warehouse. An eerie fanged smile spread across its face.

"Fuck me, what is that?" he murmured in horror. Regret pooled in his stomach and he wished he could take the words back. A glance to Izzy showed her skin paling at his words. "Izzy, I don't mean..."

"No," she shook her head, "it's fine. I...I agree. It is creepy. Like they are waiting...hunting."

But would they hunt him? Since putting together the pieces of what he saw and heard in The Antisociété, he wondered if on a primitive level they could sense something off about him. Something sinister.

It hadn't stopped Izzy though.

His grip twisted on the steering wheel. He wished he could ask Charlie if his idea worked. But even if Charlie lived, Emilien would never give him a way to reach out again. He would be as good as dead within the ranks of The Society.

They followed the road as it skirted around the outer edges of downtown until it opened up, allowing Noah to press harder onto the gas pedal. No more shadows lurked in the darkness around them and in a few more minutes, they were speeding over an empty bridge, crossing into Arkansas.

Izzy let out a long, heavy sigh and relaxed into her seat.

"I never thought I'd find a place worse than this state," she murmured, hand rested on her forehead as she stared out the window.

Noah cracked a smile. "Arkansas? What did Arkansas ever do to you?"

She flashed a sideways look at him, her green eyes twinkling from the sides of her sunglasses. "Existed."

His smile widened and his grip on the wheel loosened. "There are still a few more hours until we are in St. Louis. I figured we can find a gas station in the next hundred miles or so to siphon some gas from to make sure we get there without any issue."

"No gas delivery on speed dial, chauffeur?"

Her joking tone fluttered in his chest. "Not today. We are in Arkansas, after all."

He almost crashed the car as a smile cracked across her face, stealing his focus.

"Now you get it." And then she turned that smile full force onto him and for a moment, he lost the memories of the past few months. The hell they endured to get to this point vanished as the only thing he saw was her and the version of them they could've been. If only he were a different man. A hard lump lodged in his throat as he turned back to the road ahead.

"So, Charlie," he broached the subject with as much grace as an alligator in a deli.

Her smile disappeared and he cursed himself for letting it happen.

"What about him?"

He ran a hand through his hair and studied the lights on the dashboard, fingers hovering over various knobs and buttons like something needed adjusting. Unfortunately, nothing would fix the words tumbling out of his mouth.

"It just seems you two have...gotten close...-er. Since I last saw you, that is," he said, clearing his throat and training his face into the stoicism that fought against the mix of emotions within him.

She huffed out a sound. "I don't know how *close* we got but he was...conveniently around when I needed him to be." A torment tore on those last words.

"And The Society? How did that come about?"

Her brows furrowed and she turned to him, suffocating him under the weight of her stare. "I refuse to be interrogated by you. Who was the woman you murdered in the garden?"

"That was Nadia."

A palpable silence descended over them.

"That's all I get?" she asked.

"All I got was 'he was convenient'," he replied, raising a brow to her.

She crossed her arms, her gaze roaming the rest of his body. He tried to sit up straighter, rolling his stiff shoulders back.

"*Touché*, Broussard. *Touché*."

He hid his smirk by looking out the window to his left before he said, a tad smug, "What was so convenient about him being around?"

The temperature between them dropped and he hated himself for asking. But he needed to know, needed to fill the sinking pit of unknown in his heart with something other than all the images his imagination conjured up.

"I needed...shit," she cursed quietly and played with a loose curl at her shoulder. A shaky breath filled the air, then another. "I needed blood," she blurted out on a single exhale, squinting her eyes shut as the words spilled out.

His own breath stopped.

Right. She needed blood. It was a requirement for survival, being a vampire and all. Her lips pressed against Charlie's body would have been out of necessity.

A sick sense of rage for a man who was likely dead wafted over him and he checked his mirrors for no reason other than to search for his callous soul.

He turned to see her watching him, a slight grimace on her face. He gave a curt nod.

"Who are the Reauxs?" she asked, abandoning the subject of Charlie and Nadia. It would come up again, it would need to come up again, but he appreciated the break from hard subjects. There were no secrets about the Reauxs. There never were with truly good people. His stomach dropped at the thought.

He rubbed his jaw, unconsciously switching the turn signal on to change lanes. "The Reauxs are the closest thing to a family Benji and I ever knew."

She nodded her head slowly, accepting his vague description for the most giving, caring group of people he had ever experienced in his life. No words could reduce their impact on his life and she seemed to sense that.

"And what about Benji?"

Noah choked out a cough. Hard subjects were back on the table. "What about him?"

She shifted back to face him. "He's not dead."

Noah's lips thinned and he shook his head once. "No, he's not dead."

"He's working for Adette."

"He's definitely doing that."

Her nose crinkled. "He's kind of a dick."

Noah snorted. "Yeah, you could say that."

"What happened?"

Noah blew out a long exhale and ran a hand through his hair. "Which time?"

She quirked a brow at him and he took that to mean,

continue fucking talking you idiot.

So, he filled their time going back through the last several months. The manipulative betrayal he endured from his brother and everyone else around him under Adette's watchful eye. Izzy listened with an intensity that both comforted and unnerved him. No one had listened to him since he left her side all those months ago. No one had cared what he thought or wanted.

It felt good. Dangerously good.

They found a promising exit in Cape Girardeau and hope bloomed in his chest as they pulled into a service center where actual people appeared to be working. There had to be a big community of farmers around who still needed fuel. Or not enough people who could afford the cure to shutter their business. Just normal people, living their lives like nothing changed, despite everything going completely ass over tits around them. A yearning coaxed its way into his heart as he pulled up to a pump.

Noah stuck his head into the car as the tank filled. "I'm going to run inside and see what they have for food. Do you want anything?"

"A water would be great," Izzy said. She pressed a finger to her lips and he waited. "And...if they have Oreos...I would not be opposed."

"Ah, that's a big request. You're going to be indebted to me if they do. Are you prepared for that?"

The left side of her mouth twitched up once, twice, then she ducked her chin. Not soon enough to hide from him the smile on her face. She collected her facial expression and looked up to Noah's twinkling gaze. His eyes dipped to those lips against his will.

"I think I can handle that," she said, tilting her head.

A smile spread across Noah's face and he stepped away

to close the door before he ruined the moment by replying. Something about that woman set him off his axis and he felt like a teenager again.

He spent several minutes roaming the aisles of the large convenience store, scouring the shelves for that distinctive blue package of cookies. Defeated after his second pass by the slushie machine, he went to the register to check out with the cash he had found on the yacht alongside the car keys.

"Fifty even for the gas and the grub," the cashier said, chewing his gum in an aggressive manner.

Noah looked up as he passed the picture of Ulysses S. Grant across the counter. He froze when he spotted them. On the shelf behind the cashier, a proud stack of five packages. Double stuffed and everything.

"How much for the lot?" Noah gestured to them, eyes fixated as if he looked away they would disappear.

The cashier looked at him like he grew a second head, following his gaze and smacking his gum.

"Ah, yes. You're from out of town, I'm guessing?" The cashier turned back, an amused smirk on his face.

"I'll take them all," Noah said, reaching into his pocket for another fifty. His hand grazed the cool metal of Izzy's necklace, still stored haphazardly in his pocket and every muscle in him tightened. His pulse raced as he remembered finding it in the bag of his things left for him on the barge. A series of unanswered questions washed over him but he kept the easy smile on his face as his slid the bill across the counter.

The cashier's eyes widened and the chewing stopped, the gum threatening to fall out of his mouth. Then a snicker escaped his lips and it morphed into a full-blown laugh as he turned around, grabbed the stack, and placed them into Noah's bag.

"You out of towners are nuts for these stale ass things."

"Keep the change," Noah said, swallowing his apprehensions as he grabbed his bag and left.

Noah let the necklace fade from his mind as he strolled back to the car, unhooking the gas pump and replacing it in the holder. As he moved through the motions of checking the vehicle, he counseled himself on what to say, to hold onto the feeling he had before the reminder of all that remained unspoken between them. The secrets they kept.

He pulled his door open and slipped in.

"Your debt just became absolutely massive, Ciampi." He sprinkled an extra layer of southern charm into his words as he set the bag on his lap. The zip of his seatbelt pulling across his body filled the deafening silence in the car. He looked at Izzy and his stomach dropped. Despite it all, he had still managed to say the wrong thing based on the pale, bleak expression on her face.

"Izzy, I'm so sorry. You don't actually owe me anything. This isn't even my money so I don't give a fuck," he said hastily. He studied her, searching for an ounce of reassurance but she remained unmoved by his words. Worry washed over him and he scanned her body, dread filling his stomach that something horrible had happened while they were apart. That's when he saw her hand and the way they shook violently around the illuminated phone there. Her phone. He hadn't seen his since that day in the cell when Benji taunted him with it. Tortured him with the messages left unread.

"What," he started to say and then his vision snagged on the name at the top of the screen.

NOAH

He gulped. *What the fuck?*

As if she finally sensed his presence, she turned to him and passed the phone slowly over. He gently pried it from her grasp, sticking the bag of cookies on the back floorboard.

The first few messages were words from a distant past. Of quick stolen glances and flirtatious back and forth. Of hope for a future and a life outside the hell that chased them. Of home.

His heart dropped to his stomach at a recent message he had never seen before, a deep ache settling in its place.

IZZY

I miss you

His heart completely stopped when he saw a reply from himself, five minutes ago. Only not from him.

NOAH

What the fuck did you do to my brother?

EPILOGUE

Benji steadied himself as Malik approached, shaking hands hidden as he pocketed the cell phone and pulled out the silver switchblade instead. He shook out his shoulders and straightened, letting out a deep breath. The tenderness in the other man's eyes pierced Benji's heart as he swallowed his concern, and betrayal, for Noah. He could deal with that issue later.

"Hey good looking, any updates?" Benji asked, cracking a smile as he flipped the knife open and closed a few times.

"We're ready." Malik's clipped response stung but Benji didn't let it show, continuing to flip the knife as he followed him down the bright hallway. Always the serious one, Malik.

Well, not always. A flash of their morning together popped into his mind and the very un-serious way Malik looked as Benji dipped below the sheets with a sly grin on his face.

He kept his expression neutral though as Malik assessed him over his shoulder. The man could smell the slightest change in someone and as his dark brow rose, Benji looked straight ahead, following at his heel.

They walked down the stairs into the dank basement of The Roosevelt and a slight pang of regret filled Benji's mouth. All those months spent trying to convince Noah of the good happening here, wasted. Parenting him when they were younger hadn't been that hard. He was an easy kid, self sufficient and smart. But trying to get him to see the light as an adult turned out to be an insurmountable task. Stubborn, pig headed, holier-than-thou Noah, unable to open his fucking eyes and see the good happening to their city. Their *home*. All at the hands of The Antisociété and the genius of Adette and Henry.

Benji flexed his fist as a metal door groaned on its hinges, opening into the cell that had housed his brother for a good portion of his stay here. A black-haired man sat shirtless on a chair in the middle of the room. His head hung below his inked shoulders, a twisting vine of flowers and serpents weaving their way along the planes of his body, up his neck and down his chest and chiseled abdominals. The design disappeared beneath the waistband of his pants and as Benji's eyes roved over him, his curiosity to what lie beneath the fabric spiked. He wouldn't be disappointed by having him amongst their ranks when Emilien finished whatever he had planned for him. In fact, their whole reason for being there had been for Emilien to show them "something great" to better their cause. And a man like Charlie Valentini would definitely better their cause.

As if sensing his gaze on him, a set of piercing blue eyes shot up and connected with Benji's, setting his pulse off kilter. They narrowed, almost disappearing behind the dark lashes lining them.

Malik turned to him as if sensing his elicit thoughts, raising a brow before walking over to the tall man in the corner, a fleur de lis tattoo etched into his hand. Benji broke his gaze away from Charlie to study the man speaking in hushed tones with Malik. Collin? Cal? Benji couldn't remember.

"Aight, the way this will work can be a tad...gruesome if you've never witnessed it before. Emilien's methods are a bit unorthodox, but usually effective. You're welcome to look away. Fuck knows I've had to a couple of times and well," the British man flashed his fangs at Malik. Benji watched his lover's hand flex tight around the knife at his waist as the man's silver-grey eyes flickered on the edge of immoral delight. He made his way back over to where Benji stood, brushing his shoulder against his as they both studied the vampire in the corner.

As if summoned by his name, Emilien Dumas stalked into the room, followed closely by Adette, Henry right behind her, a hand on her lower back. Benji studied the dynamic between the three but didn't try to understand it. It didn't serve him to know their relationship. He just wanted to see his world returned to normal and as far as he could tell, the only people capable of doing that were Adette and Henry. If Emilien factored into that, it wasn't for him to know how.

"*Sommes-nous prêts*[60]?" Emilien asked.

"*Oui*," Charlie growled from the chair.

A flicker of rage passed over Emilien's face and he turned to Adette, whispering something in her ear. Her eyes widened and she turned to Henry. Whatever she said to him caused him to pale, eyes flickering to the man in the room with concern. The orange haired man placed a hand on Adette's arm and they both shuffled out of the room, the loud clang of the door closing behind them rang out across the room. They peered in through the dusty window at the top of the door with a guarded sense of curiosity. Benji glanced to Malik who only shook his head slightly and returned his focus to the scene unfolding before them.

Emilien's persona seemed to grow, fill the room as he turned back to the rest of the room. His eyes roved over the two men not associated with him as he rolled the sleeves of his dark blue linen shirt to his elbows, a shallow sneer growing on his face as he did. He looked at the other man standing when he spoke.

"Have they been prepared of what's to come, Callum?"

Callum smirked. "Prepared enough, boss."

"*D'accord.* The door remains closed until we are finished. Is that understood?"

Benji and Malik shared a glance. Bile rose to Benji's throat in anticipation. Blood had never been his thing, he saved the dirty work for his brother.

"We need to know where they went, Benji," Malik whispered, reaching a hand up to cup his cheek.

Benji nodded into the touch and turned back to Emilien. "We're ready."

Emilien moved in a flash, imperceivable until his fangs sank into the inked flesh on Charlie's neck. Charlie grimaced, breathing roughly through his mouth, spittle coming out his clenched teeth. Several long pulls worked along Emilien's throat before he lifted, taking a breath. The feral sense of need on his face removed him entirely from that of a man. Benji gulped. He had seen vampires feed loads of times. He had even seen Emilien feed. He had never seen the way craving could overcome a typically composed man. His eyes were nearly black, his dilated pupils pushing out the color, and a mad sneer creased his crimson coated lips.

A look of concern flickered across Callum's face and he made a minute move toward the vampire. An inhuman growl emanated from deep in Emilien's throat, stopping Callum in his tracks, and then he dove back in, biting into Charlie's wrist. Charlie grunted on impact, hands flexing into involuntary fists. Deranged delight radiated off Emilien as he gulped down a few more swallows before lifting up only to ferociously bite into the inked flesh of Charlie's side, just below his heart. An indecent moan escaped Emilien's lips as Charlie's desperate panting filled the air and if Benji hadn't been watching the horror unfold before him, he might have found himself aroused.

Then Emilien ripped off Charlie's pants, letting them fall around his ankles before plunging his fangs into the tattooed flesh on his inner thigh. A pained, long grunt morphed into a roar as Emilien took heavy swallows of blood. Charlie shook uncontrollably in the chair, blood spilling crimson lines across his flesh out the pairs of red dots scattered across his body. A mix of determined rage and fear etched into the deep creases of his grimaced face.

Benji glanced at Malik and saw a reflection of his alarm in his eyes. Neither of them dared to move, to breathe as they watched the horror unfold before them. A eerie feeling of being prey crept up Benji's spine, raising the air on the back of his neck as Charlie's labored breaths coursed through the air like the lapping waves of the incoming tide on a windy day.

Callum cleared his throat. "Um, boss, let's see if he's willing to talk now."

A deep, gurgled growl sounded from Emilien's throat as he took another swallow of blood. As if against his will, Emilien released his lips from the man's flesh, ripping it as he went. Charlie breathed in and out quickly, gulping the stagnant air as if he had been running for hours. His skin had paled to a sickly grey color.

"Tell us what the fuck happened, Charlie," Emilien growled.

Charlie lifted his weak head and pierced Emilien with a murderous glare. Then he spit on the man, a wicked grin spreading across his otherwise exhausted face.

"Fuck, Charlie," Callum said, rubbing his cropped hair as he started to pace.

Emilien wasted no time with words and latched his fangs into the thick muscles connecting Charlie's neck to his shoulder.

Charlie let out another roar of pain as Emilien drank and drank. Color rapidly drained from Charlie's face. Despite the fear and rage written plainly on his face, a look of acceptance and satisfaction crept in along the edges. As if he knew when he walked back onto the plantation that morning he would end up here. Accepted it. *Wanted it.*

"Come on, Charlie, she's not worth it," Callum pleaded as he gaze bounced from his boss to the man in the chair succumbing to his death.

A sick, heart-wrenching laugh escaped Charlie's lips.

"If you believe that," Charlie grunted through the pain, "then I'm sorry for what your future holds."

Emilien paused. He looked over at Callum and nodded. The man let out a relieved exhale, dropping his hand from gripping his hair and fished out a vial and syringe from his pocket. He stuck the needle into the small glass bottle, pulling the liquid quickly into the tube of the syringe. Then he knelt beside Charlie and stuck the needle into a weakly throbbed vein on his arm.

Callum stood. "You have about five minutes before it'll kick in."

"*Bien,*" Emilien said, reaching a hand up to Charlie's limp head. He lifted his chin so they looked into each other's eyes. "Charlie, unfortunately, I cannot let you die. But I can let you live forever, on the brink of death, begging for its sweet release until you give us some answers, *non?*"

Charlie's scowl narrowed on Emilien as he spoke, tears

pouring down the sides of his face. Emilien's sick smile froze Benji's heart, and then sank his fangs into the flesh just above Charlie's heart, taking in long gulps. The amount of blood he had lost would have killed anyone several minutes ago yet Charlie endured as Emilien drained him, like he said, right to the brink of death.

Emilien finally lifted from the man, standing back to observe, as Charlie's breaths labored, the pallor of a morgue growing across his body. His pulse slowed in the visible veins along his muscular arms. The smug smile on Emilien's face faltered.

"Good luck," Charlie whispered. Then a long, strained breath escaped his lips.

And never came back in.

Emilien's face fell and a small sense of unease filled the room.

"Ce qu'il se passe[61]?" Emilien barked at Callum.

"Did you drain him too much?" Callum asked, frantic notes of panic in his words as he rushed over to Charlie and pressed a finger to his neck.

Emilien stood with his mouth agape, red smeared down his chin and over his lips. "I, *non*, I did as I've always done. I took him right to the edge but he should've..."

"Fuck, Emilien, he's dead," Callum shouted. He quickly unstrapped the heft of Charlie's body from the chair and placed him on the ground. As he started performing compressions on his chest, a ringing filled Benji's ears as he watched. Dead.

Emilien ran a hand through his hair and took a step back. As if just realizing Benji and Malik stood in the room, his gaze snapped to them.

"This has never happened before. I promise. The cure, *c'est infaillible*[62]," he pleaded with them.

Benji swallowed and looked at Malik. A confused rage flowed in Malik's deep brown eyes as he challenged the man.

"What do you mean this has never happened before?" Malik shouted.

"*C'est impossible*[63]," Emilien whispered. A trembling hand went over his mouth as he backed up, his knees buckling as he fell to a seat on the small cot along the wall.

Callum spoke through strained breath as he pressed rhythmically into Charlie's lifeless chest. "We normally drain them right to the edge of death, right before their body's natural instincts kick in and they get a burst of adrenaline. That adrenaline speeds the cure through their veins and quickly gets to work repairing and replenishing their blood supply. But something went wrong here. It's like...the cure didn't work."

Callum's words were more like an academic's stream of thoughts as he worked out a problem. Most of what he said went over Benji's head. All except for that last bit. It rang out across the cell, bouncing off the damp yellowing concrete walls. Absently, Benji flipped the switchblade in his hand still, his eyes wide as he processed everything he saw. Open and closed. Open and closed.

The cure didn't work.

This story continues with…
LOVE YOU TO DEATH
What lurks beneath is floating to the surface…

❦

ACKNOWLEDGMENTS

Thank you for reading this second book in La Fleur de Lis Trilogy! Imagine getting to the end of Love You Forever and thinking, "Yeah, I'll take another but make it worse." Readers are, and always have been, the backbone of storytelling. I don't mean that in a pandering way, I was a reader before I learned to write after all. I can create and let this story live in my soul but the true magic is watching how it reacts in the world with different people from different backgrounds with different personalities, lifestyles, cultures, etc. YOU make a story come to life (or, in this case hopefully, keep it a fantasy, please).

When I wrote this story, I had no idea the direction it would go. And the same could be said for my life since writing it. I could not have seen this story come to life without several people standing behind me in various ways.

Jess, you have been and will always be one of the greatest things to happen from the internet. I value your perspective as a fellow writer, as well as the friendship we've built between our made-up worlds and struggles with the English language. I'm honored to have been able to lean on you for both of the books so far in this series and cannot wait to show you how it ends. Cheers, to the woman who may love my characters just as much as I love them.

Ally, you have always been the cheerleader I needed in this endeavor. When my confidence wavers, I know I can find some in abundance from you. You're everything a girl wants in a best friend.

Stacey and Karen, you two make for the most incredible beta team. Thank you for enduring one of the worst drafts of this story, providing honest feedback that doesn't make me cry, and still coming back for more! I am not a writer without you both. Thank you, truly.

Amanda and Kori, what a light you bring to my life. This year has seen me go through so many transformations and who knew I would find such infallible support from two incredible women who just love books and yap as much as me. To know despite it all you've read my words, sent me live reactions, and made me excited to continue to share this story, means the world to me.

Emily, who inspired me to make the leap in self publishing and owning my work. Anyone who listens to a twenty-minute long voice message from me holds a very special place in my heart because what am I even saying?

To my ARC readers, thank you for your continued support, especially this year when things have been in perpetual limbo. I'm a one woman team yet you all make me feel like I'm invincible. From the absolute bottom of my callous heart that made you start to second guess your feelings about Charlie, I cherish you.

To J, and now little baby R, you both are my whole world. Love is hard to put into words but made easier experiencing it in abundance every single day of my life. Every person should know, at least once in their life, a love like this and I am so fortunate to get to with you. **I love you, madly**.

ABOUT THE AUTHOR

Growing up in the St. Louis metro area, Cortni dreamed of escape. She found it in the pages of books and fantasizing missed conversations and interactions. It took her over a decade to harness that skill into writing a novel but we all get where we're going in the end.

When not writing, she can be found on her small (read: tiny) farm in rural Kentucky with her incredible partner, new little baby, two lovingly awful herd dogs, and a horse that is an absolute menace.

STAY UP TO DATE WITH UPCOMING PROJECTS!

Website: www.authorcortnimarie.com
Newsletter: cortnimarie.substack.com
Instagram: @AuthorCortniMarie